This book belongs to...

First Printing 2010 (E. R. Hardcastle) as *The Recruit Adventure*. Re-printed in 2018 (E. Rachael Hardcastle) as *World*, part of *Finding Pandora: The Complete Collection* - ISBN: 978-1-9999688-0-9

I – Revised Edition

Published by Rachael's imprint:
Curious Cat Books, West Yorkshire, UK
www.rachaelhardcastle.com
Map designed with Inkarnate. The map is not to scale and is for entertainment purposes only.

Typesetting: Requiem, FoglihtenNo04, Aline, Old Cupboard, Old Almanac, Times New Roman. All fonts are free for commercial use.

Cover design: Rachael Hardcastle. All images are free for commercial use under the CCO License.
Copy-editing and proofreading by Curious Cat Books.
Interior formatting and design by Curious Cat Books.

TO SEE A WORLD

Harvest Fields
Mousique
Manaia Forest
Pouki's Cabin
Casper's Cabin
Orc Pit
Drakonta
Highman's Point
Wolf Territory
Recruit Lair
Haeylo City

Volcanic Ruins
Demonic Territory
Marshland
Petrified Forest
The Land Bridge
Queen's Port
Entit Sehde Palace
Rulecast Tower
The Edge
The Depths
Abandoned Dwarf Mine
The Valley
Recruit HQ
MPLE
Enzo
Enzo Beach
Drakontan Mountains
Tribal Settlement
Mirror Of The Soul
Barren Fishtail

PROLOGUE

9180AD

Deep in the desolate mountains of Enzo in an intricate labyrinth, sat a box, that although small and unimpressive, held extraordinary importance. A woman dressed in soot grey rags crouched beside it; eyes of azure fixed on the entrance to the dank cavity she called home. Beyond the reaches of her breath the labyrinth's emptiness awaited.

Zïnnyi gave strict instructions. He trusted her to protect the box from humankind's hunger for power. Pandora crawled closer, biting what remained of grungy nails. Would one more peek harm anyone?

Soon it began to plead with Pandora's already outstretched fingers. The temptation exceeded Zïnnyi's persistent warnings. So she licked her lips and caressed the panels; layers of filth disguised unusual symbols entwined around an ancient text she had tried, but failed, to understand.

Pandora's breath caught in her throat when she lifted the lid. Brilliant white beams illuminated her cave. Emotionless cavities which were once Pandora's innocent eyes welcomed the warmth and allowed it to flow smooth as a river to the farthest stretches of her mind. Her heart ached with sorrow as the howls of mankind's past mistakes echoed through narrow tunnels. Pandora's stomach churned. What had she done? She'd wasted her second chance at redemption.

It was time to run away from her responsibility and hide

within an oblivious society.

Dangerous creatures lurked in the labyrinth, many of which He'd designed to guard her. Those claws, sharp as a samurai sword and teeth, curved like a sabre-toothed tiger would surely hunt her. Pandora didn't rate the chance of survival, but keeping her head down she took her first step back into the void, leaving the box unaccompanied.

Her only plan was to shuffle with her back to the wall, fingers crossed and breath held, until she found a way out of the labyrinth.

ONE

Arriette Monroe startled awake, rescued from her troublesome slumber by a rap on the cottage door. Setting her tea cup and book on the sill, Arriette scurried to peer through the peep hole. Her heart thumped when their eyes met; his bottle-green saucers, swarthy hair and hypnotic smile were all beautiful reminders of a happy ending that might have been. The temptation to wrap her arms around him and squeeze was consuming, but she knew better.

Besides, her mother would kill her if the humiliation didn't.

"Never thought I'd see *you* again," said Arriette, running a hand through her matted locks.

Kalvin Avery gave a curt nod, wiped his boots on the welcome mat, then followed her to the living room. The decoration hadn't changed; same squeaky floorboard beneath that hideous sheepskin rug, the art free stone walls and hand-crafted, ugly wooden furniture. Everything in its usual place, surrounded by leaning towers of paperback books, all coated in the expected layer of dust.

Arriette caught sight of her reflection in the mirror, gasped, licked her thumb and scrubbed at the fresh tea stain on her dress.

"Can I, uhm, can I get you a drink? Water, tea-?"

"Got anything stronger?"

"Sure," she grinned, then scratched her head. "Somewhere. I'll, hmm, I'll find it. So is this a social call?" Before Kalvin could answer, Arriette produced a bottle of red wine and two glasses. "Well it can't be for business if you're drinking this early."

Arriette gestured for him to pour as she opened the window. Fresh air carried the scent of mowed grass, ruffled her long, brown hair and circulated the sound of busy harvesters.

Kalvin watched her sit. His eyes lingered a little too long.

"Sue sent me."

Arriette shook her head and laughed off her mistake.

"Oh, of course. I don't know what I was-"

"It's good to see you though."

"I didn't think you'd ever come back here."

"Neither did I. You hated me; my 'mistake' branded me cruel. Plus, I have nobody else to visit here. Mousique holds painful memories. Anyway, I'm here for your advice."

Arriette chewed her lip, cracked her knuckles and tried to ignore the ridiculous finger gestures he used around the word *mistake*.

"Couldn't you ask someone closer to home?"

Kalvin thumped his feet up on the coffee table and folded his arms. Arriette bit her tongue.

"No. You know about magic and I trust you. City folk are too nosey."

"Everything I know I learned by reading."

Arriette sipped her wine and glanced out the window. Anything to prevent her worrying over that damn coffee table.

I'm turning into my mother!

"Doesn't alter my point."

"Are you sure you're in the right village for this? We're ninety percent human, remember? Your three-day ride was time wasted, Kalvin."

"I walked, and it's not wasted yet."

Arriette only read a pinch of books on magic but what she had, she thoroughly enjoyed. On the odd occasion, in private of course, Arriette attempted a few spells too. Here in the human settlement of Mousique magic had its limits.

"Retaining doctors were useless. They advised I find an educated human."

"I only read about supernatural theory," Arriette explained, "not human biology. I presume that's why you're here? Did you try the medical scrolls in the public library?"

"I hate that place," he grumbled. "Silent, boring and dusty."

Arriette raised her brow. "I'm your ex-girlfriend. There's no way I was your first choice, so spit it out. Who's sick?"

Of course if Arriette could offer help she would; time had healed all wounds from their goodbyes. She'd even forgiven Susan for running off to the city with him, and Kalvin for letting her.

He rubbed his eyes, sighed and removed his boots from the table.

"How about I tell you the symptoms?"

Arriette scowled at him, prepared to scold his impatience. She was only trying to understand. But then his shaky fingers found Arriette's. A once confident man, stubborn, stern and eager to set out and fulfil his dreams of joining the everlast army now crumbled before her, his forehead and palms sweaty.

Arriette shook him free and shuffled away, listening to the villagers' harvest songs drift in from the closest field. It calmed her nerves and brought with it pleasant memories of previous festivals.

"I barely made it here." Kalvin paused, "It's too hard."

"Hmm, must be *really* difficult for you." Arriette gulped from her glass and glanced away.

"You're still mad and I'm still sorry." Kalvin groaned. "Can you shut that window? I can't think straight."

You never could, Arriette thought, but hiding her disappointment she closed the window anyway and fought with all her might to hold the salty floodgates for a few more minutes.

"Why aren't you outside with the others?"

Arriette cleared her throat. "Uhm, something horrid happened last year. I, well, I don't like to talk about it. You were giving me the symptoms?"

Before she could hide her fear, both hands became clammy and her entire body trembled at the memory.

It happened just after harvest time. Arriette hung back to chat with her neighbour, forgetting the curfew; something she will never do again. Sharing a bottle of sweet white wine they took little notice of the tree line where her attacker lurked in the shadows.

"You can't have been bitten. You're still alive," said Kalvin.

Distressed, Arriette topped up her glass and took a distracting sip. *You know nothing of my pain.*

"So what happened?"

She frowned. "Does it matter?"

"Yes, vampyrs are nocturnal so how-"

"You came here to get advice, not give it."

Kalvin lived in a place with high walls and guards. Her only protection was a red cottage door and her garden shovel. Not enough to fight off a creature of the night.

Arriette sighed. "I got bit. He hid in the shade until the sun went down. I'm fine now. Happy?"

"Yes. So about those symptoms. They said humans react differently to magic. Medication had no effect."

Arriette was pleased they were back on topic.

"Uh, that's true I guess. Our bodies have natural defences against disease but not magic. We're not designed to cope with the extremities of it." She glanced out the window at the height of the sun. Midday. Now he'd made her late for lunch with Rihaana. "Magic is complicated and dangerous; born from a divine power and capable of anything. Vampyrs are one example; if Zïnnyi created those, who's to say he didn't make your friend ill too? Sure, vampyrs weren't always around but neither were most diseases."

Arriette ran a hand through her hair, worried by the incoming blanket of silence set on suffocating them.

"Does that help?"

"If you believe in a creator. Zïnnyi's your God?"

"Zïnnyi's *a* God, but that's my business," Arriette said. "You make up your own mind. Look, Kalvin, I don't want to be rude but I have plans for lunch next door."

Kalvin scratched his chin and cleared his throat. She was staring at him all the while; criticising khaki eyes studying every breath.

"I exhausted my supplies," he said. "Lunch sounds... fun."

"I'm sure it does. Go home, Kalvin. Ask an everlast for their advice. They have lots of experience and scrolls. Is that everything? I really am late."

Arriette exhaled, closed her eyes and replayed her mother's words. *Screw on your smile, Arriette. Be a good hostess.*

"I can't. Far too risky and I don't want lecturing. Just an answer. I owe too many favours to everlasts to ask for any." Kalvin lowered his head.

"Don't tell me any more," said Arriette, sticking her fingers in her ears. "You were supposed to join the army, Kalvin. What happened?"

"I did. When Susan got sick I had to quit." He shuffled, uncomfortable and weary. "May I join you for lunch then?"

"It's Susan that's sick?" she asked, ignoring his request. "I thought-"

"Sorry, I'm tired and forgot to mention it." Kalvin linked his fingers together and placed them on his head. "Susan said you'd have answers?"

Arriette felt guilty for rushing his visit when someone they both loved was ill, so she agreed he could stay for food.

"Answers to what?"

"Her illness. She's an ice sculpture; delicate and disintegrating. Her skin is bruised, her limbs are weak and her head's almost bald." Kalvin struggled to his feet and stretched. "You said we were late?"

For a man about to lose his fiancée, he sure is focused on his dinner.

"It must be magic but I can't diagnose from here."

"I was hoping you might come to the city and confirm it. So

will you?" Arriette barely had the chance to register the request before Kalvin was on his knees beside her. "I can't lose her. She's my weakness." Arriette thought his ego could do with a brief reminder of their history. "There's no reason for anyone to hurt an innocent."

"Other than moral support what use am I?" she said. "Maybe if you repay your debt with those everlasts they could investigate."

"I wouldn't be here if it wasn't life or death."

"I can believe *that*." Arriette groaned.

She tied the laces of her comfiest shoes and buttoned up her favourite cardigan. Together she and Kalvin packed enough supplies to last three days. Canteens of water, fruit, bread, sliced meat, cheese and biscuits.

"I can't believe I'm doing this. I suppose you want to eat first?" she said, shaking her head. "What am I thinking? I can't even erect a tent!"

With further encouragement, Kalvin managed to get Arriette to the door and by the time they left, their stomachs grumbled and their throats were dry.

"What are my neighbours going to think? Running off with my ex-boyfriend! I must be mad. What about the harvest? I'll miss the celebrations."

Kalvin took Arriette by the hand and led her down the garden path. She glanced back at her humble home and waved goodbye.

TWO

At her neighbour's table, Arriette took a crash course on everlast leadership. Rihaana's father was a prestigious figure at the top of the supernatural food chain; first on what most supes called the Haeyloian Power Scale and to everyone else, the HPS.

First on their minds though was a feast to fill their stomachs and lighten the mood. Rihaana served roasted chicken, honey-dipped parsnips and mashed potatoes, thick onion gravy, freshly baked bread and for dessert, juicy strawberries and sliced watermelon.

This time of year, the people of Mousique were never hungry. Harvest made them round, bellowing and joyful. Arriette knew from her attack that with wine came a wave of disaster, but eager to block such disturbing memories she leaned across the table and stabbed another piece of fruit.

"Rihaana, has the influx of crime this century affected the government's confidence? I hear there's been an uncontrollable increase in larceny, homicide and vampyr attacks within Haeylo City. Haven't the citizens lost faith in their security?"

Arriette found everlast immortality a truly fascinating subject. Rihaana explained their extensive training in many subjects including semiotics, philosophy, Haeyloian literature and politics gave them both the emotional and intellectual capability for leadership; more than enough to sit on the scale's throne.

Like all creatures on Haeylo, they too had a weakness and it laid within an oval pendant they called the *Mirror of the Soul*. Everlasts believed it was the gateway to a piece of Zïnnyi's purity; white magic, strong enough to power their crime-riddled society. A path to the creator.

Kalvin scowled. "How can everlasts guarantee the safety of the city's inhabitants? The past decade has introduced vampyrs, three new demonic species, plagues and who knows what else may march over the horizon?"

Rihaana poured more wine. "Well, on our twentieth birthday we get a pendant chosen by our closest relatives. Eventually, we find a pendant that chooses us, or so we hope. Such a bond increases our strength and our connection to other everlasts. First-class leaders don't like to announce their capabilities but pendants have saved lives and will continue to do so."

"You're *that* confident?" Kalvin asked.

"Sure am."

"Hey Kalvin, you could help find her father's ideal pendant," said Arriette.

"*Why* would I want to do that?"

"He might wipe your debts," she replied.

Kalvin muttered something incomprehensible and shovelled melon in his already full mouth.

"Though it sounds like a hopeless task," she said, deflated. "If you kept your promises you'd have friends among the everlasts rather than enemies with no need to hate them."

"I don't *hate* them."

Rihaana beamed. "Kalvin, pendants are gifts from the architect of our universe and they're such *beautiful* pieces of jewellery; used for healing wounds and self-defence. Treasure hunters are rewarded generously."

"Why hasn't your father hired a private investigator to do the job then?" he asked.

"Father said he leaves the decision in Zïnnyi's hands." Rihaana smiled and stood to clear the empty dishes. "It's a safe occupation from dark magic too. Pendants are silver and vibrant, everything vampyrs despise."

"*Supposedly,*" said Kalvin. "Nobody ever lived through an encounter to report a successful trial of that theory." He cast a cautious eye across the table at Arriette. "Except our *friend* here."

"Hey, I didn't *lie*. You can't count my incident anyway. I'm human, not everlast. No pendant, no statistics." Kalvin grunted and reached across for the bottle of wine. Arriette moved it just out of his reach and glared at him. "Being drunk won't help your sense of direction."

"If we are both to survive one another's company, I recommend it." Kalvin rolled his eyes. "No sense of humour? Look, I'm not accusing you but vampyr venom is deadly no matter the dosage. One bite and you'd be dead with little time to place blame on my habits."

"Explain how I survived then," said Arriette, folding her arms.

"Maybe he was a drunken local? No amount of sparkling everlast tat can protect you from the real thing." Kalvin turned to Rihaana, his eyes narrow and accusing. "So, spare me your lecture on the life-saving qualities of pendants. Everlasts *will* lose control of the city soon and when they do, I want to be as self-sufficient as possible." Satisfied, Kalvin slammed his fist on the table. "Rumour is you're planning to forfeit your pendant. Know something we don't?"

Rihaana stopped chewing. "Where did you hear such a rumour?"

"Don't worry yourself, *runaway*. I've met your father."

"Rihaana's trying to help you, Kalvin. Give you a bargaining ticket. Treasure hunting could help pay Susan's medical bills. As a reward Charles might find and hang the lunatic responsible for using dark magic on her."

Rihaana sighed. "I meant no disrespect. Susan isn't sick because of the crime influx *or* the government, least I don't believe so. Father has a lot of contacts and he plays golf with the magistrate; treasure hunting is a great idea."

Rich city folk could afford to blow their money on sports

like golf, fancy offices and luxury clothing for their daughters, thought Kalvin. Rihaana's dyed cotton dress and leather sandals said enough about her upbringing to disgust him especially when most villagers, including Arriette, wore patchwork rags.

"I need no further everlast contact. Local retainers would point me toward easy money if I was so desperate. At the moment the cash Susan has saved will cover her care." Kalvin snarled. "Thanks for your concern."

"Why would a retainer waste an eidetic memory encouraging people like you to acquire illegal, undeclared cash?" Rihaana asked, maddened by his disdainful comments.

"I may owe debts in high places, Miss Melovich, but I am owed far more by middle-class supes." Kalvin twiddled his thumbs. "My responsibility lies with the funeral arrangements only. I'd do the necessary to see Sue's burial go well but not so far as an everlast's charity. Charles can hunt for his own pendant."

Arriette sighed. "Look, Kalvin, we're only trying-"

"No, he's right." Rihaana sipped her wine. "Retainers are sympathetic and knowledgeable by nature; they'd help *legally* for free, but so would my father. I'd like to think him decent enough."

"If you knew any honest half-everlast, half-retainers we'd have cracked it then," said Kalvin. "Shame they don't interbreed, huh?"

Arriette threw a spoon at him and scowled. "Don't be rude."

Retaliation wouldn't encourage Arriette's sympathy so Kalvin cracked his knuckles and chewed his tongue before reaching over for the wine. This time she didn't scold him.

"I may be rude but I'm not wrong," he said.

"Time for a new subject before I change my mind," said Arriette. "Tell me where we'll stay if not with Susan."

"Local inn. Whoever hurt Sue might still be lurking in our apartment."

"So you *do* have a conscience," Rihaana said. "Let's use it before the alcohol dissolves your common sense. I'll get my map. We can plan your route around Manaia Forest."

"Quicker just to brave it."

"I take it back," said Rihaana. "You're about as *crazy* as a vampyr in the sunshine. Arriette wouldn't survive two days. No offence."

"None taken. I tried to tell him," said Arriette.

Kalvin slumped back in his chair, picking at a piece of bread in thought. "Just got to learn how to avoid the ghouls."

"This isn't a science," said Arriette.

"I disagree; I managed the journey without incident."

Rihaana reached across the table and took hold of Arriette's hand. "Without everlast funding or retaining knowledge, there's nothing you can do for Susan."

"Moral support and friendship is a start," said Kalvin. "Hey, tell Rihaana why they call it *Manaia* Forest. Settle her nerves."

Arriette grinned and raised her brow. "How should *I* know?"

"You read. Back me up."

Arriette inhaled her frustration and slapped on her most convincing smile. "Manaia is said to be the first creature Zïnnyi placed on Haeylo. He was a trusted messenger and a protector of the land. Scrolls in Haeylo City's library are said to depict Manaia as a white bird, if you believe in myth."

Kalvin bit into his bread and, proud of his knowledge, slammed a fist on the table.

"See? Nothing to fear."

Unconvinced, Arriette turned to her friend. "Isn't there any way to contact your father? I'm not betting on the bird."

"I'm their firstborn; if I can marry into another supe species within the next two years, I'm free of the everlast inheritance. Until then I'll remain invisible."

"I thought you had older siblings?" Arriette asked.

"Only step-siblings. Father has children with other women."

Arriette decided not to go there.

In her opinion Rihaana would have made a wonderful everlast and a skilled leader. One she'd be proud to follow. Giving that up for marriage to a human, retainer or any other supe seemed such a waste.

"He's too proud, Arriette."

"He's over *five thousand* years old," Kalvin said. "Proud is an understatement."

Only a lunatic would agree to this death trip, thought Arriette. Even the most respectable people in that city were hard-hearted. How could Rihaana's father be so brutal? He'd been with her human mother for over thirty years now. Surely marriage had crossed his mind?

"Charles is only four thousand years short of Haeylo's birth," Kalvin added. "Has lots of children with many women. Rihaana's step-siblings are now influential politicians."

"He just wants what he thinks is best for me," she said.

"Every one of his children accepted the gift. No wonder he's frustrated; you're the first to break the chain," he said, one eyebrow raised. "I'm surprised the army isn't out looking for you." Arriette threatened him with her fork. He held up both hands in surrender. "Sorry, none of my business."

"We're going to stay out of everlast politics during our visit," Arriette told Rihaana. "If anyone asks, we haven't seen you."

"Well if Kalvin's debts aren't with my father he won't bother you. Just behave yourselves."

Confused by the information overload, Arriette attempted to recall any laws she'd read in her books and the everlast class system. First were elders, second advisers and third new to the power. Haeyloian laws were universal, minus Zìnnyi's guidance for religious citizens. Still, how difficult could all *that* be to master?

"Looks like I'm not getting out of this journey. Would you mind packing us extra food for the road, Rihaana? My pantry was bare."

Once in the kitchen, Rihaana nudged her friend and smirked. "If you change your mind or decide to ditch him I won't judge you. I wouldn't trust his judgement. He'll get you both killed."

Kalvin sipped his wine. "I *can* hear you. Please stop talking about me like I'm not present."

"What else is there to discuss?" she asked, keeping her back to the table.

"Well, when did you move in? I'm sure that's an interesting topic."

He would have remembered a face as beautiful as hers; the way she pulled back that slick hair in a high bun, revealing a smooth chocolate complexion and kind hazel eyes. Kalvin's military training taught him to lie; how to look comfortable in a place you so obviously don't belong. Rihaana had dark secrets just like he, and she hid them about as well, from Arriette in particular.

"A few years ago," she said, watching him carefully. "A housing agent re-located me off my father's radar."

There it is, Kalvin thought. *She's protecting someone.* He pondered which housing agent could possibly risk defying an everlast and how much they were paid.

"Your father's search party will reach Mousique eventually."

"He won't find me unless *you* mention my location." Rihaana glanced out the window at the setting sun and shuddered. "So when are you going?"

"We can leave now if we're inconveniencing you," he said.

Rihaana untied her apron and slung it on the back of her seat. Then she stormed to the kitchen and began to cram the leftover food into an old sack.

"You're a piece of work, Kalvin Avery. I ought to let you starve."

Arriette shook her head at his poor manners, disappointed she didn't have anything left to throw.

"You're lucky Arriette agreed to travel given your history. Susan was too much of a doll for my liking; more worried about her appearance than her friend's feelings."

"We all have demons. If you knew Susan's you'd give her a break," he said.

Arriette excused herself from the table and escaped to the bathroom, pleased for a moment of peace. She could hear their debate through the walls as she tidied her hair. The conversation weighed heavily on her shoulders.

"You never met her." Kalvin went on, "You're being unreasonable."

"Arriette told me about your affair. That's all I need to pass judgement."

"I'm not here for fun. Sue misses her."

"That doesn't prove me wrong."

"Susan ran away; she didn't come here because she liked harvest festivals. Just like she didn't leave to marry me. Not at first. She's got history. History Arriette *needs* to hear."

"So tell her now," Rihaana said.

"It's important she hears it from Susan. I promised I'd let her explain."

Explain what? Arriette had heard enough. She splashed her face with cool water and straightened her dress in the mirror. Why didn't she buy one from the travelling tradesman? This unshapely brown sack looked awful on her.

"You can do this," she encouraged herself. "Get back out there. Take charge."

When she emerged from the bathroom, Rihaana and Kalvin were clearing the table and preparing the picnic in silence. Rihaana scowled at Kalvin and gestured for him to tell her, then continued packing.

"I need to come clean," he said, glaring at Rihaana. "Susan doesn't think she has long and-"

"Yes, I heard you. Any idea what this is about?"

"Who she really is. One of her friends came by before Susan got sick and warned her of a war heading our way. She said Susan and I should leave and had supes ready to protect us."

"Don't be ridiculous, Kalvin."

He continued regardless of her disbelief. "I'm serious. I just want to meet her final wish."

"Sorry, wait, protection from who?" asked Rihaana.

"And if there is a war on the way and it arrives when we do, then what?" asked Arriette.

Rihaana slammed the sack on the table and raised her finger.

"If *anything* happens to Arriette so help me—"

Despite her threat, he seemed surprisingly calm. "So we get in and out of there fast. Go straight to the hospital. Do whatever we can to save her. If we can't then she'll die surrounded by loved ones. That's better than the alternative."

"Which is?"

"Alone, frightened and unheard," he said.

Rihaana took Arriette by the arm and dragged her aside. She lowered her voice, keeping a keen eye on Kalvin. "You're actually buying this?"

"I have no reason not to," Arriette said.

"He didn't tell you about this war until *I* prompted him."

"Amends have to be made no matter the reason for his visit. He thinks I hate him."

"Do you?"

"No," said Arriette, proud of her quick response.

Despite such an uncomfortable history, Rihaana trusted Arriette could manage a few days of his company in a city surrounded by walls and guards. Her own feelings about Kalvin Avery were irrelevant.

"Watch him closely," she said, passing Arriette the picnic and gesturing at her scars. "Cover your neck and close your mouth. Oh, and Arriette, *try* to stay alive, will you?"

THREE

They left the paddock at dusk as Mousique's festivities began to settle for the curfew. Arriette's sweat-soaked palms skated the reigns, her feet quaked in the stirrups and despite the wonderful breeze, gentle thudding of her horse's hooves and the occasional neighbourly wave, the butterflies in her stomach scattered.

"Tell me more about the cause of Susan's illness," she said to kill the awkward silence.

Kalvin ran a hand through his dark hair, choosing a safe place to start the story.

"Retaining doctors think it's a hex." He frowned. "Don't pull that face."

"What face?"

Kalvin raised an eyebrow. "That's your disbelieving, criticizing, mothering—"

Arriette surrendered. "*Fine*, no more faces. You were saying?"

"Oh you haven't changed one bit," he said, shaking his head. "You know what a hex is, Arriette. I'm disappointed."

Arriette bit her lower lip. "But there aren't any witches on this planet."

"There's the wiccan faith," Kalvin said. "Bet you've studied that."

"Sure but they aren't powerful enough to hex someone."

"Everlasts think so. They're aspiring supes; study semiotics and mix herbal remedies, that sort of thing. They're low on the

HPS."

Arriette was sceptical. "Oh, symbols like the pentagram, you mean?" Arriette drew an imaginary star with her finger in the air and raised her eyebrow. "The symbol of power and disclosure of secrets."

"Drawing stars doesn't make you a criminal, Arriette. Let's not assume they summon evil spirits. It's kind of cliché."

Arriette sighed and forced herself not to look back at the village. They had already passed her vegetable patch and the communal fresh water well. The more distance they covered the more anxious she became. Most familiarities would soon be out of reach, like the gentle trickling sound from the nearby ravine, harvest shovels hitting dry soil and the salted taste of homegrown potatoes. Now an intriguing and terrifying alien world awaited her instead.

"You said you needed my help but I'm no expert."

Kalvin shook his head and pulled on the reigns. Arriette stopped beside him.

"I didn't expect you to be but you know a significant amount more than those retainers."

"I can only confirm their biology is human and their minds are magical." Arriette's brows furrowed in thought. "Does that help?"

Kalvin rolled his eyes. "I think you're more intelligent than you realise."

"On this topic I doubt it. Have you witnessed any of their magic? Spells, levitation, that sort of thing?"

"Not personally but Susan has. During her travels she also claims to have seen a dragon so make up your own mind as to how valid the story is." He laughed. "Crazy if you ask me."

"In Susan's defence, they existed once."

"*Once* being the important word."

Arriette felt sick when she realised why they'd stopped. This was the tree line where the vampyr latched to her throat; *drank* from her. Her scars began to pulse and Arriette pulled the collar of her cardigan up, taking deep, cleansing breaths.

"This *is* the quickest way, Arriette."

"We should pick up the pace. I have a decent head on my shoulders which is better said now than once we've entered through those trees." Arriette nudged her horse.

"Decapitation isn't a vampyr signature," Kalvin said.

He grinned and waved off her nausea with a simple hand gesture, then urged his horse to follow.

Arriette stirred her memory for wiccan information as a distraction. She'd studied magical illusions before and even tried a few. Her best-loved author was a woman named Harriet Foley who wrote about potions and chants as tools to flourish romance. Sometimes she gave recipes for healing balms and lotions, but Arriette wasn't a big believer in the spell-casting part. Those she'd tried all failed and after she'd felt rather silly. Still, the theory fascinated her.

Harriet's work would already have been studied by retainers so was of no use to Susan's doctor, but she thought she remembered a travelling tradesman tell the story of a young girl; the daughter of an everlast who died three days before her twentieth birthday. She was sure the girl was cursed so Arriette decided to ask Kalvin. He said when the girl's father refused to marry his mistress and retire his immortality she hexed his firstborn. The cause of death couldn't be verified. Magic never left much of a trace.

"Are the symptoms the same?" asked Arriette. "I read about biology so maybe I can find a connection."

"Unless she's worse since I last saw her, I told you all I know. It's like she's aged."

"So we're against the clock. How old is she?"

Kalvin's face strained. "In human years thirty-one but you don't know her history. That's why she—"

"Why she called me, yes you already said. I *read*."

Kalvin rolled his eyes. "Oh, never mind."

Arriette thought that such a vicious curse might be an everlast's method of punishment; speed up the human ageing process when their own lives would only flourish.

Kalvin leered forward to scan the opening ahead. "I wonder what the time is."

"Will you focus? How can we be so sure this was a hex?" asked Arriette, trying to get his attention again.

"You agree it's the most likely explanation." Kalvin sat back in his saddle and sighed. "You know, you're the only human for miles who reads about basic human biology. There aren't many of you about these days so you're valuable, like a self-taught retainer."

"Many of *who* about?"

"Humans are in short supply. Especially those who can read." His brow raised.

"We're not extinct," she argued, "but we're outnumbered by supes. All the best schools are in the city. I had no choice but to educate myself because unlike your retainers I don't remember everything I see."

"Finding an intelligent human would've been almost impossible." Kalvin's eyes were wide and sweeping the clearing as they spoke. His hands began to shake. "Can you believe a retainer asked where Susan's heart was? Like our biology is so different to theirs."

"I agree that's odd but I don't see how this—"

"They asked me if I knew any human doctors," he continued. "This isn't the only case so in my desperation I gave your name. Susan had that message for you anyway *so*—"

"You sold me to supes, didn't you?" asked Arriette. "In exchange for what?"

He swallowed hard. "One of the everlasts I owed money to came by. He threatened Susan's life if I didn't repay him. This seemed like the most logical way to please everyone."

Arriette curled her fingers tightly around the reigns. "Except me."

"Don't be like that. My debts are repaid, Susan can explain her story and you can examine some strange medical cases."

"What if I *can't* help, Kalvin? I'm not a doctor." Arriette shook her head. "You're so irresponsible."

"Don't be mad. *I'm* the one in trouble."

"We agree on something at least." Arriette sighed. "An everlast has *purchased* me, Kalvin. What's that even supposed to mean? Am I a slave? What if Susan dies before I reach her because I'm running errands to settle *your* debt?"

"Charles is looking forward to seeing how you diagnose other cases. Don't you want to help, for old times? Everlast accommodation is real nice."

"I don't think I've ever met anyone more selfish. And *Charles* is behind this? You predicted he'd send somebody for Rihaana once he knew her location and still you lied to her. You lied to *me*. I can't even look at you. What a scheming, disrespectful—"

"I won't apologise," he said.

"Oh, save your breath," Arriette yanked the reins and galloped in the opposite direction.

"Hey, wait!"

Arriette ignored him and bolted into the forest. When she'd been riding for an hour without finding another presence she dismounted and scanned the ground for prints.

"I'm such a fool. I'm lost in the most dangerous forest on Haeylo, alone!"

A rustle of leaves startled Arriette.

She reached for her horse's reigns and prepared a quick escape when through the trees emerged an overweight man on a black stallion. His wide eyes were a piercing green, predominant upon such pale skin. He'd tied back his greasy hair in a long plait and was dressed in a city uniform.

"Thank Zïnnyi! Can you help me, Sir? I took a wrong turn," said Arriette.

"My name is Dean Constable." He stared down at her with a bland expression. Arriette didn't hold her breath for a handshake. "I'm a retaining servant of Charles Melovich. My orders were to find Arriette Monroe and take her to him should the first agent fail."

Arriette peered round the horse to see Kalvin fighting

through the trees. He'd removed his trench coat to reveal matching attire and replaced his casual smirk with narrow eyes and a deep frown. He snatched Arriette's forearm.

"You just *had* to run, Arriette."

"What are you doing? Let me go!"

Dean Constable threw back his head and bellowed with laughter when Arriette tried to struggle free.

"Rihaana was right about you," she cried.

Bored with her fumbling, Kalvin threw her body to the ground with a thud, pressed her face to the dirt with his boot and kicked her hard in the ribs. She felt a sharp crack, a hideous stab of pain and an unbearable burning in her lungs.

"I tried to reason with you, Arriette."

"What gives you the right to restrain me?"

He reached up to take a pair of cuffs from Dean's saddle bag.

When he crouched low enough to imprison her, Arriette lashed out with her palm, showering dirt and stones across his face. With her arms wrapped tight around her chest, she struggled to her feet and made haste for the trees, leaving a cloud of dust behind her.

Kalvin shrieked. "Get her you fool!"

The black stallion gained on Arriette. She focused every ounce of energy she could muster on her legs then dived into the branches and flung out both arms, forcing twigs and leaves left and right to create a clearer view of what lay ahead. There was nothing but green for miles in any direction with only the scent of wet peat and an uncomfortable sticky humidity to keep her company. The severity of each throb in her thighs soon slowed her pace.

The stallion hung back when the bushes were too thick, giving Arriette the opportunity to crouch low in a ditch and cradle her wounds. She covered her mouth to muffle each whine of discomfort until her pursuers stopped rummaging through the shrubbery.

"If I can't settle this with reason I'll do so in blood," Kalvin said.

"You want to take Rihaana?"

"Now my only other bargaining ticket has escaped I have no choice if I'm to protect Susan from Mr Melovich."

Dean lowered his voice. "Sir, we're letting the Monroe woman go?"

"Believe me, she'll find us."

Arriette crawled until she could no longer hear their squabbling. Her dress was mangled and uncomfortable. When her body wouldn't carry her further she sat, curled up and cried. What was she doing? Poor Rihaana's fate had been sealed because of her cowardice. Without a compass and a horse she'd be lost in the forest forever. Grazes on her arms, legs and face wept thick crimson ink and she had to tear her cardigan for bandages.

Arriette had barely caught her breath when the sound of a twig snapping in the darkness startled her. Before she'd gathered enough air in her lungs to scream, she was surrounded.

FOUR

Arriette dragged herself to an imbalanced stance and faced her challengers. Glowing eyes alight like fire and skin the colour of snow illuminated their figures against the forest's cerulean backdrop.

"What do we have here?"

The first attacker licked her lips and danced around Arriette playfully. Coal coloured hair hung in shaggy ringlets at shoulder length, covering evidence of a brutal death.

Her friends had been dead for a long time too based on the condition of their clothes. Besides a ragged shirt and his one sandal, the youngest was bare. Arriette averted her eyes.

"Where do you think *you're* going."

The other vampyrs cackled in unison.

In one swift movement she ripped off Arriette's improvised bandage and inhaled the metallic scent. Arriette tried to dash beneath her hold but stumbled and fell face-first in the leaves.

The vampyr wore a torn waitress uniform and dusty name tag. Roberta, it said. This monster had once been a hard-working human.

She stroked Arriette's skin with the back of her hand, twirling her wavy brown hair like ribbon between pale fingers, then hauled her up.

"Let's not play with our food." Their leader emerged from the shadow of an overhanging tree. "This is my hunt. I have first bite."

He wore ripped black shorts and a navy shirt. His feet were

bare and matted blonde hair sprang untidily in all directions. If he were human Arriette might have found him attractive.

"Damn you, Angelo. I haven't eaten in weeks," said Roberta. "She's the first human we've seen."

In one smooth swing of her fist Roberta knocked Arriette down and straddled her. She glared up, eyes watering, at the overcast sky. An explosive crash of thunder shook the ground and Arriette screeched as a bolt of electricity struck a nearby tree, sending flames into the sky. Rain showered their fight, churned the forest floor and presented a thick bog which Arriette knew would drown her if she didn't battle to her feet. The wind picked up and the surrounding trees leered; branches pointed at her failure and mocked her weakness.

Another vampyr began to bind Arriette's limbs with rope. She searched through the forest's resources with her fingers whilst the vampyrs were distracted. With her remaining energy, she kicked out and managed to throw Roberta off balance with a broken branch, anchoring it between them.

The other vampyr released the rope to catch Roberta as she wobbled and splashed into a puddle of soggy leaves. Angelo's fangs were the first to attempt a bite.

Arriette stumbled into him and thrust the branch at his shoulder. Although the rain gave the others a small amount of camouflage against the forest backdrop, the sound of squelching and splashing gave Arriette her bearings back.

Pinned to the tree and unable to escape a savage cremation, she watched Angelo's face twist in agony but, in his final moments, turned her head to shield her eyes from his flaking remains. Bile rose in her mouth but then her pupils widened and stamina increased. The adrenaline gave her broken ribs temporary pain relief.

Roberta grabbed her neck from behind, cutting off Arriette's air supply. She tore the weapon away.

"You'll burn for this," Arriette managed, proud of what she was sure would be her last words before Roberta's fangs sank deep into her flesh.

Light at first, then fearsome and bellowing, Arriette began to hear human voices in the distance before her limp body was released. Dust from a soft blanket tickled her nose. Someone kind scooped her up and threw her over their shoulder.

Arriette's heroes escaped deep into Manaia Forest before the world, pitying Arriette's exhaustion, faded to darkness.

FIVE

Eleven; the whispered word that plagued Arriette's recurring nightmares. But now there were shadows in the distance and an unfamiliar man. Her vision was blurred and darkness consumed every corner.

"*Who are you?*" Arriette whispered.

"*Through every city shall he hunt her down,*" said the stranger. His face was covered with black cloth and his voice quivered. "*Thou follow me, and I will be thy guide, and lead thee hence through the eternal place.*"

Eager to escape it all, Arriette reached out and grasped his soft, beckoning hand.

She woke abruptly to the scent of smoked fish and fried eggs, fresh orange juice and strong coffee. At first she only noticed the bandages around her arms and torso, then the unfamiliar squeeze of soft material around her thighs and ankles. Perhaps she'd been more severely wounded than she thought.

Arriette stole a glance at her rescuers. Two broad men sat by a grand fireplace, turning their successful hunt into breakfast and a woman with short blonde hair swept the floor. All without even a glance in her direction. *What is this place?*

Knowing she couldn't lay there unnoticed forever, Arriette reached for the bite marks on her neck and came across two deep punctures. She withdrew her hand and gasped.

"Oh, you're awake," said the blonde. "Hungry? We have enough food to feed an army."

One of the men slammed down his cup. "We might have to now that Pando—"

The young woman threw a cushion at him. He grunted, retrieved it from the kitchen floor and launched it back. Then he returned to his meal with a scowl on his face.

Arriette used the rest of her strength to sit up. "Where am I?"

"You're here and alive," she said. "You have the boys to thank. They saw the fire."

She rushed to Arriette's side and held up a piece of broken mirror. There was so much to look at and too many unnatural colours.

"Bruises to prove it," she said, "but bruises fade."

"I look like death." Arriette pushed the mirror away and shuddered.

"Thank Zïnnyi for sending the lightning," said the woman. "He must owe you a favour."

"Hmm, I'm a *real* favourite."

There were hideous purple rings around her eyes. Scratch marks from Roberta's nails trailed down her neck and disappeared beneath her clothing, which she realised had been changed.

"Who cleaned my wounds; changed my clothes?"

The woman smiled. "I sent the men away, Arriette, don't worry."

"You know my name? You work with Dean, don't you? The swine I'll—"

The woman flinched, cleared her throat and hopped to her feet. Arriette's energy drained as fast as she'd mustered it. Her fight drifted, leaving her limp and tired.

Damn Kalvin! Damn him to Hell!

"Let me get you some breakfast."

Arriette tried desperately to remember how she got there. A blank mist cast over her thoughts and there was a terrible storm brewing behind her eyes. Coughing up what she presumed was rainwater and vampyr ash, Arriette remembered how thirsty she was.

I will be thy guide.
The silhouette saved her, brought her from the darkness. Before she could query it the woman returned with her breakfast and a tissue.

"So, vampyrs?"

"I guess," said Arriette. She wiped her mouth and blew her nose. "Listen, you got any water? Or pain kill—"

"Boys said you killed one."

Arriette rubbed her eyes and shrugged. It was all she could manage.

Why was this woman so cheerful? Rosy cheeks, brilliant white teeth and large ocean eyes filled with excitement. Arriette couldn't bear the sight of such happiness when she felt so groggy. She pushed the food away.

"Do any of you know Dante?" she asked.

"No, is he your boyfriend?" asked the woman.

"I, uhm, oh never mind. My memory's a little—"

"Vamps can't remember their human lives so I suppose now you understand why they're—"

"Inhumane monstrosities?"

The woman smiled. "Forgetful. When you're drained it's not just of your blood. They're more aggressive recently." When Arriette's eyes narrowed she waved a dismissive hand. "A topic for another time. Our creator must value you."

"More than I value myself," said Arriette. "I'm fast running out of luck though." One of the men turned to stare at her. "Do *you* know Dante?"

"Heard a voice, huh?" he said, raising a brow.

"Yes in a dream and there was a man," she said.

"Well voice or no voice I admire your courage," the woman continued. "Not many people survive vampyr attacks."

Arriette said, "Well this is my second. Third time lucky?"

"Third time dead," said one of the men.

Arriette studied the blonde's kind blue eyes and flawless ivory skin. Whoever she was, she glowed, filling the entire room with a warmth Arriette hadn't felt in a long time.

Friendship and trust, it felt like, although she was fresh out of both.

Her chest tightened at the memory of Susan.

"Who are you? Why am I here?"

"My name is Baby A. This is Reiko Port," she said, pointing to a man with a shiny head and two missing front teeth. He was far too wide to be her mystery ghost. "The man next to him is Tobias Shallow. He carried you home."

Desperate not to offend anyone, Arriette forced a croaky 'hello' whilst evaluating his shape with little confidence.

"They were out hunting when they heard your struggle. You were covered in ash."

Tobias beamed at Arriette from across the room, distracting her. His pearly grin, broad chest and tanned skin were every woman's dream. She presumed he and Baby A were involved so tried not to blush. Whilst Reiko was friendly enough to smile at her, his exterior sent chills down her spine. He had comforting eyes though. Khaki like hers.

Tobias was a beautiful specimen of a human with hazel eyes and mousy hair. *If he is indeed human.*

"I really can't remember," she muttered, fluttering her lashes.

An elderly gentleman in a white robe and sandals emerged then from a dimly lit corner of the room. Arriette hadn't noticed the fifth presence. He'd ensconced himself in an armchair by the window prior to his gentle shuffle toward her. His grey beard reached below a rope belt and a moustache sat thick across his upper lip.

Arriette accepted his handshake, noting how firm and strong he was for a man she predicted to be at least eighty human years old. He hadn't spoken yet but his size and shape proved promising for her mystery dream man.

"How do you all know my name?"

"I'm *so* glad you're here," he said. "My name is Casper and this is my cabin. I built it with my own hands. Do you like it?"

Arriette swallowed hard. "It's beautiful but I've taken advantage of your hospitality and I ought to be on my way."

Casper placed a hand on her shoulder. "Not at all. We're pleased to have you. I've been looking for you for a while. Of course, you've had the dreams so will know all about your calling."

"What calling? So it *was* you in the dream?"

"Perhaps I've said too much; presumed too much. Wrong year, maybe. I'm ahead of time. Still, I'm certain of my choice." Casper squeezed her shoulder and then struggled back to his chair. "Sleep, my dear, you've been through so much."

"Oh no, I need to leave."

Reiko stuck his blade into the wooden table top, startling her. "You won't make it out of the forest alive," he said. "I told you, third time dead."

The perfect words to dampen her already miserable mood. At least she was still in Manaia Forest, *somewhere*.

Baby A handed her a cup of tea. The scent of infused lemon excited her senses and she relaxed a little, breathing deeply. It cleared her head and settled her nerves.

"Do you want to talk about what happened?" asked Casper.

"There's nothing to say." Arriette held a cautious eye on Reiko's freshly sharpened knife.

"Surely there's an explanation for a young woman out at night, alone?" he asked.

It sure wasn't for the good of my health.

Arriette sipped her drink and set the cup of tea on the arm of the chair. Her headache was beginning to lift but in its place was something else; an intrusive, unfamiliar tug at her memories.

"I'd like to hear what happened," Casper said.

Arriette waited for their eye contact to break but he was strong-willed. So she told him everything she remembered from Kalvin's arrival until the attack. The words rolled uncontrollably from her lips until she had the sense to cover her mouth with her palm.

"Was Kalvin your lover?" asked Baby A, making nothing of it.

Arriette mumbled something from behind her hand, confused by the sudden change of mood.

"Was he?" asked Tobias.

"That's history. I handled it," she said, lifting her head, "until he betrayed me."

"We insist you stay and rest," Casper said.

"I can't go home now anyway. If I turn back they'll hunt me down. Dean was a brutal, disgusting creature. I should report him. Can you take me to the city to find Susan?"

The old man frowned. "Didn't Kalvin tell you what she wanted?"

"There was no truth there," said Arriette. "He just used me to settle debts. I'm still intent on seeing Sue, though, to tell her what an evil—"

"Arriette, perhaps we should presume Kalvin wasn't lying. What did he say?"

She sighed. "Susan had history and I needed to hear it direct. Kalvin wouldn't explain."

"So you *don't* think Susan's ill?" asked Baby A.

Arriette sipped her tea and said nothing. The answer was obviously no.

"Is that all he said, Arriette?" asked Casper.

"He mentioned a war," she blurted. "Susan's friend said they should go on the run and gain protection. Hey, what did you put in this tea?" She was awfully light-headed. "How do you know my name?"

Casper twiddled his thumbs. He took Arriette's temperature with the back of his hand and ordered more tea, which Reiko delivered swiftly.

"Drink, my dear."

Arriette complied, fearful that he might force it down her neck.

"Do you know how long you've been here?" Reiko asked.

"A few hours?"

"Forty-eight," he corrected. "Sleeping all the while."

Arriette felt much better after her second cup. "What are

you? You're not human."

"How can you tell?" asked Tobias. "Got a sixth sense?"

A crease formed in Arriette's brow as she considered his suggestion. She could sure have used a sixth sense. Perhaps then she might have avoided Kalvin's little visit.

"I'm just a human with a good judge of character."

"Well my species is of no importance at the moment," said Casper.

More secrets. Arriette traced the outline of a pentagram in her palm and sighed.

"Can you remember anything else?" asked Baby A. "War is a serious topic."

"Do you think there's any truth behind the prediction? Could all supes be involved? I've read scrolls foretelling such developments."

"That's a grave accusation," said Baby A. "Travellers might be fourth on the HPS but are completely harmless and dreamers will never attack unprovoked. They're peaceful by nature."

"Sorry, this is news to me. I had few problems until now."

Baby A folded her arms. "Your ex sounds like a *huge* problem."

Cheap shot, thought Arriette.

"Until he turned up at my door I'd done rather well without him." If she was anything it was independent. "Obviously you're supernatural and I've offended you. Please don't take this personally."

Baby A paced the room until she caught Casper scowling. "Well don't accuse us of being troublemakers," she said, softening. "Trust me, I'd know if travellers were waging war. Our species want only what's best for Haeylo and use their gift for the benefit of others. We return to Earth to investigate the rise and fall of our old planet."

"Hold on," said Arriette. "Are *you* a traveller? You speak of Earth in the present tense."

"We're in the present tense. To say you're an avid reader you're not too bright, are you?" Baby A turned to Casper. "Are you *sure* she's the one?"

Casper nodded but said nothing.

"Earth *exists*," Arriette gasped, more to herself than her company. "Fascinating; yes I do read but I didn't know travellers dared delve into ancient history."

"Earth is millions of years old and uninhabited now, but sure," Baby A said.

"Incredible. You've been there? For what purpose?"

Baby A rolled her eyes. She must have answered that question a thousand times.

"Perhaps we should wait," Tobias began.

Baby A continued, barely hearing his objection. "Your species isn't exactly *thriving* at the moment. I travelled to learn why you were so self-destructive. Travelled, that is. *Past* tense. I don't do that anymore. Not after, well, that's another story and I'm needed here."

Tobias interrupted, "Isn't it a bit early to be discussing this?"

"Please tell me. I have nothing else to do until I recover. You said I can't go anywhere. Say, are there books here? Reference and history books?"

"Of course." Casper sighed. "However, I'd rather talk."

"Why the sudden interest?" Tobias asked.

Arriette shrugged. "I like to learn."

He grinned. "If you heard some of our problems you'd wish you hadn't pried."

"You'll have to elaborate."

"Never mind my friends," Casper said. "Baby A was merely trying to explain her role. Her previous job is redundant. We'll leave it there."

"I thought He put you here to guard us; how can that job *ever* be redundant?"

"Because we're not capable of change," Reiko said without taking his eyes from the plate. His voice was so profound it made Arriette jump. "That's right, I'm human too."

Baby A continued. "Casper, Arriette should know this stuff." She thought for a moment and then nodded. "For thousands of years, everlasts have ordered time-travellers to go back and change minor details to test Haeylo."

"Test for what?"

"Power." Baby sighed. "Reiko's right, you're not capable of change. Individually perhaps but not as a species. You like to destroy things. If one of those tests ever proves positive, which is unlikely, perhaps we will finally be redundant. Of course, if you don't believe in the creation story, telling you all this is pointless."

Arriette smiled. "I believe."

Casper took a sip of his tea and asked Baby A to bring Arriette a warm, damp cloth. She was sweating and red in the face.

"Tests for power you say?" she asked, batting Baby A's hand away.

"Be still and I'll explain." Arriette slumped against a cushion and allowed Baby A to mop her brow. "We changed the past to see whether it increased the human population or improved their behaviour in the present. Everlasts are terrified that if your numbers get too high, Zïnnyi will remove their gifts, rendering them pointless. Supes were placed on the new planet thousands of years ago to protect the human race from themselves and help rebuild it."

"Are you following?" Tobias took the cloth from Baby A and threw it on the table. "You look pale."

Arriette held her breath and blinked away her nausea, then nodded. "I'm fine."

"As I was saying, everlasts fear a human uprising. You're the minority for now but imagine if we could change that. Everlasts are too selfish to allow it, being at the top of the HPS."

Tobias frowned. "Are you *sure* you want to know this stuff? You're just a human, *remember*?"

Arriette wasn't sure she appreciated the reminder that her species was dying or Tobias inferring she was anything but normal, but she'd take all the knowledge on the supes she could get.

"I think that's enough for now," said Casper. "Arriette's tired and feeling poorly."

A yawn and awkward stretch didn't give her any room for protest. "I don't mean to be rude," she said, "it's just all so cryptic. First Kalvin. Now you. I just want to get out of Manaia Forest. Normality and ignorance was a blessing." Using the arm of the sofa, Arriette pulled herself to a stance and staggered to the door. "I need air."

"Sit down," said Casper. "Drink your tea."

Arriette handed the cup to Baby A. "Thank you but I'm not thirsty."

"It contains rowan. It's good for you."

"Rowan causes hallucinations, no wonder I'm unwell."

"A few small drops does no harm," Casper assured her.

"Rowan berries enhance inner magic," said Reiko, tapping his heart and smiling. "It will flush out the toxins from that vampyr's venom. Blood transfusions are exhausting and you need your strength."

Arriette froze. "Where did you get the blood to do this? Who gave you the right? Rowan berries! Are you *insane*?"

Baby A took Arriette by the arm and tried to steer her to the sofa. It was clear their discussion on the creation and human population had been temporarily suspended.

"Until you're rested you won't understand. Rowan berries are very symbolic in our culture."

"Of what?"

"Protection," Baby A said.

"Are you forgetting my hobby? I read, Baby A. Please don't underestimate my knowledge. Rowan enhances black magic and is used to produce stakes, so what *are* you? Is this a coven? Are you a witch?"

The old man placed his index finger under Arriette's chin and lifted her face, studying the puncture marks on her neck. His eyes narrowed at her accusation.

"Rowan poisons vampyrs; it counteracts their venom, hence its relevance in your bloodstream. In high doses it's a hallucinogen, except your dosage is minimal. Now calm down."

Arriette thrust his wrist away and strained her body to move forward. The pain was excruciating. She fell to her knees, taking Baby A by the hand.

"I have to get out of here. I can't stay with witches. Somebody help me!"

"There's nobody around for miles," said Tobias. "We're not trying to hurt you. You have to relax. You're being irrational."

Arriette pulled Baby A's hand so hard she lost her balance and stumbled.

"Don't let the darkness consume me. There's good in you, I see it."

Baby A frowned. "I'm sorry but I can't. Now let go, you're hurting me."

"Travel back for me and fix this mess."

"*I can't,*" she said. "Don't make me do this, Arriette."

"If you won't help then what are you good for, traveller?"

Baby A's throat and chest began to glow as though she'd swallowed a hundred fireflies. The light danced to her limbs and eventually her eyes.

Arriette sobbed and scrambled across the floor on her knees but Baby A had already outstretched her arms to uncover a secondary gift. Her shirt ripped across the middle, leaving the time-traveller bare-chested.

Arriette covered her eyes. "Who *are* you?"

Reiko dragged Arriette behind the sofa just in time to avoid the next attack.

Baby A's eyes were ablaze with electricity. Bolts of it launched at Arriette from her fingertips. The display disorientated her and she squirmed in Reiko's arms for freedom, blinded by the fireworks.

"Keep your head down and eyes closed," he bellowed.

When the lightning stopped, Baby A released her wings.

Arriette clawed free from Reiko's hold and made a pass for the exit, knocking the table over and scattering food across the floor.

Tobias blocked her path. He grabbed her by the shoulders. "She's not going to hurt you."

Already in control, Casper whispered something in Baby A's ear and covered her chest with a blanket. She rolled her eyes, muttering something about white magic and human intolerance.

"You shouldn't have angered her," said Tobias.

Out of breath and still prepared to make a break for the horizon, Arriette broke free and hammered on the door.

"Get that *thing* to back off!"

Tobias held up his arms in surrender. "You can trust me. We're not witches, I swear."

"Stupid human," groaned Baby A, tucking away her wings and storming upstairs. "No wonder she was almost killed. What a performance. You've made a real good choice there, Casper. She'll doom us all. I hope you're happy."

Tobias opened the cabin door to a fresh breeze and a beautiful landscape. He aided Arriette's weak frame through the exit and out to a wooden porch, closing the door behind him. He exhaled with relief having managed to separate the women but kept a tight hold of her hand.

When they were alone he said, "Now what was that about?"

Arriette broke down in tears. "You saw what happened. She has a secondary gift. She's no supe, she's a freak!"

He draped his jacket around her shoulders. "She's not a freak, she's an angel. We saved your life. Show some gratitude. Baby A is a perfect specimen of all that's good on Haeylo and you should give her credit for that heritage. Accusing her friends of using dark magic, calling her names and telling her she's good for nothing isn't a brilliant start."

"You like her a lot," said Arriette, defeated. "I see the way you look at her. You're biased."

"Right now I am." Tobias rubbed his head. "Why did you have to go and upset her?"

Arriette wiped her nose on the back of her hand. "You're so protective, are you married?"

"Not that it's any of your business but no. We're family.

Those people in there are all I have," he said. "Of course I'm protective."

"I didn't mean to make anyone angry. I'm just so scared; you knew my name, about my weird dreams and we've never even met. What am I supposed to think?"

"There's no shame in fear, Arriette. We've all had the dreams. It's how Casper chose you. I'm many things but psychic isn't one of them."

"Chose me for what?"

Tobias sat beside Arriette on the porch swing and placed an arm around her. His skin was warm and reassuring.

"Don't worry about it yet. We only want to keep you safe."

"I'm a stranger. Why would you want that?"

"We see potential in you."

Arriette had to take a deep breath to fight back the second stream of tears. "I'm going to have to apologise to Baby A, aren't I?"

"You can apologise to each other. Don't be in such a hurry to know everything *now*. You might regret it."

"But how did he know my name?"

Tobias cringed, struggling to find a way around the question. "He's not human."

"I'm *shocked*," Arriette said, groaning.

Tobias grinned. "None of us are witches though. You're paranoid because of Kalvin's hex story. Casper is a shifter. He changes shape and could even mirror you."

Arriette hoped he wouldn't; one of her was enough. "A scale seven, I'm impressed."

"Sort of. You're smart; most humans don't know the scale so well."

"I'm not *most humans*. Hey, don't vampyrs shift to hunt?"

"One of their worst qualities," said Tobias.

"They have *good* qualities?"

She hadn't heard her attackers approach; perhaps they too had used this technique to creep up on her. Arriette would never turn her back to the woods again.

Tobias rolled his eyes; she was getting off topic. Part of him hoped she'd continue so he didn't have to explain Casper's primary gift.

"I thought he was an everlast."

"He's a little old for an everlast, Arriette."

Point taken.

Everlasts only aged until their twentieth birthday like Rihaana. Arriette envied their constant youth and beauty and would have given anything to share that fortune.

"Casper gives me the creeps."

"I'm a dreamer so be freaked out by shifters all you like," he said, smiling. "Casper's a nice guy though, you'll see."

"I didn't see *that* coming."

"I don't practice much. You have good reason to fear us, especially me. The forces of my telekinesis are so strong they can tear an average person in half," he said, providing Arriette with a visual aid using his hands. She cringed and turned her head. "I try and avoid violence unless I'm saving somebody's life. If I wanted to kill you, Arriette, you'd be dead already. Feel better now?"

"Privileged," she said, tightening her grip on the bench to hide her shaking hands.

"Fortunately for you, we're in the protecting business instead."

"I never met a dreamer. Is it true you can move things with your thoughts? Create storms of imagination? Bring your unconscious to life?"

Tobias cleared his throat. "You're nosey, aren't you?"

"Never mind. At least tell me your scale. The rest I can figure out."

"A power you *can't* place on the HPS," he said, raising an eyebrow. "I'm disappointed."

"It's a first, believe me."

"I'm a two," he replied. "Anything else?"

"You haven't told me how Casper knows me. Yes, I can tell you're avoiding my question."

Tobias grunted. "What will you do once you're well?"

"Ignorance isn't always bliss, Tobias."

He shrugged. "Not my place. Sorry."

"All right, well I'll have to face Kalvin's evil. He's in too much trouble for me to ignore and he's dragged my neighbour into this too."

"He's not technically evil unless he came from the box."

"What box?"

Tobias twiddled his thumbs. "Uhm, forget it."

"Somebody will let it slip sooner or later. Might as well tell me now."

"Baby A's right when she says you're not ready. Casper believes there's more to your problems than a dying friend and a murderous boyfriend. They are connected to our own issues."

"Ex-boyfriend, and you mean the war?"

Tobias didn't apologise but he nodded.

Arriette returned his jacket and gazed off into the distance. Surely this gorgeous dreamer wasn't selfish enough to use her like Kalvin?

"You were lucky the lightning struck that tree. We might never have noticed you otherwise."

"Zïnnyi spared me for a reason, blah blah."

Tobias was unable to think of a suitable reply but when the awkward silence became too much to bare he told her hunting stories instead.

Arriette learned he'd been in a terrible accident once and that Casper healed him. He too received a blood transfusion and before he woke he saw a shadow. Instead of taking its hand though, he fought it and won.

"I wonder what it all means," she said. "I thought maybe it was Casper." Deep in thought, they sat and rocked back and forth for a while.

"He'll explain when you've recovered, Arriette. Then you can see Susan."

"I get the impression you're rooting for me to be out of this place." Arriette crossed her fingers. Before Tobias could defend himself she began to laugh. "It's all right. No matter what my mouth says, know inside I'm glad you saved my life and I'm sorry if my presence is an inconvenience. I'd make a terrible vampyr so I owe you."

"You'll be on your feet soon," said Tobias. He replaced the jacket around her shoulders. "You have a certain quality I once saw in myself."

Arriette's eyes widened as he leaned toward her. "Which is?"

"A passion for life," he said. "Any other human would've given up back in the forest but not you. Plus, unlike me you didn't fight the ghost in your dream. You reached out."

"Which is symbolic of cowardice, right?"

Tobias frowned. "You're joking? I'll be damned if I ever hold hands with a stranger. You've got more guts than Reiko and I put together. He fought too, you know. I'd say your reaction is symbolic of courage." Tobias smiled and nudged her playfully. Arriette sighed, disappointed when he pulled away. "Either that or insanity."

SIX

Millions of stars twinkled overhead, set upon a comforting cobalt canvas. Arriette wondered how many of them were already dead or dying, and whether Haeylo would be next if a war really was on the horizon.

A war over what? I wonder.

Tobias and Reiko lay out on the grass bank, soaking in the last sights and sounds of the day. Casper stood above them, cradled a cup of tea and twiddled his moustache in thought. On occasion, they looked back at her then continued their private discussion. Sometimes their faces were smiling and excited and others, they were solemn and worried.

Whatever their discussion, Arriette was pleased she wasn't part of it.

She jumped from her skin when Baby A exited the cabin to greet her with hot tea and a piece of fresh fruit loaf. Arriette figured an offering of food was the angel's way of apologising and crammed the cake into her mouth.

"About this morning," Arriette mumbled between bites. "I never meant to offend you."

Pieces of cake dropped in her lap.

Although a little disappointed in her manners, Arriette couldn't help but take larger mouthfuls until the plate was empty. Baby A found her reaction so funny she waved off the apology.

"Hungry?"

Arriette grinned. "My appetite's returned."

"My reaction was for your own good, you know."

"I do," said Arriette, lowering her head. "I'm sorry for how I behaved."

"You're scared and alone and worried about wiccans. Naturally, considering Kalvin's diagnosis of Susan's illness but I promise you I have never invested time in the dark arts. We're all supes. Tobias told you?"

Arriette nodded. "He's been kind."

"We just want to help. Hey, if killing you was on our agenda don't you think the guys would've saved time and let the Vamps eat you?"

"A reassuring thought," she said, laughing.

Baby A smiled. "So how are you feeling?"

"Afraid. I thought you might understand living out here alone with these men."

It was time for her to cover her mouth again.

"Relax," said Baby A. "I *can* relate. I didn't arrive here during a morning stroll. My circumstances were much worse. I should have known better than to judge you. I had a blood transfusion too, though not from a bite. That's vampyrs for you."

Exhausted and terrified, Arriette did her best to remember the teachings of her biology books. She'd read something about the risks of blood transfusions which scared her more than these strangers. Now she carried unscreened blood.

She pondered how they'd found a willing donor at such short notice. It puzzled her how in just two days she'd been confronted by a time-travelling angel, fallen for a handsome dreamer, met an elderly shifter and been tasted by a ravenous waitress.

"When Casper found you, did you dream about a shadow? You might not remember. Oh, ignore me. It's a dumb thing to ask."

Baby A took her hand. "We all did. The shadow I saw called my name and tried to grab me. I remember at first, I ran, but then I thought about how many others he might attack if I didn't act, so I fought back. I risked my existence for the lives of pretend victims. We do silly things in our sleep." Baby A smiled. "When I woke I had this awful headache. Is there something wrong?"

"Oh no, it's just a stupid superstition. That vampyr must have emptied me. I can't keep my eyes open."

Arriette yawned and pulled Tobias's jacket tight around her shoulders. It smelled of smoked meat, sweat and man. It was paradise.

"Drink your tea. It's Casper's recipe but Reiko brews it because the old man's, you know, lost his touch a bit. Reiko is an excellent cook. A master, you might say."

"I can't argue with that," said Arriette, casting a cautious glance toward the men. "He's so mysterious and intimidating."

"Don't let the battle scars fool you, Arriette. Reiko's a tribal man; has tattoos in awesome places." Baby A sighed, lost in a memory and shook her head. "He looks scary but has a golden soul; a real gentleman. He spent the majority of his life in a small village in the Drakontan Mountains. He's quite religious but we don't talk much about our pasts. The future's far too exciting especially now you're here." She paused. "I'm sorry about before, you know with the tea?"

Arriette shrugged. "Drugs were unnecessary. I could feel the berries in my head, clouding my judgement."

"Reiko makes all kinds of remedies but the one we gave you had been modified."

Arriette swirled it around, staring into the cup. "What's in this one?"

"Sunflower, lemon, rowan berries and juniper. Casper and Reiko scavenge once a week for our ingredients. The mix represents patience and inner peace. The berries are to enhance magic. The dose won't cause hallucinations, don't worry."

What purpose would magic have in my tea?

"Well it's scrumptious. How long have you lived here?"

"Casper pulled me from the river when I was twelve years

old. Never explained how he found me. He finds it too painful to discuss so I don't pry. He named me Baby A because I'm the youngest of the group, and all they knew about me was my power. Ten years later I'm alive and happy. That's all that matters."

"Back in the cabin, you said you didn't travel anymore."

"Ah, well for a while I worked freelance," said Baby A. "Travelling back to determine how people's relatives died for a fee. Dishonest work, really. Charging humans for closure. I didn't feel good about myself, *believe* me. Casper talked me into giving it up. I learned so much about the old world that sometimes I thought about staying on Earth."

"Why didn't you?"

"My place is here," she said, smiling. "Casper said Haeylo would lose a protector if I did and besides, can you imagine how bad the Earthlings would freak out if I sprouted *wings*? Supes were fictional characters in books." Arriette loved how animated her hands were when she spoke. "The old man thinks all Angels are blessings from Zìnnyi."

"I see." Arriette glanced at the others. "Tobias doesn't use his gift much, does he?"

"He's too controlled. Drives me insane; he used to be so fun and easy-going. I miss him a little." Reminiscing brought a tear to her eye. "It's a dangerous gift."

"Is dreaming *really* a scale two?" asked Arriette.

Baby A waved at him from the porch and grit her teeth. "Could kill me with one snap of his fingers. All that teasing over the past few years; I'm surprised I'm still in one piece." That put Arriette ill at ease. "Casper encourages us to use magic in case we need it. To be honest it's no fun unless you have a real purpose. Life or death. Tobias's fast and light on his feet. Dodging arrows is just a dance with death for him; wins *every* time."

The few spells Arriette had practised at home, although they ended badly, were fun to prepare but she couldn't imagine duelling with a scale two.

"When you're pretending it's embarrassing," Baby A said, "but when it's real and you have to save an innocent there's an awesome adrenaline rush."

Tobias and Reiko jogged up the bank to join them. Casper walked slowly behind, leaning on a crooked wooden stick for support. Baby A squashed on the swing beside Arriette to make room for the others and pushed off with her bare feet.

"You made friends," said Reiko.

"Your tea is delicious even with the drug," Arriette told him. He wasn't sure whether to thank her or apologise. His face lit up with delight at the compliment anyway. "Can I have the recipe to brew when I'm home?"

"I, uhm—"

"Hey Arriette, we're all going to the river for an evening dip," said Tobias, rescuing his friend. "Fancy a swim?"

"No thanks," Arriette said, shaking her head. She'd listed at least five reasons for her decision before Baby A interrupted, insisting she should clean her wounds and bathe. "I'm being hunted by Kalvin. I can't put you in danger. Say, is there a bathtub here?" A midnight plunge and pleasant company *did* sound inviting but Arriette's head overruled her heart. "I don't have a suit and Casper said it'll take days until I'm at full strength."

"You're a similar size to me, Arriette. You can borrow one of mine." She winked. "I'll talk to Casper."

"Not like you haven't enough of them. Every time that travelling tradesman comes by here you're exchanging food for a new dress or something," said Tobias. "I don't hunt for *fashion.*"

She prodded him in the chest with her index finger. "Don't show off in front of our beautiful guest. She's not interested in your ego."

"Arriette, you said that without opening your mouth," Tobias joked.

"You know I can travel back to the day you were conceived and ensure the thing your parents did to create you doesn't take place. I'm attractive enough to distract your father."

Reiko found a comfortable spot on the porch step by Arriette's feet. She leaned down and tapped his shoulder.

"She's serious, isn't she?"

Reiko smiled wide enough for Arriette to examine the gap in his teeth. She wondered how he'd lost them but thought better of asking the history. Something caused him to leave the tribe; a fight for leadership perhaps or a volcanic eruption. The mountain always had been unstable.

Tobias stuck out his tongue and chased Baby A across the porch, trying to tickle her. Then her body began to fade.

She burst into laughter; her voice carried across the forest, shaking the ground and rustling the trees. Reiko took hold of Arriette's hand as the tin roof rattled and the swing creaked. The wind picked up, sweeping around Baby A's body like a tornado.

"Whoa, hold on a second!"

Baby A reappeared by Tobias's side and rolled her eyes. "Did you see his face?" She punched him lightly in the chest. "I can't believe you fell for it!"

Casper joined Reiko and Arriette at the swing and propped open the cabin door with a wedge of firewood. Reiko crammed another slice of cake in Arriette's mouth, most likely to prevent her expression of disgust at their practical joke. He poured several more cups of lemonade and sat them on the armrest of the swing.

"Maybe you could join them for a swim," said Casper. Baby A smiled. "When you get back we can talk about your dream."

Tobias and Baby A nodded with approval when she cast a worried look their way.

"Are you going to do that again? I thought we were in the midst of a natural disaster."

"Baby A travels in space as well as time. She can explain later," Casper said.

Arriette didn't feel up to it. "The blood transfusion—"

"Is a four-hour procedure. Reiko and Tobias promise to take care of you. Good company is an ideal therapy," said Casper.

"We'll set off in an hour or two. The water glows at night like the fireflies are celebrating. It's a sanctuary," Tobias said.

"Hmm, I look forward to it."

A blatant lie but he couldn't blame her lack of enthusiasm. The forest hadn't done Arriette any favours.

"Let's remove those bandages then," Baby A said.

She wiped her grubby fingers on her dress and knelt beside Arriette to slide them under the bandages, holding each one away from the wound whilst Casper leaned in with a knife.

Heat radiated from the many lacerations, most of which Arriette couldn't remember getting, and they throbbed so hard Arriette swore they'd developed a heartbeat of their own.

Casper struggled to remove the bandages around her legs and ankles until Tobias intervened. He ripped them in one smooth motion and repeated this for the bandage around her ribs. All the while Arriette tried not to stare at his muscles.

How could Baby A live with such a handsome dreamer and *not* fall desperately in love?

She sat back in relief when Casper shooed them all off the porch.

"How do you feel about swimming with supes?"

Arriette forced a smile. "They're growing on me."

"Good, now go and put something substantial on your feet. The river is one mile north of here and the route is uneven," said Casper. "Your old shoes were torn to shreds and your clothes destroyed. You'll have to borrow from Baby A."

Casper aided Arriette to a stance and walked her to the cabin. She suffered little pain now considering her many bruises. Evidence of a transfusion was minor in comparison to the dark rings around her eyes and the punctures on her neck.

She replaced Tobias's jacket on the coat stand and followed Baby A upstairs.

Reiko and Tobias had rooms across the hall from Casper. Probably so he could keep an eye on their mischief, she thought. Baby A's room was petite but beside the bathroom. Arriette knew she'd had her say in the matter, being the only female.

"You have so many empty rooms," she said, sticking her head in a few with wide eyes. "All of them lovely."

"One could be yours soon if you decide to stay in Manaia Forest. Casper has distant friends. He's always cleaning just in case they drop in. The male we know is missing and the female lives on the other side of the forest but you'll meet her tonight. Her name is Dion Delavious."

"Is she supernatural? What scale?"

"Vampyr," said Baby A.

She explained that demons were technically a scale eight on the HPS.

Arriette gulped. "You're friends with a demon?"

"Dion's vegetarian. Humans make her sick so you have nothing to fear."

Arriette was far too aware that Dion must have tasted human blood to dislike it.

Baby A unlocked her bedroom door. The walls were plain and the only furniture was a double bed dressed in silky white sheets and a closet. She handed Arriette a black swimsuit.

"There are ointments, soaps and cosmetics in the bathroom. If the suit fits you, it's yours. Here are your shoes."

Arriette closed the bathroom door and was suddenly pleased to be alone. When she glanced at her bruises in the mirror her chest tightened. She shut her eyes, deciding the reflection wouldn't improve for at least a month and then slid into the shoes. They were too small but she'd have to make do. Her wounds were soon coated in Baby A's balm and an hour later they both headed downstairs to greet the men.

They trekked through the forest, pausing for a break halfway. Reiko offered Arriette a canteen filled with Casper's lemonade before they ploughed on, following the compass north until they reached the river. Arriette was pleased for the frequent rest stops; her legs were still like jelly.

The gorgeous turquoise bath ran from beyond Mousique, through the forest and eventually to the ocean, descending as it intertwined across Haeylo. With it drifted Arriette's thoughts and fears.

Rooted in the present she began to see things through their eyes; how peaceful and natural the life of a supe, no matter their scale, could be.

Each ripple of water, falling leaf and reflection in the surface opened her heart to a part of Haeylo she'd never seen. The gentle waterfall beckoned them, casting spray across the surface of the water and over the rocks.

The plants and vines glowed, attracting thousands of fluorescent bugs that buzzed and hummed. Arriette listened to their singing and wished she could be part of their world every night.

"Come on in Arriette, the water's warm," said Tobias.

She sighed. "Here goes nothing."

Arriette's soul inhaled a breath of fresh air as she dropped her towel and plunged into the water.

SEVEN

Arriette flinched when vampyr Dion moved to greet her with a hospitable hug. It was too out of the ordinary. Vampyrs weren't affectionate by nature and neither, Arriette soon realised, was she. Vegetarian or not, Arriette was going to question Dion to within an inch of her life before accepting the gesture, or what was left of her life anyway.

Baby A gave Dion a pat on the shoulder before leaving them to get acquainted. Arriette's brow furrowed and her arms folded.

"So how's the diet?"

That was her opening shot? Arriette kicked herself for being so rude.

Dion picked a piece of imagined fluff from her shirt.

"Humans make me sick. It's animal blood or death. At least diets are tolerable."

Her voice was harmonious; a siren's call. It had to be because vampyrs used the weaknesses in human nature to hunt, lust in particular.

"You're very beautiful for a—"

Dion rolled her eyes and shook her head at Baby A. "Really, are ya kiddin' me?"

Arriette flinched. "What?"

"She's goin' for looks?"

"For a dead girl you're not so bad," Baby A laughed, rejoining them. "Take the compliment."

"I didn't mean to offend you," Arriette said.

Baby A threw her a towel which she ran over her body,

keeping one eye on the predator.

"Have you even tried human blood, like a whole body's worth?"

"I'm not goin' to answer that." Dion turned and grabbed her things.

"Wait, don't leave because of me. My track record with your kind isn't great."

"Most don't live to ask questions. Other vampyrs and I might look the same but on the *inside*, we're different creatures."

"You're not like them," Baby A assured her. "You're Vamp by blood but human by nature. Arriette, come here for Zïnnyi's sake! Don't be so pathetic." Baby A pointed to Dion's luminous eyes and gestured for Arriette to get closer. "I'd have thought you of *all* people would love how the whites of her eyes glow in the darkness. Research, right? Like a walking textbook."

This vampyr didn't look anything like Arriette imagined. Vamps were cold, heartless creatures and frozen in time; they walked in wounded, mangled corpses.

"I've got heightened senses too, an' I can change the colour of ma hair," she said.

Arriette relaxed into the conversation, pleased to be learning this direct from a specimen rather than another book.

"Camouflage, how interesting."

"We all got faults, don't we? Instincts are mine," she said, reaching out for Arriette's hand. "It's not like ma fingers are gonna drop off. Ma death was easy. I'm in one piece."

"Instincts don't just disappear," she said, interlocking her fingers. "Ma warned me never to trust supes with evil souls."

Tobias emerged from the water, distracting her. With his hair slicked back, Arriette thought she'd died and awoken in Heaven.

"I told you, use 'evil' with caution because—"

"I think that's enough of that for now," said Baby A, splashing him with water.

Tobias swam away and Arriette gazed after him, watching the muscles in his back move the tattooed image of a black and white butterfly.

Encased within the branches of an endless wrap of leaves extending to his neck, arms and across his chest, each branch seemed to tickle a different part of a perfectly formed body Arriette could only hope to examine further.

On each wing of the insect was a rune; the first Teiwaz and the second Inguz.

"No, let him talk."

Arriette crouched beside the water and beckoned him over, her eyes inspecting each marking as though her life was dependent upon them. If not for fear of embarrassment, Arriette would've reached out and traced each vine with her fingers.

"Don't concern yourself with myth," said Baby A.

"Is it true vampyrs go to Hell and humans to Heaven?" Arriette asked Dion. She aided Tobias out of the water and handed him her towel. "Isn't that what you wanted to say, Tobias?"

"Kind of," he said. Tobias buried his face in the towel and ran it down his chest. "Though it's more complex than good or bad, right Dion?"

"Y'all are too quick to judge," Dion replied. "Humans are equally cruel." She wiggled her fingers, beckoning Arriette to take them. "I can prove maself worthy. Baby A tells me of ya troubles and fangs scare away any enemy. Better to 'ave 'em on ya side."

"Your body is designed to hunt me," Arriette said. "How can I be sure I'm not dessert?" Dion sighed as Arriette tried to make a quick decision; shake her hand or turn away her friendship. "I've made this mistake twice."

"Being bitter ain't gonna change ma fate but I didn't *ask* to become this. We 'ave a mother or father; he or she who makes us, trains us to feed an' breed. Mine left me to fend for maself."

"You had a real family," Arriette said, "before you died."

Dion ran a hand across her belly. She had been on the path to motherhood before being made vampyr against her will.

"What happened?"

"Doesn't matter now."

"Can't you ask a traveller to take you back?"

Baby A took Arriette's hand and squeezed. Of course, they'd already thought of that solution, perhaps even tried it. They wouldn't all be talking by the river had it worked as planned.

"I just wanna get on with life."

"I'm sorry," Arriette said.

"One day, should ya ever take ma hand, I'll tell ya the story."

Arriette smiled. "For the record, I think you're very nice."

Dion excused herself. She hopped gracefully from branch to branch until she reached a treetop then threw her body into the water. Her physique was that of a skilled gymnast; light on her toes and elegant as a swan.

Her vampyr interior was a brick wall lined with lustrous white skin but before Dion was turned her hair had been a natural red and her eyes sea green.

Arriette envied such beauty.

During their chat, Reiko had been gathering some firewood for the camp. Arriette tried to light it and twirled a stick between her hands, faster and faster until the wood below began to smoke. Impressed, he sat back and stretched, revealing unusual tattoos of his own.

"Are you just going to leave it there?" asked Tobias, breaking her trance.

Arriette jumped. "Don't sneak up on me!"

He shook his body like a wet dog, ruffling his mousy locks. Arriette had to pinch herself and close her jaw.

Baby A threw him a canteen and rolled her eyes.

"Sorry but it's kind of awkward, don't you think?"

"What's awkward?" Arriette blushed. "I'm sorry I—"

"You might have hurt Dion's feelings," he finished.

Arriette exhaled and narrowed her eyes at the angel. Tobias fed more wood to the fire.

"We are what we are, Tobias. Dion's a predator."

"And you're stubborn. Are you afraid? She's just a person."

She's not a person, she's a vampyr.

Feeling guilty, Arriette got up and made it clear to Tobias

with a low grumble how ridiculous this was. When Dion sat to dry her legs, Arriette slumped on the grass bank and pointed to a gold wedding band which the vampyr twisted.

"You're married."

Dion startled and let go of her distraction. "Don't force ya self, Arriette."

"I'm not forcing anything. Please, tell me about him."

"He's ma ex-husband and I'm the least of his worries."

"Didn't know what he had until he lost it," said Arriette.

Beginning to realise how awful Dion's life must be, she sighed and tried to relax. The vampyr grinned, releasing her fangs at the memory of her partner. Arriette flinched but fought the urge to scamper.

"He always hated supes yet he married a dreamer."

"Dreamers are overrated," she said, licking her lips.

Tobias stuck out his tongue and pulled his shirt on. "Uncalled for," he said, grinning.

"Start a wild love affair with Reiko instead."

She gestured with her thumb at the bald-headed hunter, sharpening sticks with a long knife and poking his tongue through the gap in his teeth.

Dion shuddered. "Arriette, I've never met another like me. Nobody is willin' to begin a relationship with a predator. Ya won't even shake ma hand." She pointed at the rabble attempting to construct a decent camp and smiled. "Those howlin' supes are all I got."

I suppose you're not that bad," Arriette said, "and I *do* need protection."

Dion's eyes lit with interest. They had a lot in common; Arriette just didn't know it yet.

"And you're *sure* you're vegetarian?"

Dion flung her powerful arms around Arriette's waist and compressed the air from her lungs before she could object to physical contact.

"Ya won't regret it," she said.

Arriette crossed her fingers. "I hope not."

The fire blazed as they walked along the river bank. Tobias flashed his perfect teeth at Dion when she threatened to push him in, but missed. He dive-bombed backwards, covering them in water then swiped Arriette's ankles. She hopped to evade the attempt and shook her fist, averting her eyes from his see-through white shirt.

Baby A propelled her body off the rocks and released her wings, soaring above them and performing a corkscrew. Arriette caught sight of her blue eyes sparkling in the darkness, like distant stars.

"Say, can't vampyrs change shape?"

Dion's excited arms went to grab Arriette before remembering she didn't appreciate the invasion of personal space. Then she became a bat, an owl and finally an angel, mirroring Baby A's actions and together they landed on the bank of the river. Her change was swift and gentle, which reminded Arriette of a rolling wave.

"I can't tell you apart," Arriette said.

Dion shrugged off her disguise and Baby A patted her shoulder in congratulation.

"That was amazing." She turned to Baby A. "How did you get two gifts then?"

"My father was a time-travelling scientist. My mother must have been an angel, though I barely remember her. A first-class everlast sent Father to the year 1999. He worked as a Corrector, changing events in the past to improve the future like I did. I never saw him again. After that my memory gets fuzzy." Baby A strained her neck, drawing Arriette's attention to the thick black markings behind her ear. "My injury knocked the important stuff right out of me. I don't hold much hope of seeing either of them again. They don't live in our old home anymore. I checked. At least I *think* it's my old home." Baby A scratched her chin. "These guys call me Baby A because we have no idea what my birth certificate says. Some memories never returned, for example, I don't remember having brothers or sisters, grandparents or friends. Not even if I put it in context; it's a huge void. Like a curse or something."

Baby A reached into her bag and handed Arriette a fading photograph of a blonde woman.

"That's all I had in my possession when Casper found me. The colours are faded and the edges are worn but it's precious. Hey, does having a secondary power push me up the scale?" Baby A tucked her blonde hair behind her ear, covering the runic markings of Isa and Thurisaz.

"Ya can't add ya scores. That's cheatin'," said Dion, smiling. "So how'd ya end up 'ere, Arriette?"

She offered Arriette a canteen of water which she gratefully accepted.

"I'm complicated," she said.

"Oh *please*. Ya know so much 'bout our lives yet we know so little 'bout yours."

"I beg to differ. Still, what do you want to know?"

"Got any family? Friends?"

"My mother and my neighbour. I had a long-term partner until he left for the city with my best friend. Kalvin's the reason I'm in this mess. He visited to tell me she's ill; some wiccan put a hex on her and he wants my help." Dion frowned, not fully understanding the situation. "I was tricked. Kalvin sold me to an everlast to settle a personal debt. I ran away and the rest is self-explanatory. My journey here began with Kalvin and ended with vampyrs."

Arriette moved her hair to allow Dion to analyse the bite. "Third time dead, right Baby A?"

Baby A shrugged. "If number three is Dion then it's third time blessed, I'd say."

EIGHT

Having enjoyed their time in the water, the girls walked to meet Tobias by the fire and perched in a circle surrounding it. Arriette kicked off Baby A's shoes and toasted her toes. The waterfall's spray was cool and refreshing, circulating the scent of moist soil and flowers all around them. A silent, gentle peace settled upon their camp.

She'd never felt more at home.

"Kalvin is the artist of those patterns round ya eyes?" asked Dion, ruining her moment.

"I don't know which bruises are his and which are from the vampyr attack."

Arriette made a claw with her hand and faked the fight, much to Dion's amusement.

"How did ya get away?"

"I burned him alive." Arriette gestured at Baby A's ear. "Speaking of artists."

She flinched and ruffled her hair to hide the runes. "Oh they're nothing."

Dion swallowed hard. "So do ya know much 'bout us? The history of vampyrs is thrillin'."

"I read a lot," Arriette said, casting a sideways glance at the angel. "Two fangs to inject venom and suck blood. To be turned, human blood must be drained and replaced with venom. Vampyrs lay the victim to rest and later they'll rise as one of them."

"Ya done ya homework," said Baby A. "That was almost

textbook."

"Never hung around long enough to ask one myself," said Arriette.

"It's usually 'bout twenty-four hours," Dion confirmed. "The venom must make its way to ya heart. Shuts down ya organs. Then, the Vamp must feed ya their blood to replace what was taken. This forges a connection. Vamp parents call that Tōgædere."

Baby A twirled the end of a stick and nudged Arriette. "You read any of Foley's work, Arriette? She formed part of my earliest study as a time-traveller. 'Forming covens of their own, feeding in groups of four or five, some vampyr parents will turn only one in their time. Others, hundreds.'" Baby A grinned, "That's right, I read too."

"We didn't always exist," Dion said.

She cracked her fingers and slid closer to the fire. The flames licked and curled through the air. The vampyr never winced. Despite fire being a demonic weakness, her body remained completely relaxed. Arriette wondered how she died and whether her nerves registered pain or if she ever felt cold.

"There's a myth. Says we're the children of evil. The Source gave us what we needed to survive Zïnnyi's livin' guardians."

Her fangs popped down, startling Arriette.

For the next hour, Baby A told her everything about the Source; presumed to be a woman the Recruit had hunted for thousands of years.

Her name was Pandora.

Now the original Recruit descendants had separated, interbred and lost interest in history it was unlikely they'd ever find the Source. Certainly not unless they bound together as an army and combed every blade of grass and wisp of cloud. Such power would give the Source endless possibilities to hide yet still cause havoc. The return of demonic activity over the past one hundred years meant Pandora was still alive.

"The Recruit vowed to rid Haeylo of Pandora's influence," Baby A said.

Tobias gave Arriette a startling pat on the shoulder. "Can you imagine if she decided to begin an uprising? *Then* there'd be a war!"

"Don't scare her," said Baby A, whacking him with her towel.

"Ya heard of the Recruit, then?" Dion asked.

Arriette nodded. "Hasn't everybody? Do *you* believe there's a source of evil?"

"Of course. Only two kinda people know 'bout evil," said Dion, shaking a finger. "Like *really* know. Pandora an' the Recruit. Includin' how to eliminate it, strengths an' weaknesses, habits an' with vampyrs, allergies. Silver will burn right through skin this fair."

"There's got to be a way of preventing the change from human to vampyr permanently. I mean, once somebody dies they can't be turned, can they? Surely the Recruit would study these facts or make themselves known to most religious leaders?" Arriette asked. "Form a patrol to watch for signs of Vamp intervention at funerals and such?"

"I'm sure they would but why advertise your work if you haven't the manpower to act upon any accusations?" Baby A said, casting a nervous glance at Tobias. "Besides, without Tōgædere vampyrs go rogue. Kill for fun, not food, making them more dangerous. More protection for and distractions from Pandora."

"That's when ya get variations like me. No bond. No responsibility. Ma *parent* gave me memories, experiences but thankfully not his lust. The Recruit got worse evils to worry 'bout than rogues, though." Dion noticed Arriette's discomfort and continued on a positive note. "By puttin' up a headstone and markin' the death of a loved one ya can tell the vampyr they've been gone long enough for the grave to settle. Even if they *were* turned it prevents the corpse from diggin' their way out."

"So that's the purpose of funerals?" she asked.

Dion nodded but said nothing further on the topic.

"They aren't easy to kill," Baby A said. "Arriette managed in the pouring rain. What do you think about that?"

"That ya either brave, owed serious favours by Him, or ya bonkers."

"The word Tobias used was *insane*," said Arriette. The girls laughed together. "Perhaps I'm just special. Baby A believes Zïnnyi sent me a beacon of hope and Casper *chose* me, whatever that means. Lightning struck a tree; that's how I killed the Vamp and how your friends found me."

"We hate fire," said Dion, "an' stakes. We've had practice at dodgin' 'em."

"No kidding," said Arriette, rubbing her sore spots.

"Maybe He saw ya future an' took pity?" Baby A swatted Dion with wide, pleading eyes. She took the warning. "Uh, anyway, Tobias and Reiko said the female planned to turn ya, Arriette." She patted her black swimsuit dry. "Ya had a fortunate escape."

"I owe your friends my life. I'd do anything to repay that debt."

Smiling, Tobias placed a hand on Arriette's arm. She glanced down in horror, inhaling deep to control the burst of adrenaline and excitement. Heat radiated from his palm; a wonderful sensation of comfort and lust washed through Arriette's entire body until she had to pinch herself.

"Are you ill?" he asked, worried.

"Oh, sorry, never better," she said, brushing his arm away.

"Did you talk to Casper?" he asked.

"No, he promised we'd chat back at the cabin."

"Don't s'pose ya wanna talk now?" asked Dion, offering her a drink from a canteen.

The water was delightful as it gushed down her throat. Arriette wiped her mouth, then her forehead and let the cool canteen rest on her bruises. She prayed that alongside her scraggly hairstyle, pale complexion and unshaven legs that they didn't make her look like a wild animal.

"If Casper won't be offended," she said.

"Casper's too omniscient for his own good," said Tobias.

"Arriette, in your books did you read anything about human blood types?" asked Baby A.

When Arriette shrugged and shook her head, Tobias said, "Not even the rarest?"

He pulled a penknife from his bag and made an incision across his palm. He tossed the blade to Baby A and then Reiko who repeated this action. They linked their hands together.

"Are you saying we share the same blood?"

Reiko passed Arriette the penknife. She flicked it open, glaring at the droplets of crimson in panic.

Eyes wide and afraid, Arriette dropped the blade and staggered away from him.

"I'm *AB Positive?* You were *all* my donors."

"Casper saved our lives and we saved yours," said Baby A.

Arriette's village rarely saw the travelling tradesman, never mind a retaining doctor. Knowing her blood type would have cost hundreds. Expensive surgery and medication simply wasn't an option in her little village.

"You were going to die, Arriette. They had no choice," said Reiko.

"*They* and not us?"

"Supe blood is immune to human disorders. Donating my blood carried too many risks."

"Why didn't you tell me this earlier?" she asked.

Tobias lowered his head and held out both hands as an act of both defence and resignation.

"You were so frightened I couldn't bear to add to your terror."

"I can understand that I guess," she said, her voice minuscule and powerless against his. "I won't say I'm not afraid. Supernatural blood runs in my veins and magic travelled with it, right?"

"We can explain that later," said Baby A. "I'm just glad you didn't run."

"You expected me to?"

Baby A's eyes sank, following the ground until they rose to

meet Tobias's. She'd taken the news well for an inexperienced human. Not well enough, though.

"I can't say I want super powers but I'm not shallow enough to bolt," Arriette said. "You underestimated my strength."

"Inner strength comes naturally to born leaders," said a familiar voice.

Casper's white beard and moustache emerged from the shadows. Concealed by the looming trees he was able to hear every word, scrutinise her reaction and evaluate her loyalty. A faithfulness Arriette hadn't yet realised she'd pledged but one Casper recognised when he laid eyes on her. She tried to apologise for not waiting to hear the confession from him but he waved a dismissive hand.

"As each of us joined our group they inherited my blood to save their lives. Quite coincidentally they were already AB positive before I met them; another sign my choices were golden."

He took Arriette by the hand and led her to the fireside, his eyes focused on her face.

"There's no such thing as coincidence and signs," she said.

"I didn't think so either but everything supernatural happens for a reason. Zïnnyi brought you here," he finished.

Although he never blinked and his content expression remained unchanged, Arriette could read how strongly he believed that. Bewilderment forced Arriette to her knees as she stared down at her palms.

"Are you saying you saved my life because Zïnnyi instructed it? I didn't take you as a God-fearing man," she said, her eyes narrow and uncertain.

"I'm many things," said the old man. "God-fearing is not one of them."

"Do you even believe in Him or is this all just talk; a reason to pull me into a war I never wanted a part of?" she said.

"The Recruit need no reason to 'talk'," Casper said. "Do not imply I am dishonest."

Tobias lifted Arriette to a stance and lingered behind her. His presence was somehow comforting; his strong frame waited, eager to catch her should she fall.

"Oh this is priceless." Arriette began to laugh, nerves overwhelming her. "You think you're the Recruit, don't you?"

"You don't believe us?" asked Tobias.

Arriette span, her head jerked up; their eyes met in judgement. "No, I don't. I thought you supes were different. Obviously, I was wrong. You speak of Zïnnyi to suggest power; strike fear into those you're going to manipulate. Let me guess. You need my help, want to strike a bargain or train me to be your puppet. All because Zïnnyi willed it? Am I close?"

Casper chortled. "Is *that* what you think we're doing? Befriending you so we can use your knowledge? There are many retainers I could turn to for such chores. I need no human pets."

"Why didn't you let me die then? *I'm* human."

"Not anymore," Tobias muttered, his breath titillating the back of her neck. The hairs on her skin prickled. "Kalvin awakened something within you, Arriette. Zïnnyi led you to us for a reason."

"I believe he needs us to harness that energy, enhance and channel it," said Casper.

"You didn't share supe blood with a dying human out of pity, so why did you?"

"On the horizon there is only death and suffering awaiting the human race. Protecting them was an oath I swore before you were even conceived. I chose you because I have a job lined up, destined to fall in your hands. I don't need to claim allegiance to the Recruit if I am the Recruit."

"Try me," Arriette grumbled.

"You already believe. Denial is just some ridiculous human coping mechanism," Reiko said.

"If not for that oath I'd be a vampyr though," she said, casting her eye toward Dion.

"Perhaps, but if you think I hide behind Zïnnyi's name for power over one human, you're mistaken." Casper paused and lifted her chin. "You're a *survivor*, Arriette. I saw it the second you entered my cabin. A valuable soldier I can use on the front line."

"Where's my choice in this? I'm a prisoner," she spat. "Of you, your God and your cause." Arriette cradled her head in her hands. "I thought we were becoming friends."

"We *are* your friends," said Tobias, "and he's our God."

"Recruiting me without my knowledge, agreement or loyalty makes me your prisoner or your slave. Neither is how I plan to spend the rest of my life. Failing to tell me you were the Recruit is the final strike." Arriette stood abruptly and forced Casper's hand away. "I deserve a better explanation than 'I was chosen'."

"I do as my oath binds me," said Casper. "Take this as a compliment."

Arriette shook her head. "You should have saved me because you're decent, not for personal gain."

"I trust in the creator with every breath I take; it's only because of him that I take it and it's only because of us that you take yours."

"It's the truth, Arriette. Before we were saved we dreamed of shadows, bright lights and whispers," Reiko cut in. "None of us took the hand of our visitor though. *You did*."

Arriette gasped, suddenly less willing to get away. "What does that have to do with anything?"

"It's a test of will, bravery, courage and leadership," said Baby A. "Of all those Casper tested only you took the next step."

"What about Dion? vampyrs don't dream."

"She offered herself to Casper's cause of her own free will. Imagine a Vamp emerging from the darkness, seeking shelter and aid and friendship in the most unlikely of places. The creator drove her to us too."

Arriette shook her head. "You're following him because of a recurring dream."

Dion reached out to console her. Arriette startled and warned her away.

"Fearin' me now won't rewind time," she said.

"Then tell me what's *really* going on because I don't believe any of this."

"They're friends as much as colleagues," Dion explained. "We're freedom fighters. We do as the Recruit's ancestors once promised."

Disbelief had clouded Arriette's judgement.

She bound her arms around her body.

"Which makes you outlaws fighting for a better future," said Arriette. "Zïnnyi didn't order whatever tragedies you suffered. Nor has he ordered Casper to hold you captive."

"We're not captives," said Tobias, angrier now. "I'm free to go as I please. None of us are shackled to Casper despite receiving his blood."

"So go," she said, gesturing at the tree line. "Be free. Return to your family and friends. Blood doesn't bind you, loyalty does."

"I choose to stay because I have no family or friends. Do you know how I wound up here? I got shot with an arrow during an expedition," Tobias said. He pulled off his shirt, turned and pointed to a scar masked beneath the tattoo. "When my *friends* realised they hit me instead of the deer they ran away. Left me for dead. Casper saved my life. He saw potential in me."

"My tribe banished me when I challenged our leader because he whipped a twelve-year-old boy for stealing an apple. Winter stole the crops, the livestock and his sanity," Reiko explained. "When I left and got lost in Manaia Forest trying to find somewhere to keep warm, Casper took me in. He saw potential in me too."

"You'll learn soon enough who ya real friends are," said Dion.

Arriette rubbed her aching head, trying to make sense of their stories. "If I'm to believe you saved them all, explain why they cannot shift shape."

Casper ran a hand down his beard in thought. The fire

reflected in his eyes, igniting deep wisdom and control but sending uncertain shivers through Arriette's veins. His power irradiated through those eyes; she could sense his anger at her disobedience and it scolded her ego.

"Most supernatural beings can, to some extent, control their abilities enough to prevent an inheritance. Shifters would change beforehand to a being who's unable to pass on their gift," said Casper. "I, on the other hand, simply chose not to until I met you. Well, until I *recognised* you, but if you can't believe the basics of who we are you will never believe *that* story."

"All scale seven and above can power save," said Baby A. "The more active the power the greater the results. Shifters lie at seventh place on the HPS. Dreamers in second, travellers in fourth and Angels in sixth," Baby A said, her face full of fury at Arriette's ungratefulness. "You owe your life to that scale. Casper used it to reserve his gift when saving ours and we used it to share them when saving yours. He deemed you worthy of becoming a unique supe with unimaginable powers."

"Take them back. I don't want them," she said.

Baby A grabbed her towel and stuffed it furiously in the top of her bag, barely noticing the handful of dirt and leaves accompanying it.

"Welcome to the scale," she spat.

"I may be more inclined to use said control," Arriette growled. "Especially on those who didn't ask for the burden."

"It is no burden to be alive," said Casper. "If you'd rather I kill you now then say so, though it will no doubt doom the Recruit and our cause." When Arriette didn't reply, Casper continued. "Now that's settled we can move on. You'll stay and learn to use your gifts as we did."

"And if I refuse?"

"Without guidance, your power will eat you from the inside out. Pandora may even emerge and hunt you down. After all, the box senses power."

"*What* box?" she asked, puzzled.

Reiko ignored her and nudged Baby A. "It'll lead the Source right to her."

"Hey, I'm not your magnet!"

"That's enough! This is compulsory; I cannot unleash such a creation upon the world and not take responsibility for it. So you'll stay," Casper said.

Arriette scowled. "This time next year you'll be claiming credit, old man, not responsibility. You have no idea what this *human* is capable of even without magic."

"Of that I'm certain. You're the product of our goodwill, forced to learn your trade before you decide to abuse it. Then and *only* then will I be satisfied you're of sound mind to opt out. The choice will be yours soon."

"In the meantime, we'll help each other," said Baby A. "Casper thinks our problems are connected."

Tobias smiled. "We need you. You need us."

Arriette cocked an eyebrow and folded her arms across her chest. "I need only myself. Still, I can't deny my curiosity."

"Curiosity is where it begins," said Dion. "So are ya gonna help us or not?"

"Suppose I'll have to," she replied. "What do you need from me?"

"A member of our group is missing. His name is Stefan," said Baby A. "We think his disappearance is something to do with this rumoured war, except it's not a rumour."

"Why didn't you just tell me that before?"

"And risk an irrational reaction?" Tobias joked.

"What about my hunters? They'll do anything to harm me, even turning their forces against you. Those everlast debts haven't yet been repaid and Kalvin won't rest until he's free of them. I'm a liability."

"Nonsense. We protect one another. We'd like to have a chat with Susan about her friend," Casper added. "See what that retainer told her, where she sourced such information and who she works for."

"Maybe she's self-employed," Arriette said, smirking. When

her joke was ill-received, she sighed and rubbed her eyes. "There's no sanity in this. What could she *possibly* know about Stefan? They never met."

Arriette began to bite her nails; their argument had boiled her blood and she needed a safe outlet for her anger.

"Susan knows too much which is why she's lying in a hospital bed. Whoever hexed her needs her silenced. We've seen it happen before. My money is on a connection between Susan and the impending war."

"That an' Pandora's lovely little box," said Dion.

Tobias offered Arriette a hand in time to halt her questions. "Please take it. I'm sure after your training you'll begin to appreciate your gifts and your new friends."

Friends don't deceive you, lie to you or hold you captive, thought Arriette. Real friends were in short supply. People like Rihaana Melovich, who'd always cared enough to listen to unhappy stories and share her table.

"They're all lies," said Arriette. "Kalvin invented it all to settle his debt. It's nonsense."

"You don't say something like that unless you mean it," said Reiko. "*War is coming.* From which direction and by whose hand is unknown. We could be looking at global destruction, who knows? Before Susan dies she's going to tell us everything we need to know to prepare. Either Susan or that retainer."

Casper linked his fingers and sighed. "Arriette, what Reiko is so dramatically explaining is that this war is likely to be initiated by Pandora. You have only ever known a world filled with vampyrs and demons. The box birthed all that; before her, Haeylo was peaceful and innocent. We think, within the past 100 years, it has been re-opened."

"When supes are threatened they will do anything to keep control, even wage war. Everlasts more so. Good reason to train you quickly and efficiently for your own protection," Baby A said. "These past hundred years, Haeylo's suffered immensely because of Pandora's box."

"What if Stefan was recruited to serve in the war against his will? You're no fan of imprisonment. Susan could find him," Tobias said, almost pleading.

"Everlasts kill for power. Considering Susan's death sentence are you not the least bit curious?" asked Baby A. "You're so much more than flesh and bones now. Show them your strength. Make them regret kidnapping you. You carry our blood; we can teach you about our world."

Casper beamed. "Think of the scale, Arriette. Fourteen fascinating species. Fourteen weaknesses. All with histories and memories and knowledge you'll not find in any textbook. This planet is evolving all the time. *We* are evolving. You like to learn so let us teach you."

"I'm a danger to myself until you train me. You can't risk using me to fight a war yet."

"Until we speak to Susan there's no clarity in any of this, hence the urgency to meet her," Casper explained.

Reiko said, "I know you don't believe us. You think Kalvin lied and that Susan's fine. You think Pandora's box is an ancient fairy tale and this is an awful practical joke."

"A box nobody will explain!" Arriette ground her teeth. "You're so infuriating."

"You're the offspring of four supernatural enhancements," said Baby A. "There's nothing you can't do."

"So what exactly *am* I? I don't exist according to the HPS. I'm a freak."

"You're unique," said Casper. "Forget about the HPS. You'll demolish it."

They were behaving as though they'd given her the greatest gift on the planet, but through Arriette's eyes, this was another burden on her freedom. Had they plagued her, possessed her or just given her a means to survive? Only time would tell. Time they were fast running out of. Arriette closed her eyes and exhaled.

"If Susan is ageing and Kalvin wasn't lying, Susan will die soon."

"If we leave tonight we can reach the city before that

happens," said Dion. "Don't judge us too soon. Only an hour ago ya called me friend an' followed a bunch of strangers into the woods."

"I need time," said Arriette. "Trust is earned."

"Have ya given thought to *why* Kalvin behaved the way he did?" Dion asked. "Why Susan wanted to talk to ya in person? Sounds to me like Kalvin was under a lot of pressure to find ya."

"How do I know Charles won't just kill me when I arrive at the gate?" she asked. "No amount of gossip is worth that. Not even the chance to examine death by magic."

Casper lowered his body beside Tobias and stretched out his legs. Beneath his robes appeared two wrinkled feet and upon them, Arriette saw another marking she recognised; the rune Gabo, signifying a partnership, had been tattooed above his toes.

"If Kalvin captured you, Charles wouldn't have killed you. He protects what is his. Trust me, I know. Charles disapproved of Rihaana's plans to marry and leave the city, then threatened to imprison her. She was already engaged to a retainer but his loyalty to Charles prevented their union so she ran away, heartbroken. It's a death sentence Charles chose not to pursue."

Saddened to hear that her one true friend had suffered, Arriette let him speak. "Vampyrs take advantage of weakness. Tobias staked those who wouldn't disperse and brought a rescued Rihaana to me."

In disbelief, Arriette turned to Tobias. "She never mentioned you, *not once*."

"Even friends keep secrets," he said.

Casper continued. "I searched for a village she could live in safely. Mousique seemed quiet and far enough from the city. A house had recently been vacated."

"Next door. *You* bought Susan's cottage? Then why not use her as you're using me? Force additional gifts upon Rihaana."

"Rihaana's beliefs stray as far as the end of her nose," Casper replied firmly. "I cannot afford to enlist cowards in

Zïnnyi's army. A nice girl, but when tested, of no use to us."

"Yet you saved her life and found her shelter."

"I don't turn my back on the innocent," he said. "Even if they aren't ideal for your role."

Tobias interrupted and explained. "When you told us your story we wondered if Charles sent Kalvin to your village having discovered Rihaana's location. Of course, then you explained it was actually Susan who sent him."

"He knocked on *my* door," said Arriette. "He didn't see me as the cause of Rihaana's hiding. I introduced them. Not to say he won't tell Charles I was her kidnapper. Outlaws are easier to blame. Speaking of knocking on doors, why didn't you speak with us all before locating her in Mousique? How did you deem it safe?"

"A feeling I suppose," he said, "although I regret the decision now knowing you lived next door. I've been searching for your face for thousands of years, Arriette."

She didn't know how to answer such a compliment but having let Arriette loose in Manaia Forest, Kalvin and Dean would have returned to Mousique for Rihaana. She'd jeopardised her friend's freedom to save her own skin.

"If training is being forced upon me then at least allow me to ask one favour," she said. "Return me home to save Rihaana and I'll let you teach me about the supernatural. Tell me everything about the gifts I've inherited and how to use them. I suppose at least I'll have a way to protect myself or fight should the rumours of war be true. After all, a war was foretold because I read it myself. I can't just walk away knowing what Dean and Kalvin will do to Rihaana."

"No you can't," said Casper. "Nor would we let you."

Baby A fussed over Arriette's wounds. "She's not well enough to fight a war yet."

"Or emotionally ready to fight off Kalvin," said Dion, laughing.

Arriette bound her hands to fists. "He may have a rather large ego," she said, "but I guarantee the rest of him is disappointing. Nobody knows that man better than I. Inside and out. He's a narcissistic brat with no common sense. I *won't* fall victim to him again."

"Baby A's right," said Tobias. "Until your ribs and bruises heal you should rest. Baby A's angelic blood is already working and you appear willing to gain revenge. Reiko and I can find Rihaana. The rest of you go to the city to find Stefan and Susan."

"You want us to separate in a place like this, at *night*?" asked Arriette. "How can I ever consider trusting you people if you're determined to get me killed?"

"If I'd wanted to kill you, I only had to blink," said Tobias. "Any other objections?"

NINE

Arriette found herself traipsing through the dense forest with a scowl on her face. She'd never been so weary, so achy, so sweaty. She was disgusted with her fitness level and couldn't keep up to Baby A who danced around bogs and hopped over fallen trees with ease. Arriette could only stagger after her. She hoped inheriting angelic blood would increase her stamina. At the moment it only made her hate the situation more.

"I've found a clearing," Baby A said. She hacked at the branches in their way. "Need a rest?"

Arriette refrained from cursing her. "If everyone else does," she said, gasping for breath.

Dion retrieved a shovel from her pack. "Bedtime," she said.

"What's *that* for?" Arriette slumped against a tree. "A rather uncomfortable pillow choice, don't you agree?"

"I'm using it to dig a grave. The sun's comin' up," she said, scouting the tree line for a suitable spot. "Don't look so troubled, Arriette. See ya at sunset."

As Dion disappeared into her moist tomb, Arriette began to gather branches to build the skeleton of her tent. Casper threw Baby A a rock to use as a hammer and they fashioned a roof from damp towels. But feeling unstable on her feet, Arriette wasn't much help. She tied back her matted hair and took a swig of warm water from Baby A's canteen.

"I was wrong about Dion," she admitted, wiping her mouth, "and I'm sorry I judged her. Is she going to be safe in the dirt?"

Casper smiled. "She's stronger than us all; physically and emotionally. Don't be fooled by those big eyes and tiny waist. She's a weapon."

"Her gift incorporates everlast and shifter abilities," Baby A said. "Give her credit."

"She has better people skills than I do. I'll give her *that*."

"Dion understands how difficult it can be when you're away from home. The forest has been mine for years now. As a supe Dion's only twelve months older than you. If you're homesick, she's probably the best friend you could have right now."

"I do miss Mousique but this beats reading all day," said Arriette, shocked at her honesty.

"Perhaps you belong with us then," Baby A said. "We'd teach you to use magic, let you live in the forest with us."

"I've practised magic before and I'm not the best sorceress."

"Why ruin the possibility of adventure? By limiting your expectations don't you worry that in fifty years you'll be at the end of your life with *nothing* to show for it?" asked Baby A.

"I wouldn't say I'd have nothing," Arriette said defensively. "I've done lots of things."

Baby A paused and shook her head, one eyebrow raised sceptically.

Arriette hadn't had a project since meeting Kalvin. She'd always thought of true love as an adventure in its own right and, until his betrayal, never imagined she'd be this excited to begin a new one.

"Don't you want to explore? There are creatures on this planet so impressive and unique, each with skills and powers we can learn from."

"Such as?" asked Arriette.

"Well there are kingdoms even the Recruit haven't visited so I'm sure there are animals and supes we've not found too."

Arriette raised an eyebrow and shook her head. "How do we know they even exist?"

"Who?" Baby A frowned.

"The Recruit," said Arriette. "Or the *rest of you* anyway."

"Are we not proof enough?" Casper asked.

"I'm not denying your good intentions but claiming to be the Recruit? The last scroll I read said there were eleven powers but fourteen on the scale. time-travel, everlasting life, retaining memory, potion mixing, invisibility, mind-reading, sorcery, Wicca, dreaming, angelic flight and shape-shifting," said Arriette, "but other than you guys, I only know Rihaana and Kalvin."

"You still don't believe there are more of us?" asked Baby A.

"More supes I can accommodate but I'm not so sure about the Recruit. What if they aren't *saviours* after all but are evil, hunting Pandora when actually they're destroying anyone threatening their way of life. You claim allegiance to them, but have you met any others?"

"Just because you haven't met every Recruit supe doesn't mean they don't live," Casper said. "We're quite aware who we work for and their long-standing goals."

"Fine, I can make my peace with the whole 'seeing is believing' thing, but surely if Zïnnyi wanted Pandora gone he'd just kill her himself? Demons and orcs are on the scale and someone must have created them."

Casper inhaled deeply. "Arriette, your agnosticism is exasperating."

"Stop winding one another up," said Baby A. She winked at Arriette. "Hey, imagine if you could master *all* the powers! To see a world—"

"Don't change the subject," Arriette said.

"That's impossible," Casper said, hammering at their makeshift pegs a little harder than intended. "Don't fill her mind with such fantasies."

Baby A laughed. "I might know of someone who—"

"That's *enough*, Baby A. It's not your place to share the secrets of others."

She rolled her eyes. "I'm only saying, humans on Earth thought gifts like ours were fiction; made up stories from the imaginations of their writers. I always thought imagination itself was a gift. I mean, dreamers use it to assist their telekinesis. Nothing is impossible then, is it?"

Casper agreed. "Though it's a bit more complicated. Still, humans and Haeyloians aren't so different with the removal of magic."

"Biologically humans have never changed," said Arriette.

Casper said, "This is how Zïnnyi intended it. Physically humans are well designed but they are destructive and emotional. They needed guardians in the beginning."

Casper pronounced his name 'Zee-en-yee', which Arriette had never heard before. She had always called him 'Zin-yee' and had never been corrected.

"The powers halted human nature at first," Casper said. "Soon greed brought the guardians down too and we, the Recruit, were all that remained." He lowered his head.

"So what else could there be besides those eleven abilities?" Arriette asked, excited by the possibility of endless discoveries. "Ogres?"

"Ogres aren't real," said Baby A. "The Recruit take in lost souls and teach them to be practical and loving but there may be variations on the scale; mutations even."

"Like me?"

"Oh there's nobody else like you," Baby A said, smiling.

"How did Zïnnyi know we wouldn't kill Haeylo too?" Arriette asked with a roll of her eyes. "Surely if we destroyed Earth we couldn't be trusted with Haeylo?"

Casper thought for a moment and ran his fingers through his beard. "Second chances are earned. Remember that we were created in his image."

"How about vampyrs? Were *they* created in his image too?"

"No, they were born from Pandora's box," Baby A said.

Arriette's eyes lit with interest. "Are you finally going to explain that damned box?"

"Pandora was the first to betray Zïnnyi, then became the Source and the others her followers. The Recruit has dealt with her in the past. All fell quiet until one hundred years ago so we know she's active again. But there are other versions of that story."

"In all honesty most of what you hear about supes is hokum," Casper said.

Baby A and Arriette waited for him to continue work on his shelter before chatting further.

"According to humans on Earth when a person dies, depending on how well they behaved during their existence, their soul passes on to either Heaven," Baby A pointed to the skies. "The alternative is Hell." She cringed and patted the ground. "Mythology from Earth says a box was the birth of this horrid place. Can you believe that? A box! It belonged to a girl who was instructed never to open it. Her curiosity doomed mankind."

Arriette imagined a heavy marble frame with intricate golden décor. Something she'd love to store all her secrets in and bury.

"I'd like to think it was expensive and covered in jewels," Baby A said.

"You research Haeyloian history and I read up on Earth's. We make quite a team."

Casper threw Arriette a slice of bread. She caught it with a sharp reflex.

"Hey, you're healing," said Baby A.

Arriette was barely listening as she watched Casper use basic magic. He smacked his hands together and rubbed them, creating friction. All questions were held in awe.

"Monibah," he said.

Between Casper's hands shot a bolt of electricity and Arriette jumped a foot in the air. The spark set fire to the wood.

"Stay and you could learn that."

"I'd love to," she stammered. "If anything was to go wrong —"

Casper clapped his hands together again and Arriette ducked. "Magic can be passed freely with little or no medical consequence. Imagine a gift as a disease. A pregnant woman carrying a baby is responsible for the child just as I am responsible for you. To some extent, even *humans* can choose not to pass something on. No smoking. No drugs. No wine. Supernatural beings have simply evolved to be able to make such choices *naturally*. We placed our faith in that when we saved you."

"Do you mean supernatural children don't automatically inherit magic from their parents?" asked Arriette, shocked to be hearing this having been told the opposite in her books at home.

"The gene will be passed on. That can't be controlled," said Baby A, "but why do you think only the firstborn of an everlast inherits the gift of endless life? Or why a retainer can only be born if both parents have the ability?"

"Nature," Casper smiled. "Natural selection determines who *needs* the abilities. In this case, it allowed us to determine that ourselves. Back at the cabin when Baby A told you about everlasts hiring time-travellers like Baby A to test the planet, should they succeed in raising the population of humans, natural selection will phase out supes like us. That's why they're hoping for a negative result. More women will become less fertile. Species will become extinct because nature always wins. It's Zïnnyi's will."

"So even now the eleven powers are still selfish?" Arriette asked, shaking her head. "And here I thought our government was kind and protective of humans."

Baby A continued regardless of Arriette's sarcasm. "Only because it benefits them. Of course, the everlast power is only valid on bodies younger than twenty years anyway which is why you don't find many 'made' supernatural beings like you. Retainers are different but this conversation could go on forever."

"Are there rules for every species?"

"If you're referring to nature's rules, each supernatural being can only inherit gifts that are compatible with their biology. You're a born human so you were a clean slate," she said. "I can teach you the ins and outs of supe biology but that's a lesson for tomorrow."

Arriette sighed. "I'm getting a headache. Which of the gifts did you give me?"

"You have each of our gifts. Nothing you can't handle." Casper returned to the firewood. "This is one of my favourites."

Casper clapped once more and whispered; his pronunciation of the word sounded like 'Moo-neigh-baa' and seemed to produce fire.

"I'm clumsy enough without mixing Haeyloian words with my powers."

"Everything supernatural happens for a reason, Arriette. You inherited our blood because it was nature's way of giving the world what it needed. You believe in the creator."

"Sure but I'm far from being needed," she gasped, examining the wounds in various places around her body. "I'm walking pandemonium."

"Arriette, you survived two vampyr attacks. Bites are usually fatal. Enough said."

Dehydration being the biggest killer in the forest, even after vampyr attacks, Arriette took another swig from the canteen. Tobias and Reiko would be heading back soon which she took comfort in.

"I'll introduce you to other beings on our travels if you stay. Magic is tied to your emotions which is all you need to know for now," said Casper.

"Can you teach me to use Monibah safely?" She clapped her hands together frantically, her tongue poking between her lips.

"You're not in the right place yet." He tapped her head and smiled. "Get some sleep."

"Shouldn't we discuss plans for the city?"

Casper said, "No amount of plans can predict the unpredictable."

"Then can we talk about perhaps removing my responsibilities when this *war* ends?"

Baby A slouched beside her and pulled a bottle from a pocket in her bag. She thought for a moment, hesitated, then handed it to Arriette.

"I was saving this for the day I'm reunited with my mother. It's a potion, but don't turn up your nose it's good stuff."

"Wiccan?" asked Arriette, sniffing it.

"This one is courtesy of Casper."

"A *potion*? Did you see what he did back there?"

"He just summoned the knowledge to light the fire and used it to keep us warm. This, though, isn't magic. See for yourself."

After swirling the clear liquid around and tipping the bottle upside down, nothing happened.

"What's it for?"

"It's a blend of herbal remedies designed to strip a supe of their gifts. It isn't permanent though. Lasts approximately twelve months. Casper made it for me although he was reluctant."

Arriette cradled it like gold. "What's in it?"

"Extracts of various natural ingredients. Not many supes know it exists."

"But you're such a beautiful angel, how could you?"

"I want a normal life. Humans have nothing to worry about, nothing to control. At least not until recently. It took a lot of convincing for me to pass my gifts to you because humanity is sacred and fast decreasing."

Arriette sat the bottle between them on the ground and stared at it. There was no doubt in her mind that she'd want to be rid of magic once Casper's wishes were fulfilled, but she hadn't yet tried and tested any of her powers to know how fun they were.

"Take it. You need the potion more than I do," said Baby A. "Like I said, it's temporary."

"You're so good at what you do and you use it to help people like me."

"When you're trained, the war is over and you're safe in Mousique," she said, "look in the mirror and say that before you drink what's in the bottle. We made the choice to save your life but it's up to you to live it. Now get some rest. You're going to need it."

TEN

Arriette's nap was cut brutally short by a sharp scream. She listened for snapping twigs and doughy footsteps and after gathering the courage to investigate, Arriette rolled over to survey the clearing. She had to squint to make out the dark figure approaching and, leering forward for a finer view, realised her visitor was Dean Constable.

She opened her mouth to scream but there was no sound. His foul hands were reaching in to seize her.

Frozen, her initial thought was to wake from this nightmare.

"There's no hiding from a retainer. I know this forest like the hairs on my knuckles, Monroe. You're coming with me."

Dean dragged Arriette from her shelter and through endless leaves and dirt. She dug in her fingers and clawed at every branch, rock and vine she saw, but Dean was too strong. He flipped her, hooked a strong arm around her neck until Arriette's air supply fell short, then reached for his dagger as she spluttered to breathe.

Arriette waited until he bent then slashed at his face with her broken fingernails. Dean cursed and flung her across the clearing toward her friends, unaware she'd drawn enough blood for it to appear he'd been weeping it.

Arriette hit the ground with a thud, then doubled over in pain.

"Casper," she coughed. "I'm sorry. I'm so, so sorry."

The shape-shifter crouched with his head lowered and although he appeared to be uninjured, Baby A was shackled and the skin at her wrists was raw. The right side of her face throbbed and her left eye was swollen.

"I'm so *pleased* you're safe," said Kalvin, running his finger down Arriette's arm.

Her eyes widened. "*You!* How did you find me, Kalvin? It's impossible."

"Careless breadcrumbs," he said, grinning.

Baby A spat at his feet then huddled closer to Arriette.

"You're going to regret disrespecting me," he said.

With enough force to knock her over, he back-handed Baby A across the mouth. Arriette flinched at the sound.

"Damn you, Kalvin."

"See what you made me do?" he said. "This is *your* fault!"

Kalvin drew a curved blade from his belt. Arriette's eyes were drawn to the shimmer, illuminating the initials KA beneath the moonlight. A scimitar like that was expensive. *Everlast* expensive.

"Look, Kalvin, I paid this girl to take me to the city. They're innocent locals."

He gripped Arriette by the hair and dragged her up.

"How naïve do you think I am?"

"We should kill them here," said Dean, polishing his boots with saliva.

"No, we'll go deeper into the forest," said Kalvin, tightening his hold. "We keep Arriette alive."

Arriette squirmed. "What do you want?"

"To repay my debts."

"What about Rihaana, will you let her go?"

"Oh, let's just say Charles will owe *me* a debt when I'm through with her," Kalvin replied.

Arriette wriggled free and lunged for his throat. Dean shoved her aside and knocked her down before Kalvin's boot finished the job.

Arriette cried out in agony.

"Strike one, Monroe," Dean spat.

"I don't know where Rihaana is; I haven't been to Mousique

in days."

Dean growled and rolled up his sleeve, revealing the Raido rune beneath his elbow. Arriette's eyes locked onto it, believing the R-shaped symbol to be a marker identifying this beast as a retainer. She stole a glance at Baby A's I-shaped Isa beneath the P-shaped Thurisaz on her neck and swallowed hard, realising these presumed tattoos were, in fact, supe birthmarks. Although she didn't write about runes specifically, Harriet Foley had mentioned them a few times in her earliest scrolls.

"She's nothing, Kalvin. A pitiful human. Just kill her now."

"No, Arriette lives. Susan said—"

"Susan will be dead before we deliver this human to her," Dean growled.

Arriette scrunched her knees to her chest and tried to concentrate on breathing. Her palms were sticky with sweat and her pulse raced, turning her stomach to water. Casper remained uncommunicative and Baby A's eyes scanned the area for a means of escape, but neither tried to help Arriette. She couldn't blame their lack of loyalty.

"They're innocent," Arriette pleaded. "Let them go."

"If you won't act on this nonsense," Dean said, "then I will."

He pressed his dagger against Casper's throat. Arriette screamed and lurched between them.

"No! I was your original bargaining chip."

Dean knocked Arriette aside and ragged Casper from the ground by his robes. The blade was beginning to draw blood.

"Your value is diminishing," Dean said, grinning.

Arriette's eyes met Casper's. Why wouldn't he fight back or shift shape? If anyone had the means to escape Dean's fury, he did.

"Strike two, Monroe." Dean began to count down from five.

Kalvin thrust Baby A to the floor, face down against the earth. Arriette shut her eyes and used precious time to debate with her conscience. If she gave Rihaana up she'd betray the one person who'd always stood by her. Refusing such traitorous intelligence would cost the lives of two supes she was beginning to appreciate.

"Four, three, two—"

"Free them and I'll take you straight to her," she blurted, thrusting her wrists forward. "Shackle me if you wish but let the innocents *go*."

Happy with the offer, Dean released her friends.

Kalvin told them both to walk straight until they reached the edge of the forest. Once out of range, Baby A pulled the old man to her and cradled him. They disappeared without so much as a backward glance.

The knots in Arriette's stomach tightened.

Dion would be rising any second and Arriette needed to stall if her half-hearted plan was to succeed. Dean Constable may have been a retainer, but like most supes she'd encountered recently, he underestimated her.

Arriette swallowed hard, her throat dry. "Perhaps you'd be willing to bargain?"

Dean's brow creased. "Your friends are of no use to us, Monroe."

"For their *protection*. How can I be sure you won't kill them once you get Rihaana?"

Arriette struggled to the shelter, limping from a twisted ankle and passed Baby A's potion to Kalvin.

"I met the man who brews it and I can make a long-standing deal for more."

Kalvin licked his lips. "There's no label."

Dean swiped for the bottle but Kalvin was faster. He protested, "Don't be a fool, Avery. I think we ought to—"

"Lay off," Kalvin said. "I'm sure we can come to some agreement."

Arriette backed to the tree line and was pleased to find Casper and Baby A crouched low in the shadow of an old venom tree.

Were they waiting to see how this ended by putting their own lives at risk? Arriette gestured for them to leave despite wishing they'd stay.

Kalvin popped the cork and Arriette's mouth hung open in awe. He couldn't resist a drink.

What's going on? Baby A mouthed.

Arriette raised a finger to her lips.

Kalvin took a swig, burped and handed the bottle to Dean. He sniffed the liquid and once pleased his companion hadn't choked to death, he finished the rest.

Whilst Baby A would have lost only her powers and not her memory, Dean's power was his memory. But before Arriette could truly marvel at the genius of her last-minute plan, Kalvin's breathing became laboured.

"I thought I could smell human."

"Dion!" Arriette raced forward and skidded to a halt. "Thank Zïnnyi you're here."

"You k-know this m-monster?" he stammered. "Tell her to b-back off."

Dion tripped and straddled him, causally manoeuvring his face to squelch in the dirt. Perhaps she'd been watching his antics and planned suitable revenge, or maybe she wasn't vegetarian at all. Either way, Arriette would owe her.

"Can I eat him?" Dion glanced at the dark stain on Kalvin's pants and lowered her fangs to his throat. "Fear is a luscious scent."

"Oh please d-don't." Kalvin began to cry and pointed at Dean. "Take him, n-not me!"

Arriette nodded for Dion to release her hold. "This must be ya lucky day. Take ya mangy friend and get lost before I change ma mind."

Terrified, Kalvin dragged Dean who was frozen in confusion and ran from the clearing. At the trees, he span to face Arriette. She heard the swift whistle of the scimitar and ducked just in time to dodge a beheading. It stuck in the trunk of the nearest tree, free for the taking.

Dion hissed. "*Now* can I eat him?"

"Susan will be so disappointed in you," Kalvin said, then disappeared into the shadows.

Dion leaned down to pick up the empty potion bottle and cackled. "Good for nothin' little—"

"Oh, I know what he is," Arriette finished. "I did warn you. He's sticking by that Susan story though so perhaps he wasn't lying after all."

"They'll be back," Dion replied.

Arriette said, "I'm not so sure."

Casper dusted down his robes and tidied his beard, then gently lifted Baby's face. She gasped as he cleaned her wounds.

"That's going to scar," he said.

"Sure, trade *my* beauty for Kalvin's shame," she grumbled. When he'd finished she strode to Kalvin's blade and yanked it free of the bark. "Least now I can kill him with his own weapon. *Curved*; an interesting signature."

"Hey, why didn't you change shape?" Arriette asked Casper, snatching the scimitar from Baby A and examining it. "It's an everlast blade, most likely a gift. Rihaana has one and it would seem I need this more than anyone, being human and all. Casper, you were almost killed."

"But we weren't," he said.

"And you're not human anymore, for the *millionth* time." Baby A folded her arms.

"How could you jeopardise your lives?"

"I had faith," he said.

"Oh, that's *fine* then." Frustrated, Arriette slumped against a tree and scowled, examining her foot. "Nobody ever won wars on faith alone, Casper."

"It's a compliment," he said. "I believed you'd save us and I'm not disappointed."

Arriette stormed past and went to shake Dion's hand. "For a moment there I thought you were actually going to kill him," she said, then decided an embrace was far more appropriate considering the vampyr had saved their lives.

"I saw the doubt in ya eyes. I'm a good actress."

Arriette backed away. "Look at you, you're filthy!"

"Ya would be too if ya slept like me. Hand me that canteen."

Dion poured the liquid over her hands and face. "Baby A, did they hurt ya wings?"

"They didn't know I was angelic. Arriette's quick thinking saved me *that* conversation."

Baby A stripped off her jacket and released her wings. They all embraced before Casper excused himself to clean up, then she took to the skies to check on Reiko and Tobias. Arriette stared at the clouds until Baby A was out of sight.

"She'll cool off," said Dion. "Her pride is hurt, that's all. She's angry cos' I let him live and cos' he ruined her face. Not like it'll stay that way. Angelic blood is so pure that scar will fade within a week, and it won't take long for your ankle to stop aching."

"I'm pleased you spared him." Arriette knotted her fingers and blinked back tears. "I shouldn't be but it's true. I loved him once; hard to accept he's succumbed to such low behaviour just to settle a debt." Arriette shook her head. "Never felt so helpless in my life. Not even when the Vamps attacked me."

"This time it wasn't just ya own life at stake," Dion said. "Ya protected others, just like the Recruit."

Arriette shuddered. "Don't say their name, *please*."

Dion retracted her fangs and smiled. "Sorry, but for the record, ya handled that well."

"You're kidding. I could hardly breathe at one point. Felt like the entire universe was resting on my lungs."

"I can't believe ya powers didn't kick in though," Dion said. "They're tied to emotions."

"Yeah, I could've used a magic cure for that pain in my arse."

Laughing, Dion wrapped both arms around Arriette and squeezed.

This time, Arriette hugged back and allowed the metallic scent of vampyr to comfort her.

"I'm pleased ya were there to help my friends," she said. "First step Kalvin. Next step war."

"Wait, I just predicted you'd be rising. I did *nothing* else."

Dion shook her head. "Ya did more than ya think. So I guess we still have ya gifts to look forward to."

Dion pushed Arriette away and guided her to a fallen tree, indicating she should sit and catch her breath. Arriette still couldn't help but enjoy the thrill of adrenaline despite feeling responsible for the entire ordeal. Having survived her first Recruit fight, her thirst for knowledge only increased. Now she was curious about the war, Pandora's box and the Recruit's history. She was even eager to go in search of such things.

"We're nearing the edge of the forest," said Casper. "Where's Baby A?"

Dion pointed to her outline against the moon's glow. "Where do we go from here?"

"If we move fast we could reach the gates by dawn."

Baby A's feet landed on the forest floor with a thump.

"Tobias, Rieko and the everlast girl are a few miles behind us. There's a small demonic patrol not too far from here. They might miss us but I can't predict their course. Now it's dark we should move on."

"What do we do about the patrol?" Arriette asked.

"Nothing, we've just got to keep walking," Casper said, aiding her to a stance. "How's your foot, can you walk?"

"Already feeling a little better. How can I fight a demon in this state, though?"

"We may not have to," Baby A said. "Looks like all three species are out tonight anyway. If our paths cross, we're reliant on luck."

"Well how do I know which species is the most dangerous?"

"Until ya meet 'em, ya won't know."

"The shadows are hardest," Baby A corrected. When Arriette glared at her she said, "What? I have experience in the field." Baby A demonstrated firing an invisible arrow and Dion faked her death. "Orcs are merely minions who have human biology. Kill them like you'd kill your own. The demons who rule them are distinctive horned brutes with atrocious tempers. They look difficult to kill but their armour isn't so impressive."

"I don't like the sound of any of those."

"Then if we get in trouble, run. Don't try to fight. The boys will be here soon anyway," said Casper. "The three of us are no match for a demonic army. I know a place we can hide."

"Tobias and Reiko know of this sanctuary?" asked Dion.

"About a mile from here there's a track that leads out of the forest. We'll see them pass us."

Arriette said, "Nobody would dare attack a vampyr and two hunters their size."

"Ya don't miss havin' protection, ya miss *Tobias*," Dion said.

There was little point in trying to defend herself. Angels were naturally talented at picking up on human emotion and vampyrs, especially red-haired ones, were just plain nosey.

"We live miles in opposite directions. We're of different species." Arriette rubbed her bare arms. "It's so cold out here."

Casper gasped and turned his back to the group.

"What's going on? I feel *weird*." Having looked down at her missing clothing she squealed and dived behind a tree. "What's *happening* to me?"

Dion burst into laughter. "Thinkin' 'bout Tobias, huh?"

Arriette popped her head out and scowled, measuring the distance to her shelter. "Was not!"

"Then why are you *naked*?"

Casper pulled a pair of trousers from Baby A's bag and threw them at her. "You're naked because you want to be," he said.

"Stupid dreamer. Why didn't Tobias warn me how embarrassing this power could be?"

The temperature increased as fast as it had dropped and Arriette glanced down to find her original clothing in its rightful place. She patted herself from head to toe, then stepped to the centre of the group.

She sighed. "Happy now, Dion?"

Before Arriette's nerves had steadied, a harsh burning began in her chest. She slapped a hand across her heart and clawed at her shirt, freeing the itchy skin beneath. Baby A's eyes narrowed; she reached out and ran her healing fingers across what at first appeared to be a bruise. Then, as the pain ceased, a beautiful squared figure eight in fine black ink appeared.

Baby A gasped and turned to Casper. "Dagaz. That's incredible."

"What the hell is Dagaz?" Arriette snapped. "And why is it trying to kill me?"

"*It's a rune.* It symbolises a breakthrough. Thinking about Tobias sexually triggered your change and the disfavour cancelled the dream. I believe you're now a dreamer, Arriette. Congratulations."

"No thanks to Tobias!" Sweating, Arriette examined the brand. "I knew your tattoos were identification markers but I didn't think *I'd* get any."

"Dagaz looks like butterfly wings, which is a dreamer's birthmark," said Dion. "Tobias has one, 'cept his was modified with an *actual* tattoo."

"Well that's just dandy," she grumbled.

"Hey, it's not all bad," said Dion. "At least now ya the same species."

ELEVEN

Worrying about the demonic patrol on their journey to the cabin distracted Arriette from her shame. Horned brutes, ghosts and orcs?

No way can I win that *fight,* thought Arriette.

Dion and Casper strode several metres ahead. Arriette thought she'd use their privacy to pick Baby A's brain. The angel would chatter for as long as Arriette would listen, especially about magic.

"You really need a dreamer's advice," she said.

"You *know* I can't tell Tobias what happened," Arriette said, itching her rune.

Baby A groaned. "Leave that thing alone."

"It *hurts*," said Arriette, digging at the brand with her finger nails.

"Yeah, you think?" Baby A pinned back her hair. "Got two of my own. Thurisaz is a gateway marker, identifying me as a time-traveller and Isa is a standstill marker, indicating I have influence over time and space."

"And mine indicates what? That I'll whip off my clothes at a moment's notice?"

The angel rolled her eyes. "You know dreamers are a scale two, right?" Arriette nodded. "Good, well, a dreamer's thoughts and feelings are projected from their bodies," she said. "What happens in the unconscious mind is fed in as part of reality so dreamers can manipulate their surroundings. Dagaz is a breakthrough marker for telekinesis."

"For dreaming then?" Arriette asked.

"Exactly. Each half represents the wing of a butterfly."

"Meaning *psyche*," said Arriette, raising her brow.

"I'm impressed. The translation means 'soul', which is precisely where a dreamer's power originates. In the wrong hands such a gift is extremely dangerous, Arriette."

"Yeah I read somewhere that butterflies were seen to bring death and reincarnation."

"In some cultures yes, but two butterflies symbolise love and marriage." She winked, sending shivers down Arriette's spine. "Tobias can explain better than I, being what he is."

"I'm not sure telekinesis alone is worth so much hassle."

"They're architects too, using each level of their consciousness as building blocks for practically anything. Draw on a memory, link to a relevant emotion, isolate your power and, should you wish, shoot a fireball from your palm." Baby A demonstrated, using her hands and explosive noises for added effect. "Bye bye enemy."

"Oh my, I spoke too soon."

"Tobias's energy is so condensed that his flames are blue. Anyway, dreamers go through phases of development so you'll get there soon, but if I tell you any more *I'll* be the target of Tobias's next dream."

She kicked a rock, fed up with travelling and from explaining another person's job.

Arriette scratched her head. "I thought the gift was telekinesis centred though?"

"That's only half of the power," she said. "Tobias learned to control his telekinesis years ago. That's the physical aspect. He can distinguish between thoughts to leak and those to contain. He doesn't use it much, which is a shame because he's quite the weapon. There is a spiritual aspect but it's all beyond me."

"How do I control it?" asked Arriette.

"No idea, ask Tobias. Just hide your attraction to him when you raise this topic."

"Can you at least guess?"

Baby A shrugged. "Learn thought control and positive thinking, try to stay calm, collected, detached. The more emotionally involved in something, the more easily you're manipulated. You'll find it harder to make friends now you're a dreamer, that's for sure."

"I'd have expected it to be easier," she said. "Knowing nobody can harm me."

"There are people out there who'll grind your bones. You're going to want to use that gift on *a lot* of people. Tobias prefers to be secluded."

"So he lives in the forest with you."

Perhaps that's why they all live in exile, she thought. *Nobody wants the responsibility of self-control.*

Arriette nudged Baby A playfully, blushed and bit her lower lip.

"Do you think he knows?"

"About your crush? He's no reason to. Aren't you curious about *my* gift? My developments are far stronger than dreaming, Arriette. Especially my angelic half."

If I don't kill myself using this first power, thought Arriette.

"Travelling is the physical aspect; the opening and controlling of wormholes. When a traveller moves they leave a trail. Others can follow like a tunnel to another time and place until it closes, depending on the initiator's strength."

"But what if I'm pulled to a random era and can't get back?"

"It's best to take somebody with you; somebody experienced." Baby A thought for a moment. "Practise a lot. First just travel in space. It's easier to correct your place than your time."

Arriette nodded. "Got it. Would I leave these wormholes being half-human?"

"You're *one-fifth* human. What I'm trying to say is I can bring you home if you panic." She placed her index finger on the rune and smiled. "You saved my life. It's the least I can do."

They jogged at a steady pace to catch up with Dion and Casper. Arriette's muscles throbbed from the exercise but it felt good to stretch her legs.

Through the trees ahead stood a multi-storey cabin. Arriette stared up at it in awe. The staircase, wider at the base, trailed the side of the building and had been intricately decorated across a beautiful archway. The first carving was a house with a smoking chimney, followed by a rectangle and what Arriette thought looked like a top hat.

"Is it a magical ward of some kind?" asked Arriette.

"No this is Pouki's place," said Casper. "Those are traveller's signs. They're messages; these mean 'gentleman', 'well-guarded house' and 'danger'. He's expecting us."

"Those are a bit contradictory," she grumbled, wondering how he'd be expecting them when she herself wasn't expecting such a visit.

The group herded up the stairs and hammered on the door. Arriette peered over the edge of the second-floor railing and cringed.

"Pouki, we need a place to hide. Open the door!"

"Who is this *Pouki?*" asked Dion.

Baby A shrugged; the name wasn't familiar. Casper had never mentioned him.

Footsteps sounded and the door creaked open.

Baby A and Arriette linked arms and were the first to enter. They scanned their surroundings.

A wooden stool sat against the far wall between two beautiful tapestries which seemed to tell a story. A feathered rug lay in the centre and an old bench sat beneath the window. There was no other furniture and with the window open, the room was cool.

Arriette slapped a smile on her face and held it there. If Baby A's predictions were correct, making friends wasn't about to get any easier.

"Do my eyes deceive me?" said a light voice. "Bentiâ!"

Arriette turned and tilted her head to see a bearded man standing only three feet from the ground. "*You're* Pouki?"

"You must be Miss Monroe."

He extended an arm which Arriette accepted with a firm, confident handshake.

"What did you call—?"

"Pleasure to meet you," he interrupted. "I am Pouki Hallidae. Make yourself at home. Casper tells me wondrous news."

Baby A folded her arms. "I don't think being attacked, bitten and ambushed accounts for good news, do you?"

Casper placed a hand on her shoulder. Pouki circled her once then pottered toward the tapestries, gesturing that they take a seat.

"Pouki, what did you call me?" Arriette asked.

Dion and Baby A sat beside one another on the bench, their eyes narrowing as Casper's friend stood face-to-face with Arriette, placing his hands on her shoulders. His breath was sweet and his beard thoroughly groomed. He wore robes like Casper's which were plain, clean and smelled of sweet incense.

"Bentiâ," he said, "means you are blessed. Ben-tee-ae," he mouthed.

Arriette copied his pronunciation, trying not to laugh. "I'm hardly blessed. If it's not my ex-boyfriend trying to trade me it's vampyrs trying to eat me." Dion scowled when Pouki glared at her. Arriette promptly corrected him. "*Not her.* Is that your definition of bentiâ?"

His hands tightened on her shoulders. "Your body is weak but your power is strong. I'd mind that temper, Arriette. I haven't seen a woman naked in a *very* long time."

How did you know that?

Arriette shifted uncomfortably and tucked a loose strand of hair behind her ear.

"What are you, a demon?"

"He's a telepath," said Baby A. "I feel him in my head. Poke all you like, my guard is up."

"And a strong guard you have," he said, smiling. "You ought to train our new recruit to do the same."

Baby A groaned. "Casper, who *is* this guy?"

"Arriette wanted to meet other beings. This one is safe and convenient so be polite."

"Sorry I'm not overly enthusiastic but I'm uncomfortable knowing he can read my thoughts," Arriette said. "You had no idea we'd be coming here to arrange this so why *are* we here?"

"Arriette's right," said Baby A. "She deserves an explanation. We all do."

"Ah you're Casper's angel; de'va en demetran!" Pouki said, rudely interrupting.

Baby A scowled and opened her mouth to protest. Arriette beat her to it.

"Hey, we don't speak Haeyloian."

Baby A said, "He believes I'm pure and loving. Now about that explanation—"

Baby A could speak fluent Haeyloian?

Arriette thought the language died before her birth, but of course, if the everlasts still used it why not Angels too? Considering her gift was to protect and love every species it made sense to speak a variety of tongues. Maybe her blood could help Arriette learn too?

"De'va demetran," she repeated, sounding each syllable as 'De-va de-meet-ran'.

"How about you, Arriette?" he asked.

"What about me?"

"Are *you* pure?"

Arriette laughed. "Not since I was in adolescence. This has nothing to do with why Casper brought us here. You're just being nosey."

"I don't think he was referrin' to intimate relations," said Dion. "Angels are pure and lovin', connected to the planet because they cannot *connect* with anyone else." She gulped. "If ya understand."

"I don't appreciate the reminder," said Baby A. "Celibacy isn't fun. Angels are married to Zïnnyi. To share such a connection with another being would be an insult."

"Well I haven't been connected to anything in a long time.

Unless fangs and my ex-boyfriend's fist count? As for loving I had friends, neighbours and partners once."

Once, she reminded herself.

"Yet you killed somebody," Pouki said, stealing this information from her unprotected mind.

"No," she lied. "You have no right—"

"Who did you kill, Arriette?"

"A vampyr. Can we stop the interrogation? Casper, he's not aware that there's a gang of angry demons a mile from here, is he?"

"That was self-defence," said Pouki, "and yes I am aware but I'm not worried. The owners of the first and third-floor flats are rogue hunters. They haven't been home in weeks but those monsters don't know that. I read from Casper's mind that you needed a sanctuary. I've been waiting for you."

Dion gripped Casper, led him aside and whispered something in his ear. Casper gave her shoulder a firm pat. This was no place for a rogue but if the vampyr hunters were on vacation, she'd be safe.

"There's been a lot of noise on an evening; some kind of rally takes place. They worship their leader. It's likely those you saw are going to tonight's event. I was about to investigate when I picked up Casper's thoughts. They should be gathering at any time."

"What kinda rally?" Dion asked.

"I don't speak their twisted dialect of Haeyloian but they'll be planning to steal something expensive or powerful to gain the upper hand. No worries, though. They never succeed. Besides, Pandora's box hasn't resurfaced yet, so their powers are still limited."

Pandora's box! There were too many questions unanswered and Arriette thought it was about time her new friends filled in the gaps about the piece of dangerous treasure potentially opened within the last 100 years.

"Well let's keep out of their way," said Baby A, relaxing.

"Oh Casper, she's just as you imagined," Pouki said. "So

beautiful. So *powerful*."

"With the greatest respect, *what* are you talking about? Who cares if I killed a Vamp in self-defence?" Arriette asked, impatiently. "Kill or be killed. I don't want to die. Do you?"

"Oh no. Don't you know why I asked if you were pure?"

"Does it matter?" Arriette grimaced.

"Of course," said Pouki. "If your soul is tarnished there's no point in us continuing."

Baby A was right, people were beginning to boil her blood.

"In my line of work I am only able to help those who haven't walked the path of evil," Pouki explained. "So we'll need to have a chat about Pandora, about the Recruit and about your responsibilities."

"Possible responsibilities," she said, glancing at Casper.

"You're a religious leader, aren't you?" asked Baby A. "One of those who believe strongly that Pandora's box is the cause of evil. You think the box was opened too?"

"Yes I do, but that is something Arriette and I must discuss. I believe what is broken can, however, be fixed. Casper asked me to help Arriette. He believes she's going to need severe training."

"Are you qualified?" Arriette asked.

Pouki chortled. "I've trained supernatural beings for twenty years. This wasn't pre-planned, Arriette, I promise. I can hear but I cannot respond." Pouki tapped his head. "Your visit was coincidental."

"I don't believe in coincidences," Dion said, winking at Arriette.

"Which is your right. My questions are merely for my own protection though; I wouldn't want to train somebody who will use those gifts against me now, would I?"

"Go on then," said Baby A, getting to her feet. "Tell us about Pandora."

"All in good time. Arriette must understand the basics of the Haeyloian language first. Particular words will enhance your power," he said. "Wouldn't you like to learn?"

"Learning is what I do; what I'm good at. Kalvin said I was the only educated human for miles. You train individuals on your own, as a job?"

"Yes, once on behalf of the Recruit."

Baby A, Dion and Arriette glared at the telepath; Arriette in amazement, but the others in annoyance.

Pouki raised a brow and grinned at Casper. So *what* if their secrets were revealed?

Better now than once it's too late, he thought.

"You're a member of the Recruit too?" Arriette asked. "So you were all telling the truth? Oh my, I think I need a drink."

Pouki continued regardless of Arriette's wobbly legs.

"I began training individuals like yourself to control their gifts sixty years ago. I only left as I felt my time with the Recruit had expired; they needed someone younger. Besides, Casper has been keeping me updated regarding his everlasting hunt, which I'm so pleased has come to an end. Planning for this day was enough to keep me busy."

Casper placed an arm around her and squeezed. She stared at him blankly; he knew about Pouki's association with the Recruit and said nothing.

"I didn't tell you for your own protection." Casper turned to Pouki. "And we needed you, silly old fool. He was our most skilled trainer, you know. The quad girls were good but lacked experience."

Arriette gasped and pulled away from Casper. Her eyes were wide and accusing.

"Your arrival changes things once again," said Pouki.

Arriette grabbed Casper by the shoulders and shook him. "You're really one of them, aren't you?"

Casper frowned; Arriette's low-level accusations were a great insult. "I am more than a number," he said. "I was a leader."

Words were beyond her. Casper was the head of an organisation famous for the protection of the human existence. To keep such a history secret was either very brave or very stupid.

"Are you crazy?" Baby A asked. "You said we should wait."

"It is my place to share my past, not yours."

"I don't understand why you didn't tell me sooner," Arriette said, disappointed.

"About my role as leader? You didn't believe the Recruit were real, never mind my involvement. The Recruit are high in everyone's expectations and I didn't want to let you down," he said. "I chose you, so to have you thwarted causes me great pain. I left the Recruit of my own accord. What I was promised would find me never did; I had to progress the matter alone. Since then they haven't turned to me for guidance and most of the friends I had are either retired or dead."

"What could be of such importance for ya to leave behind everythin'?" asked Dion. "Ya never told us."

"Perhaps I ought to explain later. Tobias and Reiko should be here and Arriette needs preparation before we dig deeper."

Arriette flung her arms in the air. "So this *friend* Baby A said was missing, could he have joined the Recruit?"

Before Casper had the chance to speak, Reiko opened the door to the cabin. He let Tobias pass, carrying Rihaana over his left shoulder. Her hair sprang loose and her skin looked lifeless. She was unconscious.

"That friend is my brother Stefan," said Reiko. "He's just a human. He'd never join the other Recruit members without telling us. We'd have gone with him; met them together and joined forces."

"Here's your everlast. She's too feisty for her own good," said Tobias.

He laid Rihaana beside Dion on the bench and shook the forest dew from his hair.

"Ain't ya glad ya not the one unconscious?" Dion asked.

"I can take care of myself." Arriette rubbed her eyes and huffed. "Thanks for tracking us and bringing her here, guys." She turned to Casper. "Susan needs me if she's sick and Stefan might be hurt. Staying here, getting trained, is the right thing to do. Don't you have *any* idea where Stefan is?"

"A little," Reiko admitted. "He joined the city's resistance six months ago. There were rumours about the box re-surfacing. Charles and his peers panicked and recruited additional security for the everlasts. After that we heard nothing further from him."

"This is the famous Pandora's box, I assume? The one you all delay telling me about."

"He could 'ave just run away," said Dion. "Everlasts are demandin'."

"Or got himself killed," said Casper.

"No, I don't believe it. He's still training," Reiko said. "If I can find him and ask him about the box—"

"We're lucky you turned up when you did, Arriette," said Casper.

Tobias was beginning to look flustered. Arriette wanted to reach out and wrap her arms around him. His eyes were angry; his jaw clenched. He and Stefan must have been great friends.

"Did you know there's an army not far from here?" asked Reiko. "I heard one of them yell something about their mother."

"They spoke Haeyloian?" asked Pouki. "Not their own language?"

"No traces of Haeyloian at all. They spoke our tongue. They were chanting about their 'inanimate mother'. Weird if you ask me. We *just* dodged them."

"What's an inanimate mother?" Baby A queried.

"Presumably somethin' they pray to; what they believe protects 'em," said Dion. "Like a statue or amulet?"

"Or what *created* them," Casper corrected. His eyes met Arriette's. "We need to talk about Pandora's box. *Soon.*"

"We're goin' to wait 'ere until they pass, right?" Dion asked. "Ya can talk to Arriette now."

Pouki said, "Just stay until the rally ends. Arriette, Casper and I can chat when you're all rested."

"They're going to find us here," said Tobias. "You left footprints and mess. Did something happen?"

Arriette rolled her eyes. *You have no idea.*

"They're not going to come after you because you left footprints. Lots of creatures leave their prints in Manaia Forest every day," said Casper. "Be rational. When they've gone we'll get Rihaana to the city and figure out a way to convince Charles to free her and clear Arriette's conscience. Meanwhile, Pouki and I will fill in some gaps."

"How do you know this woman?" asked Pouki, checking Rihaana's temperature and cleaning her wounds.

Arriette huffed. "Can't you read her mind? It's a long story. Just don't get used to it."

Satisfied she would do him no harm, he knelt beside Rihaana and placed both hands against her skin. To read an everlast's mind was a privilege. Arriette later learned he had to make physical contact for it to be possible. From his findings they could learn about the city.

"An everlast of authority keeps the gates locked. Falkon, they call him. Lots of guards. Mostly retainers. Horses. Beautiful women."

"Kalvin and Dean might be there," said Dion. "Can ya see patrol routes too?"

"Unfortunately not. Haeylo City splits into thirteen sectors; I think I can draw you maps from my reading," Pouki said.

Pouki confirmed he could sketch a direct route. Arriette relaxed knowing she wouldn't have to stop for directions.

"We'll have to dodge any everlast guards," said Baby A. "If they know we have Rihaana with us, we'll be in trouble. Plus, the barracks are likely guarded and if there's someone after Susan—"

"There's just too much to do an' not enough of us," said Dion. "We'll never stick to any form of organisation."

Casper cleared his throat. "We're against the clock to find Susan. I'd say she's a priority."

"I'll find Susan alone," said Arriette. "My conscience can wait so long as Rihaana is safe. Reiko should concentrate on Stefan. Perhaps Dion can convince Charles to leave Rihaana alone? Tell him what happened to Dean. Vamps are influential."

"I think I can do that." Dion grinned.

"The information Susan has for you could be vital to the war," Pouki said.

"Or Kalvin could be lying," Tobias said. "What do you think, Arriette?"

"I can't walk away." She sighed. "I'm so confused, so torn. Do we have the manpower to fix everyone's problems in one day?"

Baby A held her hand. "We can only try. I'll come with you; I won't let you be somebody's bargaining chip."

"Poor Rihaana. She doesn't deserve any of this," said Arriette. "She's been there for me through the worst of times. She's my family."

"And you're ours now," said Tobias.

"It's not safe," she said, shaking her head. "I've got a terrible feeling about this."

"We promised you protection," said Tobias. "So that's exactly what you'll get."

TWELVE

When Rihaana woke and complained of a headache, Casper permitted her a short walk under Baby A's supervision. The patrol hadn't yet passed so everyone was on full alert; pacing, sighing, shuffling in their seat. Pouki, however, was only anxious to begin some basic Haeyloian dialect training, but Arriette couldn't concentrate. She felt mangy, self-conscious and irritated by all the fidgety noises.

After eating sandwiches and drinking lemonade, her friends decided to keep watch for straying rally participants and vacated the room, whilst Pouki and Arriette talked further about Pandora.

"You should relax first," he said. "Dion, where are you going?"

"Outside with—"

"Absolutely not. The sun will be up shortly so we cannot risk you sitting out with the others."

Dion ran her fingers through her filthy hair. "Looks like I'm with you then, Arriette. Hey Pouki, got any soap? Fresh clothes?"

"Soap? Of course I have soap! All my garments, however, will be too small."

Settling for soap and water, they spent the next hour freshening up and washing their clothes in a bucket. Dion emerged from the cubical of Pouki's shower and startled Arriette whilst she hummed her field song; vampyrs had no reflection and were light on their feet.

"I wish you wouldn't do that," Arriette said. "Can't you make more noise or something?"

"Sorry," she mumbled, running the towel through her hair. "Used to get a kick outta scarin' that lot in the mirror. Gets old *real* quick. Are ya gonna talk to Tobias?"

"Are you *crazy?* Tell him I was naked?"

Dion rolled her eyes. "He can help ya dream."

"I should learn Haeyloian first. What did Pouki call me, Bentiâ?"

Dion ran a comb through her hair. Arriette almost offered her use of the mirror before remembering there wasn't much point.

"If ya want to learn to control his gift ya don't 'ave a choice."

"I have nothing to offer him," Arriette said, suddenly sick of her own reflection.

"He's not goin' to expect payment. He can't speak Haeyloian either and if ya learn he might want lessons. Private lessons."

Arriette frowned. "That's *not* what I meant."

"Ya gotta at least try."

Arriette sighed. "No, I don't."

Once they'd washed and dressed, Arriette felt more human. Dion investigated Pouki's bedroom whilst Arriette continued to explain, far too loudly, why telling Tobias about her incident would be disastrous and doing some pacing of her own.

"I mean, what if I strip again or accidentally kill him?"

A head of fiery red hair appeared above the bed. "Do ya want him to die?"

"Of course not! What kind of a question—"

"Ya can't dream a dreamer to death. What use is their power if it works against 'em?"

"It worked on me!"

Dion threw her towel at Arriette and laughed. "When will ya learn? So ya were naked for a few minutes. Big deal. Ya did that to ya self."

"I hope you're going somewhere with this?" Arriette groaned.

"A dreamer's power won't work on another dreamer. It's a

defence mechanism."

"That's a load off."

"Arriette, the most damage ya can do to that boy is an ego boost. Dreamin' is the most active gift; it's only second on the HPS because everlasts outlive it. We all got our weaknesses. telepaths can't read demons, travellers lose their memory if they stray too far into the past or future, an' everlasts can't marry. The list goes on."

"Baby A said Tobias could move things with his mind. Is there some spiritual aspect?"

Dion cringed. "I'm gonna pretend I did *not* jus' 'ear that. As far as ya concerned, it's a lie."

Arriette borrowed some of Baby A's clothes and followed Dion out to the living room. The faint chatter of voices from the building's stairwell lingered at the other side of the door and their presence was of some comfort to her.

The two tapestries above Pouki's stool were difficult to decipher. Each told a story written in Haeyloian. Arriette tilted her head to the left, then to the right. She squinted, but it was no use.

"They're beautiful, aren't they?" Pouki said.

"What do they say?" asked Dion, mimicking Arriette's decoding strategy. "That's not standard Haeyloian."

"I see I'll have little to teach you, vampyr," he said.

"Name's Dion," she said, extending a hand.

Pouki grasped it. "Pleasure, Dion. The above is pronounced 'demetran ze lanya amandetza ze lunara'ê. Proniba et'ternan traquet'."

Arriette attempted to copy his pronunciation but failed, embarrassed by her efforts. Pouki slowed the phrase down until she managed the entire sentence.

"Some of the words are a little muddled but that's why we use pictures. The first lesson in Haeyloian is *never* take the words for face value."

"Why not?" Arriette asked.

"Remember the language is intended to be used alongside

magic. Magic draws its power from your emotions and the elements. You can manipulate the meaning through body language and tone too."

"So what does it mean?" Dion asked, running a delicate hand across the first tapestry.

"You don't need to read the words to follow the tale," he said, "but the story is about a leader who travels to the moon to grant his people eternal life. Instead, he finds power and tranquillity of his own and disappears."

"So he was selfish?" Dion asked. "Trickin' his people into thinkin' his actions were for their benefit."

Arriette sat cross-legged in front of Pouki's stool. "Should I assume this isn't fiction?"

Pouki winked. "President Kaines was far from selfish. Merely confused. This story should be familiar; I bought them from your father, Arriette." Hopeful, Arriette shuffled closer. "He worked as a travelling tradesman in the east for a while."

"How did you know we were related?"

"You're a loud thinker. I recognised your mother's face from your thoughts."

"Then you'll know Father passed away."

Pouki placed a hand on Arriette's shoulder. "He didn't deserve his fate. You'll have revenge one day. *Terrible* tragedy, how is your mother?" he asked.

"Wait, my father died peacefully in his sleep. Cancer. He'd been ill for months."

Pouki looked to Dion for an interruption. She asked, "How did ya end up meetin' him?"

He cleared his throat. "I went travelling with the Recruit. We discovered a power far worse than the Source. A proud, masked queen. We silenced her although we could not fully destroy her influence. Some of her possessions fell into the black market. Her name was Ze Entit Sehde Eyeh."

Pouki translated this to mean 'The All-Seeing Eye' and it was there he learned of the tapestries' characters. Myth said Ze Entit Sehde Eyeh was related to some of the characters and they originally hung above the entrance to her throne room.

"As I was leaving the city, Casper and I talked about finding you Arriette, although of course you hadn't yet been born. Casper *knew* you were out there somewhere. We met the tradesman on the road and he showed us these two tapestries. I saw the whole ordeal as a sign of good fortune and bought them."

"Good fortune?" asked Dion. "Her father stealin' a powerful sorceress' prized tapestries is a positive thing?"

"Oh, not that part of course, but that the road we were following was correct. For the creation story to appear as we discussed and the point of Zinnyi's plan? *Not* a coincidence. "

"When did ya take down Ze Entit Sehde Eyeh?" asked Dion.

"Oh, approximately fifty years ago, I'd say. As you can see I'm an old man now, incapable of such battles but used for the wisdom they taught me."

To have heard from a stranger that her thieving father's death deserved revenge, warned Arriette to learn as much as possible about Pandora's box, The All-Seeing Eye and the Haeyloian language to prepare herself for the day she'd deal with the truth. She could do nothing else about his slip of the tongue unless Pouki offered the information willingly.

So why, she wondered, did her father steal those tapestries? Did he know something about his daughter's future before she'd been conceived, and why did the date of her birth not correspond with Pouki's time frame?

If only she too could read minds.

Arriette sighed. "Pouki, you *must* explain something. My father worked in trade, temporarily, several months before my birth to support my mother, or so she tells me."

"Which is significant because?" Dion asked, frowning.

"Well it doesn't add up," she said, shaking her head. "I'm only twenty-eight. I'd have to be fifty myself for that history to make any sense!"

Dion glanced from Arriette to Pouki and back. "Do ya want me to leave?"

"Not at all." Pouki turned to Arriette and placed a comforting hand on her shoulder. "I think you should have a chat with your mother about the death of your father. I cannot disclose anything further, except for what I hear in passing."

"Then tell me that."

"Oh, no I cannot subject you to such gossip when it may very well be incorrect."

Arriette sighed and sat her head in her hands, but what use would sulking do miles from Drakonta and with half a story?

"I suppose that's fair."

"Shall we continue with the lesson?" he asked, smiling. When Arriette gestured he continue, Pouki said, "I'm shocked your mother didn't tell you this story as a girl. Lesson one is *always* our history, Arriette."

"Apparently there are a lot of things my mother never told me. If she read to me I don't remember. She travelled a lot and visited libraries all over Haeylo. That's how she met my father."

A father I should apparently be avenging, Arriette thought.

"Ya Ma lives alone?" Dion asked her.

"Yes, she's a farmer and keeps herself busy. She's too old to be carrying grain and harvesting but I visit and help. We're on good terms."

Until I get home, then she's in for it. Has everything I've known been a lie?

"Drakonta is hit regularly with disease," he agreed. "The population is small so it doesn't take long to spread."

"They live only a few miles from a swamp which I'm not convinced isn't contaminating their water supply. She won't move though, I've tried." Arriette took a deep breath. "It *infuriates* me."

"You think the water killed your father?" Pouki said.

"No, Cancer killed him but the water didn't help. It's already killed three men this year," Arriette explained. "She won't let me enquire about their water sources. Doesn't care to know."

By the way Pouki studied her, Arriette knew that he lingered somewhere deep in her mind, reading thoughts on Kalvin's visit, memories of family, Drakonta and trying to determine how much of what she said was the truth. At that moment he'd be reading drafted speeches for confronting Kalvin and Susan's departure, pondered letters to the city regarding Ma's water supply and a mental list of 'for or against being supernatural'. Now he'd be seeing the portrait of her parents which still hung above her mother's dining table and viewing painful memories.

Pouki pointed to the tapestry over his right shoulder, a wry grin on his face.

"Let's begin. The story is of a warrior fighting for his people. He decided to seek a better future. When their land is destroyed he agrees to begin a new settlement but he never returns for the others," he explained.

"Ya mean President Kaines of Earth who went to the moon," Dion corrected. "So he's real?"

"*Very* real, though it wasn't the moon. That's a myth. Translating text like this can be difficult. Bear with me." Pouki took the first tapestry from the wall and cradled it. "Demetran means lover," he said, "and lanya means planet. Lunara'ê is an old word for lunar – the moon, but is often used for 'star' these days. Et'ternan is eternity or everlasting. Amandetza is travel and tranquet is tranquillity. These basic words are obvious but others not so much."

"Isn't there a word for everything?"

"You mustn't think of this language as a means to communicate with friends," he said, "but to contact the elements and connect with their magic. Let me show you."

Pouki stood and moved a few paces back. He rubbed his hands together to create a source of heat and lifted them above his head. He whispered 'de'va lunara'ê' and the entire ceiling disappeared to reveal brilliant sunlight. Dion hissed until Arriette's gentle touch retrieved her from fear.

"That's amazin'," Dion gasped. "It doesn't burn."

"Lunara'ê in this context means 'star'."

"So how'd ya get the sun from that?"

"If you use it in the correct context you can manipulate this phrase to mean 'pure light'. The magic itself interprets your intentions and choice of words. My reference to both the sky and ceiling with my hands and the source of heat I created by rubbing them translated to what you see here."

"And the sun?" Arriette asked.

"Is, I believe, a star." Pouki grinned and lowered his hands gently.

"City inhabitants use this language daily?" Arriette asked. "Seems complex for school children to be learning."

"Only angelic and everlast children learn modern Haeyloian and most others use magic for personal gain," he explained. "Still, that's their problem not ours. Are you ready for more?"

"Aren't you goin' to translate the rest?" Dion asked.

"Like I said, that's not so easy," he said. "Let's see. Proniba means 'power'. In your case, Arriette, you could say 'proniba amandetza'."

"Power travels." Dion smiled and Arriette caught sight of two fangs poking between her blood-red lips.

Pouki shuddered at the sight. "In this case power travels in your blood. Ze marê fernan armeh en mightie Zïnnyi."

"Ah, well I know who Zïnnyi is," Arriette said proudly.

"These two tapestries are opposites; while the one on the left is negative, the one on the right is the story of a human becoming the leader of that same tribe only thousands of years in the future."

"So President Kaines made it then?" asked Dion. "The man in the tale found a place for his people to live? Wasn't so selfish afta all."

Casper knocked and entered the room, letting in as little light as possible. The rally was over. The sun was up. Tobias had managed to kill a hare and drain some blood for Dion. When they'd gone, Pouki and Arriette glared at one another.

"You don't have to say anything else. I'm not an idiot. I see through these little lessons and I'm grateful for them but for now, I prefer ignorance. Oh, and if you've been asked to get an answer out of me you'll have to wait until I see Susan."

Pouki frowned. "You're going to make a decision?"

"Don't play dumb. I feel you rummaging," she said scratching her head, "but I can't stay here. I'm not built for this."

"Is that what your heart says?"

Arriette shook her head and covered her ears. "I see what you're trying to do. Get me to offer the information of my own free will so you can't be punished for reading my mind later."

Pouki smirked. "You're smart, but worrying about Rihaana being alone is wasted. She's marrying a city retainer soon. She's even considering returning to confront her father, or she was before our friends kidnapped her from Mousique."

"For her own safety," she said. "How can I make a choice when I'm currently a prisoner?"

"I think that's a fair point. Don't see their gifts as prison bars though, Arriette. Be a student."

"I'll consider it," she said, paying little attention. "Do you know this retainer?"

"I think you do too," he said, re-hanging the tapestries.

Arriette closed her eyes. *Please let me be wrong.*

"Dean? But he's vicious, he chased me into the forest and almost got me killed."

"I'm sure Rihaana will be furious when she hears about his behaviour," said Pouki, but Arriette wasn't convinced he believed that.

She held her tongue when Rihaana strode through the door a few minutes later. Her skin was bruised; her matted hair tied back in a bun. She stormed toward Arriette, pulled back her fist and let loose on Arriette's cheek bone. She tried not to scream and forced herself to stand firm; take the punishment like the supe she was supposed to be beneath this miserable human exterior.

She dodged Rihaana's second swing and scrambled for something heavy for protection. Pouki gestured at the stool. As her fingers touched it she yelled 'entit proniba!' until her physical actions were unnecessary. With her feet firm on the floor and her hands thrust forward, Arriette had conjured enough power to hold the stool mid-air between them and by moving her hands, she could sway the stool in any direction. In doing so, Arriette had built the perfect barrier.

Dion emerged from the bedroom still gripping her lunch, followed by a nervous Casper.

"Arriette, ya dreamin'!"

"Congratulate me later!"

"I can't *believe* you're blaming Dean for this," Rihaana said. "You sent your minions to kidnap me. That's right, I heard you and the Dwarf talking."

Rihaana tried to side-step the wall. Arriette swished her hands to the left and, losing her balance, slammed both her body and the stool into the cabin wall.

"I didn't kidnap anyone." Arriette groaned. "I asked Tobias and Reiko to pick you up after what Dean did to me. I feared for your life, Rihaana, because when I ran, Kalvin was going to trade your life for his debts."

"Perhaps I wanted to return," she said, narrowing her eyes.

"So I hear but how was *I* supposed to know that? I can't believe you're engaged. Why didn't you tell me?"

"I wasn't sure we still were, because I ran away. *How* did you find out?"

Baby A ran up the stairs and stood between them, building a thicker, stronger barrier with her wings. Pouki picked Arriette up off the floor with a helping hand and tapped his head. Of course he must have read her mind; Arriette wondered if he was reading hers as she struggled to her feet. Her fingers tingled and a vicious headache surged behind her eyes from such severe concentration.

"Arriette was only trying to save your freedom," Baby A explained, peering back over the tips of her feathers. "Why are you defending him? He won't even remember your name."

Rihaana fell to her knees. "What did you do? He's not a criminal, he's gentle and kind and caring. *Honest.*" She ripped away the bandages and flung them at Arriette, outraged. Her fists slammed to the floor. "If you hurt him I swear—"

"I did what I had to do and saved my friends," said Arriette, taking hold of Baby A's hand. "Dean's an undeserving monster."

"*I'm* your friend!"

Still unsteady on her feet, Arriette asked Baby A to aid her to the bench. The angel tucked her wings away, ran the back of her hand across her clammy head, then gripped Arriette beneath the arms.

"Magic lingers. You're not used to the effects yet," said Pouki.

Tobias and Reiko charged up the stairs to investigate the commotion and burst through the door. Dion hissed, causing Tobias to kick it closed with his foot, blocking out the light.

"What did you do to Dean?" Rihaana demanded.

"It's my fault," said Casper, crouching by Arriette's side. "I made a potion."

"You *poisoned* him? Is he dead?"

Casper and Baby A glanced at one another. When they were happy the answer to her question was indeed no, Casper continued.

"He's alive," Casper replied. "It wiped his memory. I'm sorry we had to take such drastic measures."

"He tried to kill us," Arriette said.

Arriette's vision was blurry. She wouldn't be able to concentrate on their argument much longer, nor was she having any success defending her friends' actions.

"We'd have gone straight to the city and left you there had we known you'd behave like this," said Tobias.

"If I could make it up to you I would," said Arriette. "You were so sure about hiding from Charles, even when Kalvin arrived."

"I still had my doubts about everything; wanted to make up my own mind in my own time. You can convince my father to let Dean and I marry now though, considering he's unable to do so himself."

Tobias gripped Rihaana by the collar and dragged her toward the door. "Arriette owes you *nothing*. You should be ashamed of yourself. Considering her other troubles I'm surprised she gave you a second thought."

"Wait, let her talk." Baby A aided Arriette to a stance. "I can't fight your battles but my plan had always been to strike a bargain for your freedom. Why else would I go to so much trouble?"

"We could ask for a trade," said Pouki, his eyebrows raised.

Tobias nudged him. "Is stealing my ideas a telepathic right?" he said. "Tell him we want Kalvin's debts wiped to free Arriette's obligation, get Stefan's location, better directions to Susan and then once we're happy, we release the kid. Screw her freedom. She doesn't deserve it."

Rihaana put her hands together and begged Arriette to help. "Arriette, I don't want to be an everlast. Please just help me negotiate my freedom. You *can't* use me as leverage."

"Hey, I was human until your boyfriend attacked me," she said. "Now I'm a supe against my will."

"It's your destiny but this idiot is willing to throw away a natural inheritance," Tobias said.

"If Kalvin kept his word and escorted me to Susan we wouldn't be here. If Rihaana told her father she was returning to the city to marry he wouldn't have sent Dean. None of this is *my* fault. I'm just the mule buckling under the pressure of everyone else's issues." Arriette put her head in her hands, grumbled, then shook her head. "Why should I even care?"

"Those powers may not have been assigned at birth but they are rightfully yours, Arriette. They serve a purpose," said Pouki. "They saved your life and in turn you'll serve others to repay the debt. It's your responsibility."

"*Destiny* this and *responsibility* that. Let's just take her to the city and get this over with. I'm done with this nonsense."

"Arriette, we're not seeking revenge," Casper said. "Rihaana needs your help."

Tobias folded his arms and slumped against the wall. "What she needs is a foot up her—"

"Tobias! That's enough," said Baby A.

"What Rihaana needs is irrelevant. I need peace and quiet, a dark room, a bottle of wine and a good night's sleep. But hey, nobody seems to get what they want these days so why should *she*?" Arriette spat. "Who am I kidding? I'm a lousy supe. We all know it."

"She's your first innocent," said Baby A. "Early experiences are rarely smooth."

"I could've resolved this with one sip of that potion," she said. "Casper, can't you make a new batch and repay me for the trouble?"

"I will not repeat that potion for you," he said.

"Why not?"

"Because you're the one I've been waiting for since the beginning, Arriette. I left the Recruit for you. You're the key to returning evil to Pandora's box, the solution to her reign and I will not deprive Haeylo of their saviour."

The room began to spin and Arriette's sight flickered. Bile rose in her throat, an agonising pain shot down her spine and she staggered into Tobias, collapsing in his arms. Arriette's last thoughts were of her father and she hoped, *prayed*, she'd be reunited with him instead of awaking to this nightmare once again.

THIRTEEN

Arriette moaned and rubbed her tired eyes, realising they were no longer in the comfort of the cabin.

"She's not going to like us kidnapping her, Casper," said Tobias. "Hey, she's waking up!"

"Put me down, I feel sick."

Tobias sat her against an emerald green gate.

The smooth marble walkway beneath was cold and uncomfortable. Arriette scrambled to the edge of the path and allowed her body to eject the venom of their last conversation, emptying her stomach.

"You fainted," said Casper. "We brought you here while you were unconscious. We thought it might be easier."

"*Easier*?" Arriette wiped her mouth and frowned at him. "If you think I'm going any further than these gates then the both of you need a head examination."

She may have passed out but she certainly wasn't finished yelling at them.

"This is what you wanted. Let's go find Susan," said Casper. "The others will join us for the rest later, all right?"

"No, *not* all right. Before I continue along my path I have to find out who I'm walking it with," she reasoned, massaging her aching temples. "Bribing me with a focus on Susan doesn't wipe my memory. I know you think I'm a *saviour* but I want an explanation."

Casper leaned against the gate and dug his hands in his robes. He sighed. "What do you want to know?"

"*Why me?* You said you'd been searching since the beginning, that you were promised something would find you and when it never did, you left the Recruit. Pouki said you discussed finding me after troubles with Ze Entit Sehde Eyeh and I hear we've all had weird dreams that only *I* reacted to correctly."

"All of which is true," Pouki said.

"So out with it, old man. Was I the *thing* that never found you?"

"On the day we met something in me set alight, Arriette. I *knew* you."

Arriette sighed. "Where's your proof?"

"Besides a history you'll never believe? You're too powerful too early in your inheritance."

"Being your saviour, what does that entail?"

"It means you can help prevent a war," Pouki said. "Once you learn to control your gifts. Casper can't ignore this. If Pandora's box *has* re-surfaced, we need you. It's written in this planet's history that a saviour would be born; someone capable of protecting Haeylo from evils, repeating Earth's catastrophe and fulfilling our creator's wishes. I'm sorry but this is only the beginning."

Arriette wasn't sure she had the energy to pursue this.

She sighed, defeated by the day's events and struggled to her feet.

"Ugh, I'm *so* going to regret this," she said.

With Dion back at the cabin, the group were down one of their strongest fighters. Although her other friends soon caught up, Arriette felt nervous and naked to her enemies.

A two hundred foot wall circled the perimeter of the city, locking out travellers at one gate per sector. Arriette knew all twelve would be secured and heavily guarded, much like theirs. If the everlasts suspected Pandora's box had been found, gaining entry would be impossible without an agreeable soldier.

As Arriette glared up at their emerald nemesis, nausea and dizziness consumed her. Tobias squeezed her hand.

"You'll be fine once the side-effects of using magic wear off."

"I'm never using magic again," she groaned, her stomach still heaving.

Baby A sized up the wall and brushed back her hair. "Looks do-able. Casper, you and I can combine our capabilities."

Exhaustion had stolen the majority of Casper's will to use any form of magic. The gates were locked and as Arriette wasn't feeling too well she too was in no condition to practice her own gifts further.

"I think I can fly over," she continued. "If you can shift and meet me, we'll find a guard together. These guys will never open up without a reliable source to vouch for us."

"You're right," he replied. "Though I doubt I can hold form for long, perhaps twenty minutes or so."

"I'll only need ten," she said, grinning.

Arriette waved a hand at Baby A, gesturing for her to go ahead, then coughed up the remaining contents of her stomach.

The angel spread her feet and released her wings; Reiko ducked as she span to face the gate. She'd need a lot of thrust to make it over.

Tobias held back Arriette's hair. "We'll wait in the trees about half a mile back and let Arriette get this out of her system," he told Casper, then scooped Arriette off her feet.

They began walking in the direction of the trees just in time to avoid debris from Baby A's take-off. Even the marble couldn't take the force of her launch; a vast crack trailed beneath the gate and into the city, drawing the attention of passers by and scattering them like seeds in the wind. A guard knelt to inspect the damage then scanned the area with a drawn sword. Casper would need to be quick.

Shape-shifting was growing all the more painful for Casper as his human age increased. He removed his clothing to avoid ripping them and passed the robes through the bars of the gate to Baby A, then closed his eyes. She ducked behind the empty security shed until the guard moved along.

The snaps and cracks of Casper's bones as he re-formed were distressing for his friend, and once he'd changed back from a bird to the Casper she knew and loved, Baby A exhaled a sigh of relief.

"Are you all right? That sounded like it hurt," she said, patting him on the back.

"I haven't morphed in a long time," he said, tugging on his robes. "Come on, let's go."

The city was a foul-smelling, run-down place this close to the gate. Surrounding them were piles of horse manure and Baby A had to hold her breath. As they moved further into the city through the residential areas, Casper noticed the changes in status. From thatched cottages and shacks to stone builds with little gardens. All entwined on dust tracks until they reached the everlast sector; the place that made the money instead of spending it on taxes.

Drawing attention to themselves unintentionally was easy; an old man in dirty white robes and a grubby angel stood out in the crowd of well-dressed city folk. Even in the lower class streets they were the smudges upon a perfect portrait. Their presence attracted a tall retainer with glasses, freckles and a head of vibrant orange hair. Baby A stopped to read a sign as he approached them with caution. She jumped from her skin when he tapped her and cleared his throat.

"Oi, cretin, no loitering in sector five."

Baby A prodded him hard in the chest. "Who you calling a cretin?"

Casper cringed and ran a finger across his throat. "Don't poke the bear, pal."

"I can report you for verbal abuse," he said, taking a nervous step back. "You're breaking the law standing here."

"Well I can report you for crimes against a servant of Zïnnyi. Now do we still have a problem?"

Tugging gently on her arm, Casper knew lingering, particularly whilst arguing with a guard, would stir a level of trouble they'd hoped to avoid.

"I don't want to arrest you." The guard partly drew his sword and backed away. "Move along now, Miss."

"So it's 'Miss' now? An angel speaks to the *highest* of everlasts, so who might find me guilty of your accusation?"

"To bother any everlast, no matter their class, with something as *mediocre* as a misbehaving whatever-you-are and her grandfather would be punishable by death," said the guard.

He gripped her firmly by the forearm and tugged her from Casper's side.

Pushing buttons came naturally to a woman with such respectable gifts and Baby A was one of the proudest.

"Leave this sector before I have you both arrested."

"Baby A, the man is only doing his job. We're late anyway. We're never going to find the gatekeeper or the barracks. There are no signs for it in this sector. Arriette is waiting for us."

The retainer froze. He released his hold on Baby A, shoved her aside and held out his weapon.

"Arriette *Monroe*? There's a ransom on her head. She kidnapped Rihaana Melovich."

"Actually that's a misunderstanding," said Baby A. "Arriette's our friend. She's right outside the city waiting for us with the kid."

"Take me to her immediately or so help me—"

"Oh for Zinnyi's sake," said Baby A. "For a retainer you're not so bright. This way then."

With a cautious eye on the guard's back, Casper whispered to Baby A, "Not my first plan, but about the safest. What about finding Stefan?"

She winked and gestured in the direction of the gate.

"Who are we kidding? If he's alive he's not going to come back with us. That's Reiko's job, not ours. Besides, we can't even find the damn barracks let alone gain access. Let's focus on Arriette. This could get her into the city and finding Susan is her priority, right?"

Casper sighed. "I don't know. They think she kidnapped Rihaana. Obviously Kalvin and Dean beat us to the city. How else could such a rumour spread? Is it safe to bring her here now?"

"Got a better idea?"

Casper inhaled and lowered his head.

Unfortunately there were no other options. So they continued walking for fifteen minutes before the emerald gates were in sight and Casper's heart began to race.

Whilst he'd been staring at the guard's feet and minding his own business in that time, Casper barely noticed how much the city had changed since his last visit. Everlast buildings were getting higher. Peasant properties were run down and dull. But the roads hadn't changed, nor had the high stone walls protecting the city. If anything, they'd only grown. Casper feared the everlasts would borrow more of Earth's designs and technology and in doing so they would ruin this planet the way humans had thousands of years before.

With the outside world growing nearer, the tension settled in Casper's shoulders.

"Hey! There's movements at the gate," Tobias announced, watching him from the trees.

"Is it my father?" asked Rihaana. "Oh I knew this was a terrible idea."

"It's Baby A and Casper. There's a guard with them."

Rihaana exhaled with relief.

She took Arriette by the hand, gasping at the heat radiating from her fingers.

"You're stifling, Arriette. Are you ill?"

Arriette felt sick and disorientated again. Could she control her emotions long enough to get business in the city out of the way?

"I'm fine," she said, wiping her sweaty palms on the grass. "Let's get this over with."

The retainer accompanying their friends looked unreliable and clumsy. At an approximate human age of twenty-five, but a retaining mental age of a forty year old, Arriette dare not underestimate him. On arrival at the gate she placed an arm through the bars and offered him a hand. His all-knowing eyes studied her intentions. When his bank of information scanned her face and matched each feature to a few wanted posters, he accepted the gesture and raised an eyebrow at her flushed cheeks.

"You're the outlaw everybody's talking about. Why aren't you running?"

Tobias and Reiko sandwiched Arriette's body between them and buffed out their chests. Nausea kicked in; she wrapped an arm around Tobias and used his frame to steady herself.

She swallowed hard. "Well I've done nothing wrong. Let me in and I'll tell Charles myself. You've already met my friends Casper and Baby A. This is Pouki, my advisor, and these are my most honourable men," she lied. "My head of security and my bodyguard."

Each introduction was brief; Arriette wanted this retainer to fear her; to believe she had some influence or power over people enough to have followers and warriors.

She soon learned his name was Mitchell Blue and he'd worked as a retainer for Charles Melovich since his late teens.

"There's obviously been some kind of misunderstanding. As you can see Rihaana Melovich is perfectly safe. In fact, she's part of the reason I'm here, Mitchell. I'm looking for somebody but I'm also returning somebody. Here, take her hand if you don't believe me but you'll have to open the gate first."

He advised them to wait until he'd found a second retainer to assist. The gate's mechanism required two guards and as Arriette looked closer there were two locks. Both retainers had to turn their keys simultaneously.

"You must be expecting enemies if you're using the backup system. What's wrong with the cogs? Perhaps Reiko and I can be of some assistance closing it behind us."

"We'll manage," he said. Mitchell removed a pair of handcuffs, much to Reiko's disapproval. "It's unusual for a criminal as wanted as you to hand themselves in without a fight."

"There's no need for that," said Reiko, sliding through the gap in the slow-moving gates. "She's not a criminal. Don't make me tell you again."

Mitchell argued, "I *have* to cuff you."

Arriette placed a gentle hand on Reiko's strong arm. "Just take us to Charles. I'll go without a fight. Here, take the girl."

Mitchell hesitated. "All right," he said, passing Rihaana to the other retainer. He wrapped a blanket around her shoulders and walked her ahead of the others. "This way please."

Mitchell and his friend led Arriette deep into the heart of Haeylo's city.

"You didn't find Stefan?" asked Reiko.

Baby A shook her head. "We had a quick look for signs to the barracks for you though. This is the best we could do. There are guards *everywhere*. We were being stopped every two hundred yards."

"Any idea where we are?" asked Arriette, gazing at buildings twice, even three times her height.

Faced with unusual fashions and scents of foods she'd never tried, Arriette had found an adventure in new experiences alone. If her stomach would only settle...

"Sector five," said Baby A. "There are worse areas, believe me."

"Things have changed so much here," Pouki said. "Rihaana is beginning to panic. She's confused; lost, emotionally. I'd say we're close to her father or another everlast. They can sense one another."

"There aren't any everlasts in this sector," said Mitchell's companion, listening in. "There have been vampyr sightings. There's dark magic here now. Only thirty-six hours ago did we suffer from a swarm of bugs. Our water is sour and it's rained an awful lot recently."

"We're not Vamps. It's daytime and I have wings," said Baby A. Although unnecessary, she produced her stunning specimens and raised an eyebrow. "See?"

"This city is ninety percent supernaturally inhabited. We

don't trust unknown humans here, especially with such dark times approaching."

"I suppose Charles has this city locked up tight then?" asked Tobias. "Given your plagues and unfortunate weather."

"Yes he does. If you ask me this whole thing is biblical."

"Can you explain?" Pouki asked. "We've heard rumours."

"*War*," he said, not so surprisingly. "Pandora's box has been found by someone."

"Are you sure?" asked Casper.

"Misfortune is all around you, all the time," said Mitchell, "but Pandora's box housed pure evil. We don't know how it happened or in whose hands; we only know it's recent. There's no other explanation for such bizarre magic."

"And the origin's timescale?" asked Reiko.

"No idea but it's gradually increasing in severity."

Baby A stopped the guard. "You believe all this?"

Mitchell sighed, unsure if sharing information like this was dangerous.

They seemed genuine; what proof did Charles have that Arriette Monroe had kidnapped Rihaana anyway? Her recklessness was widely known and as a young teen she ran away often.

"You didn't hear this from me." Mitchell halted the group. "There's been a leak amongst everlast followers. He or she is suspected of sharing secrets with demonic sources outside the city. To whoever has the box, perhaps. They don't know exactly but if they find a flaw in our security we're all dead. Civilians can't fight a wave that strong."

"Your security isn't great though, is it?" said Tobias, taking Mitchell and his colleague by surprise. "I mean, you forgot to search or question us to any reasonable degree. You've told us all you know about an impending war. You haven't secured your weapons either."

Mitchell replaced his sword in its sheath and cleared his throat. "All interesting observations I will ensure are corrected. Now be on your way. The offices are in the square. That way."

He pointed down a narrow alley. "Charles uses the multi-storey white building at the far side. Don't stray from this road. I'll be watching."

Arriette nodded and set off walking. Rather than thatched roofs and petty dirt paths, everlasts built with stone, glass, vibrant paint and used Earth's architecture. Arriette gasped at the height of his office block; ten storeys at least. *Haeylo's landscape must look stunning from up there,* she thought, but of course she'd be keeping away from the windows. Any height above her own head scattered the butterflies in her stomach.

"Top floor," he called after her. "Don't make me regret letting you go, Miss Monroe."

"Imagine the stairs," Tobias said, laughing.

It didn't take long to find the square. Tobias grasped her hand and walked her through the doors of the building, leaving their friends outside with Rihaana until Arriette gave the all clear.

"You're burning up, Arriette."

"My back is aching but I need to focus on the task, not on how I feel."

Arriette caught sight of her reflection in the window and gasped. Not only at how worn and sick she looked, but how pristine and clean the lobby was. How much money must Charles make from taxes? How many employees did he order to their knees to scrub his office?

A woman with olive skin and rippled black hair sat behind a desk reading a trashy supe magazine. She wore a deep violet robe. Her face was stern, unwelcoming and drew Arriette's attention to the not-so-perfect part of this world.

"Charles Melovich is on the top floor, right?"

Without looking up, the receptionist said, "Move along before I call security."

"They're right outside waiting for me," she said, stern-faced.

"And who is *me*?"

"My name is Arriette Monroe. He's not expecting us but he'll see me, I'm sure."

"Of course," she said.

The woman leaned across the desk, studying Arriette from her matted brunette hair to her unshaven legs with disapproval.

"The top floor *is* his office. I take it you're not from the city?"

"Is it that obvious?"

The receptionist slapped on her most agreeable face and nodded. A smile filled with such strain and effort it was almost convincing.

"Are you his secretary?" asked Arriette.

"I'm *a* secretary. Melanie Starre; you won't remember me but I'll remember you." She winked.

Retainer. Everlasts just love retainers, thought Arriette.

With Melanie staring after them, they strode eagerly to the stairwell. Arriette pushed open the door and exhaled with relief.

"Thank goodness. Hey, can I borrow your jacket?"

"Are you cold?"

"I need the high neck and hood to hide Roberta's fang marks," she said.

An everlast would be interested to know how she'd acquired those. Tobias assisted Arriette with the jacket and together they began their trek up the one hundred and twenty steps.

"I feel sick again," she said, pausing.

"This won't take long. Then we can get on with what's *really* important."

"We can't predict who'll be waiting when we get up there," she said. "Melanie has probably already warned him we're coming. I can't breathe, Tobias."

"Arriette, you need to calm down. What's the worst that could happen?"

"He'll have dreaming guards ready to annihilate us on the belief that I kidnapped Rihaana," she said. "I knew Dean would beat us here. Snarling little liar."

Tobias raised an unimpressed eyebrow. "Try not to think so aggressively. Dreamers project thoughts like those, remember?" Arriette squeezed his hand. "Change the subject and keep moving."

"All right, what do you want to talk about?"

"Miss Starre seemed nice," he said. "Don't you agree?"

She squeezed a little harder. "Not at all. She was rude."

"Someone's *jealous*."

Grunting, Arriette replied, "She could have at least smiled genuinely."

"Give her a break. She just faced a wanted criminal."

"Wanted criminal versus sarcastic receptionist. I wonder who'd win *that* fight," she said, struggling up another flight of stairs.

"Don't get yourself worked up."

"I could take her," she insisted.

"All I said was I *liked* her. Now you're waging war."

"She was even reading a trashy magazine," she said. "*I* read books and scrolls on ancient history."

Truth is, Arriette wasn't surprised. Often everlasts employed retainers in such menial jobs as a means to control them; put them in their place. They were much better suited as librarians, teachers and writers. Retainers were even restricted in what they were allowed to read because the everlasts wanted control over how much people knew of the old world. They rejected Earth's technology to allow faster transport and weaponry but accepted their architecture, plans for health care and quality schooling. All this meant that poor Melanie Starre would remain behind a desk, likely for the rest of her life, with nothing further to develop on Haeylo. Her services were required only for her memory capacity, not intellect.

"Straight faces and heads high," Tobias said, bringing Arriette back to her own challenges and pushing open the office door.

Charles Melovich was taller and slimmer than she imagined. His rough facial features and black hair made him quite intimidating. Though beneath the surface hid a mild personality who idolised his daughter.

His office stretched across the entire top floor with the exception of a stairwell leading to the roof. An oak table ran almost the full length of the wall for meetings and against the other stood four bookcases, filled with what was no doubt interesting historical information. Decorations were minimal but the walls had been painted cream and there were family pictures on his desk.

"Arriette Monroe. I've been looking forward to meeting you." He stood to greet them.

"Likewise." Arriette shoved her hands in the pockets of Tobias's jacket.

The refusal of a handshake didn't come as a surprise to him. They looked one another up and down, critically at first, then with pity. City folk were rude, she'd determined, and being stuck in an office all day sounded boring. As did the life of a filthy traveller, thought Charles. Having no purpose in life, wandering across the land, never settling. Of course, he didn't know Arriette at all.

"Where is my daughter?"

"Downstairs," she replied. "You've nothing to worry about. She's my friend."

"Then why not bring her to me?"

"Are you kidding?"

Charles folded his arms. "Let her go and I'll consider a lenient sentence."

"I'm not even under arrest," she said. "Your guards let me go. I promise Rihaana's perfectly safe. I'm here on her behalf."

"I sent two men to find you both; he promised me a settled debt and I've received neither."

"Kalvin Avery and Dean Constable," she guessed. "They're savages, but of course that's hardly news to you. Tried to bring me here against my will under *your* orders. Or was he supposed to *ask* for my help, not force it."

"I am many things, Miss Monroe. An animal is not one of them. Of course I requested your help. Kalvin said you were the best woman for the job and loved such challenges. In return for his journey I promised to settle some of his financial debts with other everlasts, particularly Falkon Lou. He owes a lot of money and Falkon, unlike I, is not the forgiving type."

"Unlucky for Kalvin, neither am I. Don't you get to know your minions before you send them out? Kalvin and I have history; he's a changed man and not for the better. Once he learned of Rihaana's whereabouts he turned on her when he couldn't have me. Planned to trade her for everlast immunity. He's a monster and don't get me started on Dean."

Charles frowned. "I know them well enough. However you handled them, Miss Monroe, you did a *wonderful* job, because Dean can't remember his own name he's so distressed and Kalvin could only ramble about how you'd stolen my daughter. At least I can call off their ridiculous marriage now Dean has no memory of our family."

"He can't remember because Arriette gave him a power-stripping potion. It's not permanent," said Tobias. "Kalvin never had Rihaana. We picked her up beforehand."

"I see. Well you owe me one retainer." Charles was used to being owed things. "How about you? You're supernatural. Want to take his place?"

Tobias merely snorted in response.

"Of course he doesn't. He's not a lunatic. We owe you nothing." Charles began to protest but Arriette continued to state her case. "Kalvin turned up at my doorstep with some pitiful story about my dying friend. He used deceit to pull me from my home and then brute force to bring me here. It's a miracle I'm alive after what I've been through. Tobias went to Mousique to find Rihaana before Kalvin did. Your men ruined *my* plans, not the other way around."

"Kalvin was under orders to find her on his travels," said Charles. "Why did you intervene?"

"I didn't trust him not to hurt her. She doesn't want this life. I merely tried to save her from a future of imprisonment and depression," said Arriette. "How was I to know you thought she'd been kidnapped? Blaming me won't solve your problem."

Charles didn't seem convinced. "Your vampyr attacked my men. Liaison with a demon is punishable by death," he said.

"If you're willing to get past a dreamer first," said Tobias, taking a single step forward.

Charles quickly learned his place.

"What isn't punishable by death these days? Dion's vegetarian; she'd never harm a human. Not intentionally. Besides, can you deem her evil having learned of *Kalvin's* behaviour?"

"I see you let her drink from you too," he said, pointing at the puncture marks on her neck.

Tobias's jacket had done little to hide her wounds.

"Actually that's a souvenir I picked up escaping your men."

Charles shook his head, genuinely confused by the accusation.

Debts owed in his favour were exciting and gave Charles a sense of power. Owing them boiled his blood. Should he fail to deal with Kalvin's behaviour he'd owe Arriette a pretty big one.

"I never ordered such brutality."

"They need to be punished whether you ordered it or not. Don't you have a telepath working for you to prove I'm telling the truth?"

"You'd be willing to have your mind read?" he asked in disbelief. Criminals were never this co-operative; perhaps he'd been wrong. "Are you sure you can risk such a test?"

"Believe me it's nothing new. I have a telepathic friend and he helps himself."

Arriette groaned as her spine creaked and began to burn.

Impatience. Anger. Worry. These were all emotions Arriette couldn't allow to rule her. Her powers were unstable, which Charles was about to find out if they didn't progress the negotiations.

"What *are* you?" Charles said, his eyes narrowing at her squirming.

"I'm tired," said Arriette, "and not just physically."

Charles massaged his temples, defeated by her reasoning. "I never demanded your kidnap. How can I punish someone who doesn't remember his name?"

"Your wiccan connection from the forest might be of some use at this time," Tobias said, taking hold of Arriette's hand and squeezing gently.

Arriette had been thrown a life raft and for a short while she was happy for him to do the talking.

Charles scratched his chin in thought. "I have no idea what you're talking about."

"Don't act oblivious. Kalvin told Arriette that her friend had been hexed. It wouldn't surprise me if you put a contract on her head to secure his loyalty."

"That's nonsense." Charles slammed his fist against his desk. "I know of the woman you speak of. She had us *all* baffled. I promise you no colleague of mine ordered such torture."

"So *help* her. I know someone who can make another potion for Dean. When he's back to his arrogant self, throw him behind bars and keep him there. Kalvin too," said Tobias. "You owe Arriette that much."

Charles threw his hands in the air and began to pace. "I *am* helping her! I'm paying for her care. Bringing you here was supposed to aid the investigation. Hers and another six cases, three of which have already expired. You must have heard by now about Pandora's box. It's re-emerged. Somebody or something is attacking my people, Miss Monroe. Kalvin said you were an avid reader of human biology and Earth. You're a rare breed. You could help us."

"She *can* help you," said Tobias, noticing Arriette wince in pain. "First we want assurance that Arriette's enemies will be imprisoned and that Rihaana is free to go."

"So you want the two guards behind bars. That I can do, but how can I trust you?"

"Your daughter can explain everything," said Tobias. "I can go to the lobby right now and—"

Charles clutched his pendant, sealed his eyes and muttered a couple of words in Haeyloian which neither Arriette nor Tobias could understand. Why wait for Tobias's petty human methods when he had everlast techniques of his own?

"Elitia et'ternan Rihaana."

The red jasper and citrine stones surrounding the eye of the pendant glowed, filling the room with a beam of wonderful white light. Arriette shielded her eyes. Tobias shuffled closer, unsure of how far they could trust Charles.

The air between them became distorted and Rihaana's figure materialised. She greeted Arriette with a weak smile.

"Hello Father," she said coldly.

"If you could summon her through magic then why send your men? You could have avoided so much pain," Arriette groaned. "Speaking of pain—"

"I can request her presence but I'm not always granted it."

Charles frowned at Arriette's outburst, but his face softened when he saw her strain in agony.

"Your father needs you to clear Arriette's name," Tobias said, "and fast. We're working against the clock here. Rihaana, this is *your* fight."

Rihaana's eyes widened. "These people saved my life. Arriette is just my neighbour, not my enemy. When her friends rescued me from Kalvin's custody, I asked for her help to convince you to let me marry Dean, but she hates him."

"Were you afraid of my men?" he asked.

Rihaana shrugged. "I guess I thought Tobias and Reiko were yours. I fought them at first, then the toothless guy knocked me out and when I woke, Arriette explained everything. Considering her recent experience, I deemed their actions necessary. No grudges held."

"So long as she didn't keep you in Mousique against your will I have no choice but to let her go," he said. "I still cannot allow you to marry Dean. He's going to be in prison for a long time."

"You sent him to find me," she argued. "Why him if you are so against our union?"

"Do you know any soldier more desperate to find you? From what your friends have told me he's a wicked man, undeserving of your love. I forbid it!" Charles turned to a suffering Arriette and offered his hand, ignoring his sniffling daughter. "When Rihaana went missing I put my heart and soul into locating her. Kalvin offered to help in exchange for money to pay off Falkon. I just wanted her home safe."

Rihaana stormed toward her father with tears streaming down her face. "You cannot force me to inherit a gift I don't want."

Arriette wanted to reach out and wrap her arms around Rihaana. Losing someone you love fills you with rage; nobody knew this better than Arriette. Kalvin had broken her heart and since then she too had been made supernatural against her wishes.

"You're right," he said, taking them all by surprise. "This is my fault. Perhaps I should have listened, Rihaana. We'll talk about this later. I can see poor Arriette is suffering. Are you ill?"

"She's fine, come on Arriette." Tobias led her to the stairwell.

"Wait, please. Just a moment. I may be able to help."

Charles embraced his daughter with the warmest hold. "I've missed you terribly, Rihaana, but there's plenty of time for a reunion. Right now your friend Susan is in the infirmary. What else did Kalvin tell you about her condition?"

Arriette leaned against the wall, taking deep breaths between every word. "I'm sorry Charles but having been bitten by a vampyr, my memory isn't clear." Arriette straightened her back and found this eased the pain. "I do know that Susan wanted to speak with me herself. Until now I didn't believe the story."

"I'm surprised you're alive after two bites."

Charles placed a hand on each of Rihaana's shoulders and kissed her on the forehead. He tugged her tatty clothes and suggested she find provisions for Arriette. When she returned with some clean clothing, Charles pointed at the city from his window.

"The infirmary is west of this building. About a mile away. How can I repay you?"

"We're looking for someone else, actually," said Tobias. "His name is Stefan Port. He joined to fight in your war, so we believe."

"If he's alive the lieutenant will still be training him. Rihaana, have someone take Arriette and her friends to the barracks and assist their search."

"But Father, Arriette has to find Susan. If she's ageing then surely—"

Charles interrupted. "Of course, then perhaps Arriette should go straight to the hospital. Please also feel welcome to take advantage of our hospitality. I'm sure you've all earned a good night's sleep and a decent meal. I'd escort you myself, however, everlasts of my class are banned from the public eye until our threat level decreases."

Arriette thanked Charles for his kindness. "You should take Pouki," she told Tobias. "He'll convince Stefan to come home. I've got to visit Susan and enquire about the wiccan who poisoned her. Charles needs my help with the other cases too. I'm here now, they may as well use me."

Charles placed a hand on Arriette's shoulder. "You should know Kalvin is back on the streets. I'll ask my guards to search for him; bring him in for questioning and punishment." He gestured for them to follow him to the stairwell. "Also keep in mind that I have guards on every corner. I hope there is little truth in our presumption about Pandora but recent events have so far proven me wrong. I'd estimate the box has been open a long time—our quality of life and our luck has been declining for decades."

"Oh I think some of us know more about that box than we're letting on," Arriette said.

Charles turned before opening the door to the stairwell for her. He pointed at a plaque on the wall at the far end of the room.

"See that?"

"It's beautiful," she replied.

"It holds the names of all the everlasts to forfeit their eternal life in the name of love. I admit I'm disappointed that Rihaana's name will soon be up there but it's because of you that she learned to fight for what she truly desires. Bravery and honesty are traits many humans lack these days. I hope you find your friend in time, Arriette."

Arriette gave Charles her brightest smile, swallowing hard against the pain in her back.

"Me too," she said.

Charles had always known Rihaana would never make it as an everlast but at least he'd tried to show her how important the gift was to Haeylo. Arriette could understand the impulse of a father to protect his only child. Those tiny chiselled letters reminded him that although being an everlast kept his city, people and his financial flow alive, nothing but the thought of having an eventual end to his journey could save his soul.

"My most sincere apologies again, Arriette," he said, shaking her hand. "We'll meet again I'm sure. Good luck, and Zinnyi be with you on your travels."

FOURTEEN

Arriette shielded her eyes from the gleaming midday sunlight as they left the lobby. Tobias had offered to carry her but she endeavoured to walk behind him, moving lazily between winding dirt roads until they found the residential area of sector four.

"Where *are* they?" asked Arriette, leaning against the back of somebody's house.

Tobias pointed to a small diner on the street corner. The top of Baby A's head was barely visible through one of the dusty windows. *The Rainbow Diner,* the sign said. Arriette cradled her stomach; the pain, now crippling, caused bile to rise and burn her throat.

"Nice of them to wait for us," Tobias said.

"I'm just glad they're out of the way."

Tobias pushed Arriette to the ground by her shoulders and they crouched behind a garden wall. Tobias crossed his fingers and hoped the owner would be out. He indicated Arriette ought to stay quiet, touching his finger to his lips and *oh* how Arriette longed to be that finger.

"What is it?" she whispered. "Is it Kalvin?"

Tobias nodded and reached for her hand. Arriette was busy calculating how fast she could get to the diner to warn her friends; whether the route she chose might avoid him.

A stern-faced waitress stood outside the diner with half a sandwich in her mouth. Clueless to their hiding place she set off across the road, crossing diagonally ahead of Kalvin and the guards in his company. Their weapons were drawn and aimed at him.

"Charles keeps his promises," Tobias whispered.

Arriette hadn't realised how nervous she was. Her limbs were shaking and her palms sweaty, forcing Tobias to let go of her hand.

"He's got a knife," he said.

"They haven't confiscated it?"

"Innocent until proven guilty," Tobias said, then shook his head in disgust.

Arriette couldn't keep still. Adrenaline pumped furiously through her veins, enough to race her heart and flush her face. She bit her lip, trying hard not to scream as the seething pain along her spine continued to increase.

"Can you get to the others?" she asked through gritted teeth.

"No way, it's too risky. Hey, are you all right? Oh, *not now*. Zìnnyi I beg you." Tobias pinned Arriette to the wall with his free hand and lit a fireball in the other. "Don't you dare. Not when we're so close to Susan. We may already be too late. Damn Baby A for giving you that gift. It's your wings, I know it."

"You need to get her, I can't do this alone."

Arriette's body began to crumple beneath her and Tobias gulped when the skin on her back began to peel away. Anxious the patrol could see them at any second, Tobias extinguished his weapon and pulled her to him.

"Get Baby A!"

"I can't," he said, covering her mouth. "He's almost gone, Arriette. You have to *wait*."

Arriette pulled away and staggered to her feet, stumbling as she dove into the street. Pedestrians scattered, as did the waitress and her few customers, and the guards' attention temporarily strayed from their prisoner to Arriette's odd behaviour.

"Stay away," she cried, holding out a hand. "Don't touch me. I don't want to hurt anyone."

Tobias tackled her to the road, straddling her stomach to pin her back flat against the cold cobbles. She squirmed and tried to throw him off, shrieking Baby A's name.

"You're going to get yourself killed," he said. "Your wings are materialising, Arriette, sit still for Heaven's sake."

Arriette battled free and crawled for the diner. Her only focus was to find Baby A and have her stop the angelic symptoms.

"Get up," Kalvin ordered.

He backed slowly away from the guards, blade drawn and waving frantically at them to leave him be. Tobias grabbed Arriette under the arms and whisked her off the floor. There was nothing he could do for her now. It was too late.

Kalvin put the blade of his knife against Tobias's neck and ordered the guards to leave the sector, threatening to kill any he saw. Tobias's eyes widened when they complied, leaving behind their weapons for his use.

"I said get up!"

Arriette spat at his feet and collapsed to her knees.

"I swear I'll kill him."

"Get up, Arriette," Tobias demanded. "You can do this."

The surrounding properties were quiet and dull in comparison to the everlast buildings in the square. All except the diner were inactive or forgotten bar the odd thatched home; some of their windows boarded, the walls crumbling.

Perhaps for the safety of the everlasts, few people walked the streets.

Kalvin released Tobias and grabbed Arriette by the throat; she could no longer control her temper or her actions, fading in and out of consciousness and taking only random segments of their conversation in. Then a sudden weight on her back knocked them both off balance as she attempted to writhe her body loose with her last drops of energy.

Baby A and the others emerged from the diner and ran to Tobias.

"You won't kill her," said Baby A, kneeling beside him.

"You're still in love with her."

Kalvin laughed and squeezed his fingers harder. "Look at her. She's a disgrace."

"That's not true," she said. "She's not a criminal you can beat to death, Kalvin. It's Arriette. Let her go. *Please.*"

Kalvin thrust the blade against Arriette's throat, drawing blood. "Susan will die because of you. Why couldn't you comply like a normal human?"

"You want her back; that's why you're going to so much trouble."

"Not even in her dreams."

Tobias grinned. "You're going to wish you never said that."

Arriette's wings flung out at full power. Her stamina increased and her pupils widened. She thrashed and snatched Kalvin by his collar, launching them both into the cool Haeyloian air. He dangled in her arms like a rag doll. She could have crushed him. She *wanted* to crush him. Such thoughts only spurred her flight on and she whisked them higher and higher until her friends were mere specks of dust.

"You'll be surprised what your friends will do for you if they believe you've got potential."

Arriette dangled Kalvin upside down by his ankles and shook him. When she caught sight of the blade between his fingers she panicked and fumbled to manoeuvre her grip.

Arriette took what she thought would be her final breath as the blade plunged through her flesh. They plummeted at a ferocious speed as the road closed to greet them.

"Arriette, can you hear me? It's Baby A." The snapping of fingers awoke her. "She's awake!"

Arriette's feet were inches from the pavement, held by Baby A's fingers which desperately clutched her shoulders to keep her upright. Blood poured from the wound; Casper's gentle hands held rags to it and his snowy beard was stained with crimson.

Baby A lowered Arriette to the ground and sat her against the diner's door, using her own wings as a barrier to hold back nosey passers-by.

"Don't move, Arriette," said Casper. "Somebody help us!"

She couldn't have moved even if she wanted to. There were concerned faces staring down; too many pairs of hands on her body.

Someone called for a doctor but unconsciousness claimed her before she'd matched the familiar voice to a friendly face.

And the wound bled on.

FIFTEEN

Arriette opened her eyes to a bunch of beautiful peach flowers on her bedside table, a familiar aching across her chest and Baby A's watery ocean eyes staring at her. The sweet scent of her gift filled the room, mixed with medicine and strong disinfectant.

"You saved my life," she groaned.

Baby A smiled. "Now we're even."

Arriette fumbled with her bed sheets and leaned forward. "I need to get up."

"Take it easy. You're not going anywhere."

Concerned, the nurse from the desk outside Arriette's room hurried in. "Oh it's far too early to be gallivanting off, but you'll make a full recovery."

Baby A expressed her appreciation with a kind nod of the head. Arriette forced a smile.

"Where are the others?"

"They went to find Stefan. They've been at your bedside for days, Arriette. Reiko couldn't put that off much longer but there's no news yet."

"I promised I'd help. Is Casper with them?"

"Actually he's with Charles. He's been asking every day about your care and even covered the bill. He said he owed you; we didn't ask questions."

"You shouldn't have let him do that," said Arriette. "I can't accept his charity."

"He's just pleased you're safe and recovering. That's not

charity, it's friendship."

Arriette rubbed her aching head. "Did you find Susan then? She must be in this hospital. Let me up, I need to talk to her."

"Don't be ridiculous. You've been severely wounded."

"Is Kalvin in prison?"

"We don't have to talk about this now," she said.

A brisk knock at the door interrupted their conversation. A young woman stood tall in a neat black robe tied with a gold belt. She wore black pumps and her dark hair was poker straight. Her curious brown eyes met Arriette's.

"Arriette Monroe? My name is Scarlett Evermay. May I come in?" Baby A motioned for her to enter. "This is for you," she said, handing Arriette a crumpled sheet of parchment. "It's from Susan."

Arriette's eyes lit up. "Is she sleeping? How's she doing?"

Scarlett and Baby A gave each other a solemn look.

"She's at peace now," said Scarlett.

She *couldn't* be dead! She had time left to spare, surely?

Arriette whirled back the covers and made haste for the door. She'd been bed-bound for seventy-two hours and her body was still too weak to carry her weight. She collapsed in a heap with her arms outstretched for the door handle. Scarlett scooped her up and together she and Baby A carried Arriette back to bed. She sobbed furiously against Baby A's shoulder.

"We were so close. Where's Kalvin? Does he know?"

Baby lowered her head. "I'm sorry Arriette but he didn't make it."

"Did *I* kill him? Oh, this can't be happening. I'm a murderer."

She still had so much to say to both of them.

"Susan passed away yesterday morning and Kalvin was pronounced dead at the scene," Scarlett said.

Arriette blew her nose. "You can bring them back?"

"*Them?*" asked Baby A. "Kalvin got what he deserved."

Arriette ignored her and turned to Scarlett. "Can you?"

"I cannot resurrect the dead although I wish I could. Many

of my friends have perished and I miss them all very much. Unfortunately, though, I'm just a retainer."

"Then can I see her?"

Scarlett nodded. "I've arranged for her funeral to take place later this week. If you're well enough I might be able to convince your doctor to discharge you. Given the circumstances, I can't see why he'd refuse. You have angelic blood according to your notes. You're making excellent progress."

Arriette fumbled with the parchment. "I don't think I can read this."

"Susan and I were friends," Scarlett said. "I promised that if anything should happen to her I'd find you and give you that."

She ran her fingers over the curled handwriting on the folded cream parchment, hurt at the thought of Susan laid helplessly in the bed awaiting her arrival.

"Retainers here diagnosed a hex which caused her to age. Did you know that?" Scarlett asked. Arriette nodded. "She died peacefully. Find comfort in that. Susan spoke of you often. She missed you."

"Do *you* know who put the hex on her?" Arriette asked.

"I am yet to find out, though she is not the first to suffer a strange illness here."

There was nothing Scarlett could do now; her attention was better placed elsewhere.

Helping Arriette, hopefully.

Reiko and Tobias rushed through the door, hurrying Pouki along.

"Slow down! My legs aren't as long as yours." When he noticed the tears in Arriette's eyes he picked up the pace and hopped onto the bed. "Oh Arriette, don't cry."

"I'm fine Pouki. Don't worry about me. Did you have any success with Stefan?"

"He's alive but wants to train for the war. There's no talking him out of it."

"So he left all on his own after all?"

"Seems that way," said Tobias.

"We should be thankful he's happy and well," said Baby A.

"The barracks were pretty cool," said Tobias. "Everyone wore matching uniforms and carried huge swords; hundreds of beds all perfectly in line and whenever an everlast entered and yelled orders they marched around like puppets. I managed to scrounge you this," he said, handing her a brand new bow. "Never been used. Got you some arrows too. I'd make a good General, don't you think Arriette?"

"You'll never grow up." Arriette laughed. "Thanks for the gift. You'll have to train me to use it though."

He reached into the palm of her hand and took the parchment. "What's this?"

"Scarlett gave it to me. It belonged to Susan."

"I heard the news and I'm so sorry, Arriette."

Casper and Dion came through the door as Tobias reached over to hug Arriette. Dion shot across the room and dived over Pouki to reach her, pushing Tobias out of the way.

"Dion it's the middle of the day, how—"

"This hospital's windows 'ave a UV filter," she said. "Wanted to see ya."

Casper cast his eye around the room. "Oh, my! Scarlett Evermay, I didn't expect to see *you* here." He kissed Scarlett's hand lightly. "Still alive and causing havoc?"

"*Always*. I was a friend of Susan's."

"I see," he grinned. "Well, I've missed you."

"So you know one another?" asked Arriette.

Scarlett smiled. "We have a history."

"You shouldn't worry about that now. You gave us such a fright, Arriette," Pouki said.

"We thought you were dead," said Baby A.

"Looks like you've made another friend," said Reiko, flicking through Arriette's medical notes. "Charles is paying for your hospital bill, right? Must be growing money; he's covered the cost of Susan's funeral too."

"Now she's dead we'll never know who hexed her," said

Tobias.

Scarlett's brow crinkled in deep thought. "There are very few wiccans who live close to the city. Tracking her down would be reasonably easy, if indeed it was wiccan magic."

"Charles thinks perhaps another everlast was involved," Casper told Scarlett. "He's going to investigate the chain of events leading up to and including her hospitalisation and have his men interrogate the last people to speak to her, including you. He's also sending out the new resistance recruits in search of Pandora's box. Good luck to him."

"Anything to help find her killer," said Scarlett. "I have nothing to hide, but I can't imagine they'll have much luck in finding that box. Arriette, you and I need to talk."

"What matters most right now is Arriette's recovery," said Baby A, patting her gently on the shoulder. "Susan and Pandora can wait."

Arriette referred Tobias to the document he held between his fingers. "She might tell us who killed her."

Silently he unfolded the paper along the creases and his eyes followed every line.

"Go ahead, read it aloud."

Tobias coughed to clear his throat then shushed the group. "It's from a book," he explained. "Copied in her own handwriting. A book by Harriet Foley."

"I know of the author," Scarlett said. "Susan was quite insistent that reached you safely. What does it say?"

"In the year 2140AD, President Andrew Kaines announced to his fellow Americans that the world was in great danger. After centuries of pollution and ignorance to their planet, mankind began the destruction of their own species. In panic, communities all over the world formed an alliance to beg God for mercy. Earth was dying."

Casper closed his eyes and listened to Tobias's words carefully.

"When Zinnyi took pity on them he assigned those most trusted a very special gift, instructing them to use their abilities to save the human race. They called themselves the Recruit. Whilst the majority did exactly this, one chose to use their power for personal gain, enforcing evil and greed throughout mankind. Angered, Zïnnyi struck her down, stripping her of all power and banishing her to eternal suffering. Soon others followed and together they began to tarnish the prosperous planet Haeylo."

A mild chatter filled the room. Everyone was so excited to learn more about the planet that they hadn't realised what the textbook was actually telling them.

"There's more. Shall I read it?"

"Allow me," said Casper, taking the parchment from Tobias. "The remaining Recruit powers began to plot their battle against evil, using Zïnnyi's gifts to protect the miracle of the new world and the human existence for eternity."

Susan's book described what Arriette had feared all along. Casper held her hand knowingly but said nothing to the others. He could barely meet her gaze.

"Arriette, does this passage mean anything to you?" asked Scarlett.

"Maybe, but I can't act upon it alone."

"What, did ya think ya could get rid of us that easy?" Dion winked.

"I think Susan is trying to tell me something important."

"That you're the one Casper's been searching for?" asked Tobias, brushing back her matted hair.

"Ya sure ya wanna do this, Arriette? Ya can turn back any time now. The quest is over. Don't ya want ya old life back?" asked Dion.

"This *is* my life now," she said. "Besides, you guys need me."

"We should find the wiccan who hexed Susan first," said Reiko. "We could learn so much about dark magic."

Tobias flipped the document to the other side and tapped Arriette on the arm. "There's another note on here; a line from a poem:

'To see a world in a grain of sand.'
Does that mean anything to you, Arriette?" he asked.

"It's William Blake." She smiled wholeheartedly. "One of my favourites."

"It's also part of an old Recruit ritual," said Casper. "I swore my oath to my followers using it. Arriette, you remember the story of Andrew Kaines? He swore his oath the same way."

"Sounds to me like she expected *you* to be swearing an oath, Arriette," said Pouki.

Casper smiled broadly when Tobias read the final sentence.

"Eleven gifts to protect the miracle of the new world, and that miracle, Arriette, is you."

SIXTEEN

2140AD
The Creation of Haeylo: Part One

Mr Jim Robin, the thirty-nine-year-old assistant of the U.S. President Andrew Kaines, shook his boss fiercely by the shoulders and hauled him out of bed.

Breathless, he said, "Our prayers, Mr President, they've been answered."

Andrew sat up and rubbed his weary eyes.

The room was dark but he could just see the silhouette of Jim's wide shoulders and the glimmer of piercing sapphire eyes glaring into him.

He yawned and threw back the covers.

"I have an alarm clock, Jim."

"I'm doing as you asked last night, Mr President. After the vote, you said—"

"I've slept since then," he grumbled.

Andrew's wife, Christine slid into her slippers and wrapped a light pink nightgown around her bare shoulders. She shooed Jim to the door, brushing back her curled brown locks and shaking her head.

"We really ought to lock this door, Andy. You're President now, it's not civilized to have random workers—"

"Ma'am, pardon me but President Kaines requested he be notified at the first sign of a response," Jim said. "The staff are outside with your children already."

Jim dodged beneath Christine's arm and scurried back to

Andrew's bedside.

"The children are out of bed?" asked Christine.

"Yes, Ma'am."

Andrew dove to the window and flung the curtains open, revealing a gathering of his employees who had congregated around the grounds of the White House.

Sunlight drenched the bedroom. Christine shielded her eyes from the glare and hissed at Jim to leave them to dress.

"Yes, Ma'am. Mr President, should I wait to escort you to the chopper?"

Andy's hands began to shake.

"It's really happening. I can't believe she was right, Christine. She was right. This is amazing."

"Then I'm sorry I doubted you," she replied.

Jim opened the window and grabbed Andy's hand. The tremors were replaced by the congratulatory shake of his colleague's sweaty gesture.

"Listen to them. They're so excited. Are you coming, Mr President?"

"Yes, yes, of course!"

Christine embraced her husband. "I truly believed you and that girl from the election were having an affair. Claiming such an identity seemed, well, utterly ludicrous!"

"I can't blame you," Andrew said, then kissed her lightly on the cheek. "Still, I did it, Christine. I signed the contract like she predicted and He responded."

"We should be careful. We can't be sure this is real, you know? It might be a prank or that girl's idea of revenge on me, I —"

"Nonsense," he said, dismissing Christine's fear. "Come on, we should see for ourselves."

Andrew rushed down the hall, leaving Christine alone to dress in silence.

Outside the White House, the gathering grew by the minute. Andrew couldn't order them back to work, not at such an exciting time and not when he'd been President for less than twenty-four hours.

Some were pointing to the sky and cursing in disbelief as a luscious, amber vortex formed a perfect ring before the morning sun. It flickered red, spinning faster than the spectators' eyes could register and appeared to be expanding, like the opening of a tunnel.

Andrew saw every detail; each unique shade, flash and flame, moulding a future he'd been working toward since running for President, seven long years ago.

Christine and their twin children, eight-year-olds Mya and Eme, joined Andrew in the assemblage.

Mya clung to his left leg, Eme to his right; their bodies buried in the material of his suit and their strawberry blonde hair fluttered in the breeze.

"We have to see this," Christine said, joining her family on the lawn. "Your father says our tickets are guaranteed, so be brave."

Reluctant and terrified to agree with her wishes the children edged from their father and held hands in the congregation. Their faces illuminated as fireworks reflected in their innocent tears.

Andrew dropped to his knees.

"It's time for me to go but I'll see you again soon."

Andrew kissed his children goodbye and released their hands.

SEVENTEEN

9280AD – 12 weeks after the fall...

Breakfast was served at eight but Arriette meandered into the kitchen at ten, landing her in Ma's firing line. With a pounding head and doughy heart, Arriette couldn't care about her mother's likely reaction; she was in no mood.

Casper, dressed in his usual plain robe and flimsy sandals, had saved Arriette some pieces of crispy bacon, a mountain of scrambled eggs and a pot of hot coffee in preparation for the day ahead. She appreciated the sentiment from her trusted mentor but couldn't bear to eat with Ma's judgemental eyes watching her every move, no matter how ferociously her stomach growled.

She tucked a loose strand of matted brunette hair behind her ear, then cradled her cup.

"Good morning," said Casper, nodding his head.

She hushed him. "Not so loud."

"Oh, are we fragile?" he chuckled. "Pain is your friend, Miss Monroe, you should know from your training."

"It can be yours too old man. Sense the tone."

She didn't remember much of the night before.

The homecoming party thrown by her overwhelmed mother consisted of a few glasses of wine, embarrassing dancing, another glass of wine or two, stumbles, dizzy spells and well, Arriette's head became cloudy after that.

"Are you well enough to, you know?" he said, jerking his head in Ma's direction.

Not now, not ever.

Arriette cringed and added a teaspoon of sugar to her black coffee, then shook her head.

Casper glanced between the two of them, anxious and waiting to hear Arriette's speech as to why she'd been missing for the past few months. His gaze lingered on Ma a few seconds longer; strangely, he felt a parental connection with her, perhaps as they were both now caring for Arriette in a similar way.

Today Arriette planned to tell her mother everything.

The group travelled to Drakonta and arrived the night before but having been on the road for days, Arriette couldn't face more tears. She and Tobias practised delivering the news though; she'd begin by telling Ma she'd had a wonderful eye-opening, unplanned adventure but along the way, her biology was modified. Then she'd lie and say it was her decision to study magic, not Casper's, and explain the benefits of having new abilities.

Convincing lies were a part of her training.

She'd leave out the vampyrs, side-step the discovered tapestries, avoid Susan's fate and ignore Kalvin's murder.

Completely.

Arriette's face lost all colour at the memory.

"Don't you dare throw up on my table," said Ma, handing her an empty bowl.

"Easy on the sympathy," said Arriette. She shoved Ma's hand away. "I'll be fine, I just need fresh air. Casper, perhaps you'd like to explain to my mother where we've been for the past twelve weeks whilst I dress?" Arriette muffled her voice, "and perhaps I'll fall unconscious for a little bit."

Casper scowled and threw up both hands.

"No, Ma would rather hear it from her daughter."

Arriette's eyes narrowed and she shuffled, preparing to be chased around the kitchen with her mother's rolling pin.

"So how's life in Drakonta?"

Casper smirked at the sudden change of subject and Arriette shook her fist at him.

"The same as always," she replied.

Ma stuck her hands in a bucket of water and began to clear her friends' dirty breakfast plates.

"You're on vacation?"

Arriette glowered and grunted her reply between open mouthfuls of bacon. Cursing was forbidden in her mother's home so disapproving glances replaced the words she had eagerly armed her tongue with.

She looked forward to seeing Ma and hadn't sat still long enough to soak in her surroundings since meeting Casper. Drakonta's history had always fascinated her, so before leaving, Arriette was going to explore.

Retainers and humans populated the two hundred acres. Like any village on Haeylo they were plagued by myth and legend. Retainers imprinted such stories to pass through each generation and in this case it was a haunting by the spirit of an enraged dragon slayer. Some villagers believed their homes were built on his burial ground; that the dragon guarded jewels stolen from the palace of a powerful queen, half everlast-half sorceress.

Ma continued to potter, not so surprisingly giving Arriette the semi-silent treatment but the clattering of cutlery brought her back to reality. If she lived through Ma's scolding, Arriette planned to take Tobias up the mountain on a romantic hike.

First, she'd have to be brave.

These days Arriette hated being brave.

"I'm just going to say it." Arriette took a deep breath. "Casper gave me gifts I can use to—"

"Yes I know about the gifts," she said, her back to the table. "Casper told me last night. You were otherwise engaged at the time, dear."

Arriette shook her head in disbelief.

"I thought—"

"Did you think he wouldn't? I *am* your mother." Ma cleaned her rolling pin on her pinafore and slammed it on the table. "I may be old but I have my own power."

"To inflict what, disapproving frowns?"

"Fear," said Casper, "of being beaten to death by her rolling pin. We thought we'd bet on how many times you'd change the subject and I won."

"I'm not speaking to you, Casper." Arriette turned her attention to her food. "Ma, I just thought you'd be worried."

"Nothing ever happens around here," she muttered, "frankly it's given me something to think about. I've cleaned your old room and fitted fresh sheets for your stay and I've been talking with that girl. The blonde. She's got wings. Did you know?"

Arriette swallowed hard. "I had no idea."

Casper could only shrug when Arriette mouthed 'you're dead' across the table, sliding a finger across her throat.

She stood and rolled up her sleeves to dry the dishes.

"So you're not mad?"

"Concerned," Ma said.

"You didn't have to clean my room. I've booked into the Watch Tower Inn with my friends."

"I predicted last night would end in, well, this," she said, tutting. "You'll stay here where I can keep my eye on you."

Arriette grumbled. "This being my presence in general, or were you gesturing at my morning hairstyle?"

What more could Arriette do to evade her mother's nagging? She didn't want to impose either. Her baggage was much heavier than it had once been.

Besides training gear and the new clothes Charles bought for her, now she carried the burden of being a supe; supernatural responsibilities, aches, pains and the looming knowledge of her being the next best thing to happen to Haeylo, if Casper wasn't full of horse manure.

If she could have dumped that baggage back in the city, she would have.

"What exactly do you do for a living?" Ma asked Casper, folding her arms.

"He's a manager," Arriette lied.

"That sounds boring and lonely."

"Ma! Oh, Casper, I'm so sorry—"

"Oh, no offence taken," Casper said. "My colleagues are all supernatural. The day is never dull."

Arriette grumbled. "You make it sound easy."

Ma's stern face melted. "I suppose managing others is rather difficult. I can barely manage my own daughter. Arriette's been alone for too long. I'm glad she's found loyal friends. You employed her?" Before Casper replied she said, "It's about time she got a decent hands-on job."

"I can hear you," said Arriette, hands on her hips.

"You could say she works for me but you know as well as I that she'll do as she pleases and nothing more. Still, she is family now."

Now Ma knew, Arriette took the opportune moment to break the news about her favourite almost-son-in-law. Though not on purpose, Arriette had killed her ex-boyfriend and nothing could erase that disturbing memory.

Sharing it caused her great pain; how could she inflict such nuisance information on her elderly mother too?

Arriette couldn't shake the pleasure she got from knowing Kalvin wasn't around anymore but Ma wouldn't see the benefits.

As well as his death, Arriette had to tell Ma she'd be selling the cottage. Tobias and Reiko had offered to build her a cabin if Arriette trained to dream like a born supe.

Pleased as she may have been to be wanted, Arriette would miss Rosewood Cottage and Mousique's peaceful harvest season. Most of her furniture would travel with her, but what remained could either be sold or passed to her mother.

"Casper tells me he owns land in Manaia Forest that has a beautiful view of the river," said Ma.

"Yes, we swam there one night. I was considering relocating. Casper's friends are going to build me a cabin. I have some wooden furn—"

"I presume you're referring to the two men I met earlier? Tobias and oh what's his name? The big bald one with the crooked teeth?"

"Reiko," Arriette corrected, disheartened. "His name is Reiko. He's a hunter and a brilliant chef and he doesn't have any teeth. At least not front ones." She cringed. "So as I was saying—"

"It's an appealing offer."

She rolled her eyes. "Ma, don't read between the lines. They only want what's best for me."

"Are you sure?"

Arriette bit her lip.

She'd imagined them together since the day she laid eyes on Tobias's muscles. They were becoming more than friends.

She pictured his ruffled mousy hair, strong arms and runic tattoos. The last she remembered of the party was dancing with him and laughing *a lot*.

"Arriette's a good girl," Casper interrupted. "I assure you there is nothing to worry about. Tobias and Reiko have asked nothing but friendship of Arriette. In fact, they're going to help with your gardening."

"Ma, despite the welcome we actually came to give you some bad news so you might want to sit."

Ma poured a second cup of coffee and gestured for Arriette to begin.

"My legs work well enough."

Arriette hesitated, unnerved by Ma's straight face.

"Uhm, all right, the thing is—"

Arriette's heart pounded. Her sweaty palms were advising she abort the mission and run.

Magical gifts Ma could accept but what if only in theory? She didn't need to see her child sprout feathers but if Arriette didn't start breathing again soon, she might not have a choice.

She stood and paced, studying her feet which would soon be hidden under leather boots; Baby A's idea of a confidence boost but she'd never been able to walk in anything other than pumps.

Everything about Arriette's appearance announced her inexperience, right down to her underwear.

Casper cleared his throat. "What Arriette is trying to say is

—"

"Kalvin died," she said.

Quick and painless, thought Arriette, until Ma's eyes widened and the colour drained from her face.

Arriette thought she was going to faint.

"How did he die?"

"I, uhm, I killed him."

"Oh my, is there any wine left?" Ma asked.

"Don't be so overdramatic, Arriette. Kalvin's death was accidental," Casper corrected. "Your daughter was mistaken for a criminal and Kalvin tried to harm her. In self-defence Arriette accidentally killed Kalvin. Believe me, my first impressions of that man were not pleasant."

"Arriette, how could you? I suppose you zapped him with your laser vision or turned him into a toad," she lectured, pinching her nose to relieve the pressure.

And there it is, thought Arriette.

"I'm sure with a little practice I could have!"

Retaliation wasn't going to solve anything. Arriette straightened her back.

"He hurt me. I've been in the hospital."

Casper frowned. "Arriette, now is not the time."

She threw a bread roll across the table at him.

"I think you've said enough."

Casper ran his fingers across his lips as if to zip them and gestured at her mother. She was a big girl and could deal with her own troubles.

When he folded his arms Arriette offered a rude finger gesture and scowled.

"Heaven knows I've taken all I can of this nonsense. Kalvin lost his life because he tried to take mine. I'm pleased he's gone. Rather him than me."

Ma slumped in her seat and set her hands on the kitchen table, defeated.

"Are you finished?"

Not even close.

Casper sighed. "Excuse us, Mrs Monroe."

He took Arriette by the hand and dragged her into the living room, then gripped her chin, forcing her khaki eyes to meet his blue.

"Now you listen to me. You owe your mother an apology. We expected her to react this way and prepared suitable responses."

Arriette snagged her face back. Ma was never going to understand.

"I thought Tobias had you recite a speech?"

"Oh that was pointless from the start, Casper. She's my mother. She's supposed to be forgiving. Three months ago I was laid out on your sofa struggling for my life. After all that I'm still the same person, aren't I? These gifts can change the world, Casper. You said so yourself. Why can't she just be pleased for me?"

"You're not even pleased for yourself. Look, I'm sure she'll be thrilled when she's had time to think things through. Time to grieve."

Arriette's spine ached terribly and her head pounded. She didn't have enough room left in her heart for guilt.

"Agree to disagree. I think you can count that an apology."

Casper adjusted his robes and smoothed his long grey beard, then rolled his eyes when he realised Arriette wasn't going to move.

"I'm going," Arriette said, finally deflating.

"I think I'll wait here. Give you some space."

Arriette stole a glance at her mother's living room before venturing back to the kitchen. She'd cleaned the huge window, dusted the small table they'd carved together from an old venom tree and shaken the sofa cushions.

Ma took care to perfect every detail and Arriette had thrown it in her face.

After verbally scolding herself she strode through the door, ready to offer a weak apology for her outburst.

"Maybe I shouldn't have yelled—"

The air from her lungs was stolen.

Arriette grabbed the rolling pin and held it at arm's length.

There was a dagger to Ma's throat.

The creature she faced had seized Ma by the neck and she coughed and struggled to breathe. Tears streamed down her cheeks and her hands were shaking.

The attacker was cloaked in soot-coloured robes but his long slimy nose and piercing green eyes were dominant in the darkness. His face was scale-covered but because of the thick grey hair on his chin, Arriette thought he looked like some kind of mutant sewer rat. He was thin and shrivelled; the stench of his breath utterly vile, rousing the settled alcohol in her stomach.

Arriette cried out Casper's name but seeing the second opponent the creature dragged Ma backwards and pressed the dagger to her skin.

"Casper, *do something!*"

He raised his hands in the air. "Mightie proniba!"

Ma's thatched roof collapsed in on the four of them, creating a dust cloud in the centre of the kitchen. Arriette saw the opportunity to get closer and in doing so noticed his wispy white hair sprouting around a bald centre. His breathing was laboured and his heart rate was much quicker than any human.

Wherever this beast has been living it was dark, damp and dejected.

Arriette fought for breath until Casper wrapped his arm around her waist and hauled her away.

"What *is* that thing?"

"An orc," said Casper. He covered his nose with the sleeve of his robe. "Must be the servant of a more determined demon. Thirteen on the HPS so he's not as dangerous as he thinks."

"I hardly think the Haeyloian Power Scale matters right now if he's in control. Oh, and what was that supposed to achieve?" she asked, pointing at the mess in the kitchen.

"I'm a little rusty, Arriette," said Casper. "At least now we have a safety barrier."

The orc's dagger skimmed through the air, catching Arriette's eyelid and slicing her forehead. She screeched and threw back her head in time to avoid a worse fate, then fell to her knees with her palm covering the injured eye.

She slapped Casper's legs. "You were saying?"

"Arriette Monroe," it growled.

"What do you want?"

She squinted through the blood.

Arriette could make out his figure by the window. The orc shattered it with his elbow and ordered Ma to climb.

"I want you," it replied.

Arriette flicked vigorously through what she remembered of her demonic research. An orc's biology matched that of a human, almost, so it would be like hunting an animal with soft flesh and a fragile skeleton. They were the only species of demon capable of surviving sunlight.

If she could aim the rolling pin at the ideal angle, she could knock the orc unconscious. But with one eye blinded her judgement would be poor.

"What do you want with me?"

Casper pulled Arriette back. "We can't stay here."

"I won't leave Ma."

"And I won't leave you," said Casper. "So what do you propose we do? Let him think he's in control." Casper pointed at the door. "Arriette, we're not alone. Tobias and Reiko will have heard the window smash."

The orc followed Ma through the window. She screamed and Arriette lunged with one eye covered through the debris. She clambered outside to see Ma's neighbour howling at two shadows moving past her garden gate.

But where were her friends?

Arriette realised she had no chance of closing the gap so stopped in the centre of the road and outstretched both palms. She flexed her fingers and imagined the two of them being carried toward her, picturing a thick rope.

She wove the length in her mind and cast it out.

Arriette tugged her elbows in tight to her waist and opened her good eye to judge the distance, then pulled the rope as it materialised.

The creature wrestled her power.

When he was close enough, Casper kicked a mound of dirt in his face and aided Ma to a stance. She limped to the gate and collapsed against a fence while the orc writhed on the road, dazzled.

"Get up!" Arriette demanded.

The orc began to crawl in the opposite direction. Out went Arriette's arms again, this time lifting him inches above the ground and holding him still. But the weight of his body on her mind worsened Arriette's headache and after only a minute or two she had to drop him, making sure it hurt like hell.

The Dagaz breakthrough rune on Arriette's skin burned brighter than ever. Her fingers itched to scratch at it.

"I didn't realise telekinesis was so tiring," she said to Casper, hunching over to catch her breath. "Am I still supposed to feel the singe from this tattoo?"

Casper nodded. "You always will. Dagaz is a dreamer's rune, Arriette. The wings of a butterfly are the most painful to carry. You're a reader, you may wish to brush up on your insect symbolism." He winked.

Arriette kicked the orc in the chest. He spat out a thick ash-coloured liquid.

"That's for waking my rune, assho—"

"Arriette, they're here," Ma gasped.

They were joined by three of their friends. Arriette's brown-haired and hazel-eyed crush Tobias Shallow dominated her line of sight. He wore brown cargo pants beneath a khaki tank top which highlighted every muscle. Beside him, the group's time-travelling angel, a thin blonde woman wearing a cream dress and sandals, frowned with concern. Her name was Baby A. She and a strapping bald-headed human named Reiko Port, dressed in similar attire to Tobias, rushed to Ma's side.

Arriette couldn't let the orc go yet. If she did, in twelve hours

Drakonta would be swarming with his friends.

Thinking clearer, Arriette yelled at each neighbour to go inside and lock their doors. She had to ask some of them twice.

Orcs weren't afraid of the light and would gladly raid their homes given an opportunity, taking slaves back with them.

"Where have you been?" she asked Tobias. "I thought you were gardening?"

Tobias wiped his muddy hands on his shirt.

"The travelling tradesman came by. We got distracted. I think Pouki's checking his bags in at the Watch Tower too. Are you hurt?"

He examined her eye and mopped at the blood lightly with his top.

"You'll live," he said. "Might need stitches."

Arriette said, "See to Ma first."

Reiko crouched beside the orc and examined him.

"I've never seen one this close before. You got a name, pal?"

Tobias reached for his hunting knife. When the creature caught sight of the shimmering blade he tried to scramble away.

"Coyote," it mumbled. "Name Coyote."

Tobias gave Arriette a firm pat on the back for controlling her gift so well. She stumbled toward her mother, drowsy from the use of telekinesis.

On the outside she was battered and exhausted but on the inside, Arriette's ego gleamed.

"How is she?"

"*She* is your mother," Ma interrupted.

"Thanks to me you're still my mother, not a demonic dessert."

"She twisted her ankle," said Baby A. "What did it say its name was?"

"Coyote," said Arriette.

"It's not a name at all," said Casper. "It was an animal. The word in Haeyloian means 'trickster' but coyotes are extinct now."

"Coincidence? I think not," Arriette said.

"He's hurt," Reiko said, "so won't be escaping."

Arriette grinned. "You all know I'm good at dropping people. We should still tie him up."

Tobias unfastened his belt and handed it over.

Arriette was saddened to think the first time he'd unbuttoned his trousers in her presence was in the middle of a busy Drakontan street.

Reiko wrapped it around Coyote's hands and tied him to the fence a few meters away.

Tobias fumbled with his pants to secure them.

"She looks pale," said Baby A. "Maybe we ought to get her to the infirmary?"

"To think I only came to sightsee and say hello." Arriette sighed. "Wherever I go I seem to drag trouble behind me. How did this creature even find us?"

Arriette put her hands on her hips and squinted against the morning sun.

"It's unusually hot out here. How is he alive?"

"Maybe we can thank the box for the weather. Ask Pouki about the orc when he gets here," Baby A said, tapping her head.

Arriette looked forward to seeing their telepathic colleague again. When beside Casper, the two were almost identical in all but their height; Pouki stood only a few feet from the ground.

He'd stayed a while in the city during Arriette's hospitalisation then returned home to his cabin. Shortly after, the vampyr hunters from his building returned and told Pouki all about their training for the upcoming war on evil. There was a lot of truth behind the Pandora's box theory, apparently.

"Pouki can't tell me why I'm such a danger magnet. Still, he'll have plenty of gossip. I'm surprised my mother hasn't disowned me, especially after Coyote's act."

"You're more like her than you think," said Tobias. "She's strong-willed and powerful too in her own way."

"You weren't there for the Kalvin conversation."

"Kalvin deserved his fate," said Baby A.

Of course he did. Her happy memories of Kalvin Avery had been tainted and no longer resonated as valuable to Arriette. If like a retainer she could wipe him from her thoughts forever, she'd jump at the chance.

Casper disagreed. "Nobody deserves to die. We're not at a loss because he did but I'll bet Susan loved him."

"Susan doesn't have an opinion anymore."

"Which was nobody's fault," Tobias interjected.

"Which is your opinion," said Arriette. "I'm sorry, I'm just tired and angry that whilst I have the cause of Sue's death to track down and Pandora's box to research, now I have this fool to deal with."

"Perhaps they're linked?" suggested Reiko. "Susan's death and the orc's attack?"

"Let's find out shall we?"

Tobias cracked his knuckles. He swung his fist and punched Coyote, catching him between the eyes.

The orc's nose cracked and seeped a fluid which Casper later explained was demonic blood; a midnight blue tar. It smelled of sour milk and sewage water.

Tobias tugged back his hood revealing pointed ears and hideous sharp teeth. Arriette gagged and turned away.

"What do you know about a woman called Susan Petter?" he asked.

"None," it mumbled.

This time the blow to his face came from Arriette's heel, swung at the gritty sound of the orc's lie. She regretted the blow at once and hopped away, cursing under her breath.

"Vampyr," it cried. "Vampyr, no?"

"You're a liar," said Tobias.

Scarlett Evermay, Susan's retainer friend from the city, had escorted Arriette to Susan's funeral so how could she be a vampyr? They all witnessed her go to ground.

"I hope you're not lying to me, trickster. Get him inside, I'm going to lie down."

"What, now?" asked Tobias.

Arriette narrowed her eyes and winced. "If I don't lie down I'll fall down."

As she made her way to the bedroom to rest her aching head, Arriette cursed her poor luck.

"And so it begins, again," she said.

EIGHTEEN

Arriette dragged Coyote behind her using Tobias's belt and threw the orc gracelessly on a wooden chair. In the bedroom, she'd laid back to relax and realised just an hour later there was no way she'd be able to sleep after their morning fiasco.

Her muscles throbbed to the beat of her pounding heart; each pulse disabling her will-power to continue this escapade. She was sure the harrowing migraine forming behind her eyes would grip her powers, entwine and unleash them on her depleted body like ravaged dogs.

Perhaps she hadn't thought this through.

"What are you thinking?" asked Tobias.

She was thinking that kidnapping an orc would be difficult to explain if they ran into its master. Spirit demons were near impossible to kill and those holding a physical form often had sharp ivory horns, extended fangs and arched claws.

Arriette imagined such creatures as animated suits of armour. If she sourced decent weaponry the gang would be able to battle a scale eight in spite of her personal doubts, but no matter how far down the food chain this orc was, evil watched evil's back regardless of their personal disputes.

Arriette kicked the base of the chair and the orc flinched. She threw Tobias a bundle of her mother's washing line.

"Something doesn't smell right and it sure isn't my mother's cooking. He needs interrogating."

"His master's probably got others out searching for him,"

Tobias said, winding the line around the orc's waist. "Shouldn't we be concerned?"

"I'm more worried we'll attract an everlast," said Casper. "They like to be in charge and will take Coyote into custody if they find us."

"Better make it quick then," said Arriette. "Still, I don't see any everlasts around here, *do you*?"

As orcs were terrified of vampyr venom, Baby A suggested they wait for Dion to arrive.

Rather like a snake bite to a human, Vamp venom to an orc would be paralysing and after several hours of torture, deadly.

Dion was vegetarian but whilst being the most intimidating of their little group, she also liked to laugh at other peoples' expense.

When the orc was successfully restrained, Arriette asked Reiko and Tobias to give her a hand in the kitchen. She couldn't ignore the mess and Coyote wasn't going anywhere soon. Ma was independent but in her old age needed more frequent help with housework.

"Are you *sure* you're up for this?" Reiko asked.

Arriette had not long since been out of the infirmary following her fight with Kalvin in Haeylo's city. The bruises were still tender but for snot-nosed retainers, the doctors there did well to patch her up so quickly.

Also, Kalvin got what he deserved and that settled much of Arriette's emotional pain.

"I'm fine, I'm just tired. It'll pass. Can we fix the damage?"

"You know, when girls say they're fine, they're not fine," said Tobias, folding his arms. "You should take something for the pain. Reiko, can you fix her some tea?"

"There's no time for tea," Reiko said. "You'll be fine, right Arriette?"

Arriette raised the eyebrow of her good eye, pleased the other was already healing from Baby A's blessed angelic blood.

"Do I have a choice?"

She would've quite enjoyed a cup of tea but let the moment

pass.

"Sure you do," he grinned, then clambered over the debris to assess the damage.

"We'll have to patch the ceiling first, I'd say," said Tobias. "Casper's stronger than he looks, even though he's out of practice."

"The walls are filthy too," she added.

"Grab that cloth, Arriette and start cleaning. In the meantime, Reiko and I will do our best to make this place weather-proof."

Not without making a fuss she wouldn't.

Arriette loved her mother but she'd never allow her to live this down. The longer Arriette stuck around to help fix the problem the more she'd have to listen to how she'd almost gotten her mother murdered.

Almost.

"How long is this going to take?"

"We don't have tools or the money," Reiko said.

"And one of us should watch the orc," Tobias asked, then slapped his friend's arm and laughed. "Not it!"

Reiko grumbled. "Damn you, Shallow!"

Frustrated by his eagerness to turn their latest nightmare into a joke, Arriette said, "You can't just forfeit orc duty. We should all take a shift. So back to Ma, we're looking at a few days tops?"

The less squabbling the better, she thought.

Tobias nodded and climbed up on a dusty chair to inspect the damage.

"I'd say so. What's your plan then?"

"Isn't one orc pretty much like the rest?" Arriette asked. "Can't we interrogate him and then dump him somewhere?"

"That's not very Recruity of you, Arry," said Tobias. "Are you suggesting we let him go?"

"Recruity isn't a word and it's Arriette," she said, hating that nickname more than her new inheritance.

"But it's cute," Reiko joked.

Arriette narrowed her eyes. "I'm not going for cute. Besides, Susan used to call me Arry."

"Sorry," said Tobias, lowering his head. "I didn't—"

Arriette sighed and wiped the sweat from her forehead with the back of her hand.

"Forget it. I can't stay here, so let's crack on."

Reiko frowned. "But Drakonta is lovely this time of year."

"You don't know what she's like."

Reiko frowned. "Who?"

"My mother!"

"She's not the most agreeable creature, I'll admit," Tobias interjected, "but we can't leave yet. There's too much to learn from Coyote. Don't you want to know why he came after you?"

Arriette kicked her way through the debris.

"I already do. Same reason everyone wants to kill me recently." She groaned. "If we're not using magic to fix this mess one of us will have to go for supplies." She stole a glance at Reiko and smiled. "Not it!"

"That's getting old real fast."

"And with what money?" Tobias continued. "We can't afford these renovations. If Ma has the money then—"

"I can't," said Arriette, throwing her arms in the air. "She didn't ask for this."

"Neither did we."

"I know, I know," she sighed, allowing the hunter to wrap an arm around her waist. "We'll have to figure something else out. She hates me enough already."

"Ma doesn't hate you," said Reiko as he sifted through a mound of shattered cups and bowls. "There's one way to find the money. You and Tobias are both active dreamers so why not combine your gifts and create it."

Tobias's face lit up with delight.

"How about it, Arriette? An ideal opportunity for practice."

"That's not moral," she said and pulled away from him. "Sorry, I mean it's not Recruity. How could I live with myself having forged cash? If Dean found out he'd throw us in prison."

"Don't worry about him, Arriette. Charles promised he'd rot in that dingy cell forever," said Tobias.

Arriette bit her fingernails.

"I'd get it wrong; I can't control my gifts. I have a headache that won't help my concentration and I'm exhausted!"

"We have nowhere else to be right now," Reiko said.

"How about hunting down Susan's killer?"

Tobias shrugged. "Susan's dead; she's not going anywhere. We're not going to be any closer to the killer in the next hour. Be reasonable."

"Why can't I dream the roof back the way it was?"

"You're a young dreamer and I'm a bit out of practice. Building a roof takes deep concentration, capability and control."

"Everything I don't have." She groaned.

"Two dreamers working together will get this job done in no time. Then Ma can make her own mind up as to the restorations. Besides, I don't see any everlasts around here, do you?" He winked.

"I should know this stuff," she huffed. "Personal gain is common sense."

"Then sit still long enough for us to teach you."

She punched Tobias gently in the arm.

"Later. Right now I should get started interrogating that orc. It's not fair to leave this for Dion. Hey Reiko, can you make a start here?"

Reiko agreed to begin Operation Clean Up.

Tobias and Arriette made haste for the living room. The sooner they finished one job, the sooner they could begin the other.

Coyote spat at her feet the moment their eyes met.

"We need to talk," said Arriette, shaking the saliva off her foot.

She sat opposite him, resting her arms on the back of her own wooden chair and glared at his stern expression.

"Your first punishment is to clean my shoe."

"You will kill me?" he asked, his head cocked to the side.

After a short pause, Arriette replied, "No."

"I am hostage? Untie me. We friends."

Behind him Tobias was shaking his head. She wasn't going to untie the demon now, was she?

"I don't trust you," she said, kicking off her shoes. "Or your filthy habits."

"If no kill, must let go."

"Where's the logic in that?" asked Tobias. "He'll return with hundreds of his kind and wipe Drakonta off the face of Haeylo."

"In orc culture such actions are punishable by death. His master will kill him for failing whatever task he was given," said Casper. "Better to live as a free demonic traitor than die a worthless slave."

"I have enough blood on my hands, Coyote," Arriette said.

Tobias stood with his chest to Arriette's back and scowled at the orc, daring him to try the escape he'd so obviously been considering.

"She also staked a vampyr," he added. "We don't want to add to the body count."

Coyote didn't flinch but Arriette did.

Why did the reference to Kalvin's death still tug her conscience?

"My death on hands."

"Coyote, I'm not going to kill you," she said.

Coyote's eyes pressed into Arriette's mind and followed her gaze. Unease and pressure overwhelmed her. Knowing the intimidating contact was only a test to learn her weaknesses, she tried not to blink.

"Why did you take my mother?"

"My prize."

"Me or my mother?"

"You. Take leader's hand."

Arriette threw up in her mouth a little bit.

"I presume you mean marriage, but why?"

"Complete process."

Well he wasn't afraid to talk. If his master knew he'd explained 'the process', which would no doubt be to conquer Haeylo because evil plots were all the same, then Coyote would be executed.

What did he have to lose? His master would kill him anyway, failure or not.

"You're not my type," she said.

"Marriage for life eternal."

"Says who?" asked Tobias.

"Says legend," Casper interrupted. "I read it in Haeylo's library many, many years ago, except it said this applies to all demons, not just orcs. It has, of course, never been proven."

"Likely a myth if you ask me," Tobias grumbled. "The notion of marriage to gain eternal life is ridiculous, especially when you look like this guy. Who's going to marry that?"

"Obviously he didn't do his homework as your mother isn't one of us. His language skills are poor for an orc, which is unusual," Casper finished.

Tobias laughed. "He's delusional!"

"I'm a limited edition then," Arriette said, dabbing at her weeping eye with the palm of her hand. "A faulty one. He's got a good aim though, I'll give him that."

"You're Coyote's chance at freedom."

Casper rubbed his eyes, exhausted with the whole ordeal.

"This 'process' he speaks of, however, is news to me. He must have taken Ma to provoke you. Have you chase him into the woods and then attack when you're alone and vulnerable."

Arriette leaned forward and grabbed the orc's robes. Their faces, now inches apart, were both solemn and twisted with pain.

"What process does your master need me for?"

"Be mortal," said Coyote.

"I don't like the sound of this. You're his daytime messenger." Casper groaned. "Now I understand. You're going to marry Arriette because he can't, am I close?"

"I beg your pardon?" Arriette's eyes widened. "So you're not even marrying me because you want to, it's for somebody else? *Now* I feel loved!"

"Control of Underworld." Coyote struggled against his restraints. "Be mortal!"

At least he's honest, thought Casper, even if he didn't make much sense.

Unlike vampyrs, orcs weren't allergic to the sunlight and so spiritual demons and other creatures used them as their slaves and messengers. If Coyote's master couldn't marry Arriette to gain eternal life, this foul little beast could do so for him.

"Let me get this straight," said Tobias. "Your master sent you to marry Arriette to make you human? You'd be stepping down a scale, not up."

"Wants death," Coyote groaned.

I would be more than happy to assist, Arriette thought. This whole situation made her nervous.

The fewer orcs who knew of their whereabouts and procedures the better, but the more they knew about demons the easier eliminating them would be.

"If he wants to die I can fix that without vows and bells," said Tobias. "We'll make you a deal in exchange for the whole story. We release you on Haeylo's surface rather than in your boss's territory. Save your life. Forgive this little escapade."

Coyote fell silent, contemplating the benefits.

"Do take your time. You die, I sleep better at night. There really is no rush."

Casper tapped Arriette gently on the shoulder and she leaned back, willing to accept his input.

"Pouki may be able to help, Arriette. I believe an orc mind is one of the few demonic signals he is able to read. He could pull more information mentally than we can via verbal conversation."

"Oh, *you're in for it now,*" Arriette told Coyote.

"I know you," it said, taking her by surprise. "I, I *know* you. Memory—"

"Lots of people know me," she defended, taken aback by his

sudden ability to construct a sentence. "I'm not pleased, but it's true."

Arriette tightened the rope around his hands.

Demons didn't feel pain like humans. They were merciless and cruel and whilst they understood emotion they were all incapable of guilt, sorrow or mercy.

For that, she secured the restraints until his wrists bled.

"Why should I believe *any* of this?"

"You shouldn't," said Pouki.

He dropped his luggage at the door and straightened his robes.

"He's lying."

NINETEEN

Pouki Hallidae, although talented after years of reading minds, was limited in skill when it came to most demonic species. However, Arriette was overjoyed to learn he had few problems with orcs.

"Right on time as usual," said Casper.

Pouki rolled up the sleeves of his robe, ran a curious hand through his snowy beard, then grabbed Coyote by a stray tangle of hair and yanked back his head. The bones in the orc's neck cracked and Arriette's stomach tightened.

"Do I need to introduce myself?"

"Telepath," said the orc, sniffing him like prey.

Pouki shook his head. "Pathetic creatures, aren't they? Well, he's not who he thinks he is. That much I can confirm."

"So he's not lying, he's brainwashed?" asked Arriette, hoping, despite his behaviour, that they wouldn't have to kill him.

Pouki circled, examining his clothing, skin and his thoughts.

"There's a block on his memories. Orcs aren't usually so careful. There's something strange about Coyote; I can't quite put my finger on it."

"Work on it," said Arriette. "I'll ask him some questions; see if we can free his mind with prompts. Will that work?"

"I should think so," he replied.

Arriette scratched her chin. "Alright, here goes." She cleared her throat. "Why does your master want to be mortal?"

Pouki lifted a finger to indicate he'd found an answer.

"Heaven is his destination. Coyote's master needs to be human before the creator can judge his soul," said Pouki, picking the information freely from the orc's mind. "He wants mortality to conquer the sunlight and to mend his ways."

Coyote stared straight ahead in concentration.

"Nothing out of the ordinary for an evil mind. They're always trying to conquer something. In this case it's the daylight."

"You don't believe he wants to change?"

"Do *you*?" When she didn't reply, Pouki continued. "I believe Arriette has another question."

Arriette threw him a look of disapproval; he was only supposed to read the orc's mind.

"Where did you come from?" she asked.

"East of here by High Man's Tree. There's a tight opening in the rocks. First you'll see a bridge crossing the river. Then you'll hit the tree line. Demonic territory lies beneath it," said Pouki.

"How long did it take you to reach us?

"He was injured before you dropped him so I can't be sure. Time is distorted in this orc's memory, it's very odd."

Pouki's grin widened. Was he enjoying putting his weird talent to use? Arriette hadn't caused the orc's limp so after a wild guess she presumed his master inflicted the injury. Was he opening his mind to avoid being returned there?

Pouki's face creased with concern.

"Sunlight burns," Coyote said.

"You're not allergic to sunlight," Tobias argued.

Arriette jumped, barely noticing he'd left the room during their interrogation to make her a cup of tea. She cradled it between her palms, closing her eyes for a moment to appreciate the lemon scent.

"He's lived underground most of his life," Casper explained. "He burns easier than we do."

"How old is he, Pouki?" asked Baby A.

Frankly, Arriette didn't care but any information was better than being blind.

"Twenty years."

Only twenty years old?

Arriette had many years on this creature and was in far better shape. Some supernatural creatures lived for thousands of years. Baby A told her angelic blood would heal wounds quicker and age skin slower. The years would pile on but the wrinkles wouldn't.

Pouki didn't seem too happy with his feed from Coyote's brain. He leaned closer and placed a gentle hand on his shoulder. Touch amplified his reading of thoughts and emotions but still his brow creased.

"Could you find your way back to the opening?" Arriette asked.

Pouki clenched his shoulder and the orc startled. The telepath was brawnier than he appeared.

"The activity in his head seems almost human, Arriette. I can't understand. If it weren't for the way he looks I'd have read the mind from a distance as semi-supernatural."

"Not fully?" Arriette asked.

"Human but gifted, a little like yours. Born supes read differently."

Casper reminded Pouki he'd had little experience in reading the minds of demons and so a misinterpretation of brain activity wasn't surprising.

Although Pouki was relieved to find out he wasn't going crazy, Casper's face still held doubt about the true identity of their companion.

"Coyote, can you lead us to that opening?"

"If he can't, I can," said Pouki. "His memories are interesting but there's a haze like a passing storm. It's almost as if—"

"Do I need to beat it from him?" Tobias asked.

Arriette shoved him hard and shook her head.

"No, it can't be."

"Pouki, what is it?" Baby A prompted.

"As if he's been hexed," said Pouki. "An insane thought given Susan's death but an orc having memory loss is unlikely."

"So this isn't a coincidence? It's all interlinked?" asked Tobias. *"Oh for the love of—"*

Arriette considered showing some leniency; good will. Coyote didn't look like he weighed much and as her powers were growing stronger, so was her confidence. In a fight she'd certainly have the upper hand.

"Let him go."

"What? He could be lying!"

"I'd know," Pouki said. "Tobias, I've got this. If he considers escaping I'll hear him."

Perhaps Coyote set out to find Arriette because he thought she'd help him escape the pressures of a demonic lifestyle.

Maybe somebody intercepted him and wiped his memory, preventing whatever message he carried from reaching her.

No matter the reason, Arriette couldn't cage him like an animal, not if he was suffering as Susan had.

Pouki said his brain activity passed as semi-supernatural. What if beneath the smelly outer shell was a frightened man clawing his way out?

"When Dion wakes at sunset she can guard him," said Arriette. "He tried to kidnap and assault my mother and came at us with a knife. He's not going anywhere alone. Besides, he hasn't told us anything useful about Susan. I sympathise with the hex but until we learn more about Susan's circumstances, I can't trust him."

"Vampyr!" Coyote insisted.

Pouki sighed. "He believes it."

"I know, and I'm starting to but I can't take this right now."

Arriette left the room and headed to the kitchen where Reiko was scrubbing furiously on his hands and knees. She dumped her cup in the wash bucket and surveyed the damage.

Tobias followed close behind. He gave her a tight hug.

"Don't worry about Susan now. Pouki's going to see if he can get anything else from Coyote's head. You still up for dreaming? If we're going to do this you need to stand fairly close."

Arriette stifled a grin and hugged him harder.

"I think I can do that."

"You need to imagine this in context. Perhaps think of the money as rain."

They joined hands, left to left and right to right. She closed her eyes, blocking out the surrounding filth and tried to imagine they were alone. Concentration was easier having drowned her other senses and the pain in her head was dissipating.

"Let's fill the kitchen sink. That shouldn't take too much imagination. You've got to really want it, Arriette."

"Believe me, there's nothing I want more than to get out of here."

Eventually, Arriette strained out the sweet sound of his guiding masculine voice and replaced it with the chink of overflowing coins in the kitchen's stone sink.

Arriette opened her eyes and studied Tobias's calm face. How could she focus on money when all she wanted to do was kiss him?

No matter how hard she imagined the event, dreamers had nothing of an influence when it came to other people's emotions.

Arriette ignored her impulses and the tingle in her palms. When she did, from her right she heard a faint noise.

Had Reiko dropped something?

No, it was getting louder and more frequent like the jangling of keys.

Arriette briefly checked her clothing to be sure she wasn't naked again and then wrapped her arms around Tobias's neck, jumping with delight when she saw what they'd accomplished.

"We did it!"

Ma shuffled through the kitchen door snuggled in her gown and slippers. She gasped at the sight of the full sink and steadied herself.

"What's going on in here?"

"Don't get too excited, Mrs Monroe," said Tobias.

She gasped. "Did you do this?"

Tobias held up his palms and backed away.

"This was your daughter's doing. She'll get in a lot of trouble if the authorities find out, though. Can you keep this a secret?"

"I don't know what to say." Ma wiped her eyes. "I've kept many a secret in my time, Tobias, but this is beyond belief."

"Just promise us you'll use it to fix the roof."

"Yes of course." She turned to thank her daughter. "Oh, Arriette, I guess those gifts of yours aren't so bad after all."

TWENTY

2140AD
The Creation of Haeylo: Part Two

The helicopter engine fired up at ten o'clock and Andrew climbed in without hesitation. If he didn't witness this from the air—be a major part of history—he'd regret it for the rest of his pathetic human life. This was his responsibility, so he buckled in and pulled a chunky grey headset over his ears then gave his pilot a confident thumbs up.

As the vortex accelerated, Andrew's stomach churned and his entire body trembled.

This is it, he thought, there's no turning back now. He glanced out the window at his two children who waved frantically and Andrew waved back, excited to discover the new world; a world he'd guaranteed them.

Christine knelt beside Eme and Mya and stroked their hair; her mouth pressed to a thin line and her brow lowered when Andrew's gaze drifted from her encouraging smile to the journey ahead.

"Are you hungry?" Christine asked the children. From her handbag, she pulled two apples and handed them to her daughters. The girls were eager to fill their stomachs. "We're skipping breakfast today so make sure you eat the whole apple."

Eme and Mya bit down hard.

Down Christine's cheek escaped a single tear when her husband turned his back to their family, just in time to miss his children sink into an endless sleep.

They dropped their apple cores by Christine's feet. She wiped her eyes and held them tight, then she too turned her back to a life that could have been, and retreated back to the house.

TWENTY—ONE

Arriette gathered her belongings and stuffed them grumpily into Baby A's bag, thinking about the journey ahead.

She'd packed essential items for their trip; warm clothing, shoes, a comb and her canteen.

The climate was usually a consistent sauna in summer and thick with snow in winter. Arriette had been told to prepare for the very worst, especially since there was talk of Pandora's box being found, and the lines between seasons were fading.

Casper said the box caused natural disasters on Earth. An ice age, volcanic eruptions and severe storms. Considering what else Pandora's box caused, Arriette changed her clothes, strategically manoeuvring each garment over her ribs which still ached a little from her fall.

Susan's letter had been folded up with her clothes for safe-keeping during their walk to Mousique.

It took all of Arriette's strength not to re-read it.

"Ready to go?" asked Baby A, standing at the bedroom door.

Arriette pushed the bag out of sight.

"Almost."

Baby A checked under the bed for any forgotten items and gave her a nod of approval. Then she grabbed her own bag from the bathroom.

"Is there any chance I can slip away undetected?"

The angel beamed at her. "Negative."

Arriette followed Baby A as far as the kitchen. To avoid debris spreading to the living area, Tobias had closed the door and laid Ma's old curtains over the furniture.

After using her dreaming to ensure Ma could repair the roof, Arriette felt less guilty about leaving the house in such a mess.

She found Reiko and Tobias in the living room with Coyote still strapped to his chair. Arriette frowned and untied him, dragging him along behind her by Tobias's belt.

"You're going to lead me to your friends," she said.

A narrow path ran the length of the house but due to Ma's deteriorating physical health it had overgrown and been uneven for twelve months. Arriette forced her body through the shrubbery and lunged out the other side to catch her breath.

Tobias threw the orc out after her.

"I walk," said Coyote.

"I wonder how well you *fly*," said Tobias.

Arriette had already suggested Ma use the remaining cash to pay a gardener. Of course, she was too proud to admit she couldn't manage to weed on her own.

"If I use that money for anything else it will be to get that new tarmac," said Ma. "Arriette, *you'll* know all about it. People used it to lay roads and pavements on the old world. The everlasts have it."

"Why don't we, then?" asked Reiko.

"Everlasts control our technological and architectural evolution," Arriette said. "I read it in a book. We have retainers to remember that stuff, but everlasts are scared if we follow suit we'll kill Haeylo too."

"Who will?" he asked.

Arriette sighed. "Humans."

"Well *I* don't remember seeing any of this fancy tarmac," said Reiko. "Unless it's been introduced in the past few weeks."

"You can still put in a good word with your everlast friend," Ma said. "Right?"

Arriette had to pull the plug on the conversation before Ma got any other ideas.

She and Charles weren't friends, merely allies. Favours cost in the city and Arriette couldn't afford any repayments.

"I see no reason why not. Rihaana owes you," said Tobias.

He flinched when Arriette tried to crack him across the back of his head. What did he have to agree to that for?

"There's a lottery running this year," Casper said. "Jackpot is five thousand and would pay for the entire street's tarmac." He caught Arriette's eye and winked. "Tickets are cheap. The travelling tradesman is due to arrive back in Drakonta later this week. What do you think, Arriette?"

"A great idea," she smiled. "Will the traveller bring news of the winner?"

"I'll have to ask him," said Ma.

Reiko smiled. "You can pay him with your delicious home-baked cookies, Ma."

"We should get going," said Baby A. "Before he starts drooling."

Ma hugged each of Arriette's friends, leaving her daughter for last. Their embrace was awkward and forced but Arriette knew, having taken on a new role with the Recruit, that she may not see her mother again for a long time.

She had to make the best of their time together no matter how crazy they drove one another.

"You've all been a blessing," she told them. "Zinnyi has an amazing route planned for you, Arriette Monroe. I truly believe you'll do wondrous things. You should begin by keeping in touch more."

Startled by Ma's unexpected moment of weakness, Arriette gave her a kiss on the cheek and inhaled her mother's perfume. She smelled of lilies and rose petals. A scent she remembered from her childhood.

"Take care of her for me, handsome."

Ma grabbed Tobias by the collar and kissed him firmly on the cheek.

Blushing, he grabbed his gear and picked up the pace, wiping her lipstick away with the back of his hand.

Arriette rolled her eyes and stifled a laugh, vowing to interrogate her mother should they survive their journey on the topic of her father's history. She needed to figure out his involvement in those tapestries and, more importantly, how he'd really died.

Right now, though, she just didn't have it in her.

"If you don't make a move with that one, I will," Ma whispered.

Arriette flushed. "*Goodbye*, Ma."

Ma wished them well and sent them on their journey with plenty of supplies, travelling east.

If they could pick up the pace, their red-haired vampyr friend Dion could meet them at High Man's Point after sunset; a steep hill with an old oak tree for travellers to rest under. Research into the many landmarks of Haeylo had always interested Arriette. Harriet Foley, her best-loved author, believed High Man's Tree to be of great symbolic significance to Haeylo's history.

In her book, The Tree of Life, she said the leaves of the tree could heal the sick. Arriette planned to pluck one and examine it further but wasn't sure she believed it. Present since the beginning of time, it stood proudly with a view of several miles in any direction. Arriette thought it had more character and personality than most human beings.

Midday brought with it an incredible heat, torturing the orc as he strode lazily behind Arriette.

Coyote didn't look forward to meeting Dion. He'd considered trying to escape but his injury and the intense sunlight would hinder his journey.

"He's struggling," said Pouki. "Emotionally and physically. Heat tires him."

"What else have you discovered?" asked Arriette, taking a swig of water from her canteen.

Pouki glanced back at the demon, concerned.

"Not much. I see flashes of a child. Perhaps his daughter. Obviously whatever their connection, Coyote is oblivious to it.

She looks human though."

"We'll break for the night at High Man's Point. We should rest before we let Coyote take us further. Dion's going to bring the cart so we'll create a canopy with the materials we have and keep him cool."

"Perhaps you should be practising your magic," said Casper, "and not worrying about the demon."

"Arriette, I'm picking up on your doubt," said Pouki. He held up his hands quickly. "I'm not snooping. You're feeling very—"

She threw her hands in the air and stormed ahead.

"*Violated?*"

"I was going to say worried." He sighed, "I'm sorry. Control your aura, Arriette. Being a telepath isn't about taking memories and thoughts but receiving them. If you're so intent on something you give off a scent. I'm merely acting upon it."

"Well don't."

Arriette bound her hands into fists and growled.

"I know why you're intruding on my privacy," she said, tapping her head. "You think I'm going to screw up. It's my first real assignment; finding this opening and dealing with the orc."

"I'd say after the few months we've had that you're likely on your fifth assignment, so I'm not doubting your capability."

"You must understand," said Casper. "Pouki is only trying to help you. He doesn't read our minds intentionally. Not all the time."

"We agreed you wouldn't unless I allowed it," she said. "I need to be free to think in peace. Oh, and I'm not worried. I'm researching; trying to remember what my books said. No more unauthorised telepathy. I feel you in my skull. I don't need you giving me a headache."

"We had better get a move on," said Casper, checking his compass. "We don't want to miss Dion."

On arrival at High Man's Point Arriette took off her shoes and poured some cool water over her blisters. Using the back of her hand, she wiped the sweat away. The hill was much steeper than she'd pictured it.

Dion's fiery head was visible at the peak and she ran to greet Arriette with a hug.

"How was Drakonta?"

"We'll talk about that later. We have bigger problems right now," she said, gesturing at their guest.

Dion's eyes flickered a violent blood-red to match the colourful twirls of her hair. It stood on end like a panic-stricken feline.

"Tell me what happened," she hissed.

Tobias kicked Coyote to his knees. They glared at one another for a short while.

"This is Coyote," Tobias said. "Tried to kidnap Arriette's mother. Failed, miserably."

"A messenger?" she asked, creeping nearer and examining every inch of him. "He smells *different*."

Reiko interrupted. "Pouki said his mind reads like a semi-supe."

"Shifter?" asked Dion, turning to Casper.

"Pouki doesn't think he's demonic," Reiko said. "What are your thoughts?"

Inhaling his scent seemed to throw her, so she ran her fingers down his skin, examined his clothing and his mannerisms.

She hauled him up.

"Looks authentic," she said. "What does he want?"

"Mortality according to his thoughts. Didn't say much so Pouki plucked what he could throughout the questioning."

Tobias scratched his head.

"Casper, you have friends in high places, right?"

Arriette didn't like the urgency in Tobias's question but curious, allowed him to continue.

"Say he was brainwashed or hexed or whatever you want to call this. How are we going to reverse it? We can't let him go in his current state. That opening will be swarming with orcs now. I'm thinking you take us to the Recruit and we, well, hand him over."

"Can she be crowned before we take him there?" Pouki

asked. "The timing may not be great, but what other option do we have?"

Arriette felt sick to her stomach. *Crowned?* They were obviously talking about her; blatantly ignoring her presence and discussing matters involving her future as they had many times before.

But would being crowned, whatever the procedure involved, reduce the long list of creatures who'd want her dead?

Evil had a habit of trying to claim her. Roberta and Angelo. Dean and Kalvin. Could the Recruit offer her protection from them, or at least additional support?

"Casper, you never mentioned a throne."

"I presumed Pouki had explained all this."

Casper frowned at the telepath and lowered his body to the ground using High Man's Tree for support.

Pouki cringed and cleared his throat. "I would have covered the topic whilst discussing her father but we were rudely interrupted by Rihaana's outburst."

"Susan's parchment told you most of what you need to know," said Casper, "but in order to serve Zïnnyi as I have, there is a ceremony. It's by no means a throne, Arriette, merely a position. It allows you to take over."

"It makes you their official leader," said Pouki. "See, I was supposed to explain to you all about Pandora's box. The history, theories and mythology. If we weren't interrupted we wouldn't be having this conversation."

"Well we are," Arriette said. "I already know a little about Pandora; you think the box was found and used. Second-hand information is useless though."

Arriette picked a few stray pieces of grass and watched them float to the ground.

"If you want my opinion, we're wasting our time with this orc. If he's not going to tell us anything about Susan what's the point in holding him? Crowning me won't increase our chances of survival or camouflage us against incoming threats."

"What are you saying, Arriette?" Tobias interjected. "We

can't kill him. We need him for information."

"Look at him, Tobias. He's a clean slate. He knows nothing; whoever did this practically deleted everything he is. We should just let him go. At least then we can get down to what's really important and that's everything you should have told me about Pandora. I know he's been hexed like Susan but if he can't tell us what happened, why keep him in tow?"

Coyote was getting restless, huffing at every opportune moment. Arriette sympathised. Nobody could think clearly in such high temperatures.

Reiko shook his head and began to load their luggage onto the back of Dion's cart.

"I'll play no part in it," he said. "We're the good guys. We shouldn't be murdering innocent creatures. For all we know he was a friend of Susan's and this whole orc disguise was forced upon him by that wiccan. I won't have his blood on my hands."

She grabbed Tobias's penknife and gripped Coyote by the throat. The group watched in silence as she pressed the blade against his skin and closed her eyes.

Would all this go away if I slit his throat?

"It won't ease your pain," Pouki said, gesturing for Arriette to hand him the blade. "You're not a killer. Whoever Coyote is we can help him and in doing so help ourselves."

"If I can't kill him at least let me throw him back in the hole he crawled from," she pleaded. "One or the other."

"Give Pouki the knife," said Baby A. "He's our only lead to finding out what happened to Susan."

"And what of your friends in high places?" she asked Casper. "What of my crown?"

"I'll explain all that, I promise. For now, let's forget about it."

Casper threw Pouki a stern look.

Arriette pushed the orc to his knees and threw the penknife with such force it stuck in the ground. Their only lead was a brainwashed demon with nothing to offer them. He'd use up their supplies, slow them down and constantly remind Arriette of the trouble she'd caused.

More than anything, she just wanted to be rid.

"I'll take no part in his care then," she said. "You think he can lead us to Susan's killer, then be my guest."

After everyone else had fallen asleep beneath the stars, Arriette sat with her back against the tree, staring at the orc in disgust.

Dion returned from her successful hunt and asked for Arriette's help in the skinning and draining of the two rabbits she'd caught, purely to distract her.

"So why'd ya do it?" she asked.

Arriette flinched. "Do what?"

"Ya almost killed ya only lead. Coyote can take ya to Susan's killer."

Arriette sighed and ran a hand through her hair.

"Ugh, you won't understand."

"*Try me.*"

"All right," said Arriette, putting down her half skinned rabbit. "He serves as a constant reminder of my failure. Whenever I look at him I see my mother's terrified face. I see Kalvin's pleading eyes. I think back to how suited I was with life before Coyote turned up just when I was beginning to love our little vacation, just like Kalvin did in Mousique before the harvest."

Dion frowned. "Ya didn't think things would stay like that foreva, did ya?"

"Actually I did. Of course, I wouldn't have had Pouki explained this crown to me."

"Don't blame him," she said. "He tried his best."

She sank her fangs deep into the corpse of the animal and began her breakfast. Arriette tried not to stare at the process she had yet to learn more about.

"If he says he's gonna explain, he will."

"How can I trust somebody who keeps secrets from me?"

Dion shrugged. "We all got secrets, Arriette."

"I feel cheated. I should know all this. I knew Casper had other friends but he never said they were of great influence. It's like my entire life is on display; I'm just his puppet."

"Nah. Ya just easily influenced. Changes with time. Especially when ya meet these 'friends in high places'. The puppet becomes the puppet masta."

Dion threw the remaining meat onto a slab above the campfire so Arriette could have some.

"Casper promised he'd tell ya everythin'. Trust in Zïnnyi; after all it's ya God ya servin', not ya mentor."

"If he's my mentor he's taking his time teaching me," Arriette said. "Thanks anyway, though. It's nice to talk and be listened to rather than lectured to. I didn't even want to be the next leader. Casper wouldn't let me leave having given me these powers; his excuse was that I'd become his responsibility."

"If ya save a life, ya gotta be the one to take it."

"What do you mean? Like, Casper can kill me if he doesn't think I'm doing a good job?"

After a short, uncomfortable pause, Dion grinned and pointed to the sleeping hunters.

"Tobias tells me ya movin' in with 'em?"

Arriette tried not to read too much into Dion's slipped tongue, but she blushed.

"Not quite. The boys are building me a cabin like Casper's in exchange for letting them train me. Against my will, might I add. This was never voluntary. Hey, how about I ask them to make it UV safe?"

"Ya want me to live with ya?" asked Dion, dropping her food.

"You're currently homeless and I'm not. This is logical. It'll be big enough to hold meetings for official Recruit business. Not that I know what any of that's about. There's plenty of room for a vampyr."

Dion smiled and began twiddling her thumbs.

"Has Casper said anything 'bout meetin' 'em?"

"If by 'them' you mean Casper's friends, then no. I'll no doubt be a huge disappointment. I have absolutely no combat training or control of my powers. All I have is what I've read in books. Besides, I get the feeling Casper doesn't know where they are."

"The leader always knows the whereabouts of his followers," she said. "When ya ready, he'll introduce ya."

Arriette flipped the meat with a stick and sat back against the tree, deflated. She reached up to pluck a few leaves and shoved them in her bag to study at a later date.

"Casper and the Recruit haven't seen each other for a very long time. If he knew their whereabouts why didn't he approach them; ask for help in locating me?"

"Casper found 'em all, one by one; wasn't their job to find ya, Arriette. Was his." Dion paused, then smiled. "Thanks for ya offer. Sure, I'll live with ya."

"It's going to be awesome to have somebody to talk girl talk with."

She confirmed this meant gossip when Dion raised an eyebrow.

"Now I've got you alone, can you teach me more about your kind?"

Arriette and Dion talked through the night, discussing how a vampyr hunts, where they live, how they breed. She learned that a parent passes the child their memories to help teach the ins and outs of hunting and stalking and why they never remembered their lives before their death. Also, why vampyrs were so beautiful and light on their feet.

Arriette soaked it in and enjoyed every second of their conversation.

"Do you think that's what happened to the orc? He was attacked by a Vamp?"

"Nah, I think Pouki's right 'bout the hex. I think Sue's killa is his killa."

She told Arriette that from her parent's memories she predicted she had approximately twenty other demonic siblings, all of whom she'd not yet met and didn't particularly want to. It was up to them to approach her, which Arriette feared they may do at any time.

Dion reassured her she would be able to sense them and then pointed to a large wooden box she'd made herself. It didn't look big enough to house a sleeping Vamp but apparently, that would be her bedroom for the duration of their travels.

"Is that a coffin?" she gasped.

"Not named it, but I wanted to travel with ya, Arriette. We've got 'til dawn before I'm box-bound so why don't ya brief me on this 'girl talk'?"

TWENTY—TWO

Dion went to bed just before sunrise, leaving Arriette to her thoughts. At the first sign of trouble, she was to knock thrice on the coffin lid, prompting Dion to track scents and sounds, but the idea of waking a sleeping vampyr made Arriette shudder.

The sunrise was beautiful; Arriette hadn't slept and now longed to rest her head but as the gang stirred and were due to be on the road soon, there wasn't time.

Weeks had passed and still Arriette was having trouble with the basics of her powers. Although excited to master them she still wasn't overly convinced she could succeed in a serious job. Thrust upon her, she was overwhelmed with responsibility. One day she'd be the leader of the Recruit.

Baby A suggested self-doubt was part of the problem.

"Your powers are tied to your emotions. If you tell yourself you can't, then you can't."

So before waking her friends, she decided to spend time practising her dreaming to prepare mentally and physically for the strain on her body.

She began by using telekinesis to lift rocks and snap some twigs but soon grew bored. Dreamers were almighty beings with the ability to project thoughts, ranking only second on the Haeyloian Power Scale, right there behind everlasts themselves.

Tobias had, in the past, read quite a lot of Harriet Foley's work and it had become one of their favourite topics to discuss. Arriette was fascinated by her.

In Harriet's more recent work she said dreaming was one of the most active supe gifts on Haeylo as their powers projected externally to their physical presence, rather than inactive gifts such as retaining.

Arriette planned to have at least mastered her telekinesis before being interrupted.

Her canteen was floating gently between the tree and the cart when she heard a crunch of twigs. Arriette, out of instinct, hurdled the canteen over her shoulder. Casper shielded his groin.

He hopped aside to avoid impact and frowned. Arriette sighed, one hand on her chest.

"Don't sneak up on me. I thought you were a demonic attacker."

"During the day?" He laughed.

"Hey, less criticism and more praise, please. I think I've mastered my telekinesis."

"Let's see then," he said, taking a swig from his own canteen and swilling his hands and face. He took care to rinse his long moustache and bushy beard.

Arriette demonstrated her skill with the canteen and set it down at the base of the tree.

"Imagine if I met a demon. Seriously no more evil children for him, right? Where's the orc? I can test it."

Casper gulped. "Be mindful of who you throw heavy metal objects at."

"I can multi-task too."

Arriette focused on her bag and held it one foot above the grass, concentrating on her left hand to begin with. Once she got it moving she was able to take her eyes off the object long enough to lift the canteen again with her right.

"Congratulations," said a second voice.

Pouki yawned and made his way over to them.

"Tobias trained you well, I see."

"He said I never sat still long enough. I practised this alone. Are you surprised?"

Arriette felt Tobias's presence and turned to gain his agreement.

"She's right," he said, pulling on a shirt. "Now guide the water over to Baby A's tent. I want to try something."

Arriette controlled it with enough precision to fit the canteen between the gap in Baby A's makeshift tent and held it still. She was careful not to rustle the garments and towels which formed the door and roof.

"Now what?"

Tobias sniggered and nudged Arriette.

"Unscrew the cap."

"Our angelic friend will not take lightly to waking up in damp sheets," Casper warned him.

"But it's fun."

"Then it will be your funeral," said Casper.

"If she gets mad I'm blaming you," Arriette said.

He jumped up and down excitely, urging her to pour the rest of the water over the angel.

"One time I decided to hang my white sheet mid-air and make it come to life. I chased her out the cabin before admitting to staging the whole act. She ignored me for a week."

"I'm pleased we can't pick on each other then," Arriette admitted. "It's nice to be immune to your antics although it hinders my self-defence."

"Disappointing if you ask me," he said, solemnly.

"Tobias if our powers were to collide, especially if I am who Casper believes I am, things could get ugly."

"He'd deserve every bit," said Pouki.

"What, you scared?" Tobias asked, flapping his arms. "Chicken!"

"I am *not* scared."

Tobias began to squawk.

"I *said* I'm not scared," said Arriette.

"So prove it."

Arriette's spine began to creak and her vision blurred slightly. The pain in her back—a sensation she'd experienced before—seemed to consume all other feelings.

But the strain on her senses was completely new. She'd never had such a rush of adrenaline, forcing her touch, taste and smell into overdrive.

Arriette dropped the items she'd been holding mid-air and squinted at her trembling hands.

"Arriette? Are you all right?"

Pouki brushed back her hair and took her temperature with his hand.

He hissed and moved away.

"Everybody, let's give Arriette some room."

Pouki looked down at his student with concern as her khaki eyes clouded with grey speckles and her wings materialised, but in jagged, awkward movements.

From every orifice shone a brilliant white light, so dazzling Pouki was forced to turn away.

Arriette began to scream.

Baby A jumped up, knocking her tent over and staggering, weary-eyed, to Pouki's side.

"What on Haeylo is going on?" she asked. "Oh no, not now."

She knelt close to Arriette, pinning their bodies together just in time for Arriette's to begin thrashing uncontrollably.

Still unable to see, Pouki turned his back to the two women and gestured for the men to back away. If not for Arriette's biological shield, she'd be blind.

"Deep breaths Arriette. This is natural; you're receiving Zïnnyi's blessing."

She relaxed her hold a little and allowed her friend to slump against the tree. When the light faded, the group gathered around.

Baby A explained all Angels, having proven themselves to the creator, would receive His blessing. An increase in stamina, strength, self-awareness and in spirituality. Feeling closer to Him, the angel would then begin to receive messages in various ways; memories that weren't theirs, visions of pain and suffering on Haeylo and the sounds of the desperate and innocent in need of an angel's assistance. Such pain via a sense overload was His way of fine-tuning them to his calling, Baby A said.

"Service to the creator is what makes us who we are," she continued. "The physical price we pay for His blessing in the first instance is soul destroying. We'll have to give her time; Zïnnyi wouldn't have initiated the change if not for the ideal timing."

The group had been moseying close by in search of natural ingredients for a soup Reiko offered to make for dinner when Arriette finally opened her eyes.

Being first at the scene, Pouki handed her a damp cloth, her canteen and a slice of bread. Arriette had never been so grateful for the basics.

"Eat, you need your strength."

"How long have I been out?"

"About six hours," said Tobias, crouching beside her. "How you feeling?"

"I feel—" Arriette paused and stretched her limbs. "Pretty good, actually. Groggy, but, uhm, enlightened."

She hopped to her feet and released her wings. Then without further notice she took to the skies, barely feeling the feathers as they tickled her skin.

"This is amazing!"

Dancing through the sky, even at such a great height, gave Arriette a real sense of freedom and urgency. She wanted all her friends to experience this wonderful gift. She'd never felt more capable.

Baby A joined her and held her arm.

"I think that's enough spontaneity for today."

She pointed at Tobias who glared up at them with his mouth agape. Arriette told Baby A all about his plan to soak her with the canteen.

The girls winked and swooped down to grab him. Once securely in their grip, Arriette and Baby A swung him high above High Man's Tree and threatened to drop the dreamer until he begged for mercy.

"Who's a chicken now, Tobias? Don't you like heights?" Arriette teased.

"Put-me-down!"

"Learn your lesson, Tobias. With Zìnnyi's blessing, nothing can stop her!"

When safely on the ground, Tobias used his telekinesis to throw items of clothing and scraps of food at Baby A as revenge, but she could only laugh and point at his humiliation.

Arriette groaned and stretched her back.

She'd overdone it.

"How much do you weigh, Tobias?"

The huge grin and a pat on his belly said it all.

Baby A dodged Tobias's final shot and took Arriette by the hand.

"You and I need to talk," she said, "before you decide to take off again."

"I should watch the orc, it's my turn."

"Casper will take care of him."

The forest seemed to welcome them with chirping birds, blooming flowers and an increasing heat Arriette was finding easier to tolerate, although her sunburn was beginning to itch and peel.

Frustrated by the distraction, Arriette glanced down to see that what began as sunburn had developed into an I-shaped rune called Isa, representing her new control of time and space.

"I thought both Isa and Thurisaz were traveller runes?" she asked, puzzled.

"Thurisaz yes, but Angels often receive Isa because of their slavery to His wishes, travelling far and wide, often for long periods of time, merely on a hunch. Some Angels don't get one at all. Stop scratching it."

"Could have appeared in a more convenient place," Arriette grumbled, examining her forearm.

Creatures passed them by, paying no attention. Nature

continued regardless of their presence and for the first time since she inherited the blood of the supes, Arriette felt truly alive.

"I can't believe how much I was missing."

Arriette held out her hand for a butterfly to perch on and focused with all her energy on the flapping of its kaleidoscopic wings. Reds, blues, yellows and greens, all of which blended perfectly against the beautiful backdrop.

"It's almost as if I can slow down time to see everything in detail," she gasped, looking for Baby A's approval. "Is this how you always see the world?"

Baby A nodded and gestured for her to continue, fascinated with Arriette's reaction to her new senses.

"I hear the rustling of every leaf. I can even hear you breathing."

She laughed, launched the butterfly and turned to grip Baby A by the shoulders.

"Is this because of Him?"

"Zïnnyi has blessed you." She smiled. "The decision to welcome you as his defence against evil has been made."

Her face fell stern when Baby A began to explain that with such wonderful abilities would come a deep responsibility, not only to nature, to her God and to the people of Haeylo; to answer when they call, help wherever possible and find a reason behind human nature, but most of all to herself.

"Your body is a sanctuary, Arriette," she began, "and Zïnnyi expects you to take great care of yourself and to act upon what your head says as well as your heart. He will feed you sights and sounds, most of which will make little sense. Some you can act upon. Others you must let be. Do you understand?"

Arriette's attention drifted momentarily to a spider weaving a delicate web. Baby A pinched Arriette.

"Are you listening to any of this? You cannot just wander off based upon one of His messages. It may not be safe."

"Then why send them if he doesn't want me to follow?"

Baby A sighed. "Everything Zïnnyi does is to test our

judgement, Arriette. You must filter your contact with him; every second of a vision you're sent is a violation of our free will and being angelic is the ultimate test of will-power. Unlike most supes on this planet we don't have a choice when to use our gifts, nor do we have human rights like everyone else. Communication is forced upon us and only we can decide if the lead is worth the chance."

Arriette pulled her body free from Baby A and sank to her knees.

"You're telling me to ignore a person in need?"

"That's exactly what I'm telling you to do," she said, her voice firm. "Never risk your own life for that of a lost cause, Arriette. You are of much greater use to Zinnyi alive and He wants to know you're able to distinguish between life and certain death. Some are meant to die. We may not see the logic, but that's not our decision to make." Baby A softened. "You can't save everyone."

During their stroll back to High Man's Tree, Arriette shared her worries and fears with her fellow angel and Baby A reassured her that regrets were normal but ultimately useless.

"Only travellers can change the past," she said, "and even then most likely with the same outcome. You save a loved one for another to perish. Or they dodge a bullet only to then commit suicide. Angels believe everything supernatural happens for a reason and that death is not the end. It was their time and your involvement is irrelevant."

"Well that's a load off," said Arriette, wiping her forehead with the back of her hand.

"You'll be fine. This is a blessing, not a curse. Come on, we don't want to miss dinner."

"Great progress, Arriette," said Pouki when the girls returned.

"I'd love to master my other powers as easily as that. A few seconds of pain, a few hours of sleep and I'd be good as new."

"Dreaming will help with your shifting," Tobias said. "They work well together."

Reiko handed Arriette a bowl of broth and then offered one to the orc, which he refused. Arriette caught Casper's eye and gestured at Coyote. He shrugged and concentrated on his own meal.

"Besides, dreamers can practically do anything they want," Tobias said. "Even kill orcs from a hundred yards away." He winked.

"How about time-travel?" asked Baby A. "Bet you can't do that."

"All right, there's one exception."

"You said we can do anything," said Arriette.

"Sure but I don't travel through time," he said. "Being a dreamer is great for fighting, self-defence and well, entertainment. A wormhole is something else entirely. That's a job for Baby A."

"Can't I just imagine I'm Travelling?" she asked.

"I suppose it might help trigger your traveller instincts but not much more. Remember, full-blooded travellers are pulled unexpectedly through time and we can't interrupt or replicate that."

"Each power is unique, Arriette." Pouki smiled.

"Even if I go back by just a few minutes?"

"I've experimented before," he admitted. "Trust me. You'll only give yourself a headache."

Twenty—Three

2140AD
The Creation of Haeylo: Part Three

The pilot lifted the helicopter above the White House, nodded once at Andrew and ran a finger past his head, heart and both shoulders.

"Got your parachute, Mr President? We can't stay until the end. It's too dangerous. Hey, can you hear me?"

"I hear you," Andrew said, "but I won't be returning I'm afraid. This is a one-way ticket for me, friend."

"Mr Robin never said anything about this, and there's only one possible outcome, Mr President. What about your funeral arrangements and what should I tell your family?"

"Tell them I love them." Andrew smiled. "Although I'm sure they already know."

The pilot inhaled deeply and prepared to argue for Andrew's life, but thought better of it. "So now what?"

Andrew held his fingers crossed in his lap, so tight they turned white. "I'll see you on the other side, I suppose," he said.

The helicopter ventured into the vortex after what seemed like a full day's journey although they had only been in the air for about sixty minutes.

The pilot prepared a parachute and took deep breaths to calm his nerves. The higher they climbed the more Andrew worried if he'd made the right decision to stay behind and what Christine might think of him for not involving her.

"I'll be seeing you, Mr President." The pilot shook Andrew's hand and squeezed tight. "It's been a pleasure."

"Good luck," said Andrew, then heaved his pilot's body out the door.

He held his breath until the parachute opened as planned. Finally, he was alone.

Andrew lay flat on his stomach as a kaleidoscopic storm swallowed him and the helicopter.

He closed his eyes, pictured his children's future and exhaled with relief knowing he'd done everything possible to save the human race from an extinction he'd always believed they didn't deserve.

Back in Washington the streets filled with crying children, shop-lifters, emergency workers and angry drivers colliding with one another in panic. All eyes were on the sky no matter their activity.

Unbeknownst to Andrew, his contract had sparked uncontrollable panic across not only America but the entire planet.

Cities fell as riots broke out, innocent people scrambled for supplies; fought one another to protect canned goods, bottled water and baby formula.

Cars honked in endless traffic jams as far as the eye could see. All of them terrified of the apocalypse. Those predicting an afterlife took the opportunity to purge and cleanse their souls whilst others sat on the steps of their local church watching as the non-believers continued their criminal lives none the wiser.

Back in Christine's bedroom, Jim helped carry the children to the master bed, worried.

"They'll be fine," she assured him. "It's shock."

"He's coming with us, right?"

Christine frowned. "I'm not sure I understand—"

"The pilot returned without President Kaines."

"Oh, well I hope so, Jim, truly I do."

"Will we see him again, be it in this world or the next?" Jim asked Christine.

She smiled and glanced down at her unconscious children.

"I think so, Jim, and if I'm right it will be in the Garden of Eden; in paradise."
Then the skies turned black and all fell silent.

TWENTY—FOUR

9280AD

They followed Coyote from Highman's Point at noon, insisting he pick up the pace to ensure they arrived before nightfall.

Arriette was concerned for Dion in the stifling heat of her coffin and, although she wouldn't openly admit it, she was worried about Coyote's ankle too.

He'd been limping for several miles now; without him they'd never find the Underworld's entrance.

Tobias mimicked him from behind and Arriette had to bat him before he'd leave the poor creature alone.

"He's not a demon, Tobias," she reminded him. "He's bugging me as much as anyone but if we can help him we should."

"Glad you didn't slit his throat then?" Tobias raised an eyebrow. "Just sayin' you were in a hurry to slaughter Coyote until Pouki confirmed he wasn't actually an orc."

"I was wrong. I'm adult enough to admit that."

They needed him all right; Casper knew it, Pouki knew it and, as much as she'd fought her conscience, Arriette knew it too.

Now she had a theory and wanted to express her concerns before releasing Coyote, be it into the forest or the Underworld. The decision was hers after all. If she trusted anybody to give her an honest opinion, it was Casper.

"What powers do orcs have?" she asked, initiating the

discussion. "If any."

Tobias moved away, leaving the two of them to handle their dispiriting topic. Casper smiled and gave Tobias an approving nod of the head.

"They rank thirteenth on the scale."

Arriette rummaged in her memory for the other ten. Everlasts, dreamers, ten others she had yet to place and in final position– ahead of mere human beings—was the orc.

The Haeyloian Power Scale, or the Awen as most supes called it, was a list devised by the everlasts to determine which of the powers were the most influential, with the most active power.

The Awen rarely changed and consisted of fourteen very different species. The symbol– three rays of light pointing to three points of interest, encased by a perfect circle—reminded supes of what they had in common: the past, the present and the future.

"Stop me if I'm wrong: everlast, dreamer, sorcerer, traveller —"

Arriette hummed, contemplating the fifth on the Haeyloian power scale. Casper waved her on.

"Uhm, angel, shifter, demon, telepath, retainer—"

Once again, Arriette hit a dead end. Casper rolled his eyes and gestured for her to continue.

"Wiccan, orc and human."

"Twelve of Fourteen. Not bad."

"So they're not capable of shifting shape or mixing potions?" Arriette continued. "He couldn't have killed Susan?"

"Their sorcery is limited so no, I think not."

"Coyote was my prime suspect though. How can I be wrong? Everything fits."

Arriette felt deflated and not so eager to continue.

"What use is he to us now?"

"Quite the investigator now, aren't we?" Casper grinned. "Go on, let's hear it."

"He's not who he says he is. Somebody has cursed him;

wiped his memory. A curse like Susan's, although with the added torture of memory loss or whatever it is. Perhaps somebody with the same abilities– another supe of his species —did this to him, Casper. My theory is that Coyote killed Susan and his partner in crime wanted him silenced."

"Makes more sense for Coyote to have suffered at the same hands as whoever cursed Susan, don't you think? Maybe he protested and was then attacked himself as punishment? Whoever cursed her, cursed him. What are the odds of Coyote being wiccan too? I'm sorry Arriette but I cannot agree with your theory. Susan died of old age."

"From a hex which was only diagnosed because of one previous case between an everlast and his jealous lover! Just because retainers said her cause of death was wiccan magic does not make it so."

"If an everlast fell victim to wiccan magic, so can we," said Casper. "Besides, orcs are thirteenth on the scale. There's no chance he's responsible. He's likely a victim. We should study him further."

Impatience, if anything, was his student's biggest weakness.

"Do not blame retainers for an incorrect diagnosis. The historic case you speak of—the death of the everlast girl—was a tragic incident. Retainers stored the relevant data and used it to diagnose your friend. You must let this grudge go."

Arriette sighed, frustrated. "Who's to say on this occasion they didn't misread the hex?"

"Pouki would know. Magic leaves a trace."

Arriette made a noise which sounded a lot like tssssshk! She wasn't convinced.

"There's just something about him, Casper. You feel it, I know you do. You were all so certain I shouldn't kill him, that we could use him. Go ahead then."

"There are gaps in his memory we must first fill," said Pouki, pushing between the two of them. "I may be small but I'm quite useful."

Pouki rolled up the sleeves of his robe and called for the

group to halt. In deep thought he ran his fingers through his long white beard, resting lightly against his round belly.

"Reiko, untie his wrists. Only prisoners are bound. Innocent until proven guilty, right Arriette?"

Reiko looked from Pouki to Arriette for her approval; perhaps she had more influence than she'd realised.

Arriette shrugged and nodded her head, unsure whether Pouki was mad or had a spark of inspiration. Either way, she was beginning to lose interest.

"Can I ask why you're untying our only lead to Susan?" asked Baby A, taking the words from Reiko's mouth. "He may not be a prisoner but we need him."

"As much as he needs us?" said Pouki. "I doubt this creature means us harm; not beneath this false exterior."

Coyote cowered when Pouki approached him and repeated the word 'vampyr' several times. Babbling orcs were of no use to them, thought Arriette, but killing him now, having already threatened once before, was unfair.

"Vampyr," Coyote repeated, then half-smiled.

"See? We should prove we're here to help him."

"Perhaps his appearance is intentional?" Baby A suggested. "A disguise; a classic way to fool somebody into believing he was from the Underworld. I'll bet he's a shifter."

"There is logic behind your accusations. I can become an orc, however, I cannot see how a demonic servant links to Susan." Casper scratched his chin. "For example—"

Casper exhaled and loosened his stance, then one by one shifted his limbs to mirror the orc's appearance.

Coyote watched, mesmerised.

"He remembers seeing this before," said Pouki. "Either from personal experience or a friend's."

Casper shook off the camouflage. "If he was a shifter somebody froze him in this form. A very painful form of torture. No shifter should morph against his will or be refused the ability to take their natural shape."

"Noted but I still cannot penetrate his wards."

Casper frowned. "What are you saying?"

Arriette shuffled closer as Pouki placed his hands on the orc's face, much to his disapproval.

"His mind is a brick wall. I cannot break the boundary to learn who cursed him, if indeed he was cursed. If the wiccan responsible for Coyote was responsible for Susan we will have great difficulty decoding her magic. This will take time."

"Time we don't have," said Casper.

Arriette cleared her throat and folded her arms.

"Pouki you don't sound convinced this was a wiccan."

"I'm not," he said. "Personally I think this is sorcery of a very specific kind." Pouki paused and shook his head. "I cannot believe I'm going to say this, but the signature is that of a rulecast."

"So what?" asked Reiko. "Means nothing. They're just fancy sorcerers, right?"

"Who work mostly for everlasts," Tobias said.

"Oh now we are being silly," said Casper. "Say the orc caused Susan's illness. Following Arriette's theory. Then what?"

"There would have to be motive," said Tobias.

"Perhaps she knew something she shouldn't have. Kalvin said she had a history," Baby A interjected.

Casper hummed. "What business would Susan have with an orc?"

"How should I know?" Arriette said. "They didn't live long enough to share that wonderful tale."

"How do we know the orc didn't ask for this curse or receive it in punishment. There are rituals capable of turning a supe evil, you know," Baby A suggested.

"You cannot force evil upon another. You are born evil," said Reiko. "Casper's right, we're getting silly."

"Not necessarily," Pouki corrected. "Evil is a state of mind. Just as we are devoted to Zinnyi, an orc is devoted to his master, who is devoted to destroying the Recruit."

"Why target Susan though?" Baby A asked. "What could she *possibly* know?"

"She knew I would be the next Recruit leader," said Arriette, stern-faced. "She wasn't born with that knowledge. They wanted to silence her; prevent her from telling me the truth. If I hadn't have received that note, I'd still be in two minds about staying with you. At first this was forced, not voluntary, remember?"

Casper lowered his head. "I never meant to—"

"No but you were correct. Susan confirmed it, but how did she know about my destiny? Susan wasn't killed accidentally or as a punishment, it was a preventative measure. One that didn't work," Arriette said.

"The questions we should be asking are firstly how did she know about Arriette's future and finally, who the hell was she?" Baby A asked.

Rubbing her aching head, Arriette continued.

"She's dead now so it's too late. So is Kalvin and anyone else who may have been able to tell us. We don't know for sure if Susan was hexed; retainers diagnosed it but only based on one other case. Even then, how do we know they aren't covering for somebody? Bribed or threatened into lying to me? At this stage we know too little to judge this creature."

"Susan was murdered; whether her killer was a supe or not is irrelevant. Somebody wanted her dead. Aren't you curious as to the reason?" asked Baby A.

"If the Recruit predicted my destiny to lead them, evil could have also. Perhaps this orc is merely a pawn in the recruiting efforts of the Underworld. To brainwash decent supes and use them against us. Stop us from rising against them. Surely with a new leader, the Recruit will be perceived to be stronger."

Arriette reasoned with them, trying desperately to believe that Susan was a respectable person with little involvement in the impending war. A war she only knew was because of Pandora's box, but with nothing to confirm the hows and whys.

"No demon can stray above ground in the daylight and no intelligent supe would wander beneath the surface at night," Reiko said. "How can they recruit others in their cause then?"

"Susan was human," said Baby A. "She had no gifts to offer the Underworld. No weapons."

"We don't know that," said Casper. "Susan was a friend of Arriette's but she also betrayed her. What she did upon arrival at the city is beyond our knowledge."

"Your point?" asked Arriette, angered by the memory. "Oh, you're not suggesting Susan was killed as a message to me, are you?"

"Your emotions are tied to your powers," said Baby A. "Susan's death did rattle you. Casper's merely saying that Susan could have been involved in dark arts or maybe owed money just like Kalvin did. People will do anything when they're desperate. If she got herself in trouble, her death may have been a punishment."

"What you're suggesting is ludicrous. Somebody watches and studies me, learns I'm due to inherit the biggest responsibility on the planet and so kills my friend to hurt me?"

"Not hurt you but hinder you," said Tobias. "Send you on a wild chase to uncover secrets with little relevance to what's really going on. To blind you." Tobias sighed. "I'm not wrong. All we've done recently is avoid the main concern which is Pandora's box."

"Distracting us will make it easier for the enemy to kill us," Baby A said, bluntly. "Attack your weakness. Your pure heart."

"Or send his warriors to torment you, throw you off track," Reiko finished. "Pouki, your thoughts?"

Still concentrating on the orc, Pouki mumbled, "We can't rule it out. Yet, there is still the possibility that Susan's death was as a sacrifice to trigger Arriette's development. Since her passing your gifts have blossomed."

She couldn't stop the cogs in her brain from working overtime. They had a list of outlooks now, some of which gave Coyote a motive, others which freed him.

Arriette welcomed some form of organisation into their lives having been blind to what lay ahead.

"So how do we find out which of those pieces best fits?"

asked Reiko. "Should we try tracking Susan's killer? Perhaps return to the city and find Scarlett Evermay? It was through Scarlett you received Susan's parchment. If anybody can clarify all this, she can."

"We'll never find the killer," said Pouki, "not without a miracle. Our concern right now is Coyote. Do we risk freeing him and losing our only lead, however minor it is?"

"We can deal with him later," said Casper.

"This is about war. A war Susan was caught up in. A war she tried to warn us about in her note. Casper, you need to train me to take your place now so we can look further into Pandora's box. People fight over power every day. It has to be the centre of everyone's quarrels."

"You're so eager to learn," he said, grinning, "but why now, when only weeks ago you were accusing me of keeping you prisoner?"

"Revenge," she growled. "I can't let Susan die in vain. Someone has to pay."

"Who?" asked Pouki.

"Anyone. Everyone!"

Pouki tightened his robes and shook his head.

"You cannot avenge Susan through war, especially one we know little about."

"I can try," she said, holding his gaze. "I'm not a useless human anymore, Pouki. I can fight. I can dream. I can fly. Susan believed in me– she knew it was I who would lead the Recruit into battle. She warned Kalvin of the war just as Scarlett warned her. Don't deny me this opportunity, Casper."

Wringing his hands together Casper began to pace, occasionally glancing between the orc, Pouki and Arriette.

She was right, of course. Preparation for a war must begin if the Recruit were to hold any faith in their new leader. Arriette's training had to start soon and it was vital she meet his friends in the near future.

Coyote was a dead end.

"I haven't seen them in years."

"We'll find them together. Take Coyote with us if we have to. I'm going to check on Dion whilst you decide," she said. "As our next step, Casper, this is logical."

"Be sure you don't touch the lid." Baby A said, "Three knocks and—"

Arriette smiled. "You can't scare death, Baby A. I'll be back in a moment, I need to be sure it's still sealed."

Arriette walked away. Baby A rolled her eyes.

"How can somebody so emotional tell me to stay calm?" She laughed.

An hour later, Arriette and her friends were refreshed, rested and ready to continue.

Arriette dragged her body up and slapped a smile on her face.

Worrying about who killed Susan couldn't bring her back, she reminded herself, but still, one question niggled in the back of her mind.

Why would somebody kill her?

Baby A placed a comforting hand on Arriette's shoulder.

"How are you feeling?"

"Wonderful."

"You seem—"

"Confused? Angry?"

"Amongst other things," said Baby A. "I've given it a lot of thought, Arriette. I think Coyote's imprisonment in that body was to silence him."

"At Ma's place he looked terrified," Arriette said. "I feel a little sorry for him, actually."

Arriette watched him limp with Reiko on his heels, encouraging him to speed up and warning him not to lead them astray.

"Demons don't feel, do they?"

"Oh they feel all right, but they don't show it as we do. Orcs are regularly beaten by their masters; slaves of the Underworld and messengers. Alive purely for the benefit of the horned beasts and immortal spirits they serve. Do you think an orc would survive twenty minutes if they were to cry and cower in fear?"

Arriette's chest tightened. "He cowered, I saw it. True fear shone in those eyes back in Drakonta; confusion when we questioned his reasons behind the kidnap, like he was reciting a script and not his passion."

"If he is human beneath that shell, or a shifter, can you forgive him?"

"We *all* deserve forgiveness," said Arriette.

They strolled behind the orc for another twelve miles before their next rest stop, and by then he could barely stand.

Binding his ankle would provide some support, Pouki said, but not enough to get them as far as the entrance.

"Casper told me if he Shifts he can channel the powers of the creature he morphs into," said Tobias. "If this creature is indeed a shifter, can we not prompt him to do the same?"

"When changing into an orc isn't there a chance he also temporarily inherited the gifts?" Baby A asked.

"Orcs have no gifts," said Reiko. "Their blood is acidic, the colour of ink. Their skin is grimy and their hygiene poor. Does being disgusting and inhumane count?"

"They have no healing qualities?" asked Arriette.

"None. His only hope is to change shape. His best option is an angel," said Tobias. "Unless you'd like to donate some of your blood to the cause?"

Arriette opened her palm and flexed her fingers. "I'm only one-fifth angelic. Wouldn't work. Hey, Pouki!"

Arriette jogged to his side and called for the others to pause. "I read in a book once that telepathic minds can follow memory paths and unlock gateways, like finding your way through a maze with one key and a thousand doors."

Unsure whether this was to be a challenge or a compliment, Pouki nodded but said nothing.

"Coyote isn't going to make it on that ankle. I need you to find whatever signature you stumbled upon the first time you read his mind; you said it was semi-supe. From there, rather than following the path of his curse can you take an alternate route?"

"To where?"

"To his natural form."

Arriette grabbed the orc by the neck of his robes and pushed him to the ground. Pouki winced when Coyote cowered and pleaded in a blind panic.

Even his arms raised to protect his face, predicting violence.

Arriette raised an eyebrow and grinned, confirming their suspicions. "Orcs don't cower."

"No they don't," said Pouki, smiling broadly now. "You are very observant, Arriette Monroe. I cannot promise you success but I can certainly try. Now move aside."

TWENTY—FIVE

2140AD
The Creation of Haeylo: Part Four

Andrew was met by a sea of faces he used to know and he shook their hands, grateful for the unexpected company.

Each touch ignited a precious memory from his past; birthdays he'd barely been present at and Christmas parties at offices he scarcely remembered, each time surrounded by colleagues he had no names for.

Andrew's greetings were mere pleasantries until his eyes settled on an elderly woman in a pink pinafore, white flats and pale rose lipstick. The woman helped Andrew to his feet.

He'd been sprawled across a wooden table in somebody's kitchen, beautifully built in stone with mauve coloured walls and an open door that led to the garden. Innocent chirping sounds and the scent of mowed grass drifted through the airy space, clearing Andrew's mind.

"We've been waiting for you," she said.

Andrew rubbed his eyes. "It can't be you. I'm dreaming. You're dead, Ma."

The woman straightened her clothing and tidied her now greying hair. She chortled and placed both wrinkled hands on Andrew's face, then kissed his forehead.

"Am I? I hadn't realised." She paused, then smiled. "Silly boy, you're home!"

"Did I hit my head? I'm hallucinating, aren't I?"

"Oh no," she said.

Andrew slammed his fists on the table top. His mother startled and stepped back.

"I was on my way to the new world. The vortex was supposed to transport me so I can't be dead. You're lying to me."

"I never lie. We're all here for you during this difficult time," she replied, sympathy fragrant in her voice.

"You're all dead! He promised me. I signed a contract."

Andrew took in his surroundings. This was his mother's kitchen in the house he'd grown up in. He flung his arms around her, soaking in the comforting scent of her floral perfume.

Each of the others disappeared as a light wisp, almost as if they were never there.

"They have others to welcome," said his mother, "but they wanted to see you."

"I don't understand. What about my children? Are they alive? Can I see them?"

"Oh the new world is as I'm sure you imagined, but no, you cannot see them. Soon they'll join us and it may only seem days until you do. For them, it will have been a lifetime."

Andrew exhaled with relief.

When his nerves calmed they walked together, finding a comfortable spot on an old brick wall. Andrew looked back at his house with a warm heart, finally relaxing into his fate but not yet daring to admit it.

"My people begged our creator to save them. After years of praying, He finally answered. So I sacrificed myself, proved to Him we were willing to change and dedicate ourselves to the protection of the new world. I was to be His right-hand man. What went wrong?"

His mother listened intently.

She still looked as beautiful as she always had although her face had aged, her hair no longer golden and her soft skin wrinkled. Taken so young, Andrew was pleased to see the creator had, at least, blessed her with old age.

"You think getting the job you've always wanted is a sacrifice? Don't frown at me. Is it my appearance? This is how

I'd look now should I have survived the Cancer," she said. "I can change if you don't like it. Here we are not bound by the effects of time or disease."

"No, no," he said, "I like it. The children never knew their grandmother. It's nice to meet her myself. It wasn't your appearance that confused me."

"Then what?"

His mother reached out to take his hand but Andrew pulled away.

Not yet, he thought, *this is too weird.*

"Up there in that helicopter, I sacrificed my life for the world. Mankind would be saved from judgement day and the vortex would transport all worthy humans to Haeylo. That was our deal, Ma. I can't understand how I'm here. Presumably, this is Heaven?"

"A step on the way," she said. "If you sacrificed yourself, Andrew, then why are you surprised to be dead?"

Andrew's hands began to tremble so he clutched them together and covered his eyes with them. Tears were beginning to well.

"Sacrifices don't get promoted," she finished.

"Well He promised me a deal," Andrew explained. "A life of servitude and devotion to His wishes. I would help train the chosen ones to watch over our new planet and form an indestructible bond between the human race and mother nature. That's what the girl told me to do before the election, you see."

Andrew began to pace the length of the wall.

He continued, "If I'm here then where are the guardians He promised? I can't train them in death. Besides, the girl on Earth said she knew me, from another time; from the future! So you see, I can't be dead! How was I so easily deceived?"

"Everyone feels this way when they first arrive here," she said. "How can you be sure she didn't deceive you? How long had you known her?"

Andrew and his mother sat beneath an old tree, gazing up at the gentle glowing sky. Andrew shrugged off the question. Ma was right, he hadn't known the girl long enough to judge her honesty.

"If you won't answer that then answer this. What did you have in mind, exactly? To travel to a land far beyond the solar system. Safe from harm. Protected against evil. It's not quite so casual."

"I guess I never thought He'd just take my life and dump me here. I was so ready to lead. Then we could fulfil our purpose."

His mother sighed. "Which is what? What solid evidence did we give to prove we'd care for another planet? Did we deserve His trust? Did the human race take care of our last home?"

Andy opened his mouth to speak but nothing came out. When he finally gave in, the old woman smiled.

"Exactly," she said.

"What will happen to my children?"

"They'll grow up in a toxin, mutant and war-free environment, Andrew, just as you were promised."

"How did you know about—" Andrew shook his head and decided it best not to open up that door. "Never mind."

The old woman placed an arm around her son's waist and squeezed. His bottom lip quivered. He'd missed her loving touch.

"Your success will haunt them until their dying day. He promised you a safe journey to a new existence but who said anything about the journey being yours?"

"A contract with the creator shouldn't have small print," he said, exhausted. "I'll be here forever."

"Heaven isn't a punishment, Andrew. It's what we make of it. This is only your first step."

This startled Andrew.

Could he stay here for eternity? It wasn't so bad. The grass beneath his feet felt crisp, reflecting warm rays from the sun and illuminating buds between each V-shaped tree branch. His forgotten family members surrounded the house with beaming smiles. What more was there to want? Anyone else might have been thrilled with their afterlife.

Of course, Andrew missed Christine and the children but they would all be together again soon. Much sooner than he'd thought, according to his mother.

"I want to know this new world can provide for my people. I want to be there to see for myself. You can't imagine how awful Earth is in its current state, Ma. Chemical factories spew toxins into the air, causing illness and mutation. There are zones where the poor are trapped, fed to the mutants who've lost their sanity. And by fed I don't mean they're taken advantage of through slavery or exploitation, I mean literally fed. Cannibals are unavoidable since the Rabies virus mutated and the majority of society couldn't afford the vaccine. Some are so desperate to escape they sacrifice their organs on the black market to feed their family. Unemployment has skyrocketed and there are entire families starving. I couldn't bear to be a rich man in a hapless country."

"How awful," she agreed.

"I tried to do charity work and even ran for President to change what I could, but it took seven years to be voted in. You have such an influence from the position, but I met this girl—"

"You want recognition?" she interrupted.

"I want what any President wants," he told her. "To do my job."

"Leadership can be left to another for a change."

Andrew shook his head. "I should see it through. Something I cannot do from Heaven."

"Now you're dead the role must go to another, more able soul."

"So that's why I'm here; He replaced me?" Andrew asked bitterly. "Swapped me for a more agreeable guy."

"Woman, actually. Are you angry?"

"A little. Is she going to lead my people? She must be one of His guardians then?"

"She'll be well-trained either way."

Andrew folded his arms and cuddled himself in a pathetic attempt to hide his anger.

"Training is nothing in comparison to experience."

"What if her trainer is powerful?" she asked, one eyebrow raised. "Would this please you?"

"Power doesn't promise prosperity." Andrew groaned. "All the powerful people I've ever known have been greedy and vicious. Who is she then, and who's going to train her to be kind and caring? Humans lack such traits these days."

"She'll be born brave; a real hero. She'll risk her own life to save others without thinking twice about the consequences. Can you trust in our creator's judgement?"

"I can't trust someone I've only met in dreams, just like I shouldn't have trusted that girl on Earth. She tricked me."

"You should trust in your God. He offered you the contract for a reason. It had nothing to do with this mystery girl you speak of." Ma smiled.

"I can't settle for anything less than His promise to fix this. I'm sorry Ma. It's not in my nature to walk away from something so important."

The old lady reached into a pocket at the front of her pinafore and slid out a tiny leather book. She lifted a pair of silver glasses which hung on a long pendant around her neck and set them on her nose.

"Let's see," she began, scanning the book with delicate fingers. "Oh, you're right. It's here in my notes."

She thrust the book into her son's face and tapped against her latest entry. Andrew glanced down in a hurry.

"See a world in a grain of sand," she read.

"That's it," Andrew confirmed, excited. "The contract. It said the new leader could see Heaven in a wild flower, hold infinity in the palm of their hand and eternity in an hour. That was the deal: ultimate power. I told you!"

She replaced the journal in the pinafore pocket.

"Well that could mean *anything*."

Andrew remained silent, his face pale with grief for the life he'd let slide through his fingers. He believed he'd earned himself half the ownership of this new creation and the credit for America's success at the same time.

Why were his eyes always greedier than his stomach? Such dreams to be king of the world had been shattered before they'd taken flight and his mother couldn't even recognise it!

"He asked you to sacrifice your life to serve Him but he never said where. If you're worried about doing your job I'd say you've already fulfilled your duties, Andy. Now it's your turn to have some fun."

Andrew sobbed against his mother's shoulders. He was the contract, not the scroll he'd scribbled a careless name across in that darned dream.

"I'm a fool."

"No you did something amazing," she said. "Greed can be forgiven. So can deceit. I'd say the favour for your life has been returned."

"There were so many things I wanted to do before I died. Skydiving, which if my body fell to Earth again I suppose I could tick off my bucket list. And my wife always wanted a son having only raised girls. I guess now it's impossible."

"How strange," she said. "I wanted a girl and God gave me boys. Isn't that funny?"

"Science gave you Paul and me," he corrected.

"After all you've been through, how can you say there was no involvement? Not even in the miracle of childbirth?"

"I like to think some things simply happen."

"This new leader happened by accident."

Andrew scowled. "Don't contradict yourself, Ma."

"I believe I said she will be female. I don't remember mentioning her name or if she has any idea what's in store for her."

Andrew gasped. "Wait, so this woman is blind to her destiny?"

"You've got it easy," she said.

Hand in hand Andrew and his mother set off toward the house. Casting his eye above them he noticed the same vortex he'd seen on Earth. It hadn't been there before, he was sure.

"I prayed for this," he said. "I knew we'd make it. Mankind, that is. We're too complex to simply disappear."

"You still got to see it. You know, Heaven is also a pit-stop to help confused souls learn from their mistakes."

"I don't follow. Are you trying to tell me that I'm not yet dead?" he asked.

She grinned. "You're being held in a place I like to call Indalo."

Andrew slumped to the ground.

"So I'm alive but I have to learn a lesson first?"

"How should *I* know? *You* didn't read the contract."

Andrew spent his entire life reading small print. He drafted contracts and deeds and other documents before handing them over to an unsuspecting victim. If he landed himself in such a mess he could certainly dig a way out.

"I wish I could apologise for being so acquisitive first," Andrew said. "I just thought the people would have a reliable leader. I can be better if I'm given a second chance. I'd do anything to prove myself; I'd even find this new leader and help train her. Sure He planned for another powerful leader to do this, but I have some good tips," he said.

"Well you'd better choose a gift before you leave."

"Hang on. That's it? That's my lesson?"

She pulled out the pocketbook once again.

"Andrew, you don't think I potter around the house all day in Heaven, do you? I have a job here. See this list of names? Step one is my office. These people are all due to arrive here, most of them thrown to Indalo before their passage to your new planet is allowed. The unworthy, you might say. I work for a very powerful man now." She winked. "This whole time you've told me how He's been cruel. All you did was try to help him. Not once did you acknowledge your mistake. Your selfishness."

Andrew nodded but said nothing.

"I have a responsibility to ease newcomers like you into either death, if that's your fate, or to help wake you. To guide you down the right path. I feel you've redeemed yourself but I'm taking you up on that offer."

His mother snapped her fingers and in the palm of her hand appeared a tiny golden bag.

"In here there are fourteen gifts, eleven of which are or will one day be very special. Choose yours."

"But I can't see them," he said.

"No you can't but they see you just fine."

Andy slid his fingers into the bag and felt around for a minute or two. There were several items calling to him but none as strong as the gift with the soft outer surface. He squashed it, shaped it and decided it felt like the most fun.

When he was happy with the gift he'd chosen he removed it from the bag.

"It's just a ball of dough," he said, disgusted. "My children used to play with this stuff."

She sighed. "You have so much to learn,"

Andrew was now excited to meet the people who would inherit the others even if his gift wasn't the best.

"It's your job to find them," his mother explained. "I'm going to assign a dreamer with the power to move things with their mind. The man you're looking for will not be greedy, selfish or Shallow."

"I'm confused, what are you saying exactly?"

Ma grinned, ignoring his question. "Then I'll assign an angel with beautiful white wings. Look for golden hair and snowy skin; a woman all two pleased to waste your time."

"Time," Andrew whispered, "got it."

"Next I think I'll choose a retainer with an endless capacity for knowledge. You'll need her, she's going to save a life and bring great Hope to the gifted." Ma continued, "Are you getting all this, dear? Your next challenge will be an everlast who shall live an endless life, spreading Joy wherever she goes. Then a wiccan, talented beyond her years, who will be like a daughter to you, Andrew. Let's see," she continued, "how about a sorcerer? He'll fall from the Sky one day to teach others to respect what they cannot control. The time-traveller I've chosen will lose her Baby, Andrew. You should be there to pick up the pieces of the broken hearts to follow. There will also be an insightful telepath; sometimes it is the smallest efforts which bring the most success, Andrew. They pass on all they hear."

"Is that all?" he asked.

"No, there will be an expert in herbal remedies, potions, eager to study science, technology and nature. He'll come as if from a Portal to join your family. And finally, one who can turn invisible with Jet black hair. He or she will be the hardest, I imagine."

She placed a hand on his shoulder and lowered her voice.

"Be warned of a temptation far greater than using these powers for personal gain. As lucky as you are to be given a second chance there are others who He's deemed worthy of new responsibilities. They, however, will not be so careful to protect them and will use their abilities to render yours useless. Find the chosen ones, Andrew. Sift through the supernatural with a fine comb."

"So I'm going to the new world?" laughed Andrew, "and I get to meet these amazing people? Do you really mean it?"

"Under one condition."

Andrew fell to his knees. "I'll do anything, anything!"

"You must help the others find this new female recruit and train her as your replacement. Train her to love the planet, to respect the gifts and to join every battle there is to fight against the same evils that ruined our Earth. This isn't going to be easy. Assess everyone and everything you deem a threat. When the time is right, He shall return you here once again and I'll look forward to seeing you."

"What about my family, Ma?"

"Compared to this, your challenge will be easy. You must change your name and appearance to hide your true identity. You can't contact any previous acquaintances; you'll endanger them. It's a test of true will-power. Keep this woman safe, Andrew. Help her discover her destiny. Promise me you won't abuse this gift."

Andrew exhaled a sigh of relief. He looked forward to the day his family would be reunited in Indalo once again.

"I won't let you down, Ma. I promise.

TWENTY—SIX

9280AD

In desperation, Pouki and Arriette sat beside one another drawing triangles in the dirt. It took Pouki three minutes to locate the signature in Coyote's mind but still unable to unlock the door between the orc and his sanity, Casper suggested a Haeyloian relaxation spell to assist their access.

Drawing upon the elements of nature: earth, air, fire and water, Casper's plan was to chant their translations in order to focus Pouki's mind. From their energy and the meditative effects of the spell, he would force down the barrier and free endless memory paths in hope of discovering the orc's true species.

Arriette practised her pronunciation as Pouki finished off his final drawing. Then he drew an X in the centre to mark his position.

"Ayre. Walta. Fori. Urt," Casper said, and Arriette repeated after him. "Say it with rhythm."

Arriette nodded. "Urt. Ayre. Fori. Walta. Urt. Ayre. Fori. Walta. Urt. Ayre. Fori. Walta."

"You've done this before?" asked Baby A.

"Oh many a time," he said. "Before I left the Recruit, I knew four women. Their names all in line with the elements. Very powerful wiccans. They helped me to learn how to do this; an easy way to boost supernatural energy, especially in combat. Of course, when you're in battle you have no time to draw triangles so you must simply imagine them."

Casper tapped his head and grinned.

"It saved my life once or twice."

"Will they remember you?" asked Baby A.

"I do hope so," he replied.

"Can we trust them?" asked Arriette, breaking from her rehearsal.

"Make up your own mind. They're on our side no matter their methods."

"When we go to war," Tobias added, "we'll need all the soldiers we can find. How are their combat skills?"

"*If* we go to war, not when, and their skills are most likely out of date," said Casper. "Arriette my dear, you look troubled."

"Just thinking," she said, drawing the figure eight in the dirt by Casper's feet. "About this symbol."

"The symbol for infinity," he said. "Like your Dagaz marking."

"Well Coyote has a scar just like it," she said, waving her drawing stick in his direction. "I saw him scratching it."

"How interesting," he said, gesturing for Reiko to bring Coyote to him. "What kind of scar?"

"Burned it seems, with hot iron," Reiko said as he examined Coyote's skin. "A branding, not a tattoo or a birth mark."

Concentrating hard, Reiko poked his tongue through the gap in his teeth and scratched his head. He'd never seen anything like the mark, he explained, and he'd fired arrows and swung swords in years passed.

"A painful burden to bear," Casper said. "Likely a reminder of something; a punishment."

"Symbols are everywhere and mean many things," said Baby A. "It also looks like the number eight."

"The smallest details can be the most important," he replied.

"So what is it then?" asked Ariette.

"Infinity is a simple symbol and can be drawn in one swift, smooth motion." Casper borrowed Arriette's stick to demonstrate. "It means endlessness and is drawn horizontally so it is not confused with the number it looks like."

"But why would Coyote have one on his skin?"

"It's an everlast symbol used to mark their continuing life. Only the eldest of everlasts would brand a creature like that."

"Coyote was an everlast?" asked Tobias, helping Reiko to pull the orc from his knees. "We're not going to hurt you. Who did this to you?"

"Vampyr," Coyote replied. "Vampyr!"

"An everlast would not brand themselves," said Pouki. "Nor would a Vamp. He's merely babbling from a random memory he's retrieved." Pouki tapped his head and rolled his eyes. "Believe me."

Arriette frowned. "Then how did he get it?"

"Slavery," said Reiko, dusting Coyote's robes like a filthy child. "He hasn't spoken sense since Drakonta. What's happening to him?"

"His mind is deteriorating."

Pouki closed his eyes and stepped into the centre of the symbols.

"Only makes this harder as the curse is not complete. On the plus side this means it can be reversed. I'll have to find the branches and remove them. Get comfortable, we're going to be here some time."

Coyote had a history before taking the form of an orc messenger; living and breathing as a shifter inside the city walls or a small village like Mousique. Was his transformation and branding a punishment for trying to escape such a fate?

What horrid acts of violence had he experienced at the hands of his everlast master?

Pouki began to chant, gesturing for Arriette to join him in hope of unlocking his past.

Arriette's last thoughts were of the supe capable of disabling this shifter's mind in such an intricate way. Perhaps this symbol was not to identify a slave but as a daily reminder that their power over him would be eternal.

"Our killer isn't a wiccan," Arriette told Casper. "It's an everlast."

TWENTY—SEVEN

"A mind is like a tree," Pouki explained as he reached into Coyote's consciousness. "Each branch connecting with another, and another, and another. Each leaf is a wonderful memory. The buds are thoughts and dreams waiting to bloom and the flowers represent our past lovers. Imprints of perfection. Pieces of the soul."

Arriette's mouth gaped in awe when the symbols lit up for the first time like lanterns in the earth's dust. Symbols drawn by her hands, now illuminated as beacons marking her path to the truth.

Studying them closer proved an intriguing lesson in magic; sparks of energy were sucked toward them and through Pouki's hands, he drew it into himself, lifting it with grace and ease and inhaling nature's purity through his nostrils.

Arriette held her breath in anticipation.

Inside of Pouki's mind stirred a magnificent storm of energy much greater than any Haeyloian thunder could muster. Using the urgency of it, Pouki pressed against the barriers of Coyote's mind. On the inside, his strength was growing but on the outside, it dwindled.

Winding each web of code the rulecast had weaved around his memories into his tornado, Pouki began to tear it down.

Hours passed with no further movement.

Arriette bit her nails wondering if Pouki would ever return to them from his coma until finally the wall crumbled and Pouki dove straight for the beginning of Coyote's existence, replacing memories and nurturing a once tortured mind.

"How much longer is this going to take?" asked Tobias who lay on his back, watching the sky turn to darkness. "We're running out of time. The stars will be shining soon. We're in vampyr territory."

Pouki's eyes opened and with them, Coyote's mind.

Arriette placed a palm on the orc's hideous face. Her eyes searched for signs of recognition.

He coughed, over-blinked and finally came round. Other than losing his balance a little, he seemed healthy.

When the disorientation and drowsiness passed they were able to discuss the last twenty-four hours. Questions were asked about his past. It was a mournful tale of loss and sorrow. Coyote's daughter had been kidnapped for slavery when orcs claimed their land only three moons before his attempt on Ma's life. His wife was beaten and left to die by the roadside. His neighbours' homes burned with friends still inside and a beast twice his height dragged Coyote from the scene by his feet, bound him by the wrists and left him to bleed.

"I must have passed out," he said, rubbing his eyes, "because when I opened my eyes, this everlast towered over me. Leering. Sniggering. No regret or guilt, only amusement."

Baby A knelt beside him, offering him a sip from her canteen. With shaking hands, Coyote accepted.

"What was his name?" she asked.

"Falkon Lou. Such merciless eyes. Terrifying abysses, hidden beneath curtains of groomed black hair. I remember praying for death as his servants branded me one of them."

Baby A lifted his robes. "It's recent but not infected."

Sighing, she gestured for Coyote to drink.

"How could an everlast do such a thing? Orcs are Haeylo's enemy, particularly the brutes you're describing. Demons in their physical form are indescribable and often seven or eight feet tall. Their armies are capable of turning our city to dust. Surely an act of such violence is treason so why buddy up with them?"

"Apparently treason is acceptable if you're an elder," said Tobias. "So you tried to escape? Takes a very brave man to challenge an everlast."

"Several times," he said, "but my freedom would only come with the everlast's death. I stole a knife from his kitchen and waited beneath his bed. You see, for a while he used me as a personal servant. What did I have to lose?"

"You succeeded then?" Baby A asked.

Coyote shook his head. "His rulecast was to be my judge, jury and executioner. If you've never met one, they're hideous cloaked creatures with long nails and foul breath. A sorcerer by nature but far more complex with a darker soul."

"So what happened? Obviously, you survived death," Tobias asked.

"Falkon said death would be too nice a release; he wanted to hurt me. Turn me into the very thing I so despised. He said that a great power would be building and when it gave way, he'd work alongside it. There would be no room for mediocre attempts to stand in his way."

"He had the rulecast turn you into an orc," Baby A said, lowering her head. "I'm ashamed for him."

"So Falkon Lou worked alongside these orcs?" asked Arriette, her eyes wide. "For what purpose?"

Coyote bound his hands to fists and tore away his robes like they were tarnished with Falkon's memory.

"A pact between the orc patrols south of the city wall. Falkon agreed to leave them to plunder and squabble in the forest in exchange for a steady supply of slaves," Coyote said. "He wants to build an alliance for control of the Underworld, for Pandora's box. He's heard it's re-surfaced and that Pandora herself is now out of the picture, so the valuable is up for grabs."

Arriette turned to Casper. "Does Charles Melovich know of this?"

"I do hope not," he said. "He does not strike me as a traitor. Pandora's box, we know, has re-surfaced but if Falkon Lou is also Susan's murderer, he'd need a reason to kill her. Our discussions earlier point to him needing her silenced; to prevent her reaching you."

"I saw no slaves at the office," said Arriette, reassured by her own words. "I would have noticed when Tobias and I first met Charles. There were workers, of course, and that snooty secretary of his, but nobody in shackles. Charles can't be in on it. I don't believe that."

Pouki scrubbed out the symbols with his foot and placed a hand on Coyote's shoulder.

"Is there enough strength in your body to shift? Your ankle is likely broken."

Coyote took one look at his disfigured body, greasy skin and wrinkled hands before emptying his stomach in the grass.

After pulling himself together he changed one limb at a time, easing his body into the transition to avoid as much pain as possible. Every crack of bone and uncomfortable groan made Arriette fear her shape-shifting inheritance but she was pleased to see him walking again.

The rest of their journey was uneventful.

By the time they reached the opening Coyote remembered from his time as an orc, night was upon them and Dion would be rising soon.

"I should return and take my revenge," he said, peering down into the void. "It's so dank down there."

Only now as she gazed at his chest did Arriette begin to appreciate how handsome Coyote was. All six feet of him. Toned and tanned with inquisitive brown eyes and shaggy hair. He had a strong nose and high cheekbones.

Casper gave him some grey robes from the cart to cover his naked body. Arriette thought it a shame.

"There's a mirror; I remember glaring at it, wondering why I didn't recognise myself. Now I know and it's all because of you."

Arriette blushed. "We learned a lot about the side we're supposedly on. Falkon could be Susan's killer if he's working with Haeylo's enemies. If he killed her to prevent her speaking to us, we also know he's likely to attack the Recruit if we stand in his way of finding Pandora's box. We have our best lead yet because of you."

"What's done is done," he said, "but revenge will be mine someday."

"You could begin now. Go down there and cause havoc. Kill as many as you can."

He shook his head. "I wish I could. Dark magic binds the entrance. The mirror is indestructible. Each crack will repair as though it were water. I can't chance death now."

"Why not?" asked Baby A. "You said yourself there's nothing to lose."

"The dead cannot avenge the dead," he said. "Until I do, my safety is paramount. There's no way to access through there anyway."

Arriette peered over her shoulder at Baby A, offering a weak smile. This shifter would do anything for Falkon's blood and all he needed was a nudge.

Could she allow him to start the war they all knew was coming?

"I believe you and I have something in common," said Arriette, taking Coyote by surprise. "Oh you doubt me now but I've lost loved ones too and to crimes equally as chilling."

Coyote kicked a rock into the darkness. "I doubt that."

"Come on," she said. "Our friend will be up in a while. She'll know what to do."

Arriette thought about Dion's abandonment and the loss of her child. Yet she never spoke of revenge. Arriette was wondering why when she caught Coyote staring at her.

"Everything all right?"

"We heard about you before the orcs attacked. News travels fast if it offers hope. They say you have great proniba. That you are bentiâ."

"Zinnyi blessed me with power but to what extent we've yet to discover. You praise me in Haeyloian; save your compliments for another twelve months, Coyote."

"They say you can tell the supernatural from the extraordinary. That you are entit sehde. That the Recruit will be born again when you take the throne."

"Ze Entit Sehde Eyeh is a myth," she said.

Casper laughed. "You can still identify those capable of great things. Go ahead and test her judgement. Her skills are still developing but she'll not let you down."

Offended by how quickly Casper had offered her to Coyote as a performer, Arriette folded her arms and frowned at him.

"Whatever gift my mentor says I have is, at this time, merely a rumour."

It was easy to see he was foiled by her reply. She inhaled deeply and rolled her eyes at Casper, who only smiled in response.

"Please, what do you see?" he begged.

Arriette decided to try.

"You're not a lost cause if that's what you mean," she said. "I won't say you're pure or clean or kind because I don't know you and I can't see into your soul. A supe like you doesn't just fade though. You carry on. Determination like that lingers."

Arriette sighed and brushed back her hair hoping Coyote would nod and walk away. Still he glared at her, expectant.

Arriette was lost for words.

"What more do you want?"

"Please," he said, tapping his chest. "What do you see in here?"

"Are you asking if you're good or evil? Hold light or dark magic? You are what you believe you are. Nothing more, nothing less. Only our pain nurtures us. You should embrace it. Let the fire burning inside lead you to Falkon Lou and when your blade meets his flesh, flush those demons through the steel. You owe it to yourself."

Coyote's teeth began to grind as he imagined it.

"How? When? Where?"

"Here. Now. It's easy... you *fight*."

TWENTY—EIGHT

"I'll be fine," Arriette told Tobias as she tied a long rope around her waist.

"I don't trust that shifter."

"dreamers never trust shifters." Coyote growled at him. "The feeling is mutual."

"I trust Casper," Tobias argued.

"Like I said, they never trust *shifters*." He cast a cautious eye toward the tree line. "You're easily deceived."

"What's *that* supposed to mean?" asked Dion, swinging her legs from the edge of the cart and yawning. "Casper is a great shifter."

"That's enough. I'm going to help Coyote figure out how to enter through the glass. When Casper returns with the wood tell him I made my first judgement call as leader of the Recruit."

"He probably already knows you'll do something stupid. That's why he left you to it," said Tobias.

Hurt by his crude remark she shoved him aside and gave the end of the rope to Dion.

"This shifter probably killed Susan too, he's just too much of a coward to admit it," Tobias said.

Arriette held her breath and hoped Coyote would deny all knowledge.

"I might have been an orc when you asked me before but my answer remains the same. She's a vampyr. How many times do I have to tell you, dreamer?"

"Did ya kill her?" Dion asked, winding the rope nervously

around her fingers.

"Of course not. I was brainwashed to believe I was one of them. Orcs aren't capable of witchcraft. Nor are shifters without the use of the ancient language and I don't speak Haeyloian all too well."

"Why would he hurt her?" Arriette asked. "Or have reason to lie?"

Tobias huffed and strode away, disappearing into the trees.

"Don't blame him for his concern," said Reiko. "He loves you. We all do. Seeing you risk your life for this man pains him, especially when only hours ago you wanted to slit his throat."

Coyote frowned. "I'll try to forget you said that."

"He won't be the first man I risk my life for so get used to it," she said. "Coyote, let it go. I thought you were my enemy. You're alive, aren't you?"

Coyote nodded but said nothing else.

"Arriette, somebody wants to harm you. Why else would an orc be sent to steal your mother? Not for a demonic wedding, that's for sure. Falkon Lou might be behind this. Until we know why, you shouldn't go down there."

"Falkon is careless," said Dion. "If his rulecast hexed Coyote the signature will be the same. If Susan is one of ma kind, Pouki might still be able to trace that. Don't ya wanna be alive to see it?"

"You can read Vamp minds?" Arriette asked.

Pouki scowled at Dion. "I read their living memories right until their death. I can often witness how they perished, which is unpleasant for me."

"Falkon must really need something or someone to risk a traced signature," said Dion.

"Oh for Zinnyi's sake get out of the hole, Arriette," said Reiko. "Coyote can take care of himself. His revenge is none of our business."

"If this is anyone's business it's mine. Falkon and his rulecast are using dark magic to curse his people. Innocent people. Susan isn't the first. Do you remember Kalvin's arrangement with Charles? He wanted me to investigate other cases of strange illness. I'll bet they're all linked. This might solve a major crime syndicate."

"Well the answer isn't down there. You'll get yourself killed."

"Aren't you curious about the mirror? We might actually get to kill one of those little orc suckers."

"Killing orcs sounds like a great way to kick-start my revenge," said Coyote.

"This is ridiculous," said Dion. "If ya won't reconsider then I'm comin' with ya."

Baby A fastened the rope to their waists and secured it around a nearby tree, watching solemnly as the three of them disappeared.

"Can you see anything?" Arriette asked, her voice echoing.

Dion said. "This might be an ambush."

"You can jump now, you're almost there." Coyote pointed at the mirror. "This is the gateway I told you about. Throw a rock and watch what happens."

Arriette untied herself and chose the largest one she could find. She hauled it at the mirror, fracturing the edge, then gasped as it morphed back again.

"Shall I touch it?"

Dion said, "Ya going to alert their armies. We're in their territory now!"

"Relax, Dion."

But Arriette *was* scared.

What if the mirror sucked her in and swallowed her whole; lost forever with demons and bloodsuckers?

They shuffled closer, taking their time and trying not to quake with fear. Not only was it frightening but ice cold too.

Arriette reached out and placed a flat palm against the mirror. Nothing happened.

"I guess you'll have to hunt your orcs another way," she said. "See Dion, I told you—"

Dion froze and held out her arms. "Did ya feel that?"

"An earthquake?" asked Arriette.

Coyote said, "Unlikely in these parts."

The reflective surface faded to reveal a huge doorway with a staircase leading down to nothing but darkness. The walls of the cave cracked and began to crumble.

Arriette pushed Coyote through the gap and waved her hands at him to take the opportunity.

"Go!" she urged. "Take your revenge; who better than a shifter in disguise?"

Coyote smiled and tried to thank her but through the noise and falling rock Arriette could only read his lips.

Dion tugged anxiously at her arm.

"Climb," she said. "Climb now!"

Coyote began to run but turned and attempted to scramble back up the stairs again. Arriette frowned and reached out to him, bound to the wall by the rope and confused by his change of mind.

It was too late.

"I told ya this was a terrible idea," said Dion. "Let's get outta here."

The liquid mirror reformed before he reached the top. When their surroundings fell silent she could still hear the tapping of Coyote's fingers.

"Send them all to Hell," she told her reflection, "and when you do, think of me."

TWENTY—NINE

Arriette pulled herself out of the shaft and sprawled across the grass, out of breath. Dion shook her head and threw the rope on the back of the cart.

"Lucky, that's all. Next time we're dead, ya hear?"

"It's just an illusion," Arriette gasped.

"With what relevance?" asked Dion, disgusted. "Ya pushed that poor boy to his demise. Orcs don't brush their hair or dress appropriately so why need a mirror?"

"He wanted to go," Arriette said, "and how should I know?"

"There's nothin' down there but rocks an' dust," Dion told the others.

Angered by her decision, Casper shoved Dion aside and grabbed Arriette by the arm. Fury had set hard lines in his once calm face; an expression Arriette thought didn't suit him.

"Do you have any idea how worried I was?"

"I'm sorry I just thought—"

"You didn't think! I expected better of you, Arriette Monroe. What use is knowledge of a mirror to us? We can afford to lose a man we barely know but not you. Not our saviour."

Casper wrapped her tightly in his hold.

"What poor judgement. Now he's alone, those creatures will eat him alive. And Dion—"

"Don't blame her," she said. "They tried to stop me. Dion risked her life for my protection."

"Ya might hate me more if I didn't," Dion reasoned. "If she hadn't returned in one piece, or at all!"

Casper inhaled deeply and released his hold.

"Did you at least learn anything useful?"

"It can't be opened from the inside," she said, catching her breath and straightening her clothing. "Coyote didn't journey from here."

"So he lied?" asked Reiko. "Tobias was right."

"I didn't say he lied. Coyote recognised that place. I think that's where Falkon dumped him following his enslavement; where the orcs found him."

"So it's a drop-off point?" asked Baby A.

"Or a trap for victims. They fall. They touch. They explore. They're found and they—"

"Die, which I see you didn't," said Tobias, emerging from the tree line. "Where's your friend?"

"Most likely dead according to Casper," Arriette replied, "but you already knew that. Go ahead, say 'I told you so' if it makes you feel better. I'm not proud of myself but it wasn't wasted."

"I'm sorry I yelled at you," he said.

"Yeah, well, I deserved it."

Arriette grabbed her bag from the cart and rummaged for her canteen. Tobias offered her his.

"Yes you did, but I'm still sorry."

"Leaders don't apologise." Arriette grinned.

"They die pretty well if they don't respect their friends' opinions though," he said, grinning back.

"Lesson learned." She rolled her eyes and shoved him aside. "Hey, where's Pouki?"

"Gathering ingredients for remedies and potions. He's going to teach me a few things," said Reiko. "When you left he said he thought Falkon was behind Susan's death too; he thinks that if Susan knew you were the Recruit's next leader she might have known about Pandora's box too. Falkon didn't want you to find out so he killed her."

"If Falkon wants war it would be a shame to disappoint him," said Arriette. "Falkon's intentions are obvious. We can't just ignore his behaviour. Either he or his rulecast killed Susan and attacked innocent families for city slaves. Unacceptable. Inhumane."

"He needs punishment," said Baby A.

"Death," Arriette snarled. "He brainwashed an orc to kidnap my mother. Which of us will be next? What hideous monsters from the darkness will he send to strangle me in my sleep? I'm expected to let him?"

"Of course not," said Casper.

"We challenge him then. Falkon must know of me or Coyote would never have attacked us unless it was coincidence, which I doubt. I can find Susan's killer now."

Pouki and Casper exchanged concerned looks but eventually gave in and agreed to assist Arriette's cause.

"We should first track down Scarlett Evermay. She can tell us more about Susan's history and the document she left Arriette," said Pouki. "Maybe we missed something."

"We know what it's supposed to mean now," said Tobias. "That Arriette's the leader. Where's your note?"

Arriette fished the parchment from her bag and handed it over. She wasn't looking forward to hearing it aloud again.

"One chose to use her power for personal gain, enforcing evil and greed throughout mankind," Tobias read. "It says here that he struck her down and removed her gifts. Could he mean Pandora? Was she an original Recruit member?"

"You're on to something, but how did Susan know to leave that for me? Kalvin knew things. Important secrets. The city is a two-day hike from here. I suggest we change our clothing and find somewhere to sleep for the evening," she said. "Then we find out."

"It's Vamp territory," said Dion. "We're not safe here."

"How far must we go?" Casper asked.

"Five miles, maybe six," said Dion. "I can keep watch; none will attack having picked up ma scent."

Casper nodded. "Vampyrs are curious creatures. They might investigate but none would challenge her hunt. If Dion claims us as her own we'll be safe."

Sleep didn't come as naturally to Arriette as she'd expected. Had she truly doomed Coyote? Was she still innocent and pure? Surely Zïnnyi frowned upon manslaughter?

Without the orc to carry back and forth, Tobias and Reiko were able to discuss hunting and cooking without keeping a watchful eye on the prisoner and Arriette lay awake listening to their chatter.

"I'm glad he's gone," said Reiko. "Prisoners eat your food, drink your water and drain your energy. You ask me, Arriette did that shifter a favour."

Arriette tried not to breathe so heavily.

She sympathised with most creatures no matter their history and had no reason to feel guilty for trying to help Coyote. Once she learned who he was and what his intentions were things seemed to just fall into place. They'd got as much information from him as possible first, so they weren't at a loss either.

"Reiko sure likes his cooking, huh?" Baby A whispered. She rolled closer and gestured with her eyes at the two men. "He thinks a lot about you."

"Which one?" asked Arriette. "They were both quick to scold me for my behaviour."

"We all care for you. Tobias, however, loves you deeply. He'd take you as his wife in better circumstances."

"You should get some sleep," said Arriette as she turned her back on the angel. "You need your strength."

Morning birdsong and a cool breeze roused Arriette from her slumber early. Tobias and Reiko had already begun breakfast and were skinning a rabbit they'd caught before sunrise.

"Your brother is loyal to his cause," said Tobias, "so you should be proud. Stefan is missed but he's being trained by the best for a battle we support or may even join."

"He fights for an everlast. What if he or she is as tainted as Falkon Lou? Or worse, is Falkon Lou!"

Reiko stuck his blade in the soil and stormed away, mumbling to himself.

Tobias sighed and continued until he noticed Arriette sit up and stretch her arms.

"What's wrong with him?" she asked.

"What's wrong with the rest of us, I suspect."

"Hunger?" Arriette stabbed a piece of meat. "He said something about Pandora in the night. I heard him dreaming."

Tobias fed the fire with another piece of wood.

"He's always been a sleep talker. He thinks Stefan fights for something we know too little about."

"You fought for me," said Arriette, "before you knew my destiny. Before any of this. Saved my life. How is Pandora any different?"

"Pandora is a Goddess," said Tobias. "Mythical. Fictional. It's blind faith. If her box was re-opened and has released more unknown evils on Haeylo, how do we fight? How do we fight Falkon Lou, a powerful everlast who wants the box for personal gain? With blades and magic? Soldiers' blood? Stefan's blood?"

"Perhaps our own blood," Arriette said, yawning. "We don't know what's on the horizon. We can only fight what we see in this present moment. Concentration should be on Falkon Lou and his rulecast. Stefan is safe and should be free to control his own life. As long as he wants to fight, we shouldn't interfere."

"If Falkon Lou is so powerful, how are a time-travelling angel, a dreamer, shifter, telepath, human and you going to defeat him?"

"Hey, we've got a vampyr too," Arriette said, laughing.

Tobias threw a piece of raw meat at her, which she froze with her telekinesis and re-directed to the fire to pre-heat for Baby A.

"The Recruit will help us," she said. "Casper is slowly training me. Reiko will practise potions today, just as I plan to practise my magic and my pronunciation. By the time we reach the city, we'll be ready."

"Herbal remedies won't kill an everlast," said Tobias.

"Perhaps not but they'll help heal those who try."

Tobias ran a hand through his hair.

"You've made your point. We're all valuable. Reiko has only his brother and the two of them were reunited by fate. He feels responsible for him."

"How so?"

"Casper took Reiko in having deserted his tribe. His influence led Stefan to do the same; he worshipped his older brother and couldn't just forget about him. So he followed. Reiko and I were out hunting on a beautiful summer morning and there he was, presented by Zïnnyi as a miracle."

Arriette peered over her shoulder at the troubled Reiko, naked from the waist up and carving branches into sharp points. Each scar was a reminder of a life he'd taken or a soul he'd saved with his spear. So many and in so few years.

"Reiko relies on his physical, not emotional strength. Saving his brother required sympathy and reason which of course he has– he's no brute– but doesn't fully understand how to use. Arm him with a spear however and he'll carve you a hole in Falkon's chest."

Tobias winked and handed Arriette her canteen.

"But you can't carve a hole in an everlast army single-handedly."

Several hours passed before Arriette found the courage to mention Pandora in Reiko's presence. They now travelled from High Man's Tree toward the city where she hoped to confront Falkon Lou's betrayal.

"Pandora was an Earthling," she said, her eyes fixated on Reiko's back. "Created by a man called Hephaestus under Zeus's orders. Fascinating, right?"

Reiko turned to face her and, still walking, scrunched up his nose and shrugged.

"You read too much."

When he turned back again, uninterested by how Pandora came to exist, Arriette caught Baby A's eye and scowled.

"It is said in Greek mythology," she continued, "that another man called Prometheus stole fire from Zeus and as a punishment, he gave Pandora to his brother, Epimetheus. As their wedding gift, he bestowed a box, though some refer to it as a jar, upon Pandora and said never to open it."

"Of course she opened it," said Reiko with his back to Arriette, "Released upon the world many evils, leaving only one thing in the box. I know the story. What's your point?"

"Some say the evils escaped as moths, fluttering across the world and poisoning happiness. Spreading disease and death. Personally, I think they were butterflies."

"Because?" Baby A asked.

"They're not quite as gentle as they look."

Reiko raised an eyebrow at Tobias who cringed and shook his head, denying all involvement in the conversation. What purpose did this lesson in Greek mythology have at a time like this? If Pandora was one of the original Recruit members, surely the creator saw goodness in her enough to offer a second chance?

Tobias was confused but curious to learn more himself. He gestured for Arriette to continue.

"The spirit of hope called to Pandora and so she opened it once more, releasing it to heal the wounds her first mistake had caused."

Reiko rolled his eyes. "All right, Arriette. You're trying to reassure me that placing my faith in Pandora's box is a good idea. You want me to know that whilst I couldn't save my brother, there is always hope he will save himself and others."

Arriette laughed. "Actually no, that's not the point of my story at all but it'll do. You did better on your own than with my prompt."

Tobias gave his friend a firm pat on the back and chuckled, following Arriette ahead into the trees.

"You did well back there," he said when they were far enough ahead. "Leading him to realise for himself."

"Oh you misunderstand," said Arriette, "in all honesty, my story was merely to raise the topic. I just fell lucky."

"Let's keep that between us." Tobias nudged her playfully. "When did Casper say we would meet the Recruit?"

"He didn't but we're not far off. His posture is tense, see? I'm so excited. I want to learn all about their abilities. The gaps in my Haeyloian research will finally be filled."

"They're going to adore you," he said, blushing. "If they have any sense."

Strong trees towered above them. Their trunks fat and heavy and their leaves luminous and healthy, exactly the way a planet should be, especially a miracle like Haeylo.

"You want to set up camp?" asked Tobias.

"I think so. This place speaks to me."

"Hmm, well the whistling wind between those trees tells me to be afraid," Tobias said, waving at the others to hurry.

Arriette could sense the eyes of the forest reading her soul, exposing her deepest, darkest secrets. There wasn't another creature for miles but somehow the clearing was alive with personality. She took Dion by the hand and led her through the trees to evaluate the perimeter. Desperate to hear the whispering of the trees, Arriette stepped as gently and as quietly as she could.

"Why do ya suppose Falkon wants access to the Underworld?" she asked.

"I think he already has that. Falkon seems to want to get his hands on us. I mean, first he starts with the city dwellers to raise panic and get word out that it's not safe there. Then Susan falls ill and Kalvin, hired by another everlast to find me—the next leader of the Recruit—to investigate, then to send an injured orc to stir up trouble all in the space of a few weeks? Not a coincidence. He's either trying to hinder us or harm us. I haven't decided yet."

"What 'bout Coyote's masta?" Dion asked.

"Most likely a demon, one of those horned brutes."

"The source of all evil?"

"That's Pandora," said Arriette.

"We can't be sure though."

"Zïnnyi wouldn't lead us into battle blind," Arriette said. "Both Baby A and I carry angelic blood; he'd find a way to warn us."

Dion kicked a pile of leaves and folded her arms. "Guess I should know this stuff."

"I can't rely on you for all evil knowledge just because you're a vampyr."

Defeated by her own lack of self-esteem, Dion sat on a fallen tree and sulked.

"Everyone seems to want to train ya in their gifts. They all 'ave talent and I'm just...me!"

"There isn't anything wrong with just being you, Dion. At times like this I'm grateful for it."

A rustle of leaves caused Dion to scramble to her feet. Arriette picked up a branch and edged forward, allowing Dion time to adjust her vision to the shadows between the trees. She'd already walked the perimeter and found nothing, but something or someone had been watching.

Dion's eyes lit up and her hair shimmered a fiery red, sticking out in all directions like sharp needles. Arriette backed away.

"Show yourself, retainer."

Out of the trees staggered a cautious Scarlett Evermay, out of breath and bleeding from deep wounds across her stomach. Dion caught her as she crumbled to the ground.

"I found you."

Dion pushed Arriette away. "Get the others!"

She ran as fast as her legs would carry her, calling her friends' names and shouting for help. By the time they had all returned, Scarlett was pale and weak. Her voice had faded to a croak.

Panicked, Dion glanced down at the blood-stained leaves she sat upon and asked if Arriette might take her place. It reminded her of her hunger. It was consuming and distracting.

Reiko emptied the contents of his bag on the ground and began mixing ingredients, throwing them one by one into his canteen and shaking it wildly.

"Reiko, can't you mix any faster?"

"Healing potions take time, Arriette!"

"Scarlett, can you hear me?" Arriette shook her, fumbling in her bag for the healing leaves. "Wake up, please!"

Coughing and wincing in agony, Scarlett fought for words. Reiko knelt beside her and shook a few drops of his finished shake onto her tongue.

"He sent me to find you."

"Who did? Who sent you?" Arriette examined her lower body and pressed the leaves down. Her clothing was ripped and coated with crimson. Claws had done this; distinct, ravenous claws.

"Who sent you, Scarlett?"

"Charles."

The group fell silent as the sound of howling wolves filled the air. Were these the eyes that followed them so closely? Had Arriette killed yet another innocent person? She couldn't fight back her tears for long.

"He asked me to tell you—he said I—I have to tell you—*eleven*."

Scarlett gasped for air. After a few more seconds of struggling, she closed her eyes and her body lay lifeless in Arriette's lap.

"Scarlett? I need you!"

Baby A pulled Arriette away gently by her shoulders and led her back to the campfire. The leaves were useless; a myth. Reiko handed her his canteen, which she drank quickly, inhaling the familiar scent with gratitude.

"I shouldn't be drinking this," she said, sniffling.

Reiko nudged the canteen to her lips once more.

"It'll calm your nerves."

"Arriette, there's a note here. It's from Charles." Tobias ran to her side and dropped to his knees. "I found it in her robes."

With shaking hands, she took it from him. "I can't—"

"Let me," said Baby A. "It's a warning, written in Haeyloian."

"What does it mean?" asked Dion.

"He says 'beware, the dark armies march on Haeylo City'. It's written in his hand," Casper translated.

Dion frowned. "What's on the back? There's a poem. That's his warning?"

"It's not for entertainment. It's by William Blake again," he said. "I think it's meant to tell us something:

'God appears and God is light, to those poor souls who dwell in night'.

So," he paused. "Any ideas?"

THIRTY

Having gathered their belongings and settled Scarlett's body safely on the cart, they abandoned the campsite and disappeared into the depths of the forest, wary that whatever had mauled their friend might return.

"What do ya think did that?" asked Dion.

"Wolves," said Arriette. "Can't you hear them? They're all around us."

Tobias jogged to her side and grabbed her by the shoulders. Arriette squirmed and flinched as the howling grew closer.

"Look at her pupils," he said to Casper. "We need to get her to Charles."

"We can't until we can work this out," said Pouki. "It's too dangerous to risk the city now."

"They're coming," said Arriette.

"There are no wolves," said Tobias.

"They're getting closer!"

Then she screamed.

Towering behind them and breathing heavily stood a fearsome brute with grey fur. Its long snout barely hid a set of shiny daggers.

Arriette pushed Tobias out of the way and into a tree, knocking him unconscious. Terrified, Baby A and Dion lifted Pouki and Reiko to safety, leaving Casper to morph and save himself. Arriette prepared for flight with Tobias. Predicting her plan, the animal growled and lunged for her ankles.

She strained to keep Tobias out of reach and flying as high

as she could given the weight, managed to escape the wolf's jaw.

"Where the hell did he come from?" Baby A asked, panting.

"I told you I heard wolves."

"We can't leave Scarlett, Arriette. Leaving her to be eaten is no funeral," Baby A said.

Arriette took a deep breath. "I saw Susan's coffin being lowered beneath the ground but then I'm told she's actually a vampyr. How can we be sure Scarlett will be laid to rest if I couldn't even manage to bury my best friend? He'll follow us if we try anything now anyway. She's dead, it's too late to save her. We'll come back for the cart."

Tobias groaned and opened his eyes.

"What happened?" Noticing the wolf, Tobias began to panic. "Whoa, Arriette, can't you fly any higher? There, set me down on that tree. I can dream myself wings."

"Not yet, you're still recovering."

Arriette swung Tobias over the top of the wolf's head and set off toward the campsite. She gestured for Baby A and Pouki to go in another direction and for Casper to stay. Dion and Reiko headed towards Haeylo City.

"See if there's any truth behind this note," said Arriette. "We'll distract the wolves and catch up with you later. It's vital that at least some of us reach the city alive."

"You want us to split up?" Baby A growled.

Arriette peered at her over her shoulder, then at the wolf.

"Got a better idea?"

She grumbled a few words in Haeyloian and set off with Pouki. The wolves dashed after them.

Casper paused until they were out of sight and followed Arriette back through the trees. She set Tobias down and landed gently beside him.

"Run, now!"

"Wolves aren't that smart," said Tobias.

"They weren't regular wolves," Casper corrected. "They were werewolves. They can calculate and organise."

"So what do we do now?" she asked.

"Casper, do you still have the message?"

Arriette snatched the note from Casper and unfolded it, absorbed by the hope of finding answers in his words.

"Any ideas, Casper?"

Casper stroked his beard in thought, pacing to clear his mind. Arriette imagined the cogs of his brain ticking and linking together.

"God appears and God is light," said Casper. "That's your first line."

"He must be talking about an enlightenment, Arriette," said Tobias. "Perhaps when we found you?"

Casper continued. "To those poor souls who dwell in night."

"Which souls?" asked Arriette. "The city folk?"

"As leader of the Recruit you'll have many souls to save," Casper said, "and it goes on. But does a human form display to those who dwell in realms of day."

Tobias tapped his foot. "Must be linked to the release of whatever Pandora's box held. What else could saving souls from the night relate to?"

"No, no," said Arriette, "It's too simple. Any fool can work this out. It can't be an encrypted message. It's in Haeyloian. Charles must know his enemies cannot read the language to send it like this. The message is supposed to be easy. We're reading too much into it. It's just a message!"

"About Falkon Lou perhaps?" said Casper. "Or his rulecast?"

Tobias groaned. "We've no time for a debate. Rulecasts are fluent, surely? What does the rest say?"

"Trust no one; darkness is coming."

Arriette snapped her fingers. "Back in Pouki's cabin Dion and I found some scrolls hidden under the bed."

"You were snooping?" Tobias said.

Casper rolled his eyes.

"Oh don't tell me you didn't expect it!" she said. "He left it all there on purpose. Anyway, one of them described the end of

Earth. Judgement Day, as some called it. Oh, what did it say? That's it, it was a poem by Harriet Foley! 'Light is thrown to and from the vault, joining darkness on the Underside. Calling angels fall with no aid and tears of their failure, uhm, drop as they cry'. Yes, that was it."

"Are you sure?" Casper asked.

"Close enough, give or take a few words. Compare the two sections; written by different poets but referring to the same phenomenon. Charles is trying to tell us that we're under threat of an apocalyptic event. God appears and God is light to those poor souls who dwell in night. It means they go to Heaven. But does a human form display to those who dwell in realms of day. I think it means that evil takes an unexpected form, one capable of walking in daylight. It's not demons and vampyrs we should be fearing!"

"Congratulations," said an unfamiliar voice. "You've solved your riddle."

The creature they faced was almost human with the same anatomy, but she seemed alien. Arriette couldn't place her face although she had definitely seen her somewhere before.

"Arriette Monroe. What a pleasure." She smiled.

"I'll be the judge of that."

"My name is Harriet. You don't need to be afraid of me. It's lovely to see you again, old friend," she said, wrapping her arms around Casper's waist. "I understand your hands are full so I'll get straight to the point. We need you to return early."

Arriette was instantly envious of Harriet's long blonde hair which draped over her shoulders and down her back like a golden waterfall. Her eyes were bright and her skin a refreshing peach. Her silver dress hugged each of her curves but her feet were hardly visible beneath it, and bare.

"Arriette, cast your mind back. You've researched Earth's history," Casper said. "This lady can help us. Harriet wrote the piece from Pouki's scroll. The one you just read."

Yes, she did remember, it was from Harriet's only work of fiction, based upon the creation of their planet.

"I'm quite harmless," she said.

"I've been deceived enough times in the past few weeks. You don't look human."

"Oh well I'm a little older than my books suggest." Harriet winked. "I'm not an everlast. I just improvised."

"I trust her," said Casper. "She's the temporary leader of the Recruit. Harriet and I haven't seen each other in such a long time. She taught me all I know about potion mixing. I was quite clueless. You may not know this but originally I was just a human, Arriette. Harriet has been very kind to me over the years."

"Human like me? There's a lot we don't know about each other. That needs to change."

"Well I have some news for my leader," Harriet said, passionless and inconsiderate of Arriette's emotional state.

Casper's motivation increased. "Are you referring to me?"

"The job is rightfully yours." She cast a cautious glance at Arriette, then raised her brow and sucked her teeth. "For now, that is."

"Is this news related to Scarlett Evermay?" Arriette asked.

"Partially. If the sender of that message used my work, I deserve to know the name of the plagiariser."

"Charles Melovich."

"Oh, well he's a good man," Harriet said. "Did you meet him, Arry?"

"It's Arriette, and yes I did."

Harriet forced a smile. "I heard about that nasty accident with two civilians. I'm glad you've recovered, though."

Arriette made it clear with her silence that her accident and their travels were of no concern to Harriet.

"What was the initial message?"

"Eleven," said Casper.

"A rather obvious meaning, although using my poem is a brain-scratcher," said Harriet.

"Did a werewolf kill Scarlett then?" Tobias interrupted.

"Given the distant howls, it would appear so. We have your

cart, by the way. I've asked my friends to take a look at her body, but werewolves are excellent trackers so they probably recognised a scent and followed that. It only takes one of our three moons to be full and they're forced to change physically. It's unfortunate that they're classed as demonic in their wolf form, too, because during the day they're a lot like everyone else. It might be somebody you know, Arriette."

"I doubt it."

"Aww why?" Harriet asked tilting her head. "Are you a little short on friends?"

Arriette ground her teeth.

Is Casper blind?

"They don't remember much of what happens in their animal form so friends and family members are alerted at the earliest suspicion," she explained. "These beasts can't distinguish between strangers, enemies and loved ones. It's more of a curse than a gift."

"I suppose they must be bitten," Arriette grumbled.

"That depends. But werewolves are not why I'm here."

"Perhaps not but they are relevant," Tobias said. "If they follow scent, somebody could have unleashed them on Scarlett's trail to kill her before she reached us. It's Susan's death all over again."

Baby A's feet landed between them with a thud and she tucked her wings away, brushing her clothing with disgust. She set Pouki down gently and grumbled, tucking her hair behind her ears to reveal the Thurisaz and Isa runes on her neck that identified her as a time-traveller with power over space and time. Arriette wondered if and when she'd be getting hers. She wished Baby A could rewind time to avoid ever meeting this Earthling because Arriette didn't trust her.

"Well thank you for the information, Harriet. I did plan to question Scarlett about a first-class everlast named Falkon. Now she's dead I guess that's out of the question."

"I guess so."

Harriet turned to Casper as if to mark the end of her interest in her new leader.

"The Recruit would like to meet your new pet. They feel she is of great importance to this impending war."

"Then why did they send you?" asked Pouki. "You're only a scale ten and it's dark out; there are Vamps and demons and wolves on the prowl."

Harriet frowned. "Well, my telepathic friend, I can be very persuasive. Besides, during our time apart my knowledge of magic has increased my influence. I hold a rather powerful position now, covering for our MIA leader." Harriet lifted her dress to show her very own Uruz rune, symbolising a manifestation of power. "Not bad, huh?"

"Obviously you have been doing a fine job," said Casper, smiling. "If Zïnnyi blessed you with a supe birthmark—an unusual gift for a wiccan."

"How so?" asked Arriette.

"Because, leader-to-be, wiccans are not born, we are taught."

"So how did you know he was a telepath?"

Baby A cut in. "It's an identification spell. I can smell it. Helps her read other people's gifts and evaluate the threat."

Harriet grinned. "Oh, now there's no need for vicious insinuations, angel. Pouki and I have met before so I have little need for magic tricks." She lowered her voice. "He's never liked me, still, this lovely little tattoo of mine no longer offers him that choice."

"I can't trust somebody from the old world no matter how much knowledge or experience they bring. Runic marking or not, your Earthling mind is complex and different. I too can smell your magic so please spare us your lectures on trust."

"Casper is also different from yourselves in many ways," she said. "Yet you do not accuse his knowledge of being tainted."

"My friends are right, Harriet. It's not safe for a lonesome wiccan woman alone in the forest, especially one so low on the scale. No offence intended," Casper said interrupting a conversation he wasn't yet ready to have.

"None taken, my leader. However, despite this lovely chat, I was never alone. Carter's with me."

Harriet held out her hand and from the air appeared a tall, thin gentleman with black chin stubble and beautiful hazel eyes. Beneath his right eye sat a black J; Eiwaz was the most difficult of runes to decode, as it's meaning could be misinterpreted. Arriette remembered from a book that it was a process of spiritual becoming, meaning Jet held control of more than one plain.

Perhaps when he disappeared, he reappeared elsewhere.

His image unfolded from nothing, creating a perfect three-dimensional grown man. Arriette had to close her jaw at his awe-inspiring power.

"Jet Carter at your service, Miss Monroe."

"You're—"

"Invisible, yeah," he said, disappearing again and taking Harriet with him. "A rare gift I am honoured to own. Of course, I would be pleased to demonstrate at a later, safer, time."

Arriette waved her hand in wonder, feeling nothing but the cool Haeyloian air.

Invisibility. Was that one of the two missing powers from the Haeyloian scale, making Jet Carter either a five or an eleven? Powerful, or pitiful.

"He's a five," Pouki corrected, violating her privacy, "and he shouldn't be spending time with this woman. His gift can be put to better use."

"I can pass right through you!" said Tobias, fascinated. "I'm stunned. What else can you do?"

"Tobias, that's enough," said Pouki. "There will be plenty of time to make friends later. If this Earthling has quite finished showing off I believe there are Recruit supes for our new leader to meet. Perhaps then we can get some solid answers with regards to the opening of Pandora's box and this imminent war."

"The box has been opened, there's not much we can do about that now," said Harriet. "There is much you have still to learn from Scarlett's message and more still from my teachings. This I can remedy, however, I'm afraid before we can train our new recruit she must first meet her followers."

"Scarlett's death will be in vain if we brush aside Charles's message. The city will suffer for our ignorance," said Arriette. "Can't the Recruit wait just one more day?"

"What, and miss your briefing on the fascinating Recruit organisation?" Harriet laughed. "My dear Arriette, no matter your status, wealth, scale, runic identification or power, the Recruit wait for no one and nor will this war. Pandora's box is back and with it, endless possibilities arise. Aren't you the slightest bit curious?"

THIRTY—ONE

Arriette didn't want to admit her jealousy but beneath her confident exterior, inside she was screaming. Baby A's power outranked Harriet's but even the gorgeous angel couldn't concentrate with this creature hovering around Casper like a moth to a flame.

Pouki and Harriet agreed to leave each other alone for the time being and resolve their personal issues in privacy. Arriette was grateful—although curious about Pouki's grudge—because amongst the current chaos the last thing she needed was yet another fight to resolve.

Baby A cleared her throat. "So Harriet, how have you lived for so long? Shouldn't you be all wrinkled and frail by now?" She nudged Arriette and giggled. "Or dead?"

"I asked a friend of mine to cast the spell back on Earth when President Kaines got himself killed. It's a basic chant, but effective. She made me a temporary everlast."

"They can be murdered or forfeit their gift though," said Tobias. "And none possess your markings."

"There are boundaries to my abilities."

"Like?" asked Baby A.

"True love."

Arriette choked on her own saliva. "You can't fall in love?"

"It's like a fairy tale true love's first kiss deal."

"Oh, so you can love but not kiss," Tobias said.

"You got it."

With Tobias and Arriette's current relationship status, she

was pleased the wiccan would never be able to express any attraction she had for the handsome dreamer.

Arriette promised herself Tobias wouldn't like the skinny blonde anyway because they were practically engaged (in her over-imaginative head).

Harriet walked ahead with Casper as they shared old stories, whilst Tobias, Baby A and Arriette trudged behind like forgotten slaves.

She was used to being second best with Kalvin and to some extent her mother. They lived detached and contrasting lives, and Ma valued her own more than Arriette's or so it now seemed. Now, though, seemingly second best to Casper's new best friend, Arriette's scar burned with envy.

Baby A placed an arm around her waist and squeezed.

"I hate her already," she hissed, and they both burst into laughter. "Imagine that! She lures a boy into her chambers, takes advantage and all the time their lips never touch? Shame on any man who shares a bed with her."

Arriette had a disgusting thought and shuddered at the idea of Harriet and Casper ever sharing a bedroom. The probability didn't settle her stomach.

"You don't think—"

She gestured toward the two of them and Baby A's face mimicked Arriette's. She faked a gag and cringed.

"Casper's a respectable gentleman."

"I'm not so sure. He must have been a reckless young man at some point and if she never ages, perhaps they crossed paths," Arriette said.

"On Earth maybe but his duties have been far too important for him to be immature and risk his own safety here. He's survived this long," Baby A said.

Arriette frowned. "I don't think I understand."

"Oh, you don't know," she said.

"I can see where you're going with this," moaned Tobias. "I'll be over there."

Arriette frowned at him. "Tobias, is this something else you forgot to tell me? I'm only human—I can't read your mind!"

"One-fifth human," Baby A corrected.

"Do you want to tell me then, considering how long I've been oblivious to who our leader actually is?"

She sighed, "I can't. I only know the basics."

"The basics will do."

"What have I gotten myself into? Okay, you should probably sit down."

Arriette called to the others for a quick rest stop so Baby A could begin an engaging conversation about their wise leader.

They were travelling in the direction of Haeylo City and soon the forest would become denser and more dangerous. Baby A and Arriette slung their things down against a tree and perched on top of them, keeping an eye out for more wolves.

Arriette inhaled deeply to calm her anxiety and sipped from the canteen Tobias threw her, insisting she stay hydrated. Her skin was slick with sweat and her thighs throbbed from the exercise.

The group were missing two vital members: Dion and Reiko. They were already on the way to the city. When dawn came, Dion would need a light-tight bed and Reiko would be alone in the forest.

Arriette thought Dion might like to meet the wonderful Harriet Foley and her companion Jet Carter. She also predicted she'd hiss and take Arriette's side. If Casper trusted Harriet then everyone else should too. Still, vampyrs had a faultless sense for evil because they were the definition of it. So if her new room mate decided she didn't like the sarcastic wiccan, then in advance Arriette had chosen which side to take.

"Casper began on Earth as a human, Arriette. He's an old man; coming to the end of his lifespan on Haeylo."

"Humans abandoned the old planet thousands of years ago. Casper's only eighty," Arriette said, trying to calculate if this was even possible. "I know he said he was originally human but I never imagined he was an Earthling."

"He's been present since the beginning of time, at the request of Zïnnyi. Casper isn't aware I know, though, and you can't tell him. As an angel I'm fed images and information as you are too. I've used this little trick on several occasions but according to my source, Casper's been here forever."

"How can that be?"

She shrugged. "Most beings who are partially human don't live further than their eighties. Casper's fairly healthy and active for his age so I have a feeling he's good for another few years."

"Harriet has a spell cast upon her, perhaps Casper is the same? Did you ask your source of information?" she queried.

Baby A gestured to the clouds and Arriette nodded, getting the point, then sagged against the tree, dirtying her dress.

"All-knowing, but not all-telling," she frowned. "I don't know much more. Sorry."

"So he might be anybody?"

Baby A gasped. "Casper is a dear friend of mine and would never hurt his family."

"I'm not accusing him of anything," Arriette explained. "All I'm saying is you can't be only eighty and live for thousands of years. Do the math."

She flung her hands out in frustration and Baby A nodded, understanding how aggravating Casper's story truly was.

"You're right and I'm sorry. There's something he's not telling us."

Arriette said. "I'm just suspicious, is all."

Baby A rubbed her eyes. "He withheld that for your own good. I'm beginning to understand why. You're not very trusting, are you?"

"I'm not quite there yet," she said. "Remember, I had no choice in this ordeal. I'm here because I have to be, not necessarily because I want to be. Now you'll have to fill me in on Casper's history. You know more than you're letting on, Baby A."

The angel glanced over at Casper, deep in conversation with Harriet. They were a perfect match and yet complete opposites. Wise, ancient and on the correct side but secretive, conservative and abrupt in their own right.

"If he's been the leader of the Recruit for so long, it's obvious he's waited for you to appear, Arriette. He wanted to be sure you were the one before disclosing his identity. His prolonged existence is all because of you. I'm almost one hundred percent sure of his motives," she reasoned. "I think he's waiting for the right time to tell us he began on Earth and not Haeylo. We know nothing of his parents or of any children he had. There's got to be something stopping him."

"Why haven't you told me this previously? Why not tell Tobias and Reiko, or Dion? They're your friends!"

"I'm not supposed to repeat it," she cringed. "I have orders. Shouldn't have told you, either. I only hope He forgives me."

Arriette twiddled her fingers, praying for a similar ability. If Baby A had orders then Arriette would need a source of her own to be sure they weren't hiding anything else.

"Casper will explain eventually, right?"

Baby A shrugged. "When you take over leadership you'll need these facts for the safety and protection of your followers. If he refuses he'd be putting his family at risk."

"People shouldn't lie to me so much," she huffed.

Arriette picked up her possessions and scurried over to Tobias who attempted to remove a thorn from his leg. She knelt beside him to offer assistance but he only shooed her away and grumbled.

"Mind your business. Have you finished telling tales, Baby A?"

She growled. "Tobias, don't be ridiculous."

"What's the story from the sky this time?"

Arriette yanked the thorn from his skin and he let out a yelp. "Ouch!"

"You deserved that. Baby A's information comes directly from our creator so we can't start picking fault. Now mind *your* business. What happened to you?"

"Whilst you dawdled, I tumbled down a hill into a rose bush. Stupid boots have no grip."

"Where's Casper?"

Tobias rubbed his wound and gathered his things.

"Gee, thanks for asking Arriette. I'm fine by the way, I just slipped in the mud."

"Don't act like I don't care, Tobias."

He paused. "They set off walking a few minutes ago. I think Harriet asked for some alone time."

"I asked for a break. It's not safe for us to—"

A nervous sensation in her stomach caused Arriette to hunch over suddenly. The scar tissue along her spine creaked and then gave way, producing her wings without warning.

"What the—" Tobias examined her wings. "They've grown! Where did they come from? I thought you'd learned to control them?"

Arriette shushed him and called to Pouki who'd lagged behind.

Together they stalked the area, listening for snapping twigs and rustling leaves. Then her eyes settled on a well-camouflaged old friend. There, in the trees, backed by the wolf they'd encountered earlier, crouched three werewolves who hid low and watched their every move.

Wolves were great at tracking prey through scent and as they hadn't showered since leaving Drakonta, they left a defined trail.

Casper and Harriet were nowhere to be seen and neither was Jet. Arriette began to panic.

"What are we going to do?" whispered the telepath. "We can't outrun them. Did you know about this?"

Arriette gently edged over to him. "Didn't you read my mind?"

"You told me not to! What's happening?"

"I think somebody prompted my wings. We're being helped," Arriette replied, gesturing at the sky. "Baby A, I'd say He's cool with you telling me Casper's little secret."

"Secret?" Tobias asked. "What secret?"

"Mind your business," Baby A said, sneering.

The wolves' intentions were obviously food but why hadn't they pounced yet? They had the advantage.

"Getting anything? Images, sounds, emotions?" Arriette asked Pouki, ignoring Tobias.

"Anger and excitement," Pouki replied.

"Damn."

"Picking up on their hunger too," he said.

"Double damn."

"We're running out of time," he muttered through clenched teeth. "Do something."

Arriette closed her eyes and pounced, lifting the telepath with ease out of the way. Baby A and Tobias sat relatively close to one another and so Tobias's life would be saved until he'd managed to dream his own wings. Still in pain and distracted by his head injury, he could only shrug when she challenged the delay. He hadn't strained his powers like this in several years, Baby A reminded her.

Having two sets of wings was a handy addition to their collective abilities.

Casper could morph, Jet might become invisible, but Arriette had not thought of how to get a message to them.

They hadn't expected another attack.

The first wolf lunged and ripped the sole of Arriette's right shoe clean off before she had gained enough height to eliminate the threat.

The second wolf ran at speed for Baby A who spread her wings, hopped above his head and gripped Tobias's jacket with difficulty. Each beast circled below its hunt whilst the third sniffed the ground and took off on Casper's path, galloping clumsily to the trees.

"Tobias I need your help. Together, we're going to lift Casper, Harriet and Jet into the air. Now focus, I know your leg stings but I need you."

"What?" he spluttered. "Arriette there are three of them and only two of us. Our minds can't take the weight for more than a matter of minutes. I'm not performing well at the moment. I wouldn't trust—"

"A few minutes is all we need, Tobias. Have you got any other ideas? You need to try. Please."

Baby A cried, her face straining under the pressure of Tobias's weight on her muscles.

Pouki growled. "Tobias, just do it before it's too late."

Arriette closed her eyes and imagined the three group members hovering at an elevation out of reach of the hungry wolf. Arriette hadn't seen their surroundings so the imagery was a little blurry outside of her friends' bodies. She peaked once or twice to be sure Tobias took part and as instructed his eyes were firmly closed. Usually, his confidence allowed him to dream with his beautiful brown eyes open but given the pain from his fall, he'd opted to squeeze them shut.

Their minds became one and she felt his consciousness lock with her own. They were able to read each other's thoughts for a while; Arriette had to control her strong feelings for him. She stifled a laugh when his thoughts drifted to barbecued chicken and ale.

At a time like this?

The pressure and strain of three bodies on their abilities joined them emotionally and Arriette wondered if the task in Drakonta had been more stimulating, would this have also happened at Ma's. If two dreamers imagined similar events, the dreams normally collided and offset so Arriette was grateful for their mental union. Then the pressure died down and their eyes flicked open in panic.

Had they failed; fed their friends to a werewolf?

Arriette's muscles tingled and she struggled not to lose her grip of Pouki.

"They're in the air," said Tobias. "I feel them fighting it. Not sure how long I can hold up though."

"Baby A, Arriette, swap loads."

Baby A laughed. "Oh you're hilarious, Pouki!"

"I'm not joking. They need to keep this going for as long as possible. Their touch will enhance their powers. We can do this."

"How am I going to pass Tobias to Arriette and receive you without the dream failing and the four of us falling to our deaths?" she groaned, spitting each word at him with revolt.

Arriette sighed. "Less arguing, more attempting."

"But—"

"Baby A, Pouki's right. We have to try."

It would have been too dangerous to pass them slowly back and forth but she and Baby A were reasonably strong following Zïnnyi's recent blessing. Angels were natural survivors; programmed to rescue innocent people. Arriette had supposedly been prepared to lead the Recruit.

If they couldn't manage then nobody could.

"Don't squirm. We're going to throw you."

"No, wait—"

Tobias wriggled and Baby A had to tighten her clasp. She shook him and scowled.

"Tobias, stop it! I don't want to drop you."

"I can't help it. I don't like being manhandled."

"You have no choice," said Arriette. "You haven't used your power to a shifting level in years. Unless you can re-train your body to obey such a difficult dream in the next twenty seconds, you'll need to trust us."

Baby A added, "Don't give up trying. It might help if you can make yourself a bit lighter."

Arriette gestured for Baby A to fly higher. If they did have an accident and the boys plummeted, they needed enough time to catch them again before landing in the jaws of a predator.

"On the count of three. One, two..."

The girls began to swing their partners.

Pouki squawked and tucked his arms and legs in tight. Although Tobias remained silent Arriette had to chuckle at his reaction. For a hunter, hiding your face in your hands was a cowardly thing to do.

Baby A flew toward Arriette a little and caught Pouki perfectly in both hands, cradling him close and comforting him as he hyperventilated. He wrapped his arms around her neck for safety.

"Scary as hell," he moaned.

"Tell me about it," said Tobias.

She cringed, realising she'd caught him upside down by his left boot. Arriette leaned to grip his belt. It was an awkward few minutes of manoeuvring and cursing but eventually, she managed to haul him into her arms.

Now that they were joined physically as well as mentally they kept a tight telekinetic hold of their friends who by now would be wondering why they were levitating.

"They're still going to follow us but if we can find and notify the others whilst they're in the air then we can arrange a meeting place of some kind. Tobias, keep trying. We might need an extra pair of wings again at this rate."

Arriette called out for Casper and a short while passed before they caught up with them. They sat frozen in the air and were squabbling over how to get down, each of them trying a spell or a movement and failing.

"What's this about?" Harriet asked. "I can levitate on my own."

Casper agreed. "Why all the unnecessary force?"

"That's why!"

Baby A and Pouki pointed to the three vicious beasts and immediately Jet began to panic. The wolves began to snap at the air, hoping to catch another part of a shoe or even worse, one of their toes.

"Where d-did they c-come from?" Jet asked.

"Beats me. It's a good job someone was watching us." Baby A gestured to the sky. "We'd never have noticed the threat. They're learning."

"They've been monitoring us," said Casper. "Our previous escape meant taking to the skies so they waited until we weren't together and ambushed us."

"Then ate my shoe," Arriette grumbled.

"It's a small price to pay," said Pouki.

"Tobias and I are going to release Harriet and Casper in a moment. The second our power begins to fade use your own to levitate and morph."

"What about me?" asked Jet, panicking.

"When you're released, turn invisible. I'll lower you to the ground as far as I can. Follow us on the surface. Jet, if they can pass right through you you're safer than any of us."

Arriette and Tobias released their power once they had gained everybody's agreement. Casper became an eagle and Harriet remained in the air as her regular, irritating, attractive self. Jet turned invisible and screamed all the way to the forest floor but using his initiative kept his mouth shut when his feet touched the surface.

"Meeting place suggestions?"

Harriet held up a hand. "I have an idea."

Baby A rolled her eyes. "Of course you do."

"The Recruit need to speak with their leader. Why not meet at the lair? I'm sure there's somebody there who can answer your questions. We'll fly above the treetops so the wolves can't see or track us on foot."

With her scar aching less and less, Arriette was certainly getting the hang of her angelic ability but as Baby A explained earlier, she had the privilege to speak to a much higher source than any everlast. Would Arriette be able to do the same without letting her friends down?

Casper silently built a barrier between Arriette and the blonde wiccan as they moved steadily toward their new destination.

Perhaps she needed to keep negative thoughts about that woman hidden. You just couldn't predict the havoc she'd be facing next, especially if born from her own dreams.

The wolves were nowhere around so their plan had been successful, which calmed Arriette enough to exercise her wings more and venture higher, move faster and begin to have some fun.

"You know, we ought to notify Dion and Reiko that we'll be

late to the city," suggested Baby A. "They'll worry."

"Who are these humans you speak of?" asked Harriet.

"Dion is a vampyr and Reiko may be human but he's one of my best friends," Baby A snapped.

She enquired with such disgust and such distaste. These people had names and they were her friends; loyal, brave and kind friends. Harriet was a face Arriette was beginning to distrust.

"You're friends with Vamps?"

"With one," Baby A corrected. "As a matter of fact, from next month she will be Arriette's new room mate. Dion is a vegetarian."

"No such thing," Harriet said.

Arriette carried her weight to Harriet's side and nudged against her body to gain co-operation. She could feel Pouki pulling the emotions from her mind as she spoke without thinking and she wondered how tempted he was to join in, given their tendency to argue.

"Listen, Dion and Reiko are family, and when you insult my family you're insulting me, the next leader of the Recruit. As far as I'm aware, that's not the type of supernatural activity you should be looking to trigger. So before I say something I'm going to regret, please just direct us to the hideout and let's get this over with."

Casper's mouth fell open in awe. She was always so quiet and in control of her opinions but Harriet had, he agreed, gone a step too far.

"Arriette, mind your manners."

"No," Harriet said, now hovering above a clearing in the trees. "It's fine, Casper. I spoke out of turn."

The river ran through the middle of Manaia Forest and as the land was higher in the east than the west, water tumbled down, crashing against rocks to create a gentle flowing waterfall.

Arriette hadn't expected Casper to crack Harriet around the back of the head and order an apology for acting so childishly. When he didn't Arriette wished she had a hand free to beat him to it.

Harriet gestured below the group and in unison they each tilted their heads.

"The entrance to our lair is down there."

"Over the river?"

"I don't care where the lair is," Tobias grumbled. "I'll be glad to get my feet on the ground!"

"You'll be getting them wet, dreamer," Harriet replied. "The entrance to our lair is a short swim under water."

Baby A laughed. "Did you say under water?"

"But anyone could swim there," Arriette said.

"Demons can't swim," she explained. "There's no water in the Underworld."

"Vamps like the water," Baby A said.

"That's why this entrance only opens during daylight. We've thought of everything and have survived long enough to test the theory."

Dion would have been digging a hole as they spoke so she could understand Harriet's logic behind only allowing an entrance during the day.

Jet reappeared beneath and waved them down.

"You lot coming, or not?" he yelled.

Baby A and Arriette lowered the boys to the ground. Tobias flexed and stretched, whilst Pouki tidied his beard and retracted his nosey power from Arriette's head. The aching in her skull vanished.

"Arriette, I can't swim," he said.

"But—"

"I'll wait here."

"Oh no you wont," said Harriet. "The strong male will pull you through."

"The strong male has an issue with that," snapped Tobias. "People who can't swim panic in the water. Pouki's my family but I won't risk being drowned because of his fear."

"The boy is right," agreed Pouki.

"So you'll wait here alone?" Casper asked. "Isn't that risky?"

"The sun is almost up so I'll be perfectly safe," Pouki said.

"But you can't read the minds of evil," Baby A pointed out. "How will you sense their presence?"

"I cannot read demonic minds but orcs I can manage. Besides, I'm old and experienced enough to take care of myself I assure you."

Harriet stepped between Pouki and Arriette, offering a hand which she evidently ignored.

"Shall we?"

"I suppose I don't have a choice," said Arriette.

"Take a few deep breaths and jump. Swim beneath the waterfall and through the tunnel. Move quickly and relax. There's a cave at the other side."

"Arriette, you'll go first," said Jet. "They've been expecting you. We'll follow when you're at the other side."

Arriette cast an eye over to Pouki who winked to indicate he'd be safe alone. Being surrounded by active minds often swallowed him and Pouki, like any human on Haeylo, needed time to ponder thoughts and reflect on his own chaotic life. She envied him.

"See you on the other side then."

Arriette hopped off the rock and into the water like a pencil. The river was surprisingly cold and fast flowing and she fought against the current to steer for the waterfall, diving deeper until she located the tunnel.

She bobbed up for a gasp of air and then plunged below the surface. Then, lacking self-confidence she swam the length of the underwater chamber until a beacon of light enticed her to move faster.

Arriette kicked her limbs and pushed off the bottom with her feet once she'd entered the cavern.

After wiping her eyes and smoothing her drenched hair back from her face, Arriette realised she'd been treading water in a small pool, big enough for only five or six people but deep enough for twice that. The walls were covered in child-like drawings and she swam toward them for a closer look.

"If my eyes deceive me," said a quiet voice.

Arriette swirled in the water in search of company.

To the left stood a small, plump boy of around sixteen or seventeen years of age. He wore a long, pointed hat and his face was covered with netting that hung from the rim. His robes were of a similar grey shade and the boy's feet were bare.

"Who are you?"

The boy smiled. "My name is Sky. I can't believe you're actually here."

Sky knelt at the side of the pool and offered a hand. Arriette swam over and gratefully took hold as he hauled her out of the water. Off came the robes and straight around her shoulders. Beneath them, he wore a plain white shirt and black shorts.

"You have an unusual name."

"My birth name is Sebastian Sky, but I prefer Sky."

"I'm Arriette, but you already knew that," she smiled. They exchanged a firm handshake. "What do you do here? Are you in the Recruit?"

"I took the place of my father. He was murdered by a spirit demon before I was born. My mother believed him to be fighting a war and so came to the Recruit for help. They saw goodness in her heart and found her a home within these caves. I was born here."

"Your father must have been a wonderful man."

"He was a very powerful sorcerer," he said. "These robes belonged to him."

"Like a wizard?"

The boy laughed. "Yes, Arry, like a wizard."

"Oh, Arriette, please."

"My apologies, Arriette."

She dismissed the mistake. "You're one too?"

"Becoming a sorcerer is an art, not a gift. I studied for years to learn every trick and detail. Harriet said I am a valued member and that I am to train the latest potion master. I'm quite excited."

"A potion what?"

Sky led Arriette to a painting on the cave wall of what looked like a stick man stood by a large bowl. Steam was rising and forming shapes in the air, some easy to figure, others much more difficult.

"This is the potion master. Here he lives by a cauldron mixing potions for use in warfare, medicine and to enhance the powers of each member. The potion master is elected when the new leader is crowned. They decide who is worthy of the mixer's job."

"So when I lead they'll get their job from me?"

"Exactly. Current Recruit members can be made exempt from the ability to apply as they already play a vital role and carry a lot of responsibility."

Arriette shivered. "How do I choose someone within the lair if they have all got such huge responsibilities already?"

Sebastian Sky frowned. "I'm not sure—"

"Well if I have to choose a Recruit member, there are only eleven of us and surely random people don't deserve the position; how is this a fair judgement of capability?"

"Arriette, there are hundreds of people here not just the eleven members."

"But, this is the hideout of the Recruit."

Sky laughed and patted Arriette's shoulder. The unexpected jolt sent her stumbling forward.

"You've got much to learn about us, Arriette. There are eleven powerful members as chosen by Zïnnyi– if you remember the stories. Andrew Kaines was given the original responsibility of finding them, but many humans and other creatures join to support what we do and how we plan to save Haeylo. We've built ourselves an army."

Sky led Arriette to another painting which was above a hairline crack in the stone wall. This man held what looked like half a circle over his head. It reminded Arriette of a rainbow.

"Here is the entrance to the Recruit, Arriette."

Baby A popped up above the water. She gasped and flapped to keep afloat then paddled to the edge. Her wings were extended and she shuddered with fright.

Arriette couldn't imagine how she had fit through the narrow tunnel with such a wide wing span, but they looked like useful paddles.

"Harriet's a liar! Short swim my—"

"Come on, let's get you dry," Sky said.

Arriette laughed and moved Sky's cloak from her shoulders to the angel's. She looked drowned and tired.

"Who's this?"

"Oh, Sebastian Sky meet Baby A."

Baby A gave him the nod of approval and scrambled to her feet, slipping on the rock and sliding into her friend. Arriette grabbed her shoulders and the girls giggled.

"That right there is the entrance to their lair."

She grunted. "A crack in a wall?"

There was a splash in the water but no visible body. Arriette realised Jet had been next in the queue.

Being invisible wasn't completely fool proof as the cool temperature had triggered a flickering fault in his power.

He reappeared and nodded to acknowledge her.

"Hey Sky, how are you?" Jet said, looking past the others. "Everything all right inside?"

"Much better now she's here."

Arriette cringed. "I'm nothing special, believe me!"

"She's lying," said Tobias, emerging and doing backstroke through the water. "She's just as amazing as the scripts predicted, if not more so."

"I agree," Baby A said. "If anyone can win over the hearts of the Haeylo inhabitants, Arriette can." She paused. "Hey, where's Harriet?"

The gathering of wet supernatural travellers shivered on the banks of the pool but the one whom she suspected the most of having a split personality never joined them. When Arriette enquired it turned out she had decided to remain behind with Pouki for his safety.

Either that or to brutally murder the poor telepath.

If she worked for their suspects, Harriet needed to rid the gang of their mind reader first. After all, he'd be the only one to suspect any fowl play. But Arriette was new here and accusing people on her side wouldn't be the best start. Pouki could defend himself.

Jet moved up to the crack and placed a hand at either side. He gazed upon the symbol above the stone and whispered the word Indalo. Their surroundings shook and the two halves began to slide away. Beyond the cave, a well lit passage led to a low door with a wooden frame.

"What's Indalo?" Arriette asked Sky as they all trudged down the passageway, dripping.

The group jumped in unison when the cave slid closed behind them.

"A bridge between man and God; Indalo is the symbol for a vault of the Heavens."

"Why is it above the tunnel?"

"Because we are God's messengers. The Recruit provide a safe, reliable journey from the evils of the real world and every human being's destiny," Sky explained, "to their peaceful deaths."

Baby A placed a hand on her shoulder.

"He's referring to Heaven," she said.

"You explained that people went to Heaven or Hell determined by their behaviour," she said, "back at the cabin."

"The angel is correct. The Recruit's purpose is to rid Haeylo of evil by any means necessary and deliver all humans safely to Heaven. You may only enter our little universe if you understand the concept," Sky smiled.

Sebastian stopped at the door and turned to face them. He held out a hand, gesturing Arriette be the first to enter.

Her heart raced. The moment Hof truth.

What if they didn't like her?

What if the resistance thought the Recruit's progress might plummet if they named her the next rightful leader?

"I, I—"

"You'll do just fine," he smiled. "Ladies first."

Arriette turned the door knob and pushed forward. Beneath her feet grew fresh, luminous blades of grass and little white daisies. There were trees; tall and stunning to witness in bloom and children played around a picnic. They pointed at the strangers and tried to shake Arriette's hand until their mothers pulled them back, allowing the group to pass.

The Recruit's habitat truly was a sanctuary and Arriette wanted to lay down and cover herself in its purity.

In the distance she saw a castle with high built walls and tall towers. Stained glass windows sparkled in the sunlight. She couldn't believe the intense detail in the architecture.

Where am I?

Where did the brilliant sun shine from? Why were there blue skies and fluffy clouds under the ground?

Sat upon the horizon, offices stood proud and through their glass structures Arriette saw people running up and down the stairwells. Other buildings looked homely with thatched roofs.

Both men and women roamed free without the fear of being bitten or enslaved.

"An alternate universe," said Jet, "created by God at the beginning to provide the eleven unique powers with a safe place to blossom, reproduce and live happily. This is where it all began, Arriette; it's our Garden of Eden, our base."

"I feel, well, I don't know what I feel." Arriette gasped. "I'm stunned. Mystified!"

"No, the word is relaxed," said Baby A, yawning. "It's such a quiet, peaceful place. Right, Tobias?"

"It's almost as if we don't have anything to worry about," he replied.

Jet smiled. "You don't. Come on, I'll show you around."

THIRTY—TWO

"How big is this place?" Baby A asked the sorcerer with wide eyes.

"As big as your imagination," replied Sky.

Sebastian removed his pointy hat to give Arriette a better view of his face. Without the net, the boy's skin looked flawless and smooth. He had long auburn hair, light eyebrows and his nose was pointed, but small compared to his emerald green saucer eyes.

"Dreamers use their thoughts to create new buildings and facilities for us to use. Jet, lead the way."

The group followed him through the grass and past more cheerful children playing throw and catch with their families around a midday feast. Outside the lair, dawn drew closer, but in the lair the sun was bright and hot.

Arriette glanced at her damaged shoes and came to a halt. The others stopped behind to watch as she leaned down and untied the laces. She scrunched up her toes in the meadow's soft green grass and, embarrassingly, began to cry.

Sebastian rushed to her. "Are you hurt?"

"No, it's exactly as I imagined. I can't believe I'm walking through a replica of Earth. I'm overwhelmed."

The gang were reduced to tears one by one.

"Is this supposed to be such an emotional experience?" she asked Jet, "Am I being silly?"

"It happens every time for those too used to evil."

"I want the whole planet to taste this freedom," she said.

When entering the Recruit's city, Arriette's eyes widened at the red brick buildings and cobbled streets. A town hall stood beaming at the end of the way and Recruit followers gathered by a clock tower in the centre of a small square.

She passed by each shop window in awe of what they had created; a peaceful working city in which life could bloom without crime, hatred or death.

"I want this for the rest of Haeylo."

Arriette flung out her arms and twirled around in the centre of the road. Pedestrians pointed and laughed at the heavenly reaction.

"This is what Haeylo needs."

"Oh, you don't need to tell us, Arriette. Haeylo is destined to be evil-free," Jet explained. "With you as our leader I'm sure this will become more than an idea."

"I don't want to let you down."

"You won't," said Casper.

"But you can't see into the future."

"But I can," smiled Baby A. "Anyway, all we need is faith."

She placed both her hands on Arriette's face carefully and took a deep breath.

"Arriette Monroe, in all my life I never imaged such tranquillity. You deserve this."

"I don't unders—"

"I'll be back soon."

The atmosphere by her angelic friend juddered and the buildings and people around became a blurred mesh of colour. Baby A's body gently faded and Arriette swarmed at her silhouette.

"Where did she go?"

Tobias held her tight. "Baby A's gone to the future, to settle your jitters."

"She's what?"

"Just a little trip to put your mind at ease as a thank you for delivering us to the lair in one piece. She's considered it for a while now, but she's not going too far for too long. Don't want to ruin the surprise now, do we?"

"She's going to get a huge shock. We're already three of our group short and if it wasn't for Harriet, we'd have strolled right past this place."

Sebastian gestured for them to enter the town hall but Arriette had frozen.

Baby A once told Arriette that when a time-traveller moved in time they opened up a wormhole which others could use if within reasonable proximity. Arriette had the opportunity to speak to her future self and pick her own brains about what being the Recruit's leader might be like. She could prepare for the war so many were discussing and ensure she trained hard to deal with Pandora's box.

Without another minute's pondering Arriette span and lunged away from the gang, then threw her body at the space where Baby A stood moments before. Unfortunately Arriette hadn't remained close enough and the wormhole closed.

She tumbled tragically to the ground, hitting her head and blacking out.

THIRTY—THREE

A cool, damp cloth had been placed across her forehead and when Arriette opened her eyes, Tobias's hand clutched it. "That was a stupid idea."

"Ugh, not now."

"There's nothing to gain from meeting your future self, Arriette," he said.

Did that statement even need a reply? Of course there was something to gain!

Arriette panicked. She wanted to be ready to face how the war panned out. Would she live or die? Did Tobias ask her to marry him? Lots of people looked forward to their future but Arriette could only fear hers.

"Tobias, I haven't even been enlightened with my other powers yet and pretty soon the war between good and evil will begin, if it's even going to happen. We haven't even figured out if there's any truth behind this Pandora's box theory yet, and now there's a powerful everlast to interrogate. All those people in the streets; every shop either sold food or materials to make weaponry. I saw a boy of about fifteen years sharpening a stake. If I haven't tried to use my ability to travel or morph, when I need them I'll have no idea what their trigger is."

Tobias nodded. "We need Pouki's help then."

"Yes, but he isn't here, is he?"

Arriette sat up with Tobias's help and rubbed at her head. A lovely lump to prove her stupidity sat on the left hand side above her eye. The bruising was sore to touch and Arriette's face in general felt tender and delicate.

"You'll get a black eye to go with that, I think."

"Thanks to Baby A, not for long. I just assumed if I followed her I'd spare myself the horror of having to live through the next few weeks."

"Nice try, Arriette. You aren't escaping so easily."

"But I want to. I need to. I'll let you all down and each of you worked so hard to get me to the position I'm in at the moment. I was so reluctant and fought you, but being here I can see all the good to be done."

Tobias laughed. "You're here because of your own stubbornness, that's all."

"No, I don't mean the head injury. I mean the progress I've made."

"All we did was share a bit of blood," he said.

"No, that's just it! You did far more. You saved my life."

"So don't waste it then. The next few weeks will be a hoot. When we've met the other members and gained their support, we can visit Charles and Rihaana to speak with him about this Falkon guy. With any luck, he'll send some men who can go back to that pit, through the mirror and rescue Coyote if he's still alive. When we're free of responsibility for a week Reiko and I will build that light-tight cabin for Dion and your royal Recruitness."

"That's not a real title."

He stuck out his tongue playfully. "It should be."

"I won't be free of responsibility until I'm dead. Perhaps not even then."

"You need to try and enjoy your job. Take pleasure in your work and have fun. Leading the Recruit means in the not too distant future Haeylo will look like this lair."

"So beautiful," Arriette said, sighing.

"Yes you are, but I was talking about the planet."

They glared at one another for a short moment, then Arriette smiled.

"If that was a line, it was cheesy."

"Maybe, but I'd never lie to you."

Tobias gently stroked the skin on Arriette's neck, running his thumb across the puncture marks given to her by vampyr Roberta when she began this supernatural torture. Beneath them, slightly faded, were her previous bite marks. Tobias couldn't believe she'd survived both.

She shuddered as his fingertips wound her hair in ringlets and when he leaned and pursed his lips, Arriette wanted to kiss him so bad that the lingering butterflies in her stomach did somersaults.

Tobias pulled her body to his and just for a minute they waited. Holding him close meant prolonged safety and Arriette longed to be loved in return; have him feel the way she did when in his presence.

He placed a finger under her chin.

They were inches from each other.

Then there was a knock at the door.

"We're not interrupting anything?" Jet asked.

Behind Jet Carter stood Casper and a retainer whom Arriette had met briefly, but whose name alluded her. She was stunningly attractive and wore a black dress with a long, teasing slit up the right side. Her thigh showed and her stockings beneath it were laddered. Over the dress she wore a striped lilac shawl and her hair was tied up in pigtails.

Tobias glared at her but Arriette couldn't tell if he admired her beauty or despised her fashion sense.

"Not at all," Arriette replied.

She gave Tobias a look of sheer admiration and wound her fingers around his.

"What's up, Jet?" he asked.

"The others have requested a meeting with their new leader, Miss Monroe," said the woman.

"Arriette," she corrected her. "My name is Arriette."

"My name is Melanie Starr. We met in Charles's office. My apologies for the intrusion, Ma'am."

"Sure, I remember you, but don't call me Ma'am. When is

the meeting?"

Jet cleared his throat. "Uhm, now."

"Alright, I'll be through in a minute."

Jet and Casper left the room first. Melanie followed behind. When they were alone, Arriette let out a sigh of relief and lowered her body back to the sofa.

She took in her surroundings. The walls were wood-panelled to mimic her cabin, with a stone floor and a woolly rug. The furniture was grey but homely and comfortable; the atmosphere seemed natural and welcoming. Every detail had been perfected by a master dreamer just for her.

Tobias smiled. "I'm glad they're gone."

"Me too," she agreed. "I'd love to pick up where we left off but something tells me this meeting is life or death." She grinned. "It required three people to invite me."

Tobias kissed Arriette lightly on the lips and made her heart race. The brief but spectacular contact was unexpected.

"Come on," he said, lifting her off the sofa. "We'd better get a move on."

They followed in the footsteps of Casper, Jet and Melanie. A large wooden door at the end of the corridor awaited. Torches hung from the walls and were blazing, emitting heat and creating a soothing atmosphere. A scent of vanilla filled the air.

Beads of sweat ran down Arriette's forehead and as she wiped them away, her palm traced a small bump. Regretting her earlier actions she turned the door knob and entered the room.

Around a circular table sat Casper, Jet Carter, Melanie Starr, Sebastian Sky and three others whom she had never met. She took the opportunity to shake hands with each of them to give a decent first impression of their leader-to-be.

They all gave her a beaming smile.

The first unknown member was a twenty year old woman with straight black hair and sparkling brown eyes. She was fairly small and wore heavy make up but her clothing was upper class. Her nails were long and pink.

"My name is Joy Johnas."

Arriette offered her a second hand shake, which she accepted.

"What do you do here?"

"I'm a third class everlast," said Joy.

"I'm jealous of those nails. You'll have to show me how you do that," Arriette told her.

She seemed to like this compliment as her face lit with delight.

Joy had a firm handshake, which to Arriette signified a strong-willed and powerful lady. One she thought she might get along with just fine.

"And who are you?" Arriette asked, moving round the table to another equally attractive woman.

This girl was slightly younger than Joy. Arriette predicted approximately eighteen or nineteen years of age. She wore no make up at all as her radiance was obvious. Blue eyes suggested innocence and her shoulder length, light brown hair reflected the flickering flames of the candles around the room.

"My name is Tabitha Hope," she said.

"Are you an everlast too?"

"No but I'm equally as interesting. I'm a retainer."

"Ah, I have lots of questions to ask which I think you'd be able to help me with."

"It would be a pleasure."

The final unfamiliar face was a gentleman of around fifty years of age and he was plump. His hair was thin, grey and there was little of it. Clean shaven and sat bolt upright, Arriette immediately approved of this man because he had poise and elegance.

"Paulei Leigh, Miss Monroe. It's wonderful to meet you at last."

"Thank you, Paulei, but you can call me Arriette. What are your abilities?"

He shook her hand again before speaking. "I can read your mind."

"Another telepath?" She grinned at Tobias, then returned her attention to Paulei. "Somebody else to give me a headache."

The telepath grinned and in unison each of the three new faces stood. They bowed their heads in respect and all of a sudden, Arriette became their figurehead.

"I've been looking forward to making your acquaintance," she told them. "I'm sure each of you can help me. I'm concerned."

"What do you need?" asked Joy.

"Well, it's the answer to a simple yes or no question and then your opinion."

The three supes puzzled. Arriette gestured for them to take a seat and asked Tobias to squat beside her.

"How did you know I was coming or who I was?"

Paulei held up his hand. "That's my fault, I believe. I like to scan the area every now and again—up top that is—and as you're all such clear thinkers I was able to pick your names out from the noise."

"So you sent Harriet and Jet to get us?"

"Yes, we have some news for Casper about our situation but that can wait. It already has for thousands of years, why not another day?" he said. "You said you needed our opinions, Arriette?"

"Yes. Before I came here I met Harriet Foley."

Casper smiled. "Harriet stayed behind to ensure our friend Pouki was safe. He never learned to swim."

"But he's been here before," said Paulei.

"I understand, but he joined us through magical means if you'll cast your minds back." Casper then filled Arriette in. "One of the wiccans made a potion which allowed him to breathe underwater. The effects wore off the second he touched dry land on the outside, so he could travel back too."

Arriette nodded. "Well Harriet and I seem to hold different opinions and morals when it comes to vampyrs. We have a friend of the species. Dion was turned against her will last year. I want your opinion so I know where I stand when discussing Dion's presence in our affairs and hopefully organising a means for her to see this place too. Before you say anything, note that I have been bitten and survived a vampyr attack twice and have still found room for Dion in my heart."

Paulei was the first to share his thoughts.

"Is she murderous?"

"Human blood makes her sick. She feeds on animals. Her biology is vampyric but her mind and her heart remain human."

"Then she is as welcome here as any of us. Dion sounds like a woman with a respectable background and it was unfair for her to be turned against her will. Fangs may tear her away from humanity but personality and soul make up for appearances," Paulei said. "I'm all for her entry to the lair if you're happy."

Arriette smiled. "Dion will be thrilled to learn another member of the Recruit sees her condition the way we do." She turned to Joy. "How about you?"

She shrugged. "I can't say I wouldn't be a little frightened of her at first but I have to agree with Paulei that any creature made supernatural against their will should be free to make their own decisions as to how they live their lives"

"Dion saved us," said Baby A. "She's not evil."

"If this vampyr you speak of saved your life rather than taking it, she's welcome here," added Tabitha.

At least they weren't going to freak out if their vampyr friend was ever to step foot in the lair, thought Arriette. That's if she could figure out a way to get her there.

The three newbies were friendly and enjoyable to have as company.

"So what did you want to tell me?" asked Casper.

"Ah, we're almost ready for war and as you're our leader we wanted your permission to launch an attack."

Casper seemed worried. "I, uhm, well I'd need to know what the purpose of this war is."

"To seek and destroy Pandora's box and all who stand in our way, of course," said Paulei.

"I'm sorry but I cannot permit that. We are a peaceful organisation and I shall allow us only to retaliate in the event that we are ambushed."

They talked a few hours longer about how likely it was that the lair would come under attack before Arriette excused herself to shower and change. They could discuss the topic without her given that for now, Casper remained in charge and for as long as possible Arriette wanted to remain her inconsequential self.

As hot water trickled down Arriette's back, she thought about their encounter in Manaia Forest with the werewolves and worried about what Jet and Harriet did with Scarlett's body; who was responsible for the body? So after cleaning up, she slipped into a pair of light blue sweat pants and a white shirt. Then she made her way out of the room.

The corridor was empty but the door to the meeting room had been propped open. The gang had finished their meeting and so Arriette scurried in feeling refreshed and prepared to hear any bad news, when she saw Harriet standing there, minus Pouki Hallidae.

Arriette hadn't yet been seen and so she hid just outside behind the door and ear wigged. Joy and Tabitha were having an argument with her.

"Are you joking? She's a vampyr! It's ridiculous and I strongly disagree with this insanity," she admitted. "It's reckless and threatens our security."

"Harriet, in a few days Casper will be handing over leadership to Arriette and her rulings are going to apply. If you're too open with your objections to Dion, Arriette is in the position to cast you aside."

"She wouldn't dare release me of the Recruit."

"Why are you so sure? There is great power running through her veins and she's as determined as anyone to keep Haeylo safe and evil-free. Paulei scanned her and she's the one the scripts speak of. Casper was right to bring her here."

"Then she will need to murder the creature if she wishes to meet our expectations. Dion's evil whether she admits so or not. If evil is to be annihilated, then guess who's got to go too? You must see this from my perspective, girls?"

Joy sighed. "I understand how this might look but if Dion doesn't practice her evil inheritance she cannot be refused as a member if Arriette asks her to join."

Harriet laughed. "Oh please! To realise she is allergic to human blood she must have tasted it before."

Arriette stepped into the room. "She did."

"I didn't think you were—"

"Listening? Unfortunately yes." Arriette folded her arms. "Why not just tell me you were this uncomfortable with Dion? I'm not so arrogant as to dismiss your thoughts, Harriet. We could have discussed her in detail; you could have met her first."

"Well we're not plotting, scheming or lying," Harriet said, bitterly. "We were discussing your friend's admittance here, actually."

"Yes I heard, the one who was forced by her maker to drink the blood of a human to survive her first night as a vampyr. Her husband left. She lost everything, including her child. The man who turned Dion vampyr kept her captive for a short while to ensure she survived. When he left her, Dion was unable to continue his monstrous habits and once the blood took effect she became severely ill."

"Why?" asked Joy. "Vamps are supposed to adore the scent and taste of human blood."

"Something inside her still clung to humanity. When evil attempted to take over, it claimed Dion's body but not her soul. Dion is a killing machine with a heart of gold."

"If she has any heart at all," Harriet said.

Arriette couldn't evaluate her next move because it happened so quickly. She lunged for Harriet, planting a firm fist between her thin, frowning brows and launched the wiccan off her feet and across the meeting table. She toppled back, curving her body in an arc as she crashed to the ground.

Her nose gushed blood and her eyes watered.

Harriet swore at her future leader with a passion, naming her a traitor and a brute but Arriette hadn't expected to throw the woman so far. She flexed her fingers, impressed at her increasing strength and stamina then warned her to stay down with a sharp tone and a cautious index finger.

Joy and Tabitha glared at their leader-to-be in astonishment but could only laugh when they saw the mortified look on Harriet's face.

Few people ever stood up to this woman and it was about time she was aware of her rank, which had been merely temporary in Casper's absence.

"I warned you in the forest not to anger me."

"Arriette, that's enough!"

Casper and Tobias stormed into the room and gripped an arm each, then pulled her toward the door. Arriette threatened Harriet over Tobias's shoulder.

"Stay out of my way, Harriet. There won't be a second warning."

Arriette's legs buckled beneath her and her head became cloudy. As she reached over Tobias's shoulder to threaten Harriet again, her breath caught.

What was happening to her?

No longer did she reach with fingers but a huge stripy paw and when she opened her mouth to question it, instead she growled; deep from within her stomach it vibrated and shook her entire frame.

Tobias released Arriette and crouched behind the table to help Harriet to her feet. Then everybody backed away. She tried her hardest to explain that she didn't mean to frighten them. Her body seemed to shrink in height but grow in length and fur covered every area within seconds.

"Arriette, what's happening to you?" Joy yelled.

As she tried to provide an answer her jaw widened and sharp daggers protruded. Then came the roar. The torches on the walls flickered and the tables rattled.

Joy ran out the door, slamming it behind her.

Arriette turned to follow and panicked when she realised Casper and Tobias were now sprawled across her back, pinning anything sharp or dangerous to the floor. Arriette's legs gave way and she collapsed on her stomach, four paws flat on the carpet, in a heap.

Then she realised she'd torn through her clothing.

"Guys! Guys! Let me go!"

"Arriette? You're here!" said Tobias.

"I never left. Hey, give me your jacket."

"But you changed," he snarled, handing it over. "Into a tiger! How did you—"

Tabitha laughed, cutting him short. "Are you a shifter?"

"Yes," she grumbled. "Unfortunately."

"So why is this such a big deal again?"

Tobias hopped to his feet. "Because one minute she's swearing at Harriet over my shoulder and the next she's trying to eat her."

"Stop exaggerating," Arriette said, squirming. "I didn't try to eat anyone; not an intentional change, may I remind you. That's never happened before. It's my first ever shifter experience, Tabitha. I too was made supe against my will."

Harriet marched across the carpet and dragged Arriette down the corridor by her ankles. She forced the others aside and lifted Arriette by the collar, then threw her against the nearest door.

"I'll teach you to hit me!"

She kicked Arriette's knees until she crumpled and crushed her fingers.

Arriette let out a sharp screech, which turned into a growl, which turned into another, louder roar.

Casper told her she should never attack a human after changing shape. Hunters and other animals lurked in the forest who wouldn't think twice about taking out a random beast.

But she wasn't in the forest.

This time, Arriette could take the opportunity to exert her dominance. She dived on the wiccan and gnawed on Harriet's silver dress, then stuck the claws of her right paw in her thigh, retracting them slowly to inflict the most pain. Harriet yelped, bat Arriette's paw away and retreated to her room, leaving a trail of silver fabric and blood behind.

Casper's knuckles cracked Arriette across the nose and shocked her enough to trigger a shift back to her human form. She scrambled back into the jacket and cowered.

"I don't like you as a tiger," he said.

"I do," laughed Tabitha, helping Arriette to her feet. "Do me a favour and teach her a similar lesson every other day. Our lives will greatly improve."

"Ugh, do you have to go through such a transaction every time you change, Casper?" Arriette asked, rubbing her head.

She stood and stretched, hoping her scar wouldn't split again. The last thing she needed now was wings.

"It's not as dramatic."

"Why a tiger?" Tobias asked, buttoning up the front of his jacket to hide Arriette's chest.

"Her body chose a tiger because of her mood," Casper explained. "You have to remember that Arriette's powers are still tied to her feelings."

"My wings aren't," she said. "Not now, anyway."

"You're growing out of sprouting them without warning but each power takes time to tame. Hormones are one of the main causes of accidents in women who are supernatural. Try to keep anxiety, anger and well, arousal at a minimum."

She and Tobias glanced at one other. Arriette bit her lip.

"How long is this going to go on for?"

"All abilities take at least a month to become used to the body they're aligned with."

"I don't have another month. I mastered my wings in three weeks."

"Well you're lucky."

Arriette excused herself from the group and retreated to her chambers in silence. She inhaled deeply, shook off her nausea and knocked on Joy's door as she passed. The everlast was laid out on her bed reading. She froze when she realised the visitor was the tiger.

"I'm here to make my peace and apologise. I didn't mean to

scare you. Have you seen Pouki?"

"No I haven't. And you're new to this," she said, as more of a statement than a question.

"Obvious, huh?"

"I'm in the same boat, really. I'm a third class."

"Classed for how long?"

"One week," she said.

"Just a week? You're even newer than I am. What a relief, finally someone who understands the inconvenience. Who did you take over from?"

"My mother. She and my human step-father were married recently. Uhm, are you leaving us, Arriette?"

"Where did you get such an idea? I need to make a quick trip to the city to speak to a friend of mine though. He has answers to some pretty crude questions but I'll be back. I also need to find out where Pouki is. I didn't get chance to quiz Harriet."

"I've been looking forward to meeting our new leader. I hear Casper was amazing. My great, great grandparents followed him in the beginning."

"Born on Earth?"

"Some of my ancestors, sure."

"He's eighty years old," Arriette said. "He'd have to be an everlast to live for so long. Casper is a shifter, I saw this with my own eyes, so how—"

Joy gasped. "He's much more than that, Arriette."

"Enlighten me."

She patted a spot on the bottom of the bed and Arriette perched comfortably.

"He's honestly never told you this?"

"Baby A and I guessed in Manaia Forest but we got interrupted before coming to a satisfying conclusion."

"Wolves?"

"How did you—"

"Toby told me," she said.

"Toby? You're already on a nickname basis?" Arriette shook her head. "Not sure how I feel about that. He can't keep his mouth shut, that boy."

"Don't read into it, I nickname everyone. Except you, he said you're not too fond of your nickname. He likes you, Arriette."

"I like him too but if I hint within the next few days it's likely he'll wake up next to an alligator or an owl."

"Anyway," she continued, laughing, "Casper's one of the group's dearest friends and he talked many of us into accepting our destiny to be a part of the Recruit. My grandparents joined, also my parents and now me."

"He's very convincing," she said.

"Hmm, well after I accepted I found a book in the library which I get the feeling wasn't meant for my eyes."

"Why not if it was on public display?"

Joy blushed. "I think Casper kept a diary."

"You didn't?"

"I'm not proud, but I did. It was on the top shelf, covered in dust."

Joy Johnas read Casper's diary? Arriette had a feeling Casper's own opinions could be an interesting read.

"He spoke often of two children whom he missed."

"Casper's own children?"

"Possibly, and a wife too. A woman called Christine."

If Casper had a family once, Arriette needed to know how he wound up without them and why he never spoke of them. He didn't outlive these humans because the wise shifter wasn't of an everlast background. So what *did* happen? she wondered.

"He never mentioned anything," Arriette said.

"Casper said someone forced them apart."

"Killed?"

"No. He specified they'd live a healthy life in a new world."

He couldn't be, could he? All those discussions about who he actually was and where his power originated from; could they point to such a crude reality?

Arriette thanked Joy and left in a hurry, then ran out to the street in search of Baby A. Within seconds a beautiful blonde head appeared and the rest of her body materialised shortly after.

"What's up? I heard you call."

"Casper's the President of the U.S."

Baby A's face crumpled. "As in the old America?"

Arriette rubbed her aching head, panting and sweating from the sprint to the square.

"How do you know this?"

She shook Baby A by the shoulders.

"Joy Johnas read his diary."

They stood on the cobbles staring at each other, eyes wide. Arriette didn't believe the story, not without further evidence. She wouldn't allow the voice in her head to convince her otherwise.

Casper and Andy Kaines were the same people!

Zïnnyi spoke to Casper in his dreams; because of him Haeylo was created and balanced. Light and dark. The creation story wasn't just writing and myth but facts and historical timelines.

She had to sit down.

They walked to a wooden bench with a plaque hammered to the back. The metal read, 'God appears and God is light', which Arriette found rather fitting for their conversation and grinned when she realised she recognised the line from Charles's message.

This was all part of a pre-planned journey.

"So it's true then."

"Yes, Arriette," she said, "It appears so."

"Why didn't he tell us? How did he survive this long? Did he spend eternity as an old man? Andy Kaines was in his thirties when he gave his life for Haeylo."

"No, Andrew Kaines was reborn," said Casper.

The girls shot to their feet and turned to see Casper approaching from the town hall. Arriette looked him straight in the eye and tried to forgive him for the secrecy, but couldn't.

"This old man has lived the same life over and over again," he said, tapping his chest as he spoke. "I pledged to the almighty himself. My job was to guard Haeylo until I located the rightful Recruit members at precisely the right time to defend against a world-wide disaster; the prompt for the next apocalypse! I had to find a leader to resume my place. You, Arriette."

Arriette shook her head. "No, no! I'm not going to be reborn. Forget it, I quit."

"You don't have to," he interrupted. "You are the saviour, Arriette. You'll deliver every human to Heaven and the planet will be pure again before any of this happens. You won't need to be reborn because success is coming in this lifetime."

"The future isn't all bad," Baby A winked. "In fact, I think you'll find you may quite enjoy being the Recruit's leader."

"Somehow," Arriette sighed, "I highly doubt that."

THIRTY—FOUR

Sebastian Sky took Arriette's hand and led her away from Baby A and Casper before she could protest. "Arriette, I need to borrow you for a moment."

"Sky, I'm a little busy right—"

Eyes followed as Arriette entered a store on the cobbled street with a sign above the window reading 'Indalo'.

This being the password to the lair, Arriette was instantly curious as to the contents.

"I was in the middle of an important conversation, Sky. You can't just tear me away from something so crucial."

"Sorry, Arriette. Casper's orders."

"Why am I not surprised?" she sighed.

When the door opened a tiny bell rang and an elderly retainer came to greet them. He had dark grey hair, wrinkled fingers and wore a pure white suit and matching shoes; as though he'd been caught in a blizzard. His shop was almost empty but from the outside, the building looked busy and chaotic.

"Miss Monroe, I've been expecting you."

She sighed. "Everyone expects me these days."

"That's because you have a part to play in all our lives. You're destined to do some great things."

"I can offer one service or another, I guess. If it gets me out of here and back to my conversation."

"Well my dear, I believe *I* can assist *you* today."

Arriette had never been a nosey human, but since becoming

supernatural her senses had kicked into overdrive. Everything seemed intriguing; other people, animals, places and sounds. She needed to know more about Haeylo and the new world in order to be the best at the job she was due to inherit.

The retainer glared at the sorcerer.

"Sebastian, perhaps you might like to explain why she's here."

Sky took off his hat and sat it on the counter. He stood in the centre of the room after shooing Arriette and the old man out of the way and let his auburn hair flow freely down his back. Then, he reached into the pocket of a clean robe he'd acquired from the meeting room and pulled out a long, thin stick.

"Is that what I think it is?" Arriette gasped.

The boy smiled. "This was my father's wand. He gave the heirloom to Mother before he was killed and told her to guard his wand with every breath. Still, a wand doesn't have to be this shape and size, it can be anything the sorcerer has blessed as their symbolic item. It could be jewellery or clothing."

He lifted it gently and balanced the wood between his index finger and thumb. After a swift flick of the wrist, purple sparks shot from the instrument to summon bookshelves, cabinets and draws. Arriette wasn't sure where to stand in fear a piece of furniture might land on her.

As Sebastian pivoted on the spot the sign above of the store truly became a reality. They were in an old bookshop but behind the counter appeared something completely haphazard. Weaponry, antiques and historical documentation.

"What is this place?"

"This, Miss Monroe, is the Recruit's extended source of information. An archive." He walked to the counter. "Are you impressed?"

"Oh, yes."

Sebastian grunted. "An information source other than retainers, remember? Technically we don't need an archive but we like to keep particular things for sentimental purposes."

The shop owner laughed. "Of course, I'm a retainer myself,

boy!"

"I hate to be so, well, to the point, but why bring me here?" Arriette enquired.

"I need you to choose something from the store."

Arriette raised a questionable eyebrow. "What do you mean?"

"Choose something and it's yours. Every member or follower is given a gift—not one of the eleven's gifts mind you —as a welcome to our cause. Sebastian chose his hat and Casper his robe. Your friends will soon get the opportunity too."

So what was she most drawn to?

Well, there was a dusty hardback book on the top shelf entitled The Ancient Egyptians which certainly grabbed her interest and then a golden pocket watch behind one of the glass cabinets. Arriette's life did lack a bit of routine, but what was she thinking? Didn't she enjoy her existence now she'd got friends and abnormality? Her eyes left the watch and scanned the room for something she could defend herself with.

Other people offered their protection; Dion, Tobias and Charles Melovich. All powerful. All loving. All a part of her new family. There was still one thing they were unable to offer.

Independence.

If Casper thought she should lead the Recruit into battle against the evils of Haeylo and Pandora's box, then she'd need something to help her find the correct mindset and fight for their right to live safely.

Then she spotted it.

Slung in a bowl on a sideboard near the exit was a treasure Arriette had longed for since inheriting the blood of her supernatural colleagues.

There, on that filthy, beaten sideboard, lay an everlast pendant. A mirror to the soul of their creator.

She paced over and scooped up her find. The chain dangled between her fingers and the very excitement of hanging such a spectacular item around her neck, feeling a pulse against the stones displayed within, made Arriette want the power of being their leader more and more.

"Sky, I think I've found it."

"I haven't seen that before," said the shopkeeper.

Sebastian laughed. "I don't believe my eyes."

"I choose this," she stated with her head held high and her fingers clamped to the pendant.

"Oh, but Arriette, you can't choose to own an everlast pendant. The pendant chooses the everlast. They'll hunt forever to hang around the neck of a particular soul."

"Third class everlasts are automatically given a pendant, though," she said.

Rihaana once explained during an afternoon snack that on her twentieth birthday Charles was expected to give his daughter the gift of eternal life.

"Sure. They're given a pendant but not *the* pendant. An everlast may go all the way to first class before being united with the pendant they're destined to belong to," Sky explained. "An everlast can do wondrous things with the right source of power."

"Like what? They'll still live forever. What changes when the two are united?"

"They become brave, strong, willing to dive headfirst into battle and are eager to take control of dangerous situations. Falkon Lou joined with the correct pendant last year. Ever since it located him the man turned into someone I'd rather not be friends with."

"Full of himself," added the shopkeeper. "That pendant you're holding is new to me."

"Do you think Falkon, our main suspect, and the next leader of the Recruit finding their rightful pendants in the same year is just a coincidence?" Arriette asked. "He's our top suspect at the moment."

Sky shrugged. "There are no coincidences."

Perhaps his pendant was the reason Falkon took matters into his own hands and murdered Coyote's family, then enslaved him. He also ordered the kidnap in Drakonta. All this so the

Underworld would open its gates for Falkon to storm each cave and hideout. To rule, maybe, or to destroy. He obviously thought Pandora's box hid there.

"Sky, what should I do now?"

He delicately placed the pendant around her neck.

"Look forward to becoming an everlast, Arriette."

"But I'm older than the initiation age, I don't—"

The doorbell rang again and Arriette turned to find Casper had joined them. "You will become an everlast when you take over my responsibilities. Our most important ceremony is not far away and I believe the pendant chose you for a reason," he said.

"I've wanted one of these since I first learned what they did," she told Casper.

"They're unique and fascinating devices. Just remember, when you become leader the pendant will glue itself to you and won't want to lose its master. Take good care of your source of power, Arriette, and the power will take care of you."

Not only was she able to shift shape, allow her wildest creations and dreams to escape her imagination and fly, but within a few days she would stop ageing and live forever as an everlast. Did she really want eternal life, though?

"I'll be a third-class with little say over the others. My becoming invincible may not do this planet much good if I can be outranked by someone who has had the power for thousands of years. Charles. Falkon. Rihaana. All better candidates."

"You will soon be the leader of the Recruit, Arriette," Sky said.

"Providing I don't get killed!"

"As our leader you will become God's perfect creation. Think about this, who outranks Him?" The sorcerer continued. "You must remember, you've been united with yours before the majority of everlasts on this planet. Only a small minority carry the correct power source for their bodies. They can go forever without it, but they will be half as strong. You, my dear, shall be amazing."

"When is the ceremony?" the shopkeeper asked Casper.

"I'll resign in two days, I think."

"So I've got forty-eight hours to grasp my abilities?" She sighed. "I'm not sure I'm ready for this."

Once outside, the sorcerer took Arriette shopping through the city. Although he was young, the boy possessed great power and a large number of gold chips. If Arriette knew, perhaps she and Tobias wouldn't have bothered with the dream to give her mother riches.

This kind-hearted fellow might have stepped up if the explanation and deed were clear enough.

Although, it's never fair to expect anything of anyone, she reminded herself. Ignorance often saves the disappointment.

When Arriette protested Sky explained that as she'd ruined most of her own clothing on the way to the lair, it was only fair they replace them.

No more unshapely brown sacks, she thought.

"Can we go back to the bookstore? I need something to read."

"Recruit leaders do not concern themselves with research. Others do this for them," he smiled.

She pulled a face. "Hmm. I'm more of a DIY kind of girl. I've lived alone for quite a while. I'm not short of tools, paint, instruction manuals and firewood."

"I see. You don't agree Recruit leaders should hire servants?"

"Absolutely not."

Poor Coyote gave in to Falkon's every need and it landed him a widower. *Nobody should be forced to do anything they disagree with,* she thought.

"Casper said the same thing when we first met him. You and the old guy are much alike. Harriet insists Casper should be waited on when he's around and I agree. He's special. Unique."

"What was Casper like as a young man?"

"Casper has been a young man several times, Arriette, but when I first met him the guy was a true gentleman. A hero. A saint. A legend. An angel, without wings. I look up to him. We all do. Each member of our society is dreading the day he hands the job over."

"Well I appreciate your honesty."

"Oh, no, I didn't mean—"

"Forget it. You'll miss him and I understand."

"You're going to be a fine leader, Arriette. The Recruit won't be the same without the old man, though."

"You can still see him," she said. "I plan to. Casper will remain a member but won't be able to make those important life or death decisions. He couldn't tear himself away from contact with us for five minutes."

Sebastian Sky tilted his head. The confusion in his eyes sent the scar down Arriette's back into spasm. She had pretty much perfected the ability to release her wings and the confidence lowered the amount of pain she experienced. But that strange sensation she felt as Sky studied her caused her fingers to tingle and legs to tremble.

"That feeling, it's so strange."

"Sorry, that's my fault. But Casper has a lot of explaining to do. He's not been honest and I'd like to know why"

"How do you mean it's your fault?"

"Learning to be a sorcerer has its ups and downs. Sorcery takes a lot of concentration and attention to detail. It's kind of a defence mechanism. I seem to have developed the power to control my opponents' emotions. I've dedicated my life to their protection but still, they avoid me. No runes yet, though. Obviously not influential enough to receive a marking. I mean you no harm," he said. "I promise."

Only an hour later, Casper was being interrogated. The old man jumped when they entered the meeting room.

"Tell Arriette the truth. Shame on you."

"About what?"

Sky gave Casper the same unfamiliar glare that Arriette experienced. The boy scared her, even more so than Dion's fangs. Casper lowered his head and backed into a corner.

"You're not going to like it, Arriette."

"Since when did she ever like being a supe?" Baby A sniggered. She'd been sat in the corner with her feet on one of the desks, relaxing. "If it helps, I have a suspicion that I won't have been told either," she said.

Casper frowned. "This is going to be difficult for you to accept. All eleven members must be present first."

Baby A shrugged. "Do they all know the secret?"

"Sky and Joy do but their knowledge in the matter wasn't planned and I don't want to know how they found out either."

"Nobody else?"

"No, but Sky's correct in saying they ought to."

Arriette set off toward the door. "Let's go find them."

Casper held out a hand to stop her. "Travel to Charles's office and speak with him about the message Scarlett gave you. Once we get to the bottom of our current troubles I'll provide you with the next."

So Casper's big secret would be a weight on her shoulders, but not yet. As usual, the old shifter made an accurate observation.

The matters at hand including Coyote's family, Falkon's plot to enter the Underworld and Susan's message being fully deciphered, all needed to be fixed and forgotten before Arriette would be able to hack Casper's news. Whatever he had to tell them, Arriette wasn't going to enjoy hearing about it.

Baby A learned this from her trip to the future and perhaps figured out Casper's news in the process without realising at the time, but until he explained Sky's accusations they'd never know.

"Where did Harriet and Jet go?" Baby A asked.

"I think they're in the mortuary."

"She left Pouki, didn't she."

Sky nodded. "He asked Harriet to leave so she did. I think he discussed Dion with her too, which prompted Arriette's argument with her in the meeting hall. Don't worry about them; they've never gotten along."

"That sounds like Pouki," sneered Casper.

"Miss Evermay's body is undergoing an autopsy as we speak," Sky said.

Arriette frowned. "What for? Scarlett was murdered by wolves."

"Apparently your retainer friend was sick before the mutilation," said Sky.

Baby A sat bolt upright. "How sick?"

"Sick like Susan was," said Casper.

THIRTY—FIVE

Once in her room, Arriette took a deep, relaxing breath and began to count down from ten. With a lot on her mind, she looked forward to scratching each thing off her list of things to do on arrival at Haeylo City.

She hadn't yet unpacked the majority of her things considering the group left the luggage back at the campsite. Cramming the garments Sebastian Sky bought for her into a bag, Arriette predicted she might count down to seven or eight before some needy Recruit member would dive through the door and inform her of yet another problem.

Still, a couple of minor issues would take her mind off the enormous ones.

Ten, nine...

Tobias and Baby A agreed to rendezvous with Arriette and Casper in the small canteen the other members had built a few years back. Until then, Recruit meetings consisted of a tall glass of water to keep a speaker's voice clear and biscuits baked by the likes of Joy and Tabitha. Since dreamers had begun to explore the depths of their imaginations, the Recruit's facilities were improving daily.

Joy Johnas was a third class everlast and newer to her powers than Arriette. Her beautiful brown eyes and head of slick, black hair gave her an edge not to be reckoned with. Being the lowest class of everlast frightened Joy and although her personality stuck out in a crowd just like the polish on her nails, in a sense she became boisterous and bouncy because of her role in the Recruit.

Joy was one of the eleven, which made her powerful beyond belief. She hadn't yet been reunited with her pendant and Arriette did not want to boil her blood by parading hers in Joy's face. She hung the chain around her neck and slipped the pendant down her top, shuddering as the metal chilled her pale skin.

Eight, seven, six...

Tabitha Hope was the complete opposite of the young everlast who'd spilled the secrets of Casper's diary. Her hair sat at shoulder length and she tucked the mousy brown waves behind her ears effortlessly. Her eyes were a breathtaking blue. Tabitha wasn't too tall, but her hourglass figure was enough to get her noticed. Storing all that information meant she had a lot going for her; looks, brains and an addictive personality.

Even though they were both equally as gorgeous in their own style, Arriette couldn't recall feeling any jealousy toward either of them. But she and Harriet would never get along and Arriette didn't expect her to forgive the tiger attack in the meeting room.

Already the others seemed like distant relatives.

Five, four...

The door flung open and in stormed Harriet Foley with a flushed Jet Carter at her side. Casper and Baby A trundled after them, protesting at the privacy invasion. Harriet had changed into another, plainer dress but her hair had been tied up in a bun.

"You led them here," Harriet accused.

Arriette folded her arms and raised an eyebrow.

"What now, Harriet?"

"You're a liar, Arriette Monroe, and unfit to lead the Recruit to success."

She'd reached number four; much better than she originally thought.

So who had she led to the lair? Vamps, orcs or demons? Perhaps the entire Underworld had played trick or treat on the cave wall.

"Harriet, I fail to see how anybody possibly followed me here. We flew here together."

"Before we set off you went to the Underworld without clearance from an elder and angered the inhabitants. Now they're scouting Haeylo's surface in search of the woman who opened the gate."

Arriette and Casper locked eyes.

"How do you know about that?"

"I sent Jet to check on Pouki after he'd sent me away and when he got there the little elf was gone and orcs were marching along the river bank, heading our way."

Jet shrugged and sank into the suit he'd chosen for the earlier meeting.

"Sorry, Arriette."

"Don't apologise, you followed orders. That still doesn't answer how you know about our visit to the Underworld."

A tear ran down Baby A's cheek. "We have to find Pouki, Arriette. He could be in real danger!"

"We're not going to leave him, Baby A."

"Whilst on the subject and placing blame," said Casper, "would you like to tell me how you became aware of Arriette's actions?"

Harriet froze. "Information I do not wish to disclose."

"Well that's a shame," he said. "I didn't want to be the one to let you go."

Arriette tried to calm down before either her wings unfolded or she grew pointed ears and a stripy tail. The anger welled in her chest but she awaited Casper's decisions. He was the current leader after all and what he requested had to be actioned.

"What are you saying, Casper?"

The old man grabbed the wiccan woman, pulling her backwards and wrapping his elbow around her throat.

Arriette backed away from them.

Harriet's legs were violently kicking. He yanked her body to face him and unexpectedly kissed her. Then he held her face by his for a few moments before he pushed her toward Arriette, wiping her lipstick from his mouth.

She hopped aside as Harriet tumbled down, hitting her head on the coffee table and lying unconscious for a moment. Then her body began to peel and crumble. Her skin flaked and turned to a light, grey ash. Arriette was reminded of the vampyr attack in Manaia Forest before meeting Tobias and Reiko, and she turned her head.

Within minutes, Harriet Foley was gone.

"You killed her," Jet said, matter of factly.

"She had that coming," said Baby A, folding her arms. "Girl was a bitc—"

"Baby A, that's enough," Casper said. "I'm sorry, I can't stay here."

Arriette gestured for Jet to fetch a dustpan and brush and allowed Casper to leave the room silently. She didn't like the idea of sweeping her rival up and tossing her into the trash but Casper left them no choice.

Harriet once said she could toy with a man's mind providing she didn't fall in love and their lips never touched. Casper knew Harriet loved and respected him as their leader. All that remained was a brief moment of contact to break the spell.

Baby A placed a hand on Jet's shoulder.

"Harriet certainly made her point. How are we going to reach the city with orcs monitoring our movement on the surface?" she said.

"Run," said Jet, wiping his eyes.

Arriette grunted. "We fight."

"We and what army?" Jet asked.

She glanced around the room at Tobias, Baby A, and Jet. Once she seemed happy with the conclusion, she smiled.

"You're looking at it."

Tobias burst into hysterics. "I refuse to jog unarmed to a group of suffering demonic animals. You're forgetting we managed to sneak Coyote into their lair and left him there to do as much damage as one man is able to. I'll bet they beheaded the shape-changing trickster the second the gate closed."

Arriette lunged at him. "You're a real friend, you know that, Tobias? I pushed him in good faith, hoping he'd keep the form of an orc and have the chance to gain revenge or find out what happened to his family. You're making it sound as though I sent him on a suicide mission."

She gripped his t-shirt and forced him against the door, which slammed it shut and made the others in the room jump.

"It's not my fault!" she insisted.

"Get off me!"

He squirmed and yanked Arriette's body away. She let go of his clothing and brushed her hair back to regain a bit of dignity. Arriette pointed at Baby A viciously.

"I don't want to hear how I was wrong to do that."

She forced Tobias away from the exit. He stumbled to the corner and cursed as Arriette stormed past and into the corridor.

Baby A followed.

"Arriette, you didn't have to do that!"

"I said I don't want to hear it."

"I'm sorry but whether you like it or not, attacking Tobias the way you did, heck, you scared me," she said.

"Perhaps he'll think twice next time he wants to question me."

Arriette pushed open the door to the meeting room and rummaged around in a box of old documents and floor plans for the buildings within the lair.

"Where are the records kept for this hideout?"

She pointed to a rickety wooden cabinet.

"Most likely in there but they'll be locked."

Arriette kicked the draws in and dumped the remains behind her, tearing the front from the furniture and rummaging vigorously.

"There must be another exit to Haeylo! If I can find it we can get away from here safely and find our friends."

"You can't read confidential documents," she gasped. "If Casper finds you—"

"He'll do nothing," she said with a stern expression.

"Nothing at all. Now, are you going to help me or stand there criticising?"

Baby A nodded then began rummaging through the paperwork.

"Do you think they'd be able to trace our movements? I mean, why would God build this place if evil can access it through a panel or a tunnel?"

Arriette flicked through some hardback books.

"When I came here I was told that dreamers imagined homes and offices to suit the needs of the Recruit. Something tells me Pouki isn't the only supernatural being on this planet who can't swim."

Baby A thought about this for a moment and then began sifting through a box of files. Casper walked in and clunked the meeting room door shut gently behind him.

Baby A stopped abruptly and turned to face him.

"Arriette, I understand what you're doing and I must say whilst the idea is genius, you are not going to get much further than the exit to this town hall if you do not apologise to Tobias," he said. "I heard you arguing from my room."

"Like he cares; accusing me of killing Coyote. What a complete—"

"Watch your language."

"I was going to say a complete idiot, but now you mention bad language—"

"I agree his behaviour was uncalled for given the accidental deaths of Kalvin and Susan in the past month, but I do feel our battle might be stronger if the Recruit all get along. Are you listening, Arriette?" he snapped.

She tugged out a sheet of paper and cheered. "I found it!"

Casper hurried over and took the document from between Arriette's fingers. There they were, the original plans for the emergency exit.

"Let's go."

When they joined the others, Arriette slammed the sheet on the desk and folded her arms.

"Interrupting something, gentleman?"

"Not at all. Tobias and I were just discussing the situation," said Jet.

"Yes, he's got a lot on his plate these days."

Tobias groaned. "Look, Arry, I'm sorry. I didn't mean to blame you for this mess and I'm sure Coyote's fine."

"How many times do I have to remind you that my name is Arriette?"

"Stop it, both of you. If Coyote wasn't found and killed then we wouldn't need these," Casper added. "Evil must have located Coyote to realise we were up to something. It's unfortunate but a fact, and although Harriet accused Arriette of leading those wolves to us, I think they were sent to hunt us down."

"Is that what I think it is?" Tobias asked.

Casper nodded. "Turns out that the early Haeyloian dreamers decided they needed another means of travel."

Baby A stepped forward. "They employed my kind to open a wormhole in the lair for the use of its inhabitants."

"It got disabled shortly after as it was beginning to fade and send Recruit members all over Haeylo without warning," Arriette finished.

"Today, gentleman, we are going to re-open this wormhole and travel through it and out to Haeylo's surface," said Baby A.

Jet said, "But we need space travel."

Baby A smiled. "That I can fix. This is going to work."

Silence for a moment.

When everyone came to a mutual agreement that this plan was, in fact, feasible, they got to their feet and asked how they could help. Arriette sent Jet Carter off to the Indalo store on the main street to find some further information as to the wormhole's location, whilst Baby A and Casper decided it might be best to pack much-needed supplies and weapons. That left Tobias and Arriette to stare at each other awkwardly.

"I don't want to lose you, Arriette," he said, breaking the ice. "Can't we forget about this whole thing and pick up where we left off?"

Whilst admiring his strong jaw and soft lips, she realised Tobias hadn't shaved in days

"I forgive you but now is not the time to get all I love you on me."

"When all this is over, you and I are going to have a lot to discuss," he said, kissing her cheek gently.

His stubble riled her skin. "The first topic being the state of your face."

He laughed. "I'll hold you to that. Come on," he said, taking her by the hand and dragging her out of the building.

She hoped this would work, with all her heart and might. Once at the city gates, which were opened automatically for the group now under Charles's orders, she could report the army of orcs to the everlasts and the war would officially begin.

Out in the street there was a crowd of followers in front of Town Hall. She and Tobias trudged over to see what the fuss was, only to discover it was Baby A, hunched in a ball at the side of the cobbled road.

Tobias tried to lift her but she refused and swore repeatedly at him to back off.

Arriette knelt beside her friend and screamed at somebody to fetch Tabitha Hope. Retainers were knowledgeable as to all supernatural biology, most of the time.

A few minutes later Tabitha was at their side, searching her mental filing system for an answer and making some space.

"What happened to her?"

Arriette panicked, "I, uhm, can you help?"

"I hope so. Baby A, listen to me, you're going to have to tell me where the pain is."

Baby A groaned and rocked back and forth. "I don't know!"

Tabitha verbally slapped her. "Yes, you do!"

Baby A's wings extended and flapped at a high speed, creating whirlwinds across the street. Spectators were told to move aside for their safety and allow her space to breathe.

Arriette released her own wings and built an angelic barrier between Baby A's feathered weapons and those stood around her. She wrapped her arms around the angel's chest and held her still.

Her wings rustled and fought for freedom.

"My stomach," she squealed.

Tabitha began to examine her. "Here?"

"Lower," she replied.

"Here?"

"Lower! Lower!"

Tabitha gave a single nod and instructed Arriette not to leave the angel's side. She called Tobias over with her index finger and ordered him inside the Indalo store.

Those few precious moments seemed to last a lifetime; so gut-wrenching that Arriette thought her pendant had kicked her prolonged life into early action.

"Hold on. We'll fix you. I promise."

Baby A's eyes caught hers. They pleaded to stop the pain; to rid her of all suffering.

"Tabitha! Where the hell are you?"

"I'm here," she said, emerging from the shop with Jet in tow. "Hospital, now."

Tobias scooped her up with difficulty, trying to avoid her wings, and headed off in another direction following Jet's lead.

"Infirmary," said Tabitha.

Arriette's mouth fell agape. "In Haeylo City?"

"No, we have one here. She won't make it elsewhere."

"She'll be okay, won't she?"

The retainer placed a comforting hand on her shoulder. "Baby A's a strong woman, she'll be just fine."

Tabitha wrapped both arms around her neck and told Arriette how sorry she was for the loss. Arriette pulled away and frowned.

"What loss? What's going on?"

She lowered her voice. "I can save your friend, but there's nothing I can do for her baby."

"*Baby?*"

Arriette sank to her knees on the edge of the kerb and cried.

EPILOGUE

9180AD
The Creation of Haeylo: Part Five

When the world was young, the earliest everlasts asked the youngest retainers to read through every script they owned in relation to the old world. They wanted to remember the unique technology to preserve the knowledge and science behind human development and evolution. To avoid a repeat in history.

Most texts described Earth to have crumbled into darkness. A select few, however, knew differently.

Earth existed, though its atmosphere was inferior to Haeylo's and the weather bleak. Some travellers had been there, witnessed the earlier years. The sixties, seventies. Some, the naughties.

Contemplating the home she once knew, Pandora struggled through the caverns desperate to locate the exit.

Trembling in fear of what lurked in the underground lakes, she flinched at every unnatural sound and scurried over any uneven surfaces her fingers found.

Praying for sunlight, for nature, she bound her body tighter in the clothing she had left and battled onward, barely able to see her breath before her.

Finally, having explored every tunnel and ventured into every crevice, Pandora reached a cave at the Drakontan base of the mountain, lit mildly by a crack in the wall.

Her belly empty and her eyes blinded by the gift of natural

light, Pandora fell to her knees beside a pool of fresh water and drank her weight.

What would become of her now? Would He punish her for yet more poor judgement and lack of self-control?

She deserved his wrath and expected Him to do his worst, so Pandora waited in the cave for two moons, starving and frightened.

He never came.

Without words of wisdom or guidance, Pandora lowered herself into the water intending to end her wasted life but the lower she sank the brighter the water became, illuminating an underwater tunnel which Pandora had no doubt led to the outside world.

A chance to begin again; to reverse the evil she had released upon the world and to build an army strong enough to protect her until she did.

Death would be too easy; cowardly and final.

Life on this haunted planet was to be her self-inflicted punishment.

The HPS

THE HAEYLOIAN POWER SCALE

1: Everlast - There are three classes of everlast, all with the power of everlasting life and the ability to communicate with other everlasts through an assigned pendant (*Mirror of the Soul*).

2: Dreamer - Power of telekinesis and power to turn imagination into reality. When in large groups, dreamers can mirror another's reality for observation purposes. This is referred to as Mirroring, Jumping or Spying.

3: Sorcerer/Rulecast - Power of wizardry through the use of magical items, potions and spells. Rulecasts specifically work with/for an everlast and have a higher level of experience.

4: Time-Traveller - The power of travel in time and space by opening and using wormholes.

5: Invisibility - The power to turn themselves and their sensory footprint invisible.

6: Angel - Possesses wings and has the power to communicate with the creator.

7: Shape-Shifter - The power to change physical shape. They can temporarily inherit the power/s of their chosen form.

8: Demon/Werewolf/Vampyr -
- *Vampyr* – power to change physical shape. Power of

eternal life. Weakened by silver, sunlight and sharp wooden objects. Drinks human blood — their bite is fatal.

- *Werewolf* – there are blood born, bite born and shifter Born breeds of werewolf. They form packs or clans. They can change their physical shape to that of a wolf. The three most powerful clans are the Shoku, Tri and Shou, named after the moon/s they worship.
- *Demon* – there are two species of demon, the spirit and the horned. A spirit or shade demon's claws are poisonous. Horned demons have increased strength and armour.

9: Telepathy - The power to read minds and emotions. They can read human minds clearly and most supernatural (aka supe) minds. From the demonic family they can only read orc minds. Vampyric minds can be accessed but only until the end of their human memories.

10: Retainer - The power to control their eidetic memory.

11: Astro-Projection - The power to separate their spiritual and physical forms. Most are able to control both forms and duplicate their existence—one as a spirit, the other as a shell. Due to experimentation, some are forced to use only their spiritual forms whilst their physical shells sleep.

12: Wiccan - The power of witchcraft using basic spells and potions. The power can be taught.

13: Orc - A demonic slave with no supernatural power.

14: Human - No supernatural power, however, most potion masters are human, which is a skill that can be studied.

ABOUT RACHAEL

I'm an Amazon international #1 bestselling author from the UK, and I write (mostly) fantasy and adventure books for young adults and teens.

I believe in entertaining readers by offering them a temporary escape from reality. My stories are fun, fast-paced and addictive—the ideal vacation companion, and I aim for relatable characters who embark on meaningful journeys, get into tons of trouble, but overall discover the depths of what it is to be human.

Through my emotive *Noah Finn* novellas, I also hope to encourage you to look within; to find *your* story.

Through books, I believe we can face our darkest fears, explore infinite new worlds, and realise our true purpose. Creative writing helps me to understand what that purpose is.

Since starting my self-publishing experience in 2010, I have worked with many individuals to help make their dreams of publishing a book reality, including school children! My imprint, *Curious Cat Books (CCB)*, has been responsible for producing gorgeous children's books, memoirs and more since 2017.

***

Scan to visit Rachael's website or visit www.rachaelhardcastle.com for more information.

If you enjoyed reading this title, please consider leaving a short review and/or star rating on your favourite retailer website, as book reviews will help Rachael to reach more readers.

Thank you.

PRAISE FOR THE PREVIOUS EDITION OF
THE CHRONICLES OF PANDORA
WRITTEN AS *FINDING PANDORA*
BY READERS FAVORITE

"The world of Finding Pandora is interesting on its own, comprising a mirroring history and an assortment of creatures that will make for consuming contemplation sessions.... This is testament to E. Rachael Hardcastle's ability to choose carefully what to show and what to suggest... It is with this skill that E. Rachael Hardcastle delivers a light-pierced sombre story with a compact, multifaceted plot." - **Book One**

"There is a spiritual, moral and instructive quality to this book, asking us to look at ourselves as a civilization, our values and our actions. That is where its strength lies and that is something very commendable." - **Book Two**

"Finding Pandora beats at a pace that keeps the reader's attention and interest. The story flows remarkably. The imagination, planning and execution of E. Rachael Hardcastle's work is the strongest I have ever seen it... Finding Pandora is rich with societies, environments and cultures that are bustling with life, history and tradition... But perhaps the strongest feature of the book is found in its insightful themes and discussions on evil, morality, purpose and humanity." - **Book Three**

"It is all action, anguish, emotion, twists, blood, and light. It is laced with feelings of triumph and defeat, anguish and happiness, closure and continuance. The lean economical style of E. Rachael Hardcastle accelerates the tense, quick pace...

However, this isn't at the expense of depth... One thing is clear at the end, the Finding Pandora series is about sacrifice, the demands of living a purposeful life, and hope in the face of calamity. It is these poignant themes that make the series the moral force it is. As we close this chapter, we are reminded that this may not be the last time we see Arriette and the Recruit, and that should bring some excitement to fans because this story has more to offer." - **Book Four**

A NOTE FROM THE AUTHOR

Dear Reader,

If you've made it this far, thank you wholeheartedly. I wanted to give you a brief overview of the story's origins, as the path I took to share it with you is deeply important to me.

I started writing Arriette's adventures in 2010, when the series was titled *The Recruit Adventure* and was self-published in four parts: *World, Heaven, Infinity* and *Eternity* to reflect the poem it was inspired by: William Blake's *Auguries of Innocence*. A short snippet of the poem briefly features in the series in its honour—it brought me here, and continues to inspire me almost 14 years later. If you haven't read the full poem, I highly recommend the experience.

As with most indie titles, I've re-written and re-released the book a few times, most recently as *Finding Pandora* in 2018, which existed as a paperback collection of all four novels, or individual e-books. Whilst the production of that book was successful and beautiful, with *World* reaching #1 on Amazon's bestseller list, I always felt something was missing. I so desperately wanted to return to the adventure's origins to re-capture the magic I experienced all those years ago.

Writing a book is a thrilling, fun experience, but it's also hard work and takes dedication and time. Since 2010, many have supported my efforts in too many ways to fit on this page. I can't thank them all individually, but they know who they are and they know why they deserve a mention—that's what matters. Please know I am blessed and so grateful, whether we simply crossed paths or we are still in each other's lives today.

Finally, a note on my change of name. In 2010, I wanted to separate two sides of myself, so people I knew wouldn't necessarily associate me with my work, and I could write without fear of embarrassment. Since, I have accepted and embraced that being a writer is *awesome*; I'm ever so proud of it. I think about being E. R. Hardcastle fondly, as I will someday think about E. Rachael Hardcastle in the same way. But for now, I'm happy just to be Rachael. I've earned it.

And I'm so very pleased to meet you.

9 781739 437619